Mark Mason was born in 1971. He lives in London. *The Catch* is his second novel. His first, *What Men Think About Sex,* is also published by Time Warner Paperbacks.

Praise for *What Men Think About Sex*

'Mark Mason is one those writers whose natural voice is that of "everybloke" – the Nick Hornby of *Fever Pitch* or the John O'Farrell of *The Best a Man Can Get*' *Heat* magazine

'Full of wit and male competitiveness' *OK*

'A boy's *Sex and the City*, it will make men nod in agreement and women laugh out loud' *U* magazine

'Mason creates a thoroughly incorrigible protagonist that you just can't help but warm to' *Daily Record*

'An outrageous and entertaining romp . . . Men will identify with the ridiculous antics, while women will have a good laugh at their expense' *Vivid* magazine

'Lots of sex, plenty of pints and full of humour . . . Very entertaining' *Irish Tatler*

'Hilarious and outrageous' *Publishing News*

Also by Mark Mason

What Men Think About Sex

H

AUTHOR MASON, M.	CLASS F

TITLE   The catch

The Catch

MARK MASON

timewarner
paperbacks

First published by Time Warner Paperbacks in 2003

Copyright © Mark Mason 2004

The moral right of the author has been asserted.

A CIP catalogue record for this book
is available from the British Library.

ISBN 0 7515 3398 X

Typeset in Berkeley by M Rules
Printed and bound in Great Britain by Clays Ltd, St Ives plc

Time Warner Paperbacks
An imprint of
Time Warner Books UK
Brettenham House
Lancaster Place
London WC2E 7EN

www.TimeWarnerBooks.co.uk

The Catch

This isn't on. This really isn't on. Points? To get married?

And to think I'd been congratulating myself on how well I'd got it all planned. The top-notch restaurant, but one we'd already talked about going to so she wouldn't suspect anything when I suggested it. Saying I'd have to meet her there, allegedly because I had to work late at the office, but in reality so it'd feel like a proper, old-fashioned date and not just a meal we'd gone out for like any other couple who live together. And then the carefully worded proposal: 'I wonder if you'd do me the honour of becoming my wife?' Enough of a twinkle in the eye to stop it sounding corny, but not so much that Kirsty would think I wasn't serious.

This was, in fact, Plan B. I'd been discouraged from Plan A by Steve, who travelled this road himself a couple of years ago and so must know a thing or two about it. I ran my first idea past him, which was the way I'd dreamed about for years of proposing to someone, and which was rooted in my desire to avoid the predictable, the clichéd. I was going to wait until Kirsty was leaving the flat to nip down the shops and then say: 'Oh, a couple of things.' 'Mmm?' she'd reply. 'Number one, could you get some more orange juice? We've finished that last carton.' 'OK,' she'd say, picking up her keys. 'And number two,' I'd say, all casual like, 'will you marry me?' The romance of the unexpected and all that.

Steve thought about it, and then said that he could appreciate my desire to be different, and it was one of the reasons he liked me and had been my friend for so long, and in fact he could see it was one of the things Kirsty loved most about me, but that there were some matters in which it really was best to stick to the tried and trusted. Flowers, for instance. He respects, and indeed shares, my worry about sending them, which is that I'm lumping myself in with all those businessmen who send their wives a huge bouquet on Valentine's Day and then spend the rest of the year shagging their secretaries. Not that I am shagging anyone else, of course, but the lack of imagination flowers suggest could in itself be offensive, that's my fear. But, as Steve pointed out, you can try as hard as you like to offend a woman with thirty quid's worth of lilies, it ain't never gonna happen.

So the conventional route it was, and, like I say, I thought it was all going rather well. Kirsty looked beautiful, but then she normally does as far as I'm concerned. One of those women who's flowered in her early thirties (at her next birthday she'll be thirty-four and go two years ahead of me again, for a month). Not that I knew her before her early thirties – we've been seeing each other for three years, and living together for just under half that – but there's something about Kirsty that says 'prime of her life'. Maybe it's the shine to her chestnut-brown hair, or the way her soft, round face always seems passionate to me, even in the least passionate of circumstances. I love her for her confidence, too, and still can't totally believe that she's only five foot six. I know that I'm five inches taller than her, but somehow I don't really feel it.

I popped the question after we'd ordered but before we'd received our desserts (better not try to be romantic on a full stomach, I thought). I can't really remember now what reaction I expected. Delight, perhaps. Maybe the odd tear or two, I don't know. But surprise, definitely. Whether Kirsty was going to say yes or no, I thought the question itself was bound to come as a shock to her. But it didn't.

'I thought you might be asking that soon,' she replied with a smile. How do women know what's going on inside your head like that? *How* do they know? 'So I've been giving it some consideration.'

'And what's your answer?' I said, feeling a mite disconcerted.

Her smile, which had simply been pleasant, now became enigmatic. 'I've decided,' she said, 'that I'm not going to say yes.'

I was now a lot more disconcerted. 'Oh.' Under the table, I quietly closed the jewellery box and returned it to my jacket pocket. I hope Kirsty didn't notice. I would have looked a prat.

'But neither,' she continued quickly, 'am I going to say no.'

Eh? If we ever do get married, I thought, I hope she's not going to be like this on the day itself. Vicar: 'Do you take this man to be your lawful wedded husband?' Kirsty: 'Not telling.'

She could obviously see that I was confused. 'Sam,' she said gently, 'you've got to remember what happened last year. You know, your . . .'

'Yes, I know.' I'd thought she might bring that up. My 'Wobbly Week', as we've referred to it. Not that often, you understand, not that often at all, because it was quite heavy at the time and the emotional aftershocks took a while to subside. Briefly, what happened was that I rebelled. Against the relationship, the fact that we were living together, the

3

sheer *grown-upness* of it all. For a couple of months I'd been staying out more and more with people from work, friends, anyone I found myself in the pub with. I'd get back at half eleven, sometimes when Kirsty had cooked us something special, sometimes when I'd promised to help with a job around the house. The final straw came one night when we'd invited some friends round for dinner. I got home just as they were leaving. Kirsty waved them all goodbye, then shut the door, turned round and yelled at me for ten minutes non-stop. 'What the fuck do you think you're playing at?' was the general gist of it, and rightly so.

The answer, of course, was that I'd seen long-term couple-dom looming down on me like a juggernaut and thrown myself out of the way. My disgraceful, childish behaviour had been the swansong of young, free and single Sam. But instead of admitting that and apologising, I yelled back at Kirsty. 'I'll fucking well do what I fucking well like' was the general gist of it, and pretty pathetic it must have sounded. I slept that night on the sofa, left the next morning and didn't go home for a week. Hence the title, although, to be accurate, my wobbling had really happened over the previous months. That week, as I kipped on a succession of friends' floors, the wobbling stopped and I gradually admitted to myself what an idiot I'd been. Then I went home and admitted it to Kirsty. Things took a while to return to normal, of course. But eventually she came to accept what I'd learned myself: the wobble had been my final bit of growing up. It had got all the immaturity out of my system, all the fear about committing myself to one person, whole-heartedly, for ever.

Or rather I'd thought she'd accepted it. But now I found she hadn't. Not totally. 'I've got to be sure, Sam. This is a big question, you know. The biggest.'

There was no arguing with that. 'So what do we do now?'

She cleared her throat. 'I've had an idea.' Uh-oh. 'What I'm going to do is set a time limit – a couple of months or so – and institute some sort of points system, based on your behaviour. If, when the time's up, you've reached a certain number of points, I'll marry you.'

I gave it a few seconds. Not because I was confused now, simply because I was certain she was joking. But she just smiled, waiting for my reply. Gradually it dawned on me that she wasn't joking. 'You really mean that, don't you?'

'Of course. I haven't worked out the exact details yet, but I'm going to have a chat with my friends, and let you know when I've got it all finalised.'

And with that our desserts arrived. You'll understand, I'm sure, when I tell you that my chocolate torte didn't taste quite as magical as I'd been expecting it to. Kirsty proceeded to be, and has remained, just as charming and funny and loving as she ever was. But now she's round at Juliet's, as are her two or three closest friends, and the plan is being drawn up.

Points?

Points?

I still want to believe that she's joking.

The trouble is, I know she isn't.

Decided to take my mind off it all by going down the Mitre to see Pete. He's been working there for a while now. It's in one of the grimier corners of Aldgate and is owned by a bloke called Terry. Terry's not what you'd call a criminal. At least not to his face, if you know what's good for you. It's just that he sometimes forgets to pay the odd bit of VAT.

The Mitre isn't Terry's only enterprise (I've always thought it best not to ask about the others), so by and large he leaves the running of it to Ray, a one-legged barman from

Johannesburg. Don't go feeling sorry for him. He only lost the leg because of his boozing. Kept ignoring his mates' warnings to get a wound looked at. 'Yeah, yeah,' he'd say, downing another brandy and Coke and familiarising himself with that day's card at Kempton. They kept on warning him, he kept on ignoring them, complications arose and, wham, before he knew it he was spending half as much on shoes as he used to. This was before he alighted on the Mitre, which has proved an ideal place for him to work because it's tiny and the gap behind the bar, and also the gap between the bar and the main wall, are both narrow enough for him to swing himself along, supporting himself on the bar with one hand as he collects glasses with the other. There's an open bit at the far end which is more tricky, but Pete tends to look after that.

And when Pete's not there the regulars help out. Most of them are of a type with Terry, and when you ask them what they do they tend to reply 'this and that'. One night, soon after Pete had started working there, a couple of strangers stumbled in and got a bit rowdy. Nothing happened, but Pete decided he needed a bit of protection should things ever kick off properly since, let's face it, Ray's not going to be much use. So he took a hefty bit of piping he'd found in the cellar and put it behind the bar.

'Nice bit of kit, that,' said one of the regulars. 'Quick tip for you, though. Don't hit 'em on the 'ead, you'll kill 'em. Hit 'em on the back of the neck, on the kneecaps, or in the bollocks.' Clearly a man who knew what he was talking about.

Pete's not like that himself. He's more what you'd call a 'likely lad'. Our paths first crossed about four years ago when he used to deliver replacement bottles for the water cooler in our office. One day we started talking about football and just seemed to hit it off. He's never going to be

6

chairman of a PLC, but he's far from thick. He's got a native intelligence that means he can pick up any job in five minutes flat, and also allows him to charm the pants off anyone he wants to, often literally. His looks are a bonus in that department: he's twenty-six, tall, and can eat as much as he wants without even knowing there's such a thing as a thirty-four-inch waist. Pete was a very good bloke to go out drinking with before I met Kirsty on account of the women who'd flock round him. Now, apart from the odd occasion he has a spare ticket to the football, our meetings tend to be in the Mitre.

It was pretty quiet in there tonight. Ray was up the other end of the bar on what Pete informed me was his eighteenth drink of the day. He's tried telling him he should cut down a bit, if only because he hasn't got the same amount of blood to deal with the alcohol as he used to, but Ray won't listen. Rarely a day goes by, of course, without someone making the inevitable 'legless' gag. Pete poured me a pint of Guinness, and listened to my account of how the marriage proposal had gone. His first reaction was interesting in that it gave me a view of how I must have looked to Kirsty. Bemusement morphing into disbelief. Once I'd managed to persuade him that this wasn't a joke, however, he exhaled heavily (an interesting little barman habit he's picked up), and said: 'Christ. Bit of a turn-up.'

'Thanks for that perceptive insight, Pete. I know it's a bit of a turn-up. I'm the one it's turned up on. I was actually looking for some more constructive feedback.'

'All right, it's the worst idea I've ever heard. Who does Kirsty think she is, dictating terms to you like this? Either she wants to marry you or she doesn't. If she thinks she can piss you around with stupid challenges, tell her where she can stick her points. Bossy cow.'

'That's your idea of "constructive", is it, Pete?'

'You did ask.' He pondered the matter again, and decided to deliver his next bit of feedback as a question. 'How's this affected your view of Kirsty, of marrying her?'

My turn to ponder. 'It hasn't really. It came as a shock, obviously. Not to mention an anticlimax to the night I'd been looking forward to for weeks. But I still love her. I still want to marry her.'

'Well, it's simple then, isn't it?' said Pete. 'You'd better earn those points.'

He's right, of course. Not that it was his bald statement of the fact that convinced me. It was more how I felt watching him flirt with a couple of girls who came in later. Pete reminds me of how I used to be, when I was still in my twenties, chatting up the women who'd congregate round him. But gradually, especially after I'd met Kirsty, I realised that when you're in your thirties the agenda changes. Not because you think it should, or because you feel that what you did in your twenties was wrong in any way. It's just that you get bored with it.

Pete isn't. Not yet. He's still getting the adrenalin rush, the ego boost that comes from attracting new girls. Because that's what it is. Men don't, contrary to the popular myth, think with their dicks. They think with their egos. Orgasms are easily obtainable on your own, without a woman, without the need to buy wine, chocolates or cinema tickets. So it's not a physical need, it's an ego need. When you're Pete's age, and you're in a pub, making a couple of girls the same age as you laugh, your ego loves it. It's in an ego massage parlour.

The old me would have been across to those girls, joining in with Pete, chatting them up. But tonight I just smiled fondly at him. He was a 3-D home movie of the old me. I knew as the girls flicked their hair behind their ears and responded to Pete's teasing with more of their own that I was past all that. I knew it in my heart. My heart wants Kirsty.

So my heart wants those points.

That's it. The plan's been finalised. My instructions have been received.

Kirsty was sweetness and light as she sat me down on the sofa. She'd made us a cup of tea, and as she bent down to put mine on the table she kissed me gently on the top of the head. Then she went and sat in the chair opposite me. I got the feeling that she wanted to lend the occasion a sense of formality, to get across the importance of what I was about to be told.

'Now, darling,' she said, 'this is how it's going to work.' Her smile, which was as loving and friendly as ever, somehow jarred with the nature of what she was saying. It felt a bit like being sentenced to hard labour by your mum. 'Starting tomorrow, I'm going to award you points, based on whether your behaviour is what I'd expect from a man I was willing to marry. You'll earn points for behaviour I approve of, and lose points for behaviour I disapprove of.' Still she was smiling, and still it was jarring. 'The duration of the scheme will be twelve weeks. If at the end of that time your points score has reached one thousand, I will gladly become your wife.'

Big jar at that point. My heart thumped with joy at Kirsty saying the words 'your wife', but quickly calmed down when I remembered the other words that had made up the sentence. At the forefront of my confusion was the question of exactly how I was to earn these points. 'One thousand?' I asked. 'Is that many? Or not a lot? What do I do to earn, say, five points? Or lose ten? How many points to the euro, Kirsty?'

Her smile broadened a little, which made it sexier but at the same time more incongruous. 'That did occur to us,' she said, reminding me of how this scheme had been devised, or at least refined, by a committee of her friends. It wasn't a pleasant thought. I felt outnumbered. 'And so to help you gauge how you're doing I will, each Sunday evening, give you your running total. You'll know what you've done that week, so you should be able to develop a feel for roughly how much a point is worth.'

'Couldn't I have some specific examples?'

'Sorry, Sam. Can't be done.'

'Why not?' This was starting to get very unfair.

'Because if I tell you that a particular deed is worth, say, fifty points, you'll just do it again and again, won't you? And likewise if I let you know that another deed is only worth two points, you won't waste your time doing it, you'll concentrate on higher-value deeds.'

I could see what she meant. 'So I get a weekly total, and that's it?'

'Afraid so. But I'm sure you'll bring your deductive powers to work on it. You're a bright lad, after all, Sam. That's one of the reasons I love you.' She was teasing me now, and we both knew it. 'Any more questions?'

'Only the one I asked you on Friday. And look where that got me.'

'Right, that's that, then.' She came over and snuggled up next to me. 'Tell you what, why don't we celebrate your last night of not being on points with a takeaway? What do you fancy?'

I fancied it not being my last night of not being on points. I fancied Kirsty saying, 'Yes, Sam, I'd love to marry you.' I fancied planning a big fuck-off wedding and deciding where our honeymoon was going to be.

'Pizza?' I said.

An hour or so later, as we lay entwined on the sofa, a quattro formaggio and a bottle of Rioja having met their demise, Kirsty kissed my neck. Then she put her mouth next to my ear and, very softly, so that her speaking was little more than breathing with sounds, she said: 'By the way, Sam, you know there's one thing you needn't worry about when it comes to earning or losing points, don't you?'

Then her mouth came round to meet mine. I almost wished that that one thing was subject to points, because last night we'd both have earned thousands.

Week One

Breakfast on Monday wasn't so much a meal as a minefield. The knowledge that the day marked the start of my trial (because that's how it feels) hung over me like an executioner's axe, albeit one that couldn't fall for twelve weeks. I found myself analysing every last detail of every last thing I did, trying to work out whether it could be a points-earner or a points-loser.

I put the cornflakes back on the table – did I spill any on the way? No, good. Oops, packet lid's still open. There, closed it. But is that points earned for closing it, or points lost for leaving it open in the first place? Oh don't be ridiculous, Sam. You don't not marry someone because they've left the cornflake packet open for a few seconds. I poured myself a cup of coffee – remember to top up Kirsty's as well. One of those little courtesies that you always . . . usually perform (don't you?), but doubly important now. No, not doubly, infinitely. You weren't earning points at all for it until today.

I noticed that I was getting near the end of my cornflakes at the same time as Kirsty – get them down you so you can start washing up before she does, Sam. Surely that's got to be a points-earner? Careful, though – don't want to lose points for messy eating. As I stood at the sink, swilling out the cafetière, Kirsty came up behind me, put her empty bowl on the side and gave me a gentle kiss on the cheek. I sensed that she'd guessed the tortured calculations I was going through because she whispered 'love you' and then made a point of leaving for work before I did. No doubt she wanted to save me from too much self-analysis at such an early stage. Break me in gently to the notion of being on points.

My nerves were grateful for the rest, but the very fact that I was in this situation in the first place kept bugging me all morning. Why did I have to be on points? I could understand Kirsty's doubts about my proposal, bearing in mind that my Wobbly Week was less than a year ago. Entirely understandable that she should be worried about a possible repeat. Just because I know it's not going to happen doesn't mean she will. But either she trusts me or she doesn't. Either she feels enough confidence in me to walk down the aisle or she doesn't. What do these points bring to the party?

By lunchtime I couldn't take it any more and so engineered a joint expedition to the sandwich shop with George.

George is the same age as me, and I think the clue to our friendship is that I never really became friends with him until I fell in love with Kirsty (which was, by the way, about three months or so after I started going out with her). As my twenty-something, going-out-flirting-with-girls-with-Pete days ended, so I began to notice George more. He'd always worked in the office, and I'd always found him perfectly affable. But it wasn't until I settled down into domestic cosiness that we really started to get on. He's a bit shorter than me, and a little chubbier, and he's got, to borrow his euphemism, 'slightly more forehead' than he used to have. Never been a real party animal, but then, as I say, that's one of the reasons I like him. He's a rock of stability in an uncertain world. And regarding my current situation, I thought he'd be a better source of advice than Pete. George has got some form when it comes to serious relationships. He's lived with at least one girl I know of, although he's not seeing anyone at the moment.

We took our sandwiches to the courtyard at St Paul's. We often go there when the weather's good, but on Monday it kept reminding me, and making me jealous, of people who've got married. (Not that the royal family have had much of a track record there lately.) I filled George in on Kirsty's scheme. Initially, like Pete, and indeed like me, he assumed she was joking. This was starting to get a bit tiresome. Once I'd persuaded him that she wasn't, he gave the matter some serious thought.

'You do love her, don't you?' he asked.

'Of course.'

'And you really meant it when you asked her to marry you?'

'No, George, I was doing it for a bet. Of course I meant it.'

'Well, if you're serious about this, you're just going to have to go along with it.'

This got me no further than Pete had in the Mitre. I think George must have sensed my disappointment, because he went on: 'Look, Sam, anything that means this much to you is worth working for, isn't it?'

I nodded.

'And,' he continued, 'you've got to realise that the tables have been turned.'

'How do you mean?'

'You proposed to Kirsty. You're the one chasing her, not the other way round. She's the one with the say-so, and you assumed too easily that she was going to say yes.'

I hadn't thought of it like that before, but George was right. When men are younger, 'playing the field', which is, let's be honest, Respectable Bloke Speak for 'shagging around', we hold all the cards, don't we? We're offended by the 'c' word – 'commitment'. Girls want it, we don't, so we do everything we can to avoid it. Which is fair enough. But what's equally fair, and this is the bit I hadn't realised until now, is that when we get older and decide that the field has been played sufficiently, it's not necessarily a given that we'll be able to get the woman we want. I swanned around in my twenties having relationships but studiously avoiding anything that looked like a long-term future. Then when I decided that the time had come for all that to change, and I'd got my Wobbly Week out of the way, I assumed that the rest of the world, by which I mean Kirsty, would simply go along with the plan.

But she hasn't. The tables have indeed been turned. A woman spends her twenties getting messed around by these strange creatures called 'men', who've got one eye on her bra strap and the other on her best friend. She can't pin them down to a serious relationship for love nor money. Well, certainly not for love. Then she gets into her thirties, and finds that the men she's meeting have had their engines converted to run on commitment instead of lust, and that at last they want that serious relationship. But why should she accept the first one who comes along, arrogantly expecting to claim her for his own? Why should she flutter her eyelids in gratitude, hold out her finger for the ring and say 'I do'? Men were choosy in the old days, to the point of not choosing anyone at all – she can be choosy now. She wants to be sure she's making the right decision. She's not going to be rushed. And who can blame her? Certainly no bloke who's spent the last decade refusing to be rushed himself, that's for sure.

True as all this is, though, I still don't understand what

Kirsty's playing at by putting me on points. I can see why she might want to take her time in making a decision, weighing up how she feels about me. But what does she hope to achieve by marking my behaviour? She knows me well enough by now, she knows who I am, what I am, what I do, what I don't do. Why do I have to be on these *bloody* points?

George carefully lifted the second half of his sandwich out of the packet, making sure that the overflowing dollop of mayonnaise landed on the grass rather than his trousers. 'What, erm, what happens . . .' he began, looking slightly uncomfortable all of a sudden.

'What?'

'What happens if you . . . if you don't reach the thousand points?'

Christ! The instant George said it I felt my shoulders slump. The sheer horror of the question was like a physical force pressing them down. It just hadn't occurred to me: what *will* happen if I don't reach the thousand points? Is it all over? Do we split up?

My journey home that night was agony. I knew I'd have to ask Kirsty for clarification, but I was scared. Deep down, if I'm totally honest, I think I knew what the answer was going to be.

'Well,' said Kirsty, when I finally plucked up the courage (twenty to eleven, if you must know), 'if you don't manage to get to a thousand points, then we won't be getting married . . . and there really wouldn't be any sense in us staying together after that, would there?' She spoke quietly, with the air of a sympathetic doctor delivering very bad news, but there was a firmness in her tone that left no room for doubt.

'You mean . . .' My sentence wouldn't finish itself. I didn't know whether I wanted to cry, plead for Kirsty to change her mind or explode with fury.

'Look, I'm sure it's not going to come to that,' she continued in a much cheerier tone, before kissing me full on the lips. 'So let's stop getting ahead of ourselves, eh?'

Wednesday night was a very different story. Points, points, points, I told myself, bring on those points. Tell me this isn't the biggest points-winner you've ever heard of.

Kirsty and I were watching television. The news was on, and they'd got to the boring stories about local government and crooked car traders. My mind started to wander off on to estimates of what points I might have won or lost that evening. I congratulated myself about putting the washing on, which had to go in the plus column, but developed a nagging worry that there was still a Tube ticket in the back of my jeans, which would get pulpy bits of mess all over Kirsty's clothes, which would transfer the whole episode firmly into the minus column. Eventually I decided that I *thought* I could remember throwing the ticket away.

Anyway, that's not the incident in question. By the time I returned my attention to the TV, we were several minutes into a film. It was some chronic effort from the 1980s, starring, if that's the right word, which it isn't, someone who used to be in *Magnum*. Not Tom Selleck, and not the old British guy either. Yes, that's how bad a film it was. My hand had reached out, picked up the remote and had it half-raised towards the set before I managed to stop myself. Because I'd dimly begun to remember an incident from the past, when Kirsty and I had just started living together. I'd switched channels in the middle of an ad break without warning her, and she went berserk. Absolutely ballistic. 'I was watching that,' blah, blah, blah. Can't remember what the advert was for, but I don't think that was the point. I think it was more an involuntary outburst at an annoying habit she normally managed to tolerate.

Which is what earned me the points on Wednesday – I didn't do it. I deliberately said, 'Do you want to watch this?' (and of course she didn't) before turning over. Obviously I couldn't know for a fact that it had earned me points, but the way Kirsty smiled as she gave her reply filled me with confidence.

And when the washing machine finished, I discovered for sure that I had thrown that Tube ticket away.

Points BONANZA.

And so today arrived. Sunday. I felt more and more nervous as the afternoon wore on. We were heading towards the moment when Kirsty was going to give me my first weekly points total. Around teatime I started to wonder exactly how the information would be communicated.

'I've been thinking about that as well,' said Kirsty when I asked her. 'And I've decided that I'm going to write the total on a piece of paper, seal it in an envelope, and put it on the dining table for you. Then I'll leave the room to let you read it in peace.'

'*What?*' I shouted. 'A sealed envelope? This isn't the Oscars, you know.'

Kirsty placed a calming hand on my shoulder. 'Listen, Sam, if I tell you the total to your face you'll only quiz me about it, and ask what you earned points for, and where you lost points, and how you can earn more points next week, and it'll be awkward because I won't be able to answer your questions.'

'I won't do that.'

'You will, Sam. I know you, and that's what you're like.'

'Am not,' I said sullenly.

She raised an eyebrow.

'All right,' I said, 'maybe I'm a bit like that. But I promise not to be tonight.'

'Well, in that case it won't matter that I'm not in the room when you read your total, will it?'

Damn. She had me on that one. So at seven o'clock I was forced to look away while Kirsty took a piece of paper from the message pad by the phone, wrote a number on it, sealed it in an envelope and went upstairs for a bath.

For a good ninety seconds I couldn't even pick the envelope up, never mind open it. Not only was it difficult to get to that end of the room on account of my legs shaking with nerves, I was also trying to work out in advance what sort of a total I'd be happy with. A thousand would be nice, I thought. But then would it? If I'd got to a thousand now I'd have the rest of the twelve weeks to worry about hanging on to them. All right then, ten thousand . . . Stop being stupid, Sam. What, realistically, was I looking for here? The best answer I could come up with was that a thousand divided by twelve is a shade over eighty-three. If I'd got eighty-three points, I'd be on track. More – say, a hundred – would be nice, as it'd mean I had some to play with, in case of rogue weeks in the future. A lower score – say, seventy – wouldn't be disastrous, because I could always make up the shortfall later on. But eighty-three was the general area I wanted to be in.

I made my unsteady way to the dining table, supported myself against it for a few seconds, and then thought, sod it, best be on the safe side, sit down. I pulled out a chair and collapsed on to it. I picked up the envelope. At first my fingers refused to work properly and that irritating thing happened where tiny bits of the corner come away without actually letting you get at the envelope's contents. But eventually I engineered enough of an opening to get my finger into, and with a single rip along the top the piece of paper was mine for the taking.

I swallowed a couple of times, squinted (what for? Did I think that was going to make the total any bigger?) and took out the paper. Holding my breath, I opened it out. Kirsty had written: '27'.

Twenty-seven? Twenty-fucking-seven? That wasn't even half of what I needed to be on course. It wasn't even a third. Quickly I did the sums (it's amazing what complete despair does to your mental capacities): twelve weeks at twenty-seven points a week would come to three hundred and twenty-four points. Which would mean I was six hundred and seventy-six points short of being able to marry the woman I love.

I stared dejectedly at the piece of paper. Maybe I'd read it upside down? But no, the other way up it just looked like a lop-sided 'L' and a dodgy '2'. It was definitely twenty-seven. This was about as bad a start as I could imagine. But I couldn't see where I'd gone wrong. At least not that wrong. What sort of points tally had Kirsty and her friends come up with?

Which was when the idea hit me. Kirsty *and her friends* . . .

I made a couple of quick calls and within ten minutes was heading for the door. 'I'm going out for a while,' I called up to Kirsty.

'OK, darling.' The 'darling' grated a bit, in view of the meagre points total she'd just awarded me, but I ignored it.

The Mitre was quiet, even for a Sunday, which was good, as it allowed Pete to concentrate on the task in hand. Which I explained as soon as George arrived and we'd got the drinks in. 'I've asked you here,' I said, 'to see if you'll help me with my problem.'

'Which one?' said Pete. 'There are so many to choose from.'

This wasn't what I needed. 'You know which one. This points thing.'

He gave an indignant snort. 'I don't see why you should have to go through all this, you know. Don't see it at all.'

Neither do I, of course, but I didn't want to get side-tracked into complaining. I'm on points and that's all there is to it. 'Whatever, Pete. The question remains, though – will you help me?'

'Count me in,' said George.

The readiness with which he answered was a boost to my spirits in itself. We both looked at Pete.

'Yeah, if you think I can help.'

'I'm sure you can,' I replied, trying to build some early team morale.

'What do you want us to do?' asked George.

'Be my advisers. See if you can spot things I haven't. Generally stir up my thinking about the whole situation.' On the way to the pub I'd been thinking it through. My reason for wanting Pete on board was his ongoing contact with members of the opposite sex, and exposure to the ways they think. Whereas George could hopefully provide the seasoned, mature viewpoint. I didn't spell it out to them like this, of course, but what I'm after is a blend of youth and experience.

'You mean you want us to be a War Cabinet?' said Pete.

'Well, I don't know about the "war" bit. But yes, if you like – a Cabinet.'

'This is great,' said Pete. 'Two minutes ago I was working in a pub, now I'm a Cabinet minister. Can I be Chancellor of the Exchequer?'

'If you like.'

'I would ask to be Foreign Secretary,' said George, 'but my passport has run out.'

'Well, I'm Prime Minister,' I said, 'and I'm telling you both to concentrate. I've got to reach a thousand points in twelve weeks' time. And tonight I've been given my first total. Frankly, it's disappointing. It's twenty-seven.'

'Twenty-seven?' said Pete incredulously. 'That's not disappointing, it's catastrophic. What did you do, shag her sister?'

George and I fixed him with warning stares.

'Sorry, sorry.' Pete thought for a moment. 'It's a pity there isn't a course you can enrol on, that teaches you how women want you to behave. You know, like obedience classes for men.'

He was right. There isn't a course like that, and it is a pity.

'Listen,' said George, 'what you need to do is analyse this properly. I reckon you should make a list of all the things you've done that could have won or lost you points, and work out how Kirsty got to twenty-seven.'

This wasn't a bad idea. 'Pete, have you got anything I can write on?'

He fetched me a sheet of paper. 'While you're busy with that, I'll get us some more drinks. Same again, is it?'

I nodded, and he started pulling the pints. Ray wasn't serving anyone at this point, and hopped down to our end of the bar.

'What's that you're writing?' he asked, leaning over to peer at my list. The smell of alcohol on his breath was quite overpowering, and as I glanced up at him I remembered how incredible it is that Ray's in his late thirties. With his thinning hair, badly neglected teeth and skin so deprived of daylight it's turned grey, he could easily pass for fifty.

'Sam's listing all the things he's done that might have pleased or displeased his girlfriend this week,' said George.

Ray gave a truly nauseating grin. 'You haven't used her toothbrush, have you?'

'No,' I said, less than happy about being distracted.

'Just wondered. I used a bird's toothbrush once, and she hated it.'

'What's so bad about using someone's toothbrush?' asked George.

Ray's grin spread. 'It was what I used it for that she didn't like.'

I slammed my pen down. 'Ray, even if I believed that a woman had ever let you into her house, never mind her bathroom, I still wouldn't be interested in hearing about it. Now will you please fuck off?'

He made his way back to the other end of the bar, propped himself on a stool and carried on drinking his Smirnoff Ice.

When I'd finished the list I handed it to George.

'This all looks pretty good,' he said. 'Ironing times one. Washing-up times four. Asking before you change channels times one. Putting the washing-up away when it's dry times two. Taking the empty toilet roll off the holder and replacing it with a full one times one. Breakfast in bed times one . . . yeah, all points-earners.'

'What about buying her chocolates?' suggested Pete.

I shook my head. 'Thought about it, but she's on a diet at the moment.'

'Why don't women tell you when they're not on a diet?' asked George. 'It'd be a lot easier for them.'

Pete clicked his fingers. 'You could buy her a packet of Slimfast instead.'

'Yeah, that's a good idea, isn't it?' I replied. 'Give my girl-friend a present that says "I think you should lose weight".'

'Mmm. You've got a point.'

'The thing about a lot of these activities,' said George, 'is that you've got to be careful not to do them too much. If you start doing the washing-up fifty times a week Kirsty will know that you're only doing it to earn points, and so she'll discount the last forty. In fact she might even mark you down for them, on the grounds that they show a lack of imagination.'

'I see what you mean. Be a good boyfriend, but don't be unrealistically good.'

'That sort of thing.' George cast his eye over the list again. 'This isn't too unrealistic, though. I don't think any reasonable woman could call this an excessive workload from a prospective husband.' His lips began to move quickly and silently as he performed some mental arithmetic. 'Unless Kirsty's marking you in ones and twos for this sort of thing – and I don't think she'd be that unfair – then everything you've got down here must add up to more than twenty-seven. I mean, "changing the bedlinen and tucking the sheet underneath the mattress on all four sides, even the one that's pushed up against the wall" – that's got to be worth thirty points on its own.'

'That's what I thought.' The job had proved a total nightmare. I'd got to the last fastener on the duvet cover only to find that I'd put the first one in the wrong hole, which meant undoing the lot and starting again. I *bloody* hate it when that happens.

'You know what this means, don't you?' said Pete. 'There must be something you haven't spotted that's losing you points, dragging the total back down.'

He was right, of course, but for the life of me I couldn't think what I'd done wrong. I racked my brain for equivalents of the remote-control incident from the other night.

'Are you sure you've looked at every angle of every deed?' asked George. 'I mean, this for instance: "dusting". Did you dust *properly*? You know what women are like. Where we see a thin layer of dust they see compost.'

I thought it over for a minute. 'No,' I said eventually. 'I'm sure it's not that. Kirsty and I are pretty much on a level when it comes to cleanliness. We're not slobs, but we're not obsessive about it either.'

George drained his pint. 'Well, it's got to be something, Sam. You're haemorrhaging points here, and you'd better find out how.'

Week Two

The week began with a brainwave. Ask Steve again. He's already crossed the Rubicon, so if anyone could give me directions it'd be him. Unfortunately he's also crossed the Thames and headed deep into Sussex, on account of Mrs Steve producing the first Junior Steve. They didn't want to bring him up in London, so off to the country it was. Steve couldn't join the Cabinet, then, but as you know from his role at the beginning of all this, he was available for telephone consultations. One of which was undertaken on Monday.

'Hi, it's Sam.'

'How's it going? When have you set the big day for?'

I'd forgotten that I never got back to him with Kirsty's answer. 'We haven't. I'm not even sure there's going to be a big day.'

'Eh?'

I told him about the points scheme. There was a silence. And then: 'She's joking of course?'

If one more person . . . 'No, Steve, she isn't.'

More silence. And then: 'Bloody hell.'

'Bloody hell indeed. And what's more I've got off to a nightmare start. I'm earning points, I'm confident of that, but I'm also losing them, and I don't know how. Which is where you come in. I need to second-guess Kirsty's thinking,

27

work out what it is in my behaviour that annoys her. You and I are pretty similar, so I was wondering if you could have a word with Emily, ask her if there are any little things you do that she'd rather you didn't, any traits of the male of the species that she'd iron out, given the chance?'

He laughed. 'I'm sure if there was anything she'd have mentioned it by now.'

'But would you ask anyway, just in case?'

'Yeah, of course. I'll have a word tonight. Give you a call back tomorrow.'

'Cheers, Steve.'

My phone rang on Tuesday morning. 'Hello?'

Steve didn't even bother with a greeting. 'By the time she went to bed last night Emily had got to thirty-nine things. This morning she added another eleven. Christ knows how many there are going to be by the time I get home.'

'God, Steve, I'm sorry.'

'She said this points lark isn't a bad idea. She's thinking of putting me on them, and if I don't come up to scratch she's going to divorce me and take the baby. And if I really don't come up to scratch she's going to divorce me and leave the baby. Do you realise what you've started?'

'I'm *really* sorry.'

'Not as sorry as I am. Now will you please leave me out of this arse-brained mess of yours?'

In the circumstances I thought it best not to press him for any information. 'Of course. Sorry again, Steve.'

I heard the line go dead just before I got to 'course'.

By Friday I still hadn't made any progress on what was losing me points, but that didn't matter so much. Not to someone who'd earned as many points as I had the previous night.

Kirsty's appearance when she got back from work gave no clue as to the turmoil bubbling inside her. The very opposite, in fact. She looked particularly sexy. Her hair was slightly tousled and her eyes seemed to have a compelling intensity about them. She can still do this to me, you know. Make me catch my breath, get me excited just by walking into the room. And the sexiness she was radiating on Thursday evening made me think that her suit might be coming off, with eager assistance from yours truly, even before the wine rack was raided.

But no. As soon as the handbag hit the sofa, followed swiftly by Kirsty's own crumpled frame, I realised it wasn't sexiness she was radiating, but despair. The intensity in her eyes was simply the prelude to tears. They came quickly. There were lots of them.

'What's the matter?' I said, rushing across to put my arms round her. I kissed her hair and cradled her. 'Darling, what is it? What's wrong?'

She buried her face in my shoulder and sobbed. It was a minute or so before she could speak, by which time my shirt was soaked. 'I'm sorry,' she said.

'Don't be silly. What's wrong? What's happened?'

'No, I *am* being silly,' she said, tiny hiccups of upset still punctuating her words. 'It's just work, that's all.'

'What about it?'

'It's Jenny again.' Her boss. 'She knows how much I want that attachment, and she's doing everything she can to stop me.' This is where I'll spare you the details, which believe me isn't the approach Kirsty took. Not that I minded, because I love her and I want to help her, but there's no need for you to know the intricacies of her office politics. Suffice it to say that Jenny's not really playing ball, while other people in the office are much more on Kirsty's side and in a position to

29

help. This isn't the first time the issue's cropped up, so I knew a bit about it already. First step was to fetch the Kleenex and stem the small tidal wave that was Kirsty's crying. Then, continuing to cuddle her with one arm, I used my free hand to make a list (I'm getting used to those) of practical steps she could take to improve her chances of bagging the attachment. Asking Ian, who's one of her other bosses, to send a few well-worded e-mails, that sort of thing. As the list grew, Kirsty's sniffing gradually subsided, and by the time I reached step five she was completely composed again, if a little quiet.

'Thanks, Sam,' she said, taking the list from me and putting it in her handbag. I'd actually just thought of a sixth thing, but felt it best to let things lie. 'Thanks,' she repeated, patting my knee gently. 'I think I'll go and have a shower now.'

And so while Kirsty cleaned away her rivulets of mascara, I got on with cooking us some dinner. When she returned, looking quite pale, we sat and ate in relative silence. I tried making some conversation to take her mind off work, but understandably she didn't respond with much enthusiasm. Can't blame her, poor thing. We all have problems like this at work, don't we? And they do get to you, however much you try and ignore them. Even when you're as strong as Kirsty. I've been to a couple of her office's 'bring your partners' nights out, and it's clear that not only is she popular with everyone, she's respected by them as well. Doesn't surprise me. Kirsty can look after herself. By which I don't mean she's bolshie, but if there's something she's not happy about, things get done. That applies to cabbies going the long way home, insurance companies who think they can hide in the small print, you name it. So I'm sure her quietness tonight was due to her thinking about the list I'd made and how she could implement the steps on it.

Which is what I mean about earning lots of points. Part of me feels selfish for saying that, but then I didn't ask to be on these points, that was Kirsty's idea. And it certainly wasn't the case that I gave her help and advice just to earn points. Kirsty is the woman I love, and I have always done everything I can to help her. The items on my list, indeed, were simply refined versions of the advice I've given her about this problem before. So it's not that I was cynically using her distress to further my own agenda. It's just that as a by-product of the help I would have given her anyway, I'd bagged a few points.

So everyone was a winner.

After the other night, I'm sure you'll forgive me when I say that this afternoon's wait for my total was a little easier on the nerves than last Sunday's. Sure I was on edge, and doubtful as to whether I could have made up my shortfall and got anywhere near the one hundred and sixty-six points I need at this stage. But even assuming that I was still behind schedule, surely, I thought, I'd made some sort of progress?

Perhaps, then, you can understand my feelings on opening tonight's envelope and finding the figure forty-six.

No, I'm not having you on.

Forty-six.

Even a repeat of last week's twenty-seven, which would have been laughable if it hadn't been so serious, would have taken me up to fifty-four. Not only had I failed to increase my scoring rate, I had actually done worse this week than I did last. I had managed nineteen points. Even people who come last in the Eurovision Song Contest manage more than that.

For a good five minutes I seriously contemplated not turning up for this evening's session of Cabinet. (We've arranged them for eight o'clock every Sunday night at the Mitre.) But then I realised that would be silly. Pete and George might not be much, but they're all I've got. Plus I'd have to see George at work tomorrow anyway. There was nothing for it. Cabinet it was.

I couldn't face telling the two of them what my score was, so I handed them the piece of paper and legged it to the Gents before they could digest the information. Although I couldn't hear any cackling from in there, I nevertheless braced myself for a mild session of mockery on my return. But when I got back, both Pete and George were standing in complete silence, taking it in turns to hold the paper up to the light.

'What are you doing?'

'We just thought that perhaps Kirsty's pen hadn't been working when she wrote down the first digit,' replied George. 'Wondered if there was an indentation of a "1" in front of the "4".' He examined the paper one last time. 'No, you're unlucky.'

'Inventive,' I said. 'Futile, but inventive. Now can we get down to business, please?'

George and I perched ourselves on stools, while Pete remained behind the bar, keeping an eye out for customers. Ray was caning it, even by his standards, and to preserve his balance – always a tricky job for him, of course, even when he's sober, which is never – he was leaning against the wall at the other end of the bar, to all intents and purposes out of the picture when it came to work.

'Before you start,' said George, 'can I make a suggestion?'

'Please do. That's what you're here for. I'm struggling with walking at the moment, never mind suggestions.'

'I think you should repeat last week's exercise,' he said. 'Put down everything you can think of that might be a factor, and let's see if that gives us any clues.'

Again Pete gave me a sheet of paper, and again I went through the week in minute detail, considering every last incident to see if it could have been a points-earner or a points-loser. Eventually, when I was sure the list was totally one hundred per cent exhaustive, I handed it to George.

He studied it for a while. Then he looked up. 'Pete, I don't suppose you've still got last week's list lying around, have you?'

Pete looked through the pile of betting slips and copies of the *Racing Post* that Ray keeps by the till. Ray himself, I noticed, had fallen asleep standing up, and slid a little away from the vertical. Good, I thought, that'll leave us free from his 'witticisms' for a while.

'Got it,' said Pete, extricating the list from the pile. He handed it to George, who placed the two pieces of paper side by side.

'As I thought,' he said, looking from one to the other.

'What?' I asked.

'On the trivial stuff – duties around the house, that sort of thing – you've scored pretty much the same in both weeks. There are differences, obviously, but I think they roughly cancel out. Here, for instance: in week one you hoovered the stairs twice, whereas this week you only did it once, *but*' – he held up his index finger for emphasis – 'you've also got "achieved a whole seven days of not leaving any jam traces when using my knife in the butter", which has got to be worth a stairs-hoover of anyone's money. Hasn't it?'

We both looked at Pete, who nodded his agreement.

'So you're level on that sort of thing,' continued George, 'but you've also got your "helped Kirsty through emotional upset about problem at work" to add on. Which means that you definitely scored more, not fewer, points than last week. Which in turn means that you must have done something this week that you didn't do last week which lost you points. Or at least committed a points-loser more times than you did last week.'

'I follow your logic,' I said, 'but we still don't know what that points-loser is, do we?'

George shook his head regretfully.

I turned to Pete. 'Any ideas? Can you think of anything, anything at all, from your recent experience with women? Anything that gives us a sign of what's offensive to them?'

He scratched his head as he struggled for an answer. In the end he said: 'There was one thing. This girl I was seeing. I gave her a compliment about her mother, said I thought she was very attractive. You haven't done that, have you?'

'No.' I gloomily picked up a beer mat and started spinning it on the bar. 'Hang on, what's wrong with that? Most girls would find it charming if you complimented their mother.'

'It was the way I phrased it,' said Pete, wincing at the memory. 'Or, to be more precise, the question I followed it up with.'

For Christ's sake. 'No, Pete, funnily enough, I haven't asked Kirsty, or indeed her mother, anything like that.'

'Just a thought. I was fairly pissed at the time.'

A silence descended on us. And indeed on the whole pub – I realised that no one else was left in there. Even the jukebox had played out all its selections. The only sound that accompanied our deliberations was an irregular snoring from Ray.

Suddenly George slammed his hand down on the bar. 'Papadums,' he shouted.

'Eh?'

'What?'

'Papadums. It was something a girlfriend said to me once. We were out for a curry – and this is several months after we'd started going out with each other, mind you – that's what you've got to remember, they keep this sort of thing to themselves for ages, brood on it, let it fester – we're eating the papadums, having a really nice time, when bang, completely out of the blue the smile disappears from her face and she says, "You've done it again." "Done what?" I say, and she says, "You've eaten the last bit of the last papadum." So I look down, and she's right, the bit I've just taken from the bowl and smothered in mango chutney is indeed the last bit of the last papadum.'

Pete and I nodded, waiting to see where this was going.

'So I say sorry, and she says "it doesn't matter" in that way women have got that actually means "it matters like hell but I'm not going to say so", and I know the rest of the meal, in fact the rest of the evening, is knackered, and . . . anyway, the point is, when you're having a curry with a mate and you eat the last bit of the last papadum, he doesn't get in a mood about it, does he?'

'I don't even notice who's eaten the last bit,' said Pete.

'Precisely,' replied George. 'Blokes don't, do they? You just keep eating until you put your hand out and there's no papadum left, at which point you say "ho hum" and wait for the chicken madras. But women can't do that.'

'Of course they can't,' chirruped Pete. 'They're waiting for a chicken tikka masala.'

'No, no, no,' said George impatiently. 'Well, yes. But what I mean is, they keep an eye on who's had the last piece. And so, after Madeleine's strop, did I, the next time we had a curry. I was ultra-careful to make sure that I offered her the last piece. And do you know what?'

We both shook our heads.

'She didn't want it. She said, "No, you have it." I insisted, but so did she, and in the end I had to eat it. And I've noticed, ever since then, that when you offer a woman the last piece of papadum she'll make sure you have it. So that, dear Cabinet colleagues, is the lesson.' George leaned forward, with the air of Socrates about to deliver an eternal truth of human life. 'Women always have to be offered the last piece of papadum. But they will never *eat* the last – piece – of – papadum.'

Pete and I looked at each other.

'That's all very well, George,' I said. 'There's just one problem.'

'What?'

'Kirsty and I didn't go for a curry this week.'

George looked almost winded by the news. 'Oh.'

'Or last week. So none of my disappearing points can be explained by FUCKING papadums. Now can we get on and come up with some more relevant factors? It's my backside that's on the line here, and to be honest with you the quality of advice I'm getting leaves more than a little to be desired.'

The silence returned as we all concentrated our minds on the question. But inspiration came there none. After a while there was a brief rustling sound, followed by a gentle thump, as Ray finally tilted over and fell to the floor.

Disraeli didn't have this, you know. He wouldn't have achieved a tenth of the things he did if he'd had a Cabinet like mine. Imagine how he'd have got on with snapping up chunks of the world to build our Empire if he'd had Lord Thingy trying to fix up a threesome with his mother-in-law, the Earl of Wotsit going on about what he once had for starters, and a one-legged flunkey in the corner nicking all the brandy.

Week Three

It was no good. By the start of my third week, I'd come to an inescapable conclusion.

Women are a foreign country. They do things differently there.

I needed help from someone who knew the terrain. And in Amanda, I was sure I'd found that someone. I went to see her on Monday morning. Although she works for the same department as me and George, her office is on the floor above ours.

On the way, though, I stopped off at George's desk.

'Sorry about last night,' I said. 'Biting your head off about the papadums.'

'That's all right.'

'And I didn't mean it about your advice not being up to scratch. OK, Kirsty and I haven't been out for a curry in the last two weeks, but we probably will sometime in the next ten, so I'm sure your papadum tip will come in very handy. I'm sorry.' I'd thought about it on the way home and realised that George had a point. Women very often are like that with papadums. Certainly Kirsty is. She always insists that I have the last bit. I don't think it's just a civility thing, it's almost as though it's her wanting to look after me, make sure I'm well fed. A sort of Mother Nature thing, if that doesn't sound too pat. I hope it doesn't. I have to say that, in my experience, most women seem to have at least a bit of the mothering instinct in them.

George smiled to show that my apology was accepted. 'We'll get you there in the end, Sam.'

I thought about telling him that I was off to seek extra-Cabinet advice, but decided it might sour the atmosphere of reconciliation. I'd tell him about Amanda later.

The woman herself was in the middle of a phone call when I arrived, but she gestured for me to pull up a chair.

'Yes, Bill,' she was saying in her soft Scottish accent. 'Yes, I see . . . mmm . . . uh-huh . . . very interesting . . .' She held the phone away from her ear and waved it about. I laughed, and reflected on how right Amanda was for the task I had in mind. Slim and fair-haired, she's got bright blue eyes that can see through bullshit at half a mile. She's a month or two younger than me, and we started at the firm at the same time, but I've never been able to match her for coolness or all-round nous. In meetings, where I always keep my mouth firmly shut, she lets the preening, self-regarding males talk themselves out, then says, 'Right, we'll do this, this and this,' and everyone says, 'Yes, Amanda, you're spot-on there,' and goes off and does it.

Finally she escaped from her tormentor. 'Sorry about that.'

'Someone being difficult?'

'Not difficult. Just tedious.'

We exchanged a few pleasantries, and then I came to the point. 'Amanda, I was wondering if you might be able to help me. With a non-work problem.' I told her about my proposal and Kirsty's reply. 'And before you ask, no, she's not joking.'

Amanda looked surprised. 'I didn't think she was.' Of course not. She's a woman. She understands these things. 'In fact,' she continued, 'I was just thinking what a good idea it was. I might do it myself, if I ever find myself in Kirsty's position.' Amanda's single, although from what I know of life in the department it's not for any want of offers. 'Anyway, are you saying you want me to advise you on how to score the points? Tell you what to do, what not to do?'

I say it again: how do women know what's going on in your head like that? 'Er, yeah. I've already got a Cabinet assembled. George's in it, and a friend of mine called Pete. We've been trying to work out where I'm going wrong. But we haven't had too much success. I'm on forty-six points at the moment. If I fall any further behind schedule I'll be going backwards.'

Amanda didn't reply, but fiddled thoughtfully with a folder on her desk. I couldn't make out what was written on the cover, but I could tell from the logo that it was nothing to do with our firm. Eventually she spoke. 'Have you read any of those e-mails I've sent round about Timepool?'

I searched my memory. I could vaguely recall something about a scheme that was looking for volunteers. Needless to say I'd instantly deleted the e-mails in question, as I do any e-mails that contain the word 'volunteer'. Or 'charity'. Or 'petition'. 'Erm, yeah. Not in great detail, though.'

'Tell me anything that was in any of those e-mails, Sam.'

'All right, I didn't read them.'

She smiled. 'That's better. I didn't expect you to. No one else has. But seeing as you're here . . . The firm's signed up as a corporate sponsor of this thing called Timepool. And I've been put in charge of coordinating it. Basically they're a charity. They need people to give a bit of time each week to help people who . . . well, who need help.'

This really didn't sound like my sort of thing at all. 'What kind of help?'

'People with learning difficulties, kids who are in trouble at school, that type of thing. As a sponsor we're expected to provide a certain number of volunteers. So far we're a bit behind target.'

'I know the feeling.'

Amanda smiled, but didn't say anything else. She was obviously waiting for me to volunteer.

'I don't think I'm really cut out for this,' I said.

'Rubbish. You're just the sort of person they're after – really ordinary.'

'Thanks.'

She laughed. 'You know what I mean. They don't want heroes, anyone like Robin Williams in *Dead Poets Society*. They just need ordinary people who can spare a bit of time each week. You'd be perfect.'

'What would I have to do?'

'It depends on who you're helping. It might mean giving someone a hand with their reading, or . . . I tell you what, why don't you come along to the training talk on Wednesday? Normally they explain everything to people, and vet them, if you like, at their own place, but because we're signed up as a firm they do special sessions here once a week.'

It was perfectly plain what was happening here. 'This is a quid pro quo, isn't it, Amanda? You join my Cabinet, I volunteer for your scheme?'

'That's a very harsh way of putting it, Sam.' She tapped a pencil against her teeth. 'But an accurate one.'

What could I say? It seemed selfish to ask Amanda for help and then not return the favour. And so, despite considerable misgivings, Wednesday lunchtime found me in one of the meeting rooms upstairs, with Amanda, a couple of people I dimly recognised from another department and the guy from Timepool. Alan, he was called. I have to say, he wasn't what I'd been expecting. No beard, no brightly coloured Peruvian knitwear, no air of worthiness. In fact, he looked like any other forty-odd guy in a suit doing a job that had become not so much boring as routine. He told us how the scheme worked, which didn't take long, because the whole point is that there aren't any rules as such. Alan just matches you up with someone he thinks you might be able to help, and you spend some time with them, usually once a week. There are one or two formalities to go through, like you have to be checked to see if you've got a criminal record, which I suppose is fair enough, but apart from that it's up to you to use your initiative, see what you think of the person they've given you, try and give them whatever help you see fit. The down-to-earth way he spoke about it got rid of a lot of my misgivings. It wasn't that heavy or serious after all.

Alan called me at the office the next day. 'Might have something for you,' he said. 'Lad called Danny. He's thirteen.'

Thirteen? My misgivings came tumbling back. What would I have to say to a thirteen-year-old? I couldn't remember the last time I'd spoken to anyone that age. It was probably when I was thirteen myself. 'Right, OK.'

'In the last year or so he's developed an allergy.'

Oh God. This was sounding heavier and heavier. 'To what?'

'School.'

Thank Christ for that. Alan was being funny. After a fashion.

'It's got fairly bad,' he continued. 'The school have said that unless he signs up to Timepool, they're going to expel him. We get quite a few of those.'

I still wasn't sure this was my cup of tea. 'Do you really think I could be any help?'

'Yes, I do. Danny's mum's given up, to the extent that she was ever really bothered, his teachers can't talk any sense into him, and neither can his head teacher. Often we've found that a problem kid will listen to someone from outside their normal circle, someone they don't see as an authority figure in the usual sense. How would you feel about meeting up with Danny, seeing how you got on with him?'

I looked across at George and remembered last Sunday evening in the Mitre. Three blokes without a clue between them. I needed Amanda in that Cabinet. Desperately. Which meant . . . 'OK then. I'll give it a go.'

Alan said he'd sort something out for next week, and rang off. I went up to see Amanda.

'Very good,' she said when I'd explained it all to her. 'I'm impressed.'

'So does that mean you'll help me with my points?'

'Yes,' she said, smiling. 'I'd love to.'

'Great. Thanks.' I told her where the Mitre was and then got up to leave. As I reached the door, something occurred to me. 'This Danny thing – should I tell Kirsty about it or not? I mean, it might look a bit like I've got involved just to impress her, to earn points.'

'Tut-tut, Sam, how could you *possibly* imply that a member of the fairer sex would be so cynical?'

'It's completely unlike me, doing something like this. She wouldn't believe that I wasn't doing it to earn points, so not only would she not give me the points, she might even take points away.' I was reminded of what George said that first week in Cabinet about doing the washing-up too many times.

Amanda nodded. 'I think you're best not to tell her.'

43

She's right. I suppose mentioning the scheme to Kirsty would be safer if I explained why I've had to get involved in it. But that would mean telling her I'm getting help on the points front, which she might interpret as cheating. At the very least it'd show her how worried I am. So it's clear – this Danny enterprise has got to remain hidden from her.

Tonight's total didn't come as the shock that the first two did. Without having eased off in my efforts to score points whenever possible, I was aware that the mystery ways I'd been losing points were probably going to continue, and that I shouldn't expect anything different when it came to the total.

Nor did I get it. Seventy-one. Which meant that I'd scored twenty-five in the last week. Not as good as the first week's twenty-seven, but then not as bad as last week's nineteen. None of them anywhere near the eighty-three that should be my weekly average, of course, but that didn't concern me unduly as I headed towards the Mitre because I knew that also making her way there was my new secret weapon. Amanda.

As soon as she walked in, I felt a surge of confidence. Here, in my Cabinet, was a woman, an intelligent, clued-up woman who knew about women and what they want from men. Ray, on the other hand, felt something rather different, because he performed the particularly frisky hop he reserves for good-looking women who come into the pub. He's been known, if it's a couple of young American girls (they get quite a few in there, as the pub's near the end of a Jack the Ripper walk), to almost hop over the bar in his excitement.

This needed putting a stop to, and quickly, if Amanda's presence wasn't to be jeopardised at the outset by one of

Ray's 'ripe' chat-up lines. So before he could worm his way into the conversation I found out that Amanda wanted a vodka and tonic and set him to work on the first round. Then she said hello to George and I introduced her to Pete. After a bit of chit-chat, Cabinet was ready to be convened.

'Before we start,' said Amanda, 'I'm just going to nip to the loo.'

I could tell by the way Pete watched her all the way to the Ladies that Ray wasn't alone in his feelings for her.

'Oi,' I said.

Pete turned round to find my hand reaching over the bar and grabbing his collar. 'Don't even think about it.'

'But—'

'But nothing. I am not having my Cabinet ministers getting "involved" with each other, all right? This is a serious matter, a very serious matter, and we're here to work on it. Not on each other. Understood?'

Pete nodded. I let him go and he straightened out his crumpled shirt-front. 'Christ, imagine what you'd have done if I'd actually spoken to her.'

Once Amanda was back and seated at the bar between me and George, I opened proceedings. 'Could I start by saying on behalf of the Cabinet how glad we are to be joined this week by a new minister, Amanda.'

'What post is she going to hold?' asked Pete.

Giving him the benefit of the doubt as to whether this was a feeble attempt at a double entendre, I replied: 'She will be the Secretary of State for Understanding What The Bloody Hell Is Going On With These Points.'

The halitosis reached my nostrils just before the cackle reached my eardrums. 'Secretary?' leered Ray, appearing from behind Pete. 'That's good. Women always make the best secretaries.'

The look of repulsion on Amanda's face should have been the only clue Ray needed. But of course, him being him, it wasn't. So I had to give him another. 'Ray, which two-word phrase do we address to you most often?'

He returned to his end of the bar.

'Who is *that*?' asked Amanda.

Pete gave her a brief rundown on all matters Ray.

'And does he always dress like that?' she asked. Ray was wearing a 1974 Black Sabbath T-shirt over which he had put on, but not buttoned up, the dirtier of his two polyester shirts (a hotly contested title).

'Yes,' we said.

'Well, at least he's never going to be mistaken for being gay,' replied Amanda. 'Now come on, I want to hear about these points.'

I signalled for Pete to fetch the lists, then placed them nervously in front of Amanda. 'These,' I said, 'are my guesses as to where I've been gaining points.'

A flicker of amusement played across Amanda's lips as she glanced through the items. It was a reaction that drove me mad with curiosity, not to mention worry. 'As you can see,' I continued, 'weeks one and two are fairly similar when it comes to domestic incidents, what we might call the "small change" of points-scoring. Which led George to put forward a theory about the lack of progress in week two. George, perhaps you could give Amanda a brief summary of that theory?'

He duly ran through his comforting-Kirsty-must-have-scored-a-shedload-of-points-so-there-has-to-be-a-points-loser-we-haven't-noticed hypothesis. While he was talking, I spotted Amanda's lips twitching several more times. What was she finding so funny?

After George had finished, Amanda continued to examine

the lists for a while without speaking. The three of us drew closer, looking from her to each other and then back again as we waited for her judgement. Even Pete and George seemed to have caught my nervousness by now. Eventually Amanda placed the lists back on the bar and looked up. 'The theory's an interesting one,' she said calmly. 'As far as it goes.' Aha, I thought, she's bringing me down gently. 'And it goes in completely the wrong direction.' Oh. Not that gently then.

For a brief moment I felt like throttling George for getting it so badly wrong, but my rush of anger soon passed. He had, after all, come up with one more theory than I had, and in the end the responsibility for all this has to be mine and mine alone. It's my funeral. If it's not my wedding.

'Which direction should the theory be going in?' I asked.

'Let me check something before I answer that,' replied Amanda. 'This "helped Kirsty through emotional upset about problem at work" – what form did that help take, exactly?'

I told her about writing down the five practical steps.

Amanda smiled. 'I thought so.'

'Surely that's worth points. Lots of them. Isn't it?'

'Absolutely. Lots of points deducted from your total.'

'*What?*'

'That would have cost you points, Sam, not earned them. So George was right to spot that item as a significant one. But instead of it pushing your total up, and there being some other mystery item losing you points, that item itself was the one losing you points.'

'But I gave her lots of help.'

'No, Sam, you gave her lots of male help. Which is a very different thing from female help. You looked at Kirsty crying and thought that what she needed was a hearty dose

47

of sensible advice, actual things she could do to improve her situation.'

I looked at Pete and George to check that I wasn't going mad. Their expressions reassured me they were just as confused as I was. 'Yes,' I said. 'Of course I did. What else would I think?'

'If you were a woman, Sam, you would think, "Kirsty is crying, she needs a comforting hug, a good old bitch about how evil her boss is, lots of red wine, and at least a bar and a half of chocolate."'

'But—'

'Sam, I know what you're going to say. You're going to say, "But we already know how evil her boss is, there's no point going on about it, what we really need is to take some action to fight back against that." Aren't you?'

I'm not even asking the question any more. Women can read minds. That's all there is to it. 'Might be.'

'Well, let me tell you, Sam, women know all about fight. We know all about pain. And we're a lot better at getting through it than men. Of course we are – we have periods to endure, childbirth, bikini-line waxings. Whenever we've got a problem, we know all the steps that we'll take to rectify it, sooner or later.'

'You do?'

'Of course. Certainly Kirsty will. She's an intelligent girl—'

'She's going out with you, after all,' interrupted Pete.

'Sarcasm's a sackable offence in this Cabinet,' I told him, 'so shut it. Carry on, Amanda.'

'Kirsty didn't need you to tell her those steps, Sam. She knows her way round that office. She works there, remember?'

'So why was she so upset about it all?'

'Because sometimes women want to be upset.'

This was Alice in Wonderland stuff. 'Why would you *want* to be upset?'

Amanda gave a little chuckle. 'Because it feels good, Sam. It's our pressure valve, if you like. All that pain we're so good at soaking up, all those colds we battle through when men lie in bed for three days claiming they've got pneumonia, all that shit life throws at us day in day out – it all builds up inside us and sometimes we just want a bloody good cry to let it all out. And nine times out of ten we'll pick something really stupid and trivial to cry about.'

'So Kirsty being upset about her boss was a pressure valve?'

'Yes. She didn't want you to rescue her with your list of practical steps. She knew all those already. She just wanted to wallow for a while. You dried her tears before they'd finished. You turned her pressure valve off. You were making things worse, not helping her.'

At last this was starting to make a little bit of sense. Slowly, mind you, and only a very little bit, but at least I was getting there. 'That was how I lost my points? By not allowing her to be upset?'

Amanda nodded. 'I wouldn't be surprised if it's lost you points this week as well. Has Kirsty referred to her boss again?'

'No, not that I can rememb— . . . oh, hang on. She did say something the other night, over dinner. Mentioned Jenny in passing. Some snide comment she'd put in a report, I think. And I said to Kirsty, all chipper and cheery, "You needn't worry now you've got that list," and she nodded and said, "Hmm."'

Amanda watched me perform the reasoning with the benevolent expression a mother wears watching her child ride a bike without stabilisers for the first time. At the time

I'd thought Kirsty's 'hmm' was a contented 'hmm, isn't it a good job I had you to help me see all those things that need doing'. But now it began to dawn on me that it had actually been a frustrated 'hmm, I know I've got that list, and I wish you'd shut up about the bloody thing and just let me have a good old mope for once'.

'If I'd let her go on,' I said, 'and agreed with her about Jenny and how much of a bitch she was, she'd have been a lot happier for it. Is that what you're saying?'

Amanda gave another nod.

'And I'd have earned points instead of losing them?'

Yet another.

I looked at Pete and George. 'So if you want to help a woman, don't help her.'

The three of us slowly shook our heads in amazement at the mysterious ways of Womankind.

'I think it's a fair bet,' said Amanda, 'that Kirsty will give you another test about this some time in the coming week. So remember: don't be practical, just be there.'

I repeated the phrase in an almost hypnotised voice, which sounded strangely echoey until I realised Pete and George were repeating it with me. 'Don't be practical, just be there.'

We stayed momentarily zombified, and then all snapped out of it. 'That's great, Amanda,' I said. 'Thanks.'

'It's bloody illogical if you ask me,' said Pete grumpily.

I glowered at him. 'As you say, Pete, if I ask you.' I turned back to Amanda. 'Anything else you can think of? Any other tips?'

'I think that's enough to be going on with for now, don't you? You're doing well on the "small change" stuff, as you call it, so keep that at its current level. Then if next week's total shows an improvement, we'll know why.'

I was feeling a lot happier by now, so was content to leave proceedings there for the night. 'Another drink for the new Cabinet minister?'

'Same again, please.'

Pete didn't move.

'You heard her,' I said to him. 'Vodka and tonic, my man.'

'What about the old Cabinet ministers?' he asked. 'Don't they get a drink as well?'

'Of course. George – pint? Right. Pete – you can have a half.'

'A half?'

'I lost points for being too practical, you're losing beer for being too sarcastic.'

Pete sneered back and poured himself a pint anyway. Once he'd given me my change, he leaned casually on the bar and started talking to Amanda. It started mundanely enough with him asking where she was from, but soon there was some minor ribbing about Paul Gascoigne's goal against Scotland in Euro '96, and I could tell from the sparkle in her eyes that she was enjoying receiving the attentions of a good-looking younger man. Chatting to George, I leaned back so that I was directly behind Amanda. Then, by way of gestures towards her and Pete, and a mime of pulling a noose around my neck, I communicated what would happen to him if he pursued those attentions. He stubbornly refused to look at me, but I know he got the message all right.

And he'd better act on it. Tonight was the first bit of progress I've made in this whole sorry affair, and it was all down to Amanda. With her on my side, I think I can make some more. So I am not, repeat not, going to let that progress be impeded by Pete's testicles.

Week Four

Didn't I tell you? Didn't I say that Amanda would be the answer?

Kirsty's last two references to her problems at work had come in the evening, at the end of days when Jenny had been particularly difficult. But this week's was in the morning. Tuesday morning, to be precise, as we both lay trying to summon the energy to get out of bed.

'Ohhhh,' groaned Kirsty sleepily. 'I really don't want to go to work today.'

'Me neither,' I yawned.

'No, but you haven't got to spend all morning in a meeting with the Bitch Trog From Hell.' She burrowed her head firmly into the pillow. 'Aheddur, aheddur, aHEDDur,' came the muffled growl.

'I *know* you hate her,' I said, instinctively putting my arms round Kirsty and holding her close. Equally instinctively I opened my mouth to offer some very male help. But I managed to stop myself. Don't be practical, I thought. Just be there. And so I continued to hold Kirsty, and waited for her to make the next move.

'Shuzzabij.'

'I know she's a bitch,' I replied gently. 'She's a complete bitch.'

'Wunnagilla.'

'Killing's too good for a bitch like that. You should keep her alive, make her suffer. Horribly.'

Kirsty nodded, which brought her mouth free of the pillowy folds. 'How horribly?'

We spent the next five minutes devising uses for an office stapler that you wouldn't believe, by which time Kirsty was in a far better mood, and it was as much as I could do to stop her marching into work in her dressing gown. I knew, of course, that while her hatred of Jenny is very real, she was deliberately bringing it up again to test me. But I didn't mind. That's the whole aim of this, after all.

And I was not practical. I was just there.

Wednesday evening, on the other hand, was bloody hard work for not much reward. It was my first meeting with Danny.

Alan had arranged it for a park near, but not too near, Danny's home in Stoke Newington. 'Want it to be somewhere slightly out of his normal environment,' he explained. 'Increase the chances of him responding well.' He picked a park because it'd make it hard for Danny to pull his 'usual trick' – disappearing quickly down the nearest side street, losing whoever was supposed to be looking after him. Apart from that the only advice he gave me was that there wasn't any advice. Just treat it as a normal chat to start with, see if I could form some sort of bond with the kid. Don't steam straight in there asking about his truancy. If a chance came to tackle that once I'd bonded with him, then fine, take it.

I was a few minutes early getting to the benches where we were meeting. At least it had got me half an hour off work, I reflected, as I gazed across at some kids playing football in the distance. Half-five to half-six with Danny, home by half-seven, Kirsty wouldn't know that it hadn't been a late finish at the office. I felt strange being there, maybe even a bit nervous, but then I remembered that Amanda's points-advice had already brought results, so this was definitely a price worth paying.

Soon I saw Alan approaching. The kid walking with him was smaller than I'd been expecting. I don't know why, but I'd assumed Danny was going to be tall for his age, a real handful physically as well as socially. But he was quite slight, narrow shoulders hunched against the outside world, and he spent most of the time looking at the ground. On the odd occasion he did look up, I saw that his face was thin and pale. His eyes were dark brown, as was his badly cut hair. He was wearing jeans and an Eminem T-shirt, neither of which had been near a washing machine in weeks. Right from the first moment I saw him, the very first instant, I knew there was something strange about this boy. Something definite, a crucial, central fact – but one I couldn't quite put my finger on. Even by the time they got to the benches, it had started to bug me.

'Hi there,' I said, shaking Alan's hand.

'Hi. Here's Danny then. Danny, this is Sam.'

I automatically held out my hand to Danny, and then worried that it seemed stupid to treat a thirteen-year-old in this way. You don't shake hands with kids – do you? I didn't know. I didn't normally deal with them. Anyway, the point was academic, because Danny refused to look up. I let my hand fall back to my side.

'Danny, I said this is Sam.' This time the tone was more intimidating.

It produced a reaction, just. Danny looked up, surveyed me for about a second, more out of curiosity than politeness, grunted something that, if you were being charitable, you could interpret as 'hi', then resumed his fascination with the grass.

Alan shrugged, as if to imply this was the best we could hope for. 'I'll see you back here in an hour, all right?'

'Yeah,' I said. 'See you then.'

Danny didn't move or speak.

'Well,' I said when Alan had gone. 'Right.' Then I realised I didn't know what to say next. Looking at Danny – what *was* it about him that was bugging me? – it hit me that my repertoire of things to say to thirteen-year-olds was limited. Very.

But this didn't remain a problem for long. Incredibly, he looked up and spoke. 'Got any fags?'

'Sorry, I don't smoke.' *What?* I was apologising to a boy of thirteen because I didn't have any cigarettes for him? 'Er, hang on a minute, you're not supposed to ask me things like that.'

'Why not?' he replied, taking out a packet of Benson and Hedges and a lighter.

The cheeky little fucker. 'Why did you ask me for a cigarette if you've already got some?' Damn, it was too late, the words were out. He'd obviously not wanted to waste his own fags if there was a chance of getting one from me. But my mind didn't work like that. My mind was conventional, reasonable, honest. For which, read 'sap'. I'd got off to the worst possible start (not the first time that had happened recently). Not only had I shown myself up as naïve, I'd let him get away with lighting up in front of me. Should I tell him to put it out? No point. He clearly wouldn't, and short of wrestling the cigarette from his mouth there was no way I could make him. Even if I could manage that before he legged it, I'd probably get into trouble for assaulting him.

Besides which, I figured, smoking was clearly the least of this lad's problems. Plenty of the thirteen-year-olds in my class smoked, and now they're thirty-two-year-olds who smoke, and they've no doubt got good jobs, and even if they haven't it won't be because they smoke. No, Danny's real problem, the one that'll really mess his life up and the one that I was supposed to be helping with, was that he keeps bunking off school. I decided to concentrate on that.

But how? Opening up with 'why don't you like school, Danny?' was what Alan had advised against. In desperation, I looked around for something to talk about. Apart from a few people taking the long way home from work to enjoy the evening sunshine, the only thing happening was the football.

'Shall we go and watch that lot for a bit?' I started walking as I said it, to make it harder for Danny to say no. Perhaps it was the fact he'd got one over on me at the beginning and so didn't see me as a threat, but he consented, and started shuffling along behind me. It took a few minutes to reach the other side of the park, during which time he didn't say a single word. Neither did I. Partly I hoped the silence would intimidate him into making an effort, and partly I was still trying to work out what was so unusual about him. There was something not quite right, but I couldn't for the life of me pin it down. It was starting to infuriate me.

The game was the usual hotch-potch you get in park football. Everyone was wearing their favourite team's shirt, so there was no way of telling who was on which side and you got Barcelona passing to Crystal Palace, then Palace being tackled by Brazil. The lads were older than Danny, sixteen or seventeen. After a minute or so, one of the players managed to hit the goalpost (or rather pile of bags) from two feet away. It was a miss so terrible that even Danny couldn't resist saying something.

56

'Twat,' he sneered.

Not the most eloquent bit of commentary, perhaps, but at least it was an opinion, something I could respond to, get to grips with. 'Do you like football then?' I asked.

'S'alrite.'

'Who do you support?'

He looked at me as though I'd asked the most stupid question in the world. 'No one.'

Oh I get it, I thought to myself. To support a particular team would be too conventional, wouldn't it? It'd imply enthusiasm about something, a break with this 'fuck the world' act. That would never do, would it? But I managed to keep all this to myself. Confronting him, antagonising him wouldn't achieve anything. Instead I walked over to a spare football that was lying nearby and kicked it at him. Talking wasn't doing much good, perhaps action would be better. Being the world's worst footballer, though, I miskicked slightly, putting the ball a yard to Danny's left. It was heading for the pitch, with enough force to end up in the middle of the game if it wasn't stopped.

But it turned out to be the best thing I could have done. Danny instinctively lunged for the ball, and as it caught his foot it spooned up in the air. With one flick of his knee he had it instantly under control and waited casually for it to fall again, collecting it deftly on the inside of his right foot a few times before transferring it back to his left. However withdrawn he may have been up to now, he couldn't resist showing off his keepie-uppie skills. For a good twenty seconds the football was powerless to return to the ground as Danny bounced it off his feet, his knees, his head, his shoulders. There was no emotion in his face, no delight or pride at his achievement. He refused to lose his bored-with-life expression. But he had to prove how good he was. Only when he decided that he'd proved it enough did he let the ball drop back to earth.

So you're no doubt thinking: That was it, that was how Sam forged an initial bond with the boy, the beautiful game takes its customary role in male relations, how delightful and satisfying that must have been for you, Sam. Whereas what was really going through my mind was: You little bastard. Why can't I be that good at keepie-uppie? I'd give my eye-teeth to be able to do that. I can normally manage one bounce, two if I'm lucky, before the ball gets that bit too far away and I have one last, desperate lunge that shoots the fucking thing three miles into the distance. In fact there was a moment during Danny's display when I was thinking: If he does that ultra-flash thing where you bend over and catch the ball on the back of your neck and stay absolutely still, I really am going to have to punch him out of sheer jealousy. Petty, I know, but then I'd never wanted to do this in the first place. I'd never claimed to be interested in furthering anyone's moral or social welfare. If I was peeved about a thirteen-year-old being better than me at keepie-uppie, then that's how it was.

To admit that to him, though, would have been to lose even more face than I had with my initial wayward pass. Plus one of the goalkeepers had noticed us and was starting to look suspicious that we might be trying to nick their ball. From what I knew of Danny he could well have been right. So I started to move away. 'Come on,' I said. 'This game's boring. Let's go for a walk.'

Satisfied that he'd won round two, Danny followed.

After a while I asked: 'So what's the problem then, Danny? Why won't you go to school?' By now I'd calmed down and grown up a bit, and realised that his victories over the cigarette and the keepie-uppie might have been worthwhile, even though I'd planned neither of them. Having established that I wasn't another adult determined to cow him into submission, Danny might open up to me slightly.

"Cos it's shit."

Very slightly, it seemed. But at least this was a start. 'I know,' I replied. 'It was shit when I went there as well.'

'Well, what d'you ask me for, then?'

'Look, Danny, I know school's not exactly a barrel of laughs, but trust me, if you don't get the qualifications now, while you've got the chance, it'll be too late, and the rest of your life will be even worse than you think school is now.' There are various things you start doing after thirty that prove you're turning into your own father. Complaining about the quality of modern pop music is one of them. As is emitting a gentle sigh each time you sit down in an armchair. And with the line I'd just said to Danny, I'd found another one.

'I don't need school,' he said, matter-of-factly.

'Oh, don't you? And why's that?'

He took out another cigarette and lit it. 'Just don't.'

'What are you going to do instead then?' I was starting to get irritated now.

'I know people.'

'Really? That's very impressive. I'm very happy for you.' I stopped myself. Getting sarcastic with him, I'd already decided, was pointless. Anger was what he was used to. I had to stay calm. 'What about your family, Danny? What do they say about all this?'

'Huh.'

'Could you be a bit more specific?'

'They don't give a fuck, do they?'

I remembered what Alan had said about Danny's mother. Obviously it was true.

'Have you got any brothers, sisters? How do they get on at school?'

'Dunno. My brother went to live with my dad, didn't he? Wish I had. Wouldn't be stuck with my mum and her stupid fucking boyfriend now. That's where my problems started. One of the reports on me said that, I seen it. Said my "domestic situation was a factor".' He took a drag on his cigarette and then looked away to show that he'd said his final word on the subject.

And despite my best efforts in what remained of the hour, he had. We walked around the park a bit more and sat on a bench but he refused to say another thing, about school, his home life, anything. By a quarter-past six I'd given up trying to get any response from him and we sat there in complete silence. But still something was bugging me, the something about Danny that seemed strange. What the hell was it?

Alan arrived to collect him, saying he'd give me a call the next day to 'chat it over'. I said goodbye to Danny, who grunted at me and walked off to Alan's car. That's it, I thought, that was your last chance. You can keep your Timepool. I'm not wasting my energy on someone who can't even be civil to me. Danny, it struck me, had put me in the opposite position to Kirsty: I could understand what I was supposed to be doing (helping him) but didn't want to do it, whereas with Kirsty I don't understand what I'm supposed to be doing (trying to earn these points) but I'm desperate to do it.

On the Tube home I realised what was so weird about Danny. He was an adult, not a child. Despite the fact that he was thirteen years old, everything about him seemed adult. The look in his eyes, the way he spoke, the way he walked. He was soaked through with the cynicism of the adult world. Nothing moved him, there was no bounce in his step, no excitement in his eyes. It was as though his childhood, if it had ever existed – had it? – was over. He was an adult, a miserable, hard-bitten adult, in a child's body. I thought back to what I was like at his age. My primary interests, as far as I recall, were my Raleigh bike, Caramac bars and the question of how I could procure the phone number of the blonde one in Abba. But Danny didn't have any of that about him. Several good-looking girls had walked past us in the park, but he hadn't looked at any of them. He was terminally unimpressed by the world and everything in it. Even his keepie-uppie display had been to get one over on me, not to show off in the way that kids normally do.

This child wasn't a child. It was the most incredible thing in the world. And the saddest. In an instant my mind had been changed about carrying on with him.

On Friday lunchtime I was to be found in the newsagent's around the corner from work. Amanda's 'don't be practical, just be there' insight had persuaded me that further injections of female thinking were what this points-search needed. But where were they to be found? Walking through reception that morning, with its table full of magazines, an idea had come to me.

Only when I got to the newsagent's did I realise how much choice there was. The women's magazines shelf seemed to go on for miles. I was only glad it was the shelf immediately below the car magazines, which at least gave me an excuse for standing there that long. Which one should I buy? I could go for the lot, but not only would that get me some funny looks as I queued up, I'd also get a hernia carrying them back to the office. Plus I'm trying to cut down on my spending at the moment. New stereos and holidays to Egypt – not to mention diamond engagement rings – are all very well, but when you forget that the car insurance is up for renewal before you go buying them, things can get a bit sticky. Although I don't feel too guilty. Cruising down the Nile was when I looked at Kirsty and had the first inkling that I was ready to buy that ring.

Anyway, there I was, trying to decide which women's magazine I should choose, based on the stories advertised on their front covers. Every single one of them seemed to have a feature about women who used to be men, or men who want to be women, or men who like men who look like women. How many of these people *are* there? Do the magazines have to share them around? Beyond that, there weren't any useful indicators. What I was hoping for, of course, was a feature entitled 'What You Want Your Man To Do To Earn Points If You've Put Him On This Scheme Where That's What He Has To Do Before He Can Marry You'. Strangely, though, I couldn't spot one of those, so I chose a magazine called *Excite!* on the grounds that Kirsty was reading it the other day.

And they say it's men who are obsessed with sex. As I thumbed through the magazine in the Gents at the office, I was staggered by how many of the articles were about G-spots, sexual fantasies, spicing it up, slowing him down and God knows what else about life between the sheets. Curious as much of this was (I don't think I'll ever be able to eat an artichoke again), it was of no use to me and my points, as you'll recall Kirsty specifying that that subject was off the scoresheet. Then there were the make-up trials, and the fashion tips, and the diets, and the fitness regimes, and of course the transsexual, and the cover story, which was an interview with some Hollywood babelet, who if you believe the magazine is so hot she scorches any film she's in, and if you believe me is a bag of bones I'd never heard of before and don't want to hear of again. Read the lot, I did. Every word. Well, OK, I skipped the make-up trials, and the transsexual. And the fitness regimes. And I only speed-read the diets and fashion tips. But none of that was what I was looking for anyway. I was after insights, facts about the female view of the world that I've been missing. The babelet had precious little to offer. All in all it was a waste of one pound forty and my lunch hour. Leaving the magazine in the cubicle (I bet that'll lead to some interesting office gossip), I returned to my desk.

And no more did I think of *Excite!* until yesterday afternoon, when Kirsty and I were putting the shopping away. I'd volunteered for freezer-duty, which I'm telling you must have earned me points aplenty, because there was so much to fit in that I had to completely reorganise the top three shelves. Kirsty had a much easier time of it, faced with nothing more challenging than fitting all the tins and sugar and coffee and stuff into the big eye-level cupboards. She finished well before me.

We'd got the radio on. A news bulletin had just come to an end.

'Now sport,' came the over-earnest voice from the speaker. 'Cricket, and England have suffered a major injury blow ahead of next week's Test match.'

I tensed, waiting for the bad news.

'It's been revealed that—'

'Damn,' said Kirsty. 'We forgot to get . . .' And this is where it happened. This was the *Excite!* moment. As soon as Kirsty started speaking I began to open my mouth to quickly say 'shh' so that I could hear who was injured. But something miraculous happened: I didn't make the sound. I didn't shush Kirsty. I let her carry on speaking, informing me that we'd forgotten to get fabric softener, and drowning out the name of the cricketer. At first I couldn't work out why I'd done it. I'd voluntarily – or was it involuntarily? – stopped myself hearing the news I was desperate to hear. Why? It made no sense. But then something from the Babelet interview popped up in my mind. In the conscious part of my mind, that is; it had been in the subconscious part all the time, and was in fact what had stopped me shushing Kirsty. Babelet's approach to acting, apparently, is this: 'It's kinda like when I'm in role, you know, I'm totally myself, but, like, at the same time I'm so totally not myself, and that's the key, you know, you gotta keep those two things in your head at exactly the same moment, which I think is pretty cool if you can do it.' Stick with me here, I know you're wondering what this has to do with fabric softener, but trust me, all will become clear. 'And it's kinda like, you know, easier for me, I think, being a woman, because we can concentrate on two things at once, whereas men so totally can't. It's kinda like, with my boyfriend, when we're just chilling, watching TV, you know, he'll tell me to be quiet when the ice-hockey score comes on, and that is like, so uncool, you know, that so pisses me off.'

Told you we'd get there. I hadn't really taken it in when I read it, or at least hadn't realised I'd taken it in. But when the moment came, I did the right thing. Thinking about it, I've realised that shushing Kirsty at important moments is something I do all the time. No doubt she gets as pissed off with me as Babelet does with her boyfriend. I'm sure I've done it in the last three weeks, and it's lost me points. I bet you anything you like yesterday was another test, like the Jenny thing the other morning. Kirsty will have known I was itching to hear which cricketer it was. Maybe she even read the *Excite!* piece herself and was reminded of my habit by that.

Never having pondered this point about women concentrating on different things simultaneously, I hadn't understood how illogical, and therefore offensive, it must be to them that men tell them to shut up without any explanation. If we made it less offensive, of course, and said, 'Sorry, my love, but would you mind just pausing there for a second while I listen to the radio?' we'd talk over what we were trying to catch in the first place. Hence the curtness. It's not meant to be rude, but I can see why it looks it.

Not yesterday, though. No rudeness from Sam. As I carried on cramming the freezer with petit pois, I felt thoroughly chuffed with myself. Don't get me wrong, it was bloody infuriating not knowing who'd got himself injured. And finding out from the bulletin thirty minutes later that it was Michael Vaughan was a big disappointment. But not half as big as the thrill I got this evening when I opened up the envelope and found that my total now stands at one hundred and seventy-one. In the past week I'd scored exactly a hundred points. One *hundred*. My first three weeks scored twenty-seven, nineteen and twenty-five. Week four had scored more than all of those put together. The significance of the number wasn't lost on me. Kirsty had obviously awarded me a round hundred to show that my female-help routine on Tuesday, and my not shushing her yesterday, were exactly what I should be doing.

Down at the Mitre, I gave Pete, George and Amanda the good news. They were really pleased for me, and at the risk of sounding soppy, I felt quite moved. Even my report on the week's small change made them all smile. Especially resourceful, I thought, were 'untangling the curly bit of the phone cord' and 'allowing Kirsty to pop the foil on the new coffee jar even though it was really my turn'. Pete managed to take the edge off everything by pointing out that I was still behind schedule, and with eight weeks to go I still need more than a hundred points a week. But that'll come in time, I'm sure.

Later, as Ray was treating everyone in the pub to his rendition of 'You're Nobody Till Somebody Loves You', which I have to say lacks something of Dean Martin's style and panache, George looked across at Amanda.

'Can men really only concentrate on one thing at once?'

She nodded. 'It's the way your brains are set up.' She paused to think of an example. 'When you're navigating for someone on a journey, I bet you turn the car radio down to read the map, don't you?'

He looked at me. I looked at Pete. All three of us looked at each other, mentally placing ourselves in the situation. Then, before we could stop them, our right hands came out as if to turn down a radio. Amanda allowed herself a quiet smile.

'Ah,' said Pete, moving a bit closer to her, 'but life isn't all about car journeys, is it? There are some occasions when we men can concentrate on two things at once.' There was a significant glint in his eye as he spoke.

Amanda replied in kind. 'Oh really?'

They were staring straight into each other's eyes. My hackles rose. I leapt in before Pete could say anything else. 'Right then, Pete, same again for everyone, quick as you like, chop-chop, there's a good lad.'

I've told the little bastard before. He is *not* going to threaten my progress by flirting with the most important member of Cabinet. He can pack it in of his own accord or I am personally going to introduce a meat cleaver to the situation.

Week Five

What do points mean? Points mean confidence.

Breakfast was much easier to face on Monday, knowing that at last I'd had a productive week. A hundred points made my marmalade spread a lot more smoothly. Across the table, Kirsty was applying the finishing touches to her lipstick. I marvelled at the fact that there was a chance of this woman, this gorgeous woman, becoming my wife. She clamped her lips on a piece of kitchen towel, then folded the deep red stains inside and used the towel to wipe some stray breadcrumbs from the table. Then she looked up and realised I was watching her. She gave me an ultra-serious look for a moment, and then suddenly stuck her tongue out and crossed her eyes in a totally immature schoolgirl fashion. It made us both burst out laughing.

In one gesture Kirsty had summed up why I love her, why I couldn't stop loving her even if I tried. The lipstick stood for everything that's grown-up and sophisticated about her, the things about her that earn my admiration: her successful career, her self-confidence, her unfailing ability to reverse into even the tightest parking space. But admiration on its own isn't enough. You can respect someone for being grown-up and sophisticated, but you can't love them. Love is about being comfortable with someone, knowing that behind the sophisticated front there's someone you can have a laugh with, snuggle up to, feel close to. And I've got that with Kirsty. That's why the breakfast thing gave me butterflies of love: there was this woman, looking stunning in her trouser suit and scarlet lipstick, ready for another day of high-powered meetings and important decisions – and I was the one she stuck her tongue out to. Me, Sam, I was the one who got to laugh with her when she pulled a funny face. I tell you what, there are few things in this world more lovely, more sexy, than shared laughter.

It was a moment so removed from the notion of having to earn points before I can marry her that again I found myself asking what she's playing at. Why do I have to go through all this? Can't she see I really mean it when I say I want to spend the rest of my life with her, that the Sam of Wobbly Week is a Sam of the past? I wish you could photocopy your soul, like you can get a printout of your heart-rate. Then I could show it to her, as documentary evidence that I love her absolutely, in a way I've never loved anyone before. But you can't. So points it is.

She was opening the post.

'Oh damn, I'd forgotten about that.'

'What?'

'The balancing payment on the car insurance,' she replied, passing me the letter.

'I thought we paid that the other week.'

'That was just an initial amount. Don't you remember? The bill said something about them changing the premiums from last year, and depending on what we'd paid we'd either get a rebate or another bill.'

I looked at the figure in the bottom right-hand corner of the page. '*Four hundred and twenty quid?*'

Kirsty nodded her head. 'Well, I suppose it's not that much more than we thought it was going to be.'

What? I had the sense to keep my mouth shut at this point.

'When we made the last payment,' continued Kirsty. 'You do remember, don't you, Sam? I sat down with the calculator and last year's bill, and worked out that we'd probably owe them quite a bit more.'

'Yes, of course I remember.' This was not entirely truthful. All right, it was entirely untruthful.

'Can you pay it out of the joint account? I'll transfer another two-ten in today.' Her implication was clear. I was to transfer two hundred and ten into the joint account as well. This was not what my overdraft needed at the moment. Four hundred and twenty quid. The insurance company pull that little surprise on a Monday morning, throwing my already precarious finances into complete meltdown, and they've got the nerve to call it a 'balancing' payment?

Parasites.

Danny seemed a bit, and I do mean a bit, perkier this week. We met on Tuesday evening; our sessions don't always have to be on the same day, which is good for me as it'll stop Kirsty spotting a pattern. If she did that she might well put two and two together and get an affair I'm not having, which could lead to the odd point being deducted.

Perhaps Danny's attitude improved because we were in a proper urban setting (Clerkenwell, a couple of miles from his home) rather than a park. Alan had thought that this would give us more options for things to do. He'd also told me, on the phone that afternoon, about the latest news from Danny's education officer. Unless he goes on a special course at the end of the summer to catch up on some of the work he's missed and show some commitment, he won't be allowed to return to his school for the new academic year. Instead he'll have to go to a centre where they deposit all the most persistent truants.

'What happens there?' I asked.

'Not a lot,' said Alan grimly. 'In fact, they might as well cut that stage out altogether and send him straight to a Young Offenders' institution.'

'What have you been up to then?' I asked Danny cheerily as we walked along the north side of Smithfield market. Summer's really kicked in now, and outside all the pubs the wide pavement was thronged with drinkers.

'Not a lot.' There was cynicism in his eyes, real, grown-up cynicism. Thirteen-year-olds sometimes try to pretend they've got this attitude, to hide the childish wonderment that has shown in their eyes up till now, but you can always tell it's an act. Danny, though, isn't acting. That's the sad thing. This genuinely is what he's like. Disenchanted with what the world's shown him so far, sceptical that what's coming next will be any better. So jaded is the look in his eyes that I almost imagine I can see lines at the corners, as though he's a middle-aged man.

'What about your mum and da— . . . your mum and her boyf— . . . partn— . . .'

'You mean my mum and that wanker who lives with us?'

'I don't remember that category on the census form but, yes, that's who I mean. Have you done anything with them?'

'Kept clear of them.'

Why was I bothering with this? Why didn't I just go home now? I've got a marriage proposal I'm trying to keep alive, I didn't need any of this. 'OK, what about friends? Have you got any friends you spend time with?'

'All those wankers from school?'

'Is everyone in your life a wanker, Danny?'

'Not everyone, no.'

'Well, who isn't a wanker, then?'

'Wouldn't you like to know?'

Eh? He made it sound as though it was a secret. I'd asked the question simply to get a positive comment out of him for once. But his response was sinister. I remembered last week, when he said that he 'knew people'. What was going on here? I felt worried. 'Danny . . .'

But before I could say anything else there was a blur of activity to my right, a yell from someone, and then Danny was off at full tilt, running towards the Farringdon Road. I tried to chase after him but found I couldn't move. Then I realised that the man standing next to me had his hand round my arm. 'What the fuck was that about?'

I wrenched myself free of his grip. 'What? What happened?'

'Don't give me all that. Your fuckin' lad nicked my drink.'

My lad? The cheek. I don't look that old. But somehow that seemed too trivial a side issue to bring up. Everyone on the pavement for twenty yards in either direction was watching us. I gazed after Danny and saw that in his right hand was a bottle, out of which beer was foaming as he ran.

'I'd just put the drinks down on the table,' the guy was explaining to his friends, 'and then, wham, that fuckin' kid darted in and nicked my Pils.' He turned back to me. 'What are you going to do about it, mate?'

There wasn't anything else I could do, was there? I felt in my pocket. There was a stack of change, but Danny was getting further and further away all the time, and the least the bloke would expect was a couple of pounds' compensation on top of his replacement beer. I thrust a fiver into his hand, muttered an apology and ran off after Danny. Even without the hundred-yard headstart his natural speed combined with my natural lack of fitness would have given me no chance. But as he reached the main road a huge lorry appeared, heading up to the market. It was so long that to take the corner it had to block the road's entire width. Danny was trapped. I slowed down as I got closer to him so that I'd have some breath left to vent my anger. With the lorry manoeuvring behind him he stood waiting for me, wearing a could-have-lost-you-if-I'd-wanted-to face, and drinking the beer.

I reached him, stood so that he was backed into a corner, and tried to think of a suitably intimidating line. But I couldn't. Buzzing from my run, and furious that he'd cost me a fiver I can ill afford at the moment, all I could do was explode in anger. 'You *bastard*!' I yelled, making a lunge that was half an attempt to grab the bottle, half an attempt to belt him round the head. It succeeded in neither, but as he ducked Danny dropped the bottle, which smashed on to the pavement. At least I'd denied him the spoils of his victory.

'*Why did you do that?*' I shouted.

'Wanted a drink.'

The sheer logic of this stopped my anger in its tracks. Unable to think of a reply, I had time to calm down and come to my senses. Losing it completely, in public, on account of a thirteen-year-old boy, was ridiculous. Besides which, if I continued to rant and rave, Danny would see me as another adult he'd beaten, someone else who could only shout at him. None of the other grown-ups in his life had got anywhere by pulling rank on Danny. That was precisely the reason I was spending time with him in the first place.

And anyway, the stolen drink wasn't the real issue here, any more than the smoking was last week. What was really bothering me was what I'd been asking Danny about when

72

his thirst intervened. 'Listen, you, what did you mean back then? About there being people in your life who aren't wankers? I think you've made it pretty plain you weren't referring to me. So who is it? What are you talking about, Danny? Which people do you "know"?'

But he wouldn't even look at me. The moment had gone. I knew it. Just like he had last week, Danny clammed up. After a while I had the sense to give up. My questions were pushing the information deeper into him, not drawing it out of him. But there's something going on in that boy's life. And it's not good.

Last week's points continued to fill me not just with confidence but with an eagerness to earn more. The better you get at something, they say, the quicker you can learn it. On Friday night, I did a nice bit of learning.

It involved a food processor. Until that afternoon it had been sitting happily on a shelf in John Lewis, but then Kirsty decided to go shopping on her way home and after that there was only going to be one winner. She's always been a gadget-chef. I prefer the simple approach: a hot oven, a sharp knife and a sturdy joint of beef. The only time I've ever got at all fancy in the kitchen was when I borrowed a mate's blowtorch to melt the sugar on a crème brûlée. I'd seen Delia Smith do it and it worked a treat, but I forgot to check the blowtorch's setting before I lit it, and instead of the little blue flame I got a bloody great orange one which took half the work surface off and melted two of the cupboard doors shut. Kirsty was not impressed. It's a good job I wasn't on points then, otherwise there'd be slightly more chance of me giving birth than marrying her.

But whereas I keep it basic, there's nothing Kirsty loves more than a kitchen appliance. If it chops, slices, stirs, mashes or grinds and you can fit a plug on it, she'll be there, Visa card in hand. Her old processor was *so* out of date (in other words the guarantee had months rather than years to run), so she just *had* to treat herself to this new one. It was unbelievably hi-tech. I don't know about cooking, it looked as though you could recondition a Ford Cortina with it. There were attachments here and compartments there, and by the time Kirsty got everything out of the box there was barely enough room left in the kitchen to turn round. Then she was faced with the task of assembling it all. While that happened, I went into the other room to watch the news.

An hour and a half later she was still in there. I decided to go and check on her progress. Kirsty was so absorbed in what she was doing that she didn't even notice me enter the room. Most of the processor had been pieced together and, the tip of her tongue poking out as she concentrated, she was fiddling with the last two or three components. The assembly instructions were lying on the table next to her, seemingly unread. I picked them up and began to flick through them.

I know, I know. And if you're a woman, you'll know as well. If you're a bloke you probably won't, but read on and you'll soon learn, as I did, just in time.

When I reached illustration 3 (a), I noticed that Kirsty had failed to connect filter B to socket 4. As a result, everything from tray G upwards was in the wrong place, which was why she wasn't getting anywhere. Without that filter in its proper place she could have been there until teatime on Saturday and the processor still wouldn't have worked. She needed to be told . . .

'. . . or does she?' asked the Points Fairy sitting on my shoulder. 'If Kirsty wanted to do this by the book, don't you think she'd have read the instructions for herself by now? In fact, if she'd wanted your help at all, don't you think she'd have asked you?'

I paused, and thought about it for a moment. Yeah, Kirsty was perfectly capable of looking through the instructions. Would I be doing the right thing by tapping her on the shoulder and showing her illustration 3 (a)? Would that lose me points? I thought back to the other week and my list of solutions to her Jenny problem. Something told me there was a link between the two things. I couldn't quite put my finger on it, but it came under the heading of 'Unwanted Help'.

Still Kirsty's tongue was poking out. Still she fiddled with the last few parts. Still she failed to acknowledge me, although as I was standing right beside her she must have known I was there. Very quietly I replaced the instructions on the table and tiptoed out of the room.

Was I right in my suspicion that Kirsty didn't want any help? I know I was. You want proof? I'll give you proof. I'll give you three hundred and twenty-one bits of proof.

Yes, you heard right. Three hundred and twenty-one. Tonight's total was three hundred and twenty-one. This week's score was a hundred and fifty.

Cabinet, unsurprisingly, was something of a riot when I told them all. Pete yelled 'you fucking beauty' and punched me exuberantly on the arm. Amanda threw her arms round me with a shriek of delight and kissed me on both cheeks. George's rioting was somewhat quieter, but no less intense. 'Even if Sam only maintains his current level of one hundred and fifty points a week,' he said, eyes half closed in concentration, 'he'll pass the thousand mark in another five weeks, giving him two weeks to spare. That's the very least he can expect. If he maintains his current rate of increase, namely fifty points a week, that'll mean two hundred points next

75

week, two hundred and fifty the week after that, and then in the following week, week eight, he'll get three hundred and achieve the thousand with no fewer than four weeks to spare. If, on the other hand, he maintains his current *percentage* rate of increase, next week he'll score two hundred and twenty-five points—'

'All right, George,' said Amanda. 'If we want bar charts we'll ask for them.'

I had a warm glow inside me, because I was thinking about the one person who was especially delighted about my very good week. And not, before you leap to conclusions, me. I was thinking about Kirsty. When she left the envelope on the table tonight and retired for her now customary seven-o'clock-on-a-Sunday-evening bath, I noticed that she was smiling. Very faintly, but she was definitely smiling. For the first four envelope-placings she'd achieved an absolute poker-face, which as the first three weeks had dealt her, or rather me, some of the worst hands imaginable was no mean feat. But tonight she couldn't help betraying (or was it deliberate?) the tiniest indication of pleasure that I was, at last, on track to get my points. That made me feel all warm inside.

Once we'd settled down a bit, I asked Amanda if I'd been right to link the Jenny episode with the food processor.

'Of course,' she replied.

This isn't meant to sound conceited, but I felt quite proud of myself. I'm starting to think for myself now, get these points sussed by my own efforts. I still wasn't totally happy, though. Instinct had guided me to the right solution, but I hadn't entirely ironed out the logic of it.

George was confused, too. 'I thought it was supposed to be men who never read the instructions?' he said to Amanda.

Before she could answer, I added my own query to the list. 'I can see how Jenny and the food processor were similar. Kirsty didn't want the answers thrust on her, she wanted to wrestle with the problems for a bit. But her distress about Jenny was an emotional thing. The food processor was just a technical hitch that needed sorting. There wasn't any emotional element to it.'

Amanda recoiled in shock. 'How can you say that? You've completely misunderstood the relationship between a woman and her kitchen gadgets. It's an *entirely* emotional relationship. Yes, George, you're right, normally women *do* read the instructions. When it's a practical thing, like putting a wardrobe together or knowing how much water you should mix with the wallpaper paste. But this is the exception. This is emotional.' She turned back to me. 'You don't think Kirsty actually needs any of her kitchen gadgets, do you? There are knives and chopping boards, and unless you're cooking for fifty people you don't need anything else. Kirsty didn't buy her food processor to process food, she bought it because she wanted something to love.'

'Something to love?' I snivelled. 'Aren't I enough?'

'Of course you are,' said Amanda impatiently. 'I'm talking about a different sort of love. The love a woman has for shoes, lipsticks, handbags. She'll buy far more of them than she ever needs because she gets pleasure simply from buying them, from having them. But although that love's trivial, it's still important. And so you have to let Kirsty indulge it in her own way. Which, being a woman, means not bothering with assembly instructions. Kirsty was playing with her new toy, deepening her emotional bond with it. She was expressing love by piecing it together in her own quirky way.'

'Quirky?' said Pete derisively. 'You mean wrong.'

'Wrong in what sense?' replied Amanda. 'It's wrong if you just want to get the food processor functioning as quickly as possible. But if you want to enjoy playing with it, discovering things about it – which I can guarantee you was what Kirsty did want – then it wasn't wrong at all.'

This was starting to make sense. It was the handbags that had convinced me. Kirsty's always buying new handbags. At one stage she had seventeen. I know because I went round the flat and counted them. Every time she buys another one I ask her what she needs it for, and she always replies that she hasn't got one in this colour or that size or one that'll go with her new outfit, or some other reason that hadn't occurred to me. But the real, underlying reason is what Amanda was explaining now. Women don't buy handbags, or food processors, because they need them. Or rather they do, it's just that their definition of 'need' is different from men's. A man needs a new food processor because his old one has broken. A woman needs it because she wants something to play with.

'So you mean, by working out how to assemble the thing without the instructions,' I asked, 'Kirsty was getting more fun from it?'

Amanda smiled. 'Dead right she was. Doing it that way gave her the pleasure of discovering and correcting her mistake. Which she wouldn't have been able to do if you'd come along with illustration 3 (b).'

'3 (a),' I said.

'That was a very male correction, Sam.'

'I don't care. It doesn't cost me any points in here.'

Week Six

Looking back on it now, it seems like a foghorn sounding across the calmly lapping waters over which my points-attempt was by then sailing. But at the time, it sounded like any other ring from my mobile phone.

'Hello?'

'Sam, it's me. Where are you?'

'Pot-holing in Zambia. Pete, it's eleven o'clock on a Wednesday morning. Where do you think I am?'

'What I mean is, can you talk?'

'I am doing, aren't I?'

'No, you prat, can you talk freely?'

'About what?'

'About earning some money. Tomorrow night.'

What the hell was he on about? I retired to the Gents to conduct the conversation in privacy. 'What money?'

'Seventy-five quid, that's what money. Seventy-five quid each, I mean.'

'Each? Me and you?'

'No, you and Tiger Woods. Of course I mean me and you. Terry's paying me a hundred and fifty.'

Just the mention of that man's name brought me out in a cold sweat. 'Terry? What are you doing for him that's worth a hundred and fifty quid?'

Pete could hear the suspicion in my voice. 'Nothing to get your knickers in a twist about. It'll be easy. Next to this, Sam, falling off a log requires a Masters degree.'

'Well, if it's so easy why don't you do it on your own? Why give half the money to me when you could pocket it all yourself? And anyway, what's "it"? What's the job?'

'Delivering something. That's the reason Terry wants me to take some help along. Give me a hand carrying the stuff. He said I could pick whoever I wanted and pay them as little of the hundred and fifty as I wanted, as long as they look presentable. So that was Ray out of the question, but there are plenty of other people I could have asked, and I'd have paid them a lot less than half the money, but no, I thought, why not ask Sam, he's a good friend, and seventy-five quid could pay for a nice meal that might well earn him a few points from the woman he's trying to marry.'

This, I must admit, was the moment he really got my attention. The way my finances are, I couldn't even treat Kirsty to fries with her Big Mac. Seventy-five pounds would be very welcome right now, as would the points that went with them. But my doubts were still there. 'What are you delivering?'

'Just a few carrier bags. Gotta take 'em to the Savoy.'

'The *Savoy*?'

'Yeah, that's where Terry's friend is staying. We drop the stuff off, you take your money, end of job. Total time out of your life, less than an hour. Total money received, seventy-five quid. Total points earned when you give that seventy-five quid to a waiter at Kirsty's favourite restaurant – well, start counting, sunbeam.'

Still my brain was worrying about the words 'Terry's friend', but everything else Pete had said made sense. All I had to tell Kirsty was that I was going to meet Pete, which in itself wasn't a lie. We'd deliver these bags, I'd get seventy-five quid, I'd walk away. There was, when you looked at it rationally, zero risk on one hand, and lots of potential points on the other.

'All right. What time shall I meet you?'

Wednesday was supposed to be my Danny evening, but just as I was about to leave the office Alan called and said it was off. Danny had gone missing. Hadn't been home the night before. Not the first time he's done it, apparently, and no doubt he'd return soon enough from 'whichever friend's house he's been hiding at', but for this week I was stood down.

I was relieved at not having to go through another hour of near-silent moodiness, but also couldn't stop thinking about these 'people' he claims to 'know', the ones who 'aren't wankers'. My unease from last week returned. Alan may think that Danny goes off to a friend's house. But Danny doesn't have friends. Not of his own age, anyway. Where had he gone? Who was he with?

The next day, I decided to go straight to the Mitre from work. Pete had said I should look 'presentable', so there was no point changing out of my suit. I sent Kirsty an e-mail to let her know I was seeing Pete, and she replied that she was going late-night shopping with Juliet (and therefore, no doubt, although she didn't say this of course, tinkering with my points total), so she'd see me at home later.

I got to the pub at just gone half-six. Pete was telling a couple of the regulars to keep an eye on Ray while he was gone, make sure he didn't get pissed, or rather too pissed. Then he took me through to the back room. In the middle of the floor were four huge Giorgio Armani bags, the plush cardboard ones about two feet by eighteen inches, with string handles.

Clothes? I asked myself. But as soon as I picked up one of the bags I knew its contents weren't the original ones. The bag was unbelievably heavy and packed absolutely solid. When it banged against my leg I thought I could feel a large wooden board in there, which seemed to have a horizontal ridge carved into it. I let the bag swing round. The other side felt exactly the same. What was in these bags? I couldn't see, as each of them had been very securely sealed at the top with clear tape. Something told me that I didn't want to know what was in there. This was Terry's business. I was content to let it stay that way, and take my money with the minimum of fuss.

Pete took a twenty-pound note from his pocket. 'Terry gave me this to get a cab there. But at this time of day it won't only be cheaper to get the Tube, it'll be quicker. Why don't we make ourselves a few quid extra?'

'I like your thinking.'

'You'll like the money even more, won't you?'

Fifteen minutes later Pete and I were on a Circle line train heading towards Temple. As we trundled along, I realised just what a truly pathetic criminal I'd make. Whatever was in these bags, Terry was obviously keen to ensure that the outside world didn't get a look at it. Which was why he'd used the tape. Being Terry, he'd done a very thorough job. But I still couldn't stop myself sneaking nervous glances at the bags, just in case. The real pros aren't like that, are they? They stride confidently into the bank, secure in the knowledge that everything's as it should be with the gun concealed in their jacket. But I'd be standing there, third in the queue, surreptitiously trying to check that I'd remembered to load the thing, and that it was pointing the

82

right way up so that when I grabbed it I wouldn't find myself holding the barrel.

Despite my paranoia, of course, the tape held firm, and soon we were off the Tube and walking, as fast as our loads would allow, which wasn't very, up to the entrance of the Savoy. The famous silver frontage glistened magically in the warm evening sun. The lobby had the buzz you normally get on a Thursday evening, not quite as exciting as Friday's the-weekend-starts-here buzz, but a pretty convincing dress-rehearsal. Guests were leaving for nights out, while others were arriving back laden with the fruits of four-figure shopping expeditions. We wandered around while Pete tried to get his bearings. 'We've got to meet Deano in the River Room,' he said.

'Deano?' I replied. 'Is he from Essex?'

'No, not Deano. Dino. D-I-N-O.'

'What sort of name's that?'

'Serbian.'

I stopped absolutely dead still. 'Serbian? *Serbian?* This guy's from Serbia?'

'Yeah. What's wrong with that?'

I shook my head in astonishment. 'You told me we were delivering something, Pete, but you didn't tell me we were delivering it to a fucking warlord.'

'Don't be stupid,' said Pete dismissively. 'He's not a warlord. He's a businessman.'

I couldn't believe I was hearing this. 'Pete, have you watched any news in the last ten years? Out there those two things mean the same. In the Serbian Yellow Pages, if you look up "Businessmen" it says "See Warlords".'

'What's got into you all of a sudden?'

'What's got into me is that Terry is paying us a hundred and fifty quid – a hundred and seventy if you include the taxi we didn't get – to deliver this little lot, so God knows what Slobodan—'

'Dino.'

'God knows what Dino's paid him for it, and anyone from that part of the world who's got that amount of money is not exactly the sort of person I feel very comfortable about meeting. Even if it is in a five-star hotel.'

'Will you stop being such a ponce about all this? Everything's going to be fine.'

'I knew we weren't going to be dealing with the Archbishop of Canterbury here,' I continued, 'but someone from Serbia—'

'Oh shut up,' snapped Pete. 'You're being paid to deliver a couple of bags, not analyse world politics.'

In the absence of any signs telling us where the River Room was, he stopped a passing member of staff and asked. As I always do in a very posh setting I started to feel self-conscious and became convinced that even with a suit on and a Giorgio Armani bag in each hand people would be able to single me out as someone who didn't belong there. The feeling was heightened in this case by the fact that we were there to meet a Serbian warl— businessman. While the guy pointed Pete straight ahead, I put one of the bags down and passed a hand over my forehead. A slight coating of sweat had formed.

'This way,' said Pete breezily. Although I was annoyed with him for not telling me about Dino, I couldn't help but admire his confidence.

I followed him down the steps into the River Room. It was wonderful. Huge and ornately decorated, with a high ceiling, it oozed class. And money. Even the guy playing the piano in the middle of the room, effortlessly tinkling away at one sublime standard after another, looked as though he could afford to buy and sell the whole place twice over. As for the guests, reclining on the plush sofas that filled most of the floor space, gently clinking the ice in their drinks as they placed them back on the low, elegant tables – well, if a single one of them was wearing an outfit worth less than five hundred pounds I couldn't spot it. But none of those clothes, nor the jewels that twinkled when the women turned their heads, were at all flashy. The riches on show were all the more impressive for being so understated.

I turned to Pete. 'I can't see anyone with a Kalashnikov, can you?'

'Very funny.' He scanned the room. 'But no, I think you're right. If Dino was here he'd have spotted the bags by now.'

'Regular touch by Terry, that, is it?'

Pete nodded. 'Come on, let's go and get a drink while we wait. Apart from anything else it might calm you down.'

We made our way over to the bar in the far right-hand corner. I remember thinking it seemed a bit small to cope with such a volume of trade; there must have been at least two hundred people in there. And also, I wondered, why is there no one serving? And why are we the only ones . . .

If these questions hadn't been preoccupying me, I would, I suppose, have noticed the drinks spillage on the floor near to where we were standing. And I would have noticed that when I put my two bags down, one of them went right into that spillage. And I would have realised what this was likely to do to the cardboard that made up the base of the bag. But none of these things happened, because those questions were indeed preoccupying me. And there's nothing I can do to change that now.

Pete and I exchanged an uncertain glance, which gradually turned into a realisation of what we'd done wrong. Before either of us could say anything, though, an impeccably discreet waiter came over and invited us to take a seat, as it was in fact waiter-service. I could have kicked myself. The clue was in his title, really, wasn't it? He was the soul of courtesy, which was pretty admirable in view of the fact that he must have been thinking, Who are these cretins, and what are they doing here, standing at the bar as though they're about to order two pints of lager and a packet of crisps?

A few of the guests sitting near us were obviously thinking along similar lines, because they turned to look at us. Some of them at least had the grace to do it while pretending to look over our shoulders at something else, but nevertheless it was obvious that we'd drawn attention to ourselves. My out-of-place feeling multiplied itself by ten, and I could feel my cheeks beginning to glow red.

'Can you see any free seats?' I murmured to Pete, as though if the guests couldn't hear me talking they wouldn't be able to see me.

But there weren't any seats to be had. So we had to carry on standing there as the guests who'd looked at us gradually resumed their chattering and the pianist executed a gentle turn from 'These Foolish Things' into 'A Nightingale Sang In Berkeley Square'. And although I didn't know it at the time, this was another minute in which the bag at my feet was soaking up the drink from the floor. But, like I say, there's nothing I can do to change that now.

Then, on the far side of the room, I saw a group of people making the initial pocket-patting movements that showed they were about to leave. If Pete and I were to nab that table we'd have to be quick so I picked up both my bags and nudged him with my right elbow.

'Come on, let's grab those sofas,' I said. My right arm struggled once more with the weight of its bag. My left arm, still programmed to think that it was carrying something heavy, shot upwards as with a faint tearing sound the entire base of the other bag dissolved, and its contents fell out.

What were those contents?

The one-word answer is 'magazines'.

You want a more-than-one-word answer? Come on, use your imagination, this is Terry we're talking about.

Put it this way, they weren't *Good Housekeeping*.

Suddenly everything seemed to be happening in slow-motion, and as the foul cargo passed before my eyes I had time to register that what I thought had been a wooden board had in fact been the magazines' covers. They'd been packed on their sides, spines uppermost. So tightly had they been crammed in that the first layer could support a second one without coming apart. The slight gap explained the horizontal ridge. As each layer comprised a good fifty mags, I was looking – literally – at not far short of a hundred pornographic magazines about to hit the floor of the River Room at the Savoy Hotel.

The sound they made as they landed was far louder than anything else happening in the room at that moment. Not surprisingly, everyone stopped talking and turned to see what was going on. After all, you do that when it's a tray of glasses that's been dropped, don't you? But then you look away again, because there's nothing more to see than a pile of broken glass.

This, on the other hand, was somewhat different.

The magazines had bounced when they hit the floor. Some of them had opened out, some of them remained closed. But even the closed ones had covers that left nothing to the imagination, and the drop had been from a sufficient height that an area of floor about five feet by three was now completely covered with . . . well, still not quite able to believe what had happened, I looked down to see what it was covered with.

The only things I could find to comfort me in this moment of sheer, undiluted horror were that all of the combatants were human, and that nothing they were getting up to was what you'd call perverted. At least not seriously so. It was, to quote the old euphemism, 'good, clean fun'. But by God it was graphic. Those fifteen square feet seemed like a thousand acres to me, all of it filled with human flesh, both male and female, joined together in various combinations and various positions. Maybe it was the way the magazines had covered each other, or maybe it was the way the photographs had been cropped in the first place, but there didn't seem to be many faces on show. The focus was very much on what you might call the 'business area'. Sometimes that area did include a face, of course, but by and large it didn't. All in all, I felt a bit like I was witnessing the last days of Sodom and Gomorrah.

And so, I realised as I glanced up, did everyone else. Conversation was a thing of the past. Drinks stopped halfway to mouths. Shocked, disgusted and, in one or two cases, fascinated faces stared first at the magazines, then at me and Pete, and then back at the magazines. 'A Nightingale Sang In Berkeley Square' continued to play peacefully in the background, but even the pianist, who was facing the other way, couldn't resist turning round to see what had happened. The single wrong note he hit in his astonishment rang out, perfectly encapsulating the way in which the River Room had been shaken out of its normality.

'Tell me that didn't just happen,' mumbled Pete, who like me was standing absolutely still, gazing down at the thousand acres of flesh.

'That didn't just happen,' I mumbled in reply.

'I *really* want to believe you, Sam. But the evidence is pretty convincing.'

Still neither of us moved. Perhaps Pete was going through the same petrified thought process as I was. If we don't move, went the reasoning, no one will know that the magazines are ours. They might assume that we just happen to be the people standing nearest to this incredible pile of filth that's appeared out of nowhere. But within a few seconds my mind began to function properly again. You are the one, it told me, standing there with a cardboard bag that's got the bottom missing from it, which you're holding directly over the pile of magazines that has so gripped the attention of everyone in this room. Even the ones who didn't see it happen are going to have not the slightest difficulty in piecing it together. You are the one who has just dropped hardcore pornography all over the floor. Everyone here knows it.

As soon as this hit me, everything that had seemed so unreal became horribly, viciously real again. My first instinct was to leg it. But three factors decided me against that. One, I was having enough difficulty even standing up. Two, we still had to wait for Dino, and running away from the situation would put Pete in a difficult position with him, and therefore with Terry. And three, even if I wasn't bothered about landing Pete in it (which, to be honest, I wasn't), Terry would soon find out who I was, and I didn't fancy him coming to look for me at the best of times, let alone when marrying my girlfriend depended on keeping in her good books. No, I was going to have to stay and face the music, not to mention the shocked patrons of the Savoy Hotel.

I dropped to my knees and started gathering up the magazines. Pete, however, still seemed incapable of thought, let alone movement.

'Well, don't just fucking stand there,' I hissed at him. 'Get down here and help me.'

He did as he was told. It was only now, as I noticed the pulpy scraps of cardboard amongst the magazines, that I realised what had happened. We reduced the thousand acres to a couple of piles, undid the tape from the remaining three bags and crammed them full with the load from the fourth. Then, with Pete using all his might to squeeze the tops of the bags shut, I managed to reseal the tape.

It's never going to be easy to publicly handle large quantities of hardcore pornography while maintaining your dignity. Certainly Pete and I failed to manage it, and so I can't really complain about the people in the River Room, i.e. all of them, who gawped in amazement as we picked up the bags and carried them over to the empty table on the far side of the room. The pianist was by now playing 'Blue Moon', which may or may not have been his idea of a joke. Only when we'd sat down and made a great play of examining the menu, did the mild hubbub of conversation start up again. I knew, of course, that most of those conversations were going to be about us, and although my breathing was gradually getting back to normal, my heartbeat still felt like it was doing its utmost to prove that 'die of embarrassment' isn't just a figure of speech.

A waiter came over to us. For a moment I thought he was going to ask us to leave, but it soon became obvious that he was just as uncomfortable about serving us as we were about being there, and that he wanted to get our drinks order and move away as quickly as possible.

'Two beers, please,' said Pete, staring straight ahead.

'Certainly, sir,' replied the waiter, backing away as though we had bombs strapped to us.

'He didn't ask us which sort of beer we wanted,' said Pete after he'd gone.

'Don't be stupid,' I said. 'He wasn't bothered. And neither am I. I just want to hand these bloody magazines over and get out of here. Did you know what was in these bags?'

'Of course I did.'

'Well, why didn't you tell me?'

'You didn't ask.'

I couldn't argue with that. The very reason I hadn't asked what we were delivering was that I knew I wouldn't like the answer. The fact that I had no right getting annoyed with Pete made me even more annoyed with him. 'Where's this warlord of yours, anyway?'

'What do you mean, warlord of mine? A, he's not a warlord, and B, he's not mine, he's ours. You're on for half of this money, remember?'

'Yes, I bloody well am,' I replied angrily, 'and so while we're on the subject, cough up.'

'We haven't finished the job yet.'

'No, Pete, "we" haven't, have "we"? So why should half of "we" get to keep all the money? Hand over my seventy-five quid.'

'It's no good,' he muttered. 'You'll need to say that just a *bit* louder. Someone in room five-one-two didn't quite catch all of it.'

I glanced around. People were starting to look at us again. 'Hand over my seventy-five quid,' I whispered.

'All right, all right, if it'll make you happy.' The sofa we were sitting on had dragged Pete back into its luxurious depths, which meant that he had to haul himself up to reach into his trouser pockets. Alarm registered on his face as he felt first in one pocket, then the other, and then checked them both again to confirm that neither contained the cash.

'Oh, that's just great,' I said. 'He's only lost the fucking wages. We're delivering pornography to a Serbian warlord and embarrassing ourselves in front of the most elegant group of strangers we'll ever meet, all for the sheer fun of it. Well listen, Pete, the reason I'm here is to earn some money to earn some points to earn my girlfriend's hand in marriage, so as far as I'm concerned you're paying me that seventy-five quid yourself. We're doing the handover, then we're going to a cash point, and I'm not letting you out of my sight—'

'*Will* you shut the fuck up?' snapped Pete. 'The money must have fallen out of my pocket, that's all.' He stood up, but the space where he'd been sitting showed no sign of any banknotes. So he pulled the cushion forward slightly and bent over to feel around in the gap at the back. 'It must have gone right down there,' he said, leaning forward even more. He was supporting himself by holding on to the arm of the sofa with his other hand, but the sofa was soft and comfortable and giving and he ended up with his arm rammed right down the gap. He reminded me of a vet with his arm up a cow.

'For Christ's sake, Pete,' I said out of the corner of my mouth. 'People are starting to look again. You're embarrassing me.'

He yanked himself free and sat down again. '*I'm* embarrassing *you*? Sam, I stumbled slightly. You dropped a hundred porn mags on the floor in full view of this entire room. Which of those two do you think is the more embarrassing?'

'Stop trying to change the subject. I want my money.'

'Well, you'll just have to—' He stopped, appearing to have felt something as he shifted his weight. Reaching into the back pocket of his trousers, he found the money. 'There you are. I knew I couldn't have lost it.' He leafed through the notes, only to find that there weren't any fivers. 'Sod it. Have you got any change?'

I grabbed four of the twenty-pound notes. 'No, and I don't need any. In fact, taking into account our profit from the Tube journey you still owe me about three quid. You can give me that another time.'

'I feel honoured.'

We were prevented from further squabbling by the reappearance of our waiter, who placed two glasses of beer on the table in front of us. Then he spotted that both of us were holding cash. 'There is no need to pay now,' he said. 'I will bring you a bill when you wish to leave.'

'Yes, obviously, I know that,' I said, irritated that he assumed we didn't know how to behave in a place like this. Although on the form we'd displayed so far I couldn't blame him.

The waiter departed. I took a consoling gulp of my lager.

'Good evening,' came a quiet, deep voice from behind us. 'Would you, by any chance, be Peter?'

We both looked round. Standing there was a man slightly over six foot tall, solidly built but not muscly. His back was ramrod-straight, his clothes as unshowily expensive as those of everyone else in the River Room. There was only one slight sign of vanity: although his weather-beaten face showed him to be well into his fifties, the man's hair was as black as coal.

Pete stood up. 'Hello – Dino? I'm Pete. This is Sam.'

Dino, who had been concentrating on the bags, noticed Pete's outstretched hand and shook it without smiling. Feeling that I should do the same as my partner, I rose to my feet. It was only when I shook Dino's hand that I realised what we were dealing with. My hand was crushed until it felt like it could fit inside a toilet-roll tube. His eyes, which were just as black as his hair, were the eyes of a man who fears no one but is feared by everyone. In that bone-mashing handshake I got absolute confirmation that this was a Serbian businessman who knew how to do business. And I don't mean he was a member of the Rotary Club.

Still he didn't smile. 'This is the merchandise, yes?' His accent was thick and heavy. It dripped with Balkan menace.

'Yes,' said Pete, who, like me, was flexing his right hand to check that it still worked.

'I am glad to see that as usual Terry has taped the bags well. It would not do for all these nice people to see what is inside.'

'The very thought,' replied Pete, as I gave an involuntary cough.

'Good,' said Dino. 'All is as it should be.'

Great, I thought, can we go now?

'You will not object to waiting for one moment?'

Dino headed off. Pete and I sat down.

'Look at the bruising on your hand,' I said to him, 'and then tell me that Dino's just a normal businessman. And what's he up to now?'

'Yes, my right hand's bruised. But my left could still punch you in the mouth. So will you stop complaining? It'll all be over in a couple of minutes.'

My phone started to vibrate. Thank God I'd remembered to switch it to 'silent'. I'd done quite enough to offend the River Room's sensibilities already. The display told me it was Kirsty. In the position I was in, even looking at her name felt dangerous. My thumb went instinctively for the 'divert' button, until I remembered just in time that there'd only been three rings and that she'd know I'd deliberately put her on to voicemail. So I let it carry on ringing, ready to pretend later that I'd been out on the street and hadn't heard the call. A terrier-sized piece of guilt started to snap at my heels. But I kicked it away by reminding myself that I was only doing this to earn money to earn the points she wants me to earn. Those eighty pounds, because they were going to be spent on her, were worth eighty million to me. I couldn't wait to ring up and book the table. The anticipation of watching her delight as we ate and drank our way through the money gave me goosebumps. Making her happy was going to make me ecstatic.

These joys swept away my horrible thoughts of dirty magazines and Serbian criminals. Soon my phone gave another little judder as Kirsty's message reached it. I dialled my answerphone:

'Hi, love, it's me. Hope you're having a nice time with Pete. I'm on Regent Street. Juliet's just left me. We went for a drink – well, a couple actually – after the shops, and I wondered if you were around for a couple more, but you're not. Hey-ho. See you at home. Love you.'

The tiny kiss she blew before hanging up melted my heart. If only I wasn't here with a stack of porn and a war-lord, I thought, it'd be heaven to meet up with her and spend that eighty quid right now . . .

Hang on.

In a couple more minutes I *wouldn't* be here with a stack of porn and a warlord. I'd only be here with the prat who got me involved with it all in the first place. And I could tell him to get lost as soon as look at him. Once Dino had retired upstairs with his literature, and Pete had been dispatched with a forceful reminder that he still owed me money, the night would be mine, as indeed would the girl, if I wanted her. It wasn't too late to turn this evening around. OK, every-one else in there saw me as the guy who'd lowered the tone, but Kirsty didn't know that. I was sitting on a plush sofa in a plush bar in a plush hotel, with eighty quid in my pocket and love in my heart. These are the nights, are they not, that you look back on from your old age. These are the nights that you have to make the most of. These are the nights that you have to grab by the neck.

And if a barrel full of points falls into your lap as a result, that's even better.

'To call the person who left this message,' came the disembodied voice of my network, 'press hash.'

Hash was there to be pressed. Who was I to disappoint it? Please God let Kirsty not have got to the Tube yet.

God was listening. 'Hi, darling. Did you get my message?'

'Yeah, just got it now. Sounds as though your retail therapy's put you in a good mood.'

'You know, Sam, sometimes I think Nicole Farhi's thinking only of me when she designs her clothes.'

'And Juliet's cried off, has she?'

'Yeah, the spoilsport.'

I could tell that Kirsty was just the tiniest bit drunk. No, not drunk, just merry. And how much more merry would she be, in every sense of the word, after I'd spent my eighty quid on her? 'That's a coincidence,' I said. 'Pete's just about to leave me.'

An 'am I?' look came over him. A 'yes you are' one came over me.

'So why don't you come and join me?' I continued.

'Where are you?'

'The River Room at the Savoy.'

'Wooooo, get you. Bit grand, aren't we?'

'Yeah, well. Sometimes you feel like treating yourself, don't you?'

'I can relate to that.'

'And sometimes you feel like treating your lovely girlfriend as well.'

'I can *definitely* relate to that.' Without having to ask, I knew that Kirsty had started scanning the street for a cab.

'Don't be long, will you?'

'As if.' She hung up.

Almost as though he knew that my spirits had recovered, nay soared, from their earlier nadir, the pianist started to play 'Come Fly With Me'. I turned to Pete. 'You've only got two instructions. One, drink up. Two, stop being here.'

'You really should learn not to worry about people's feelings, you know. Come out and say what you mean.'

'Here comes Dino, look. You could give him some help lugging the bags up to his room.'

Pete flexed the fingers of his right hand, and winced. 'Somehow I don't think he'll need it.'

Dino arrived back at the table. In my eagerness to see him depart I was concentrating on the bags, wondering if he'd pick up all three in one hand or spread the load a bit. When I looked at him I saw that his earlier thunderous, about-to-break-necks-if-everything-wasn't-in-order expression had disappeared. His whole demeanour was now full of friendliness, even bonhomie, inasmuch as a Balkan gangster can be said to exhibit bonhomie. I started to feel nervous.

'All is very well,' he said. 'I have spoken to Terry and congratulated him on the work done by his new representatives. Terry was glad to hear of your good work. And so we celebrate, yes?' Dino sat down in the chair at the head of the table, his back to the entrance of the room.

Forget 'nervous', I was now panicking like I'd never panicked before. The bag-collapsing incident had just been knocked off the top of my All-Time Top Ten Moments I Have Panicked chart. Compared to this, it was now nothing more than a hazy memory of something going slightly awry. Because while it may have embarrassed me beyond belief in front of two hundred strangers, it hadn't affected things with

Kirsty. I was never going to see those two hundred people again. But I did want to see Kirsty again. In particular I wanted to see her wearing my wedding ring. Which depended on points. And if turning up to find me with a Serbian criminal and four hundred pornographic magazines wasn't a points-loser *par excellence*, then I didn't know what was.

For the second time in half an hour my mental faculties had responded to a moment of panic by going on strike. 'What do I do now?' I whispered to Pete, as Dino ordered champagne from a waitress.

'You can't leave,' he whispered back. 'You'd have to explain it to Kirsty, and that'd lose you points. Plus Dino would take it as an insult, which means Terry would do the same, and that'd lose you limbs.'

'Yeah, but how do I explain all this to her?' I whined, nodding towards Dino and tapping the bags, which were by my feet.

'Use your initiative.'

'Pete, the average potato's got more initiative than me.'

'You two are all right?' asked Dino.

'Yeah, fine,' I replied.

'Just discussing a bit of business,' added Pete.

'Ah. I understand.'

No you don't, I thought.

'I'm sure,' said Pete, pulling the bags one by one round to Dino's end of the table, 'that you would like your merchandise to be as near you as possible.'

Dino nodded. 'Thank you. It is always wise to take good care of your investments.'

I was impressed. Getting distance between me and the evidence was a good move. Pete was thinking a lot more clearly than I was.

At that moment Kirsty appeared at the top of the steps. She looked, I've got to say it, stunning. She was wearing her black suit, which although it's only from Next looks as though it's from Donna Karan when it's on her. Heads turn when Kirsty wears that suit, including mine. Tonight she looked even more glamorous than usual, as the setting, and the Nicole Farhi bags in her hand, brought out the star quality in her. And now she was about to find me in a gutter of criminality. My stomach churned in terror.

She caught sight of me and smiled. As she walked down the steps and crossed the room, I noticed several men watching her while pretending to carry on listening to their wives. Normally I feel proud when this happens, proud that of all the men Kirsty could choose she goes for me. On this occasion, however, I wanted to click my fingers, not to summon a waiter but to make Kirsty disappear. Or rather, to make Dino, Pete and the magazines disappear, so I could sit there with Kirsty and pile up the points.

'Hello, darling,' she said, kissing me on the cheek. Already her smile had dimmed a fraction at the sight of Pete. Why was he still here, she was no doubt wondering. 'Hi, Pete.'

'Hi.'

As she sat down on the opposite sofa, I leaned forward, as though I didn't want Pete to see my face, and mouthed, 'Sorry, he changed his mind.' She responded with an almost imperceptible shrug that was obviously meant to mean, 'Oh well, nothing you could do about that.'

All this time, Dino's attention had been taken by something on the far side of the room. Kirsty leaned forward herself, so that we could talk without him hearing us.

'Who's that?'

'No idea.'

'Ah, Sam, Pete,' boomed Dino, 'here is our champagne.'

Lovely. It had been the approach of our waitress that had grabbed his attention. Kirsty looked confused, not to mention a little suspicious. 'When I said "no idea",' I murmured, 'I meant—'

'And who is this that has given us the pleasure of her company?' interrupted Dino.

Oh God. 'This is Kirsty,' I said, shooting her a look. 'Kirsty, this is Dino.'

Nonplussed, Kirsty nodded in acknowledgement of Dino's grin, which was full of charm, but charm with an unmistakable intent.

The waitress was by now filling the champagne glasses. 'We will, of course,' said Dino, 'be needing another glass now.'

'Certainly, sir.'

'Here,' I said to Kirsty, 'you have mine. I'll wait for the glass.'

'Thank you.'

'Here's to a satisfactory conclusion of business,' said Dino.

I prayed that Kirsty would assume Dino was talking about some business deal of his own, which he'd wanted to celebrate with the first strangers he could find. Looking a lot less happy than when she'd first walked in, Kirsty took a sip of her champagne, then announced that she was going to the Ladies.

Dino waited until she'd gone. Then he leaned across and smiled. 'She is your girl, yes?'

I nodded. Although by then I wasn't really sure any more. And I didn't have the gumption to extricate myself and Kirsty from this awful set-up. Even the champagne – my glass had now arrived – tasted like cat's pee.

Kirsty rejoined us.

'So,' said Dino, 'how long have you been with Sam?'

She looked at me as she answered. 'Three years.' Not a trace of a smile left. I wouldn't have been surprised to hear her add, 'But I'll only be staying with him for another seven weeks. If that.'

'I see.'

Unable to hold Kirsty's stare any longer, I turned to look at Dino.

I've heard people say that in moments of complete terror they felt as though an icy hand had gripped their entrails. In my case, the icy hand decided that the entrails wouldn't be sufficiently painful, so it went straight for my bollocks. Having grabbed them, it proceeded to roll them around, at first like Pete Sampras deciding which ball to serve with, and then less gently, like a Las Vegas gambler going for a really big throw of the dice. Because I had just understood what Dino had meant when he asked if Kirsty was 'my girl'. And in enquiring how long she had been 'with' me Dino hadn't meant romance but business. Like the total and utter imbecile that I am, I had accidentally let Dino form the impression that I was Kirsty's pimp.

As the full implication of this hit home, the icy hand stopped being a gambler and became an on-edge business-man giving his stress ball the workout of its life. I was sitting here with my girlfriend and a Serbian gangster, one of whom was losing her interest in marrying me, and one of whom could at any moment make a suggestion that would vaporise what little remained of that interest. In an attempt to rid myself of the icy hand's attentions, I swallowed hard, several times. Kirsty, who was still fixing me with her stare, couldn't help but notice. 'Are you OK?' she said.

'Yes, fine,' I replied, in a voice that sounded as though I'd been sucking on helium. I coughed a couple of times, and managed to get my voice back down to somewhere near its normal level. 'Yeah, I'm OK. Bit of champagne went down the wrong way, I think.'

Pete, thank God, sensed that there was a breach, and stepped into it. 'Nice champagne, though, eh?'

Standard English Politeness kicked in.

'Mmm,' said Kirsty.

'Lovely,' I added.

'I only buy the best champagne when I am celebrating business,' said Dino.

Kirsty, playing by the rules of politeness, asked him: 'What business are you celebrating?'

And I, in a desperate attempt to prevent Dino answering, lunged at the nearest object to hand. Which happened to be the champagne bucket. I was aiming for a nudge, which would spill a bit of water over the table and create a minor distraction, but I got my angles wrong and tipped the whole sodding bucket right off the table. This created about as major a distraction as you could imagine, because its contents went all over Kirsty's feet, soaking them with ice-cold water and frothing champagne. The shock caused her to screech at the top of her voice, which made everyone in the room look round – yet again – to catch up on the latest events in Freak Corner.

'What are you doing?' she gasped, as a waiter appeared and started to clear up. Dino assisted by taking a silk handkerchief from his pocket and using it to dry Kirsty's feet. I half-registered that he was leaning over her more than was strictly necessary, but I was concentrating on explaining my own actions.

'Sorry, I was going to top up everyone's glass, and I accidentally caught the bucket with my hand.' I glanced down at her shoes, which she'd taken off. They were her dark red ones with the black stitching and the severely sexy heels. Or rather they had been. Now they were mushy piles of mis-shapen leather, with champagne bubbles oozing from the seams and no future whatsoever as shoes. 'God, I'm sorry,' I gabbled.

Kirsty looked at me severely.

'My dear,' said Dino, 'perhaps you would like to come to my room upstairs to . . . tidy yourself up.' With that he winked, put an enormous hand on Kirsty's knee and squeezed tight.

I had to stop watching at this point. I looked down at my lap. It was, I know, a complete desertion of my responsibil-ities. Any man who sits by while his girlfriend is groped by a stranger can have no excuse. Even when the groper is a Serbian gangster whose friend can sack, and do worse things to, your mate, and give you a dose of the worse things as well. You don't let someone treat your girlfriend like that.

These were no doubt the exact thoughts going through Kirsty's mind. There were three or four seconds of silence, in which she was obviously waiting to see if I'd do anything, and then a single, crisp smack pierced the air. I looked up to see Kirsty collecting her bags, throwing her ruined shoes into one of them, and then storming out of the hotel without even a glance in my direction. Then I looked at Dino, who was sitting stock-still, his eyes wide and unblinking in sheer disbelief, a red palm-print slowly developing on his right cheek.

My worries about what I was going to say to Kirsty were put on hold as I dealt with the immediate problem: Dino. I'm not sure whether the icy hand was grabbing my genitals at this point, because the main thing I could feel was a cer-tain loosening of the bowels. Backing away from Dino, who was still motionless, I started to edge along to the far end of the sofa, as did Pete, both of us ready to run like hell as soon as we'd got our legs clear of the table.

We were starting to rise, very slowly, from our seats, when Dino suddenly shook his head, blinked a couple of times, and looked over at us. We froze.

'I am sorry,' said Dino quietly.

What?

'I am sorry. I do not know what I was thinking of. I should, of course, have spoken to you about the business details first.'

I couldn't believe I was hearing this. Relief and anger coincided.

'I hope you will forgive me, Sam.'

Forgive him? I wanted to punch him. But I have a hard and fast rule about that. I will only punch people who are much shorter than me, much lighter than me, and unable to run as quickly as me. As a consequence I have only ever punched one person in my whole life. His name was Ben Rollason, and he had just tried to nick my *Sesame Street* pencil case. Faced with Dino I opted for a vague grunt, which he could interpret as forgiveness being granted and I could think of as a very rude word. After that I left Pete to bring proceedings in the River Room to a close, and ran out of the hotel in search of Kirsty.

I couldn't find her. She had, of course, got a cab. Walking through central London is a thing best avoided if you're not wearing shoes. Dejectedly I headed for the Tube. By the time I got in Kirsty was in bed and fast asleep.

It was Saturday afternoon before she'd speak to me. And even then that was only to say she was going out to buy new shoes, so could she please have a blank cheque. That was rubbing it in a bit, I thought. But when she got back she did at least have the grace to say how much she'd spent. A hundred and thirty pounds. A hundred and fifteen of that was the shoes, the rest had been spent on a new attachment for her food processor. So my net financial loss was fifty quid. The bank account creaked a little more, but that was the least of my worries. God alone knew what I'd lost in points.

I found out tonight. My trembling fingers just about managed to get the envelope open. This week's total was three hundred and twenty-two. In the last seven days I'd earned a single point.

'That's not good, is it?' said George later on in the Mitre.

'It's certainly nearer "bad" than "good",' answered Pete.

'How do you feel?' asked Amanda.

'Disappointed, obviously,' I replied. 'If I'd got the same as last week I'd be on four hundred and seventy-one now. But in a way I'm also relieved that my total didn't actually go down. After Thursday's disaster I was expecting to find myself back on zero. I thought about trying to explain to Kirsty what had happened, but decided that "I was delivering some pornographic magazines to a Serbian warlord to get some money to treat you, but I didn't know he'd still be there when you arrived, and the only reason he put his hand on your knee was that I'd accidentally let him think you were a prostitute" would probably harm my cause rather than help it.'

'Developing an almost intuitive feel for the female mind, aren't you?' said Pete.

Amanda ignored him. Which made two of us. 'You're right,' she said. 'Least said, soonest back in with a chance of earning points. And I think Kirsty's let you have a point this week as a symbol of hope. She obviously couldn't let Thursday go by without docking you points for it, but all the same, you must have earned points in the rest of the week. I bet she decided to keep your spirits up by making that total one point more than you lost in the Savoy.'

I didn't know whether to believe this, but even if it was a whistle in the dark then the best thing I could do was join in. 'Yeah. I've got to latch on to that point as a beacon, haven't I?'

'Come on,' said George, as his contribution to the whistling, 'tell us about the rest of the week. What do you think you earned points for?'

'Since Thursday, not a lot. I couldn't do right for fear of doing wrong. These new shoes, for instance. When Kirsty got them out of the bag I really did like them, but I was afraid to say so in case she thought I was creeping to get back into her good books. So I've played it safe and given her a wide berth.'

'Very wise,' said Amanda. 'And I think this coming week should be a time for quiet consolidation. This is the end of week six, right? You're halfway through the test. You've only got three hundred and twenty-two points, but if you get back to last week's scoring rate you'll soon make up the shortfall. Concentrate on your small change this week. See where that gets you.' She turned to Pete. 'Have you still got those lists from the first two weeks?'

He rummaged around by the side of the till and managed to find them.

'Let's see if we can't do some fine-tuning,' said Amanda, studying the lists. 'Ah, here we go. This "tucking the bed sheet in" thing: do you put the pillowcases on as well?'

'Of course,' I said, smirking at George as if to say, 'What does she take me for?'

'*And* put the near end inside the extra little flap?'

My smirk vanished. 'What extra little flap?'

'I thought as much,' she said, before going on to explain that there's a flap at the open end of a pillowcase that you can tuck over the pillow itself to stop it falling out. Try it. I did when I got home. It's brilliant.

'"Not leaving jam traces in the butter",' continued Amanda. 'Good, but do you apply the same principle to sugar?'

I thought about it. 'Oh, you mean not letting tea or coffee drip into it and go all hard? Mmm, couldn't guarantee that I *never* do it. Something else to keep an eye on. Ta.'

'And while you're at it,' added Amanda, 'when you've fished the teabag out of the mug with a spoon, don't use the same hand to push the bin lid open. You get brown drips all over the top of the lid.'

This was gold dust. Absolute gold dust. Amanda was on a roll. 'Don't leave the spoon under the tap so that Kirsty drenches herself.'

'I've never noticed that happen,' I said.

'Of course you haven't,' explained Amanda. 'Because Kirsty never leaves the spoon there, does she?'

God, these things are so obvious when she points them out. 'Anything else?'

'Squeeze the toothpaste from the bottom of the tube, not the middle.'

I gave her a good-natured sneer. 'Even I'd spotted that one.'

Week Seven

Only two words, but they were a defining moment. It was Monday night, and Kirsty and I were watching television, sitting on opposite sofas, plates of microwaved chicken chow mein on our laps. The soap opera was even less inspiring than the food, and the atmosphere between us was still tinged with Kirsty's resentment about the Savoy. A forced civility had broken out, but it was no more than that. I could see why she felt the way she did. Suspicious circumstances like that must have reminded her of my Wobbly Week and set her wondering if I'm ready for marriage after all.

She put down her fork and sighed. I glanced up and found she was looking at me, an intensity in her eyes that was making them shimmer. It's a look she gets very occasionally, when something important's on her mind, really important, something beyond mortgages and job offers and pension plans. The shimmering told me that what was coming next would concern me, and be either very, very good or very, very bad. Even before I knew which, it was a beautiful moment, because it was Kirsty showing that I mattered to her. I must do, otherwise I wouldn't have produced a reaction like that.

Then came the two words. They were: 'Bloody Mary?'

I broke into a smile. Kirsty makes the best Bloody Mary in the world, and by offering me one she'd signified that her resentment was over. Such an out-of-the-ordinary drink on a quiet Monday night in was unusual in itself, but coupled with the thaw in relations it marked, Kirsty's suggestion was sexy as hell. And she knew it. Before I could reply she added: 'But there'll be a condition.'

'Which is?'

'Foot massage.'

We both grinned. She could impose as many conditions like that as she wanted. The chow mein was ruthlessly side-lined, the vodka and massage led to what you'd expect vodka and massage to lead to, and in one glorious evening I felt closer to Kirsty than I had for a long, long time. Best part of breaking up is making up, et cetera. In fact it was only in the small hours of the morning, lying in bed listening to Kirsty's breathing deepen as she fell asleep, that the thought of points popped into my mind again, disturbing my bliss. Why was she judging our future like this? The closeness we'd felt tonight should have convinced her we should be together, not the number of times I changed the pillowcases or whether I left spoons in the sink. But it was no use going over that again. On points is where I am. I put the thought out of my mind, cuddled up even closer to Kirsty, and slipped into my dreams.

Alan called on Tuesday, to ask if I wanted to see Danny this week. He'd reappeared after a couple of days, refusing to tell anyone where he'd been. As a result of that and the beer-nicking incident in Clerkenwell, he'd been told that it was the park again. Built-up area privileges had been lost. If I agreed to see him at all, that was.

I agreed. I couldn't not agree. Despite a feeling that Danny doesn't deserve all these chances, I can't stop myself worrying about him. Alan said he appreciated my persistence. 'And listen,' he added, 'you remember the course I mentioned, at the end of the summer? I've got you a copy of last year's curriculum. Thought perhaps you could look through it with Danny, try and persuade him that he should go on the course.'

'Sure. If you think it'll help.'

'All we can do is try,' he said wearily.

Wednesday was another roasting-hot day, so the park was busy as Danny and I traipsed round it. For a few minutes the only sound he produced was the scuff-scuff-scuff of his trainers on the gravel path. At one point he stretched out his foot for a large pebble and started dribbling with it. His smirk confirmed my suspicion that this was intended as a reminder of how much better he was than me at football. Immaturely I bridled at this, but I also knew that his mockery was preferable to no reaction at all. It set me apart from the adults who couldn't get through to him full stop. This helped me rise above his implied taunt and I felt quite pleased with myself for that. Although is pride at not being childish in itself childish?

That's one for the philosophers. My job was to make some progress with Danny, find out where he was last week, get him on this bloody course. Light-hearted references to his vanishing act ('thanks for getting me the week off', etc) elicited nothing but silence. So I switched tack, and held the curriculum out to him.

'Have you thought about this course?' I asked.

Danny only took the stapled bundle of A4 sheets because I kept tapping it irritatingly against his arm. I knew that once he was holding it, though, he wouldn't be able to resist giving it the once-over, if only to deride it. I wasn't wrong.

'"Geography: basic rock formations"? What's the point of that?' He threw the curriculum on the grass, and carried on walking. 'I don't need any of that shit. I'm sorted. Don't need school.'

I retrieved the curriculum and looked through it as I hurried to catch up with Danny. Algebra, construction of the periodic table, eighteenth-century social history . . . He was right. I remembered exactly how it felt when I was thirteen, trudging through textbook after irrelevant textbook, learning a load of facts that I'd forget two minutes after the exam they were designed to get me through. 'Don't think I don't know what you mean,' I said to him. 'Virtually everything in here is a complete waste of time. I know, because I did it all twenty years ago, and haven't used a single bit of it since.'

He looked up at me. I think I'd succeeded in shocking him. No doubt I was the first adult who'd been that frank with him. 'So why are you on my fuckin' back about it?'

'Because the rules of the game might be stupid, but they're the only rules there are. You know this lot's a waste of time, I know it's a waste of time, even the people who set it know it's a waste of time, but if you don't go through with that waste of time, you get a crap life. Stupid, I know, but that's the way it is. You've got one chance left to accept that, Danny, or you really are going to get the crap life. Please, trust me, it's for your own good.'

Christ, I'd said it. I'd used that phrase. In the lexicon of talking-to-children clichés, 'it's for your own good' is up there with 'this is going to hurt me a lot more than it'll hurt you'. But that didn't bother me. What was frustrating was that I couldn't get the message through to Danny. He wouldn't listen.

'I've told you,' he said, as though the problem was mine, not his, 'I don't need school. Don't need your "rules". Got my own. You have to find your own rules when you've had a background like me.'

I could see this going round in circles. Equally, I knew what would happen if I pressed him about where he went last week. This kid genuinely didn't care when adults told him off or warned him. We all go through a rebellious phase, but Danny was in a much more dangerous place than that. And so he needed more careful handling. One telling-off too many and I could push him over the cliff.

At one of the gates to the park there was a snack stall. 'I fancy an ice cream,' I said. 'Want one?'

'Can't we go to the pub instead?'

'No we can't,' I replied, against all my natural instincts. 'Now do you want an ice cream or not?'

Even the most self-consciously miserable child likes ice cream. Danny hated himself for being so conventional, but couldn't resist the offer. 'If you like,' he murmured.

I sensed the chance for a small victory. 'No,' I insisted, speaking very calmly and slowly, 'if *you* like. You don't have to have an ice cream just because I'm having one, Danny. You can say no if you want to. Now would you like one?'

He fought with all his might to stop himself giving in. But it was a very hot evening. Eventually the word tumbled reluctantly out of his mouth. 'Yeah.'

The lack of a 'please' didn't concern me. I'd won, and we both knew it. I'd got him to do a normal 'kiddy' thing, to accept my hospitality, however ungratefully. As long as I could keep this link open to him, albeit a link based on antagonism, I stood a chance. I had to stop him doing what he does with all the other adults in his life, namely cutting himself off, verbally, emotionally, even – when he runs away – physically.

'This is crap,' he said after the first mouthful.

He was right too. Synthetic rubbish, white instead of yellow. One-pound-sodding-fifty a go, as well. Once you'd wolfed your chocolate flake the rest of it was a real chore. But I didn't say anything. I'd opened a seam of negativity in Danny, and if I kept my mouth shut he'd have to mine it, get me back for my victory, show me that he wasn't bluffing about not needing school.

'This is *really* crap,' he continued. 'Ones you get at the beach are ten times better than this.'

Got him. 'You go to the beach with your mum, do you, Danny?'

Obviously the answer was no. He rose to the provocation. 'Wouldn't waste my time with her.'

'Oh, so you go on your own?'

I held my breath. We were close to something here, and I had to be careful not to blow it. But after about fifteen seconds he still hadn't answered. Should I risk giving the pot another stir? 'I see. You go to the beach on your own.'

That did it. 'Maybe I know people who live near the beach.'

Come on, Sam, you can raise this another notch or two. Easy, though, don't scare him off. 'Really? You know people who live near the beach? Interesting. I wonder what they're like? I bet they're just kids, like you.' I spoke without looking at him, phrasing my comments as throwaway thoughts. Too direct a challenge and he'd pull down the shutters. I had to niggle him. 'Yeah, they'll be kids.'

Danny snorted. 'I'll tell Spider that when I see him.' As soon as he'd said it he took a huge bite of his ice cream. 'Fuck, this is really shit, I'm not eating any more of this.' He hurled it on to the grass and stood there, silent. Wasps began to buzz around the ice cream. There was an ugly mood between us now, and I knew that Danny's openness had come to an end. I'd be getting nothing more out of him today. He hadn't been able to resist giving me evidence that his 'don't need school' statements were more than just talk, but he didn't want to give me so much that I'd be able to act on it. I knew that someone called Spider was involved, and that he lived near a beach, but nothing more than that.

It was a start, though. It showed that I could get to Danny. Good, because he's got to me. It's *so* infuriating, knowing how close he is to finally, irretrievably pissing the rest of his life up the wall and not being able to get it through to him. He thinks he knows it all. If I could just show him how wrong he is.

Hang on. Is that what it's all about? Kirsty putting me on points, I mean. Has she done it to show *me* that *I* don't know it all? Is she doing with me what I'm trying to do with Danny?

I've started to realise that in working out how to earn these points, I'm working at our relationship. Hearing that phrase in the past, I automatically associated it with relationships that are in trouble. But now I'm beginning to wonder. Is it something we all have to do, even when things are going well, even when the saucepans aren't flying around the ears? Until now I've always assumed it's 'I love Kirsty, she loves me, no further effort required'. We blissfully recline in the bowl of cherries that is our relationship. But perhaps it's not that simple. Maybe that's what Kirsty's trying to show me. The minute you stop making the effort is the minute your relationship starts to go wrong. Putting me on points is her way of getting me to make that effort. All these things I've discovered which are now earning me points are things I never even thought about before. And although Kirsty obviously isn't saying that tucking the pillow under the extra little flap is grounds for marrying someone, the simple act of me thinking about things until I discover, with Amanda's help, that there are extra little flaps to be used shows that I'm willing to work at our relationship. The flaps, and the not shushing her during the sports news, and all the tiny compromises and considerations, they don't really matter in themselves – it's my making the effort that she values. Love isn't just something you feel, it's something you work on.

I'm trying to get Danny to understand something new about life. Kirsty's doing the same to me.

I wish I could tell her I've worked that out. Not to earn points, although it might get me a dozen or so, but just because I want her to know. Understanding something like this makes me feel a bit more in love with her. Can't tell her, though, of course. It'd mean telling her about Danny.

Oh well. Doesn't really matter. The important thing is that these points make a bit more sense now.

Which is a good job, because as of tonight there are even more to be made sense of. The new total is – wait for it – four hundred and eighty-two. In the last seven days I've scored one hundred and sixty points.

Amanda's reading of this was, I'm glad to say, the same as mine. 'That's ten more than your previous highest score in a single week,' she said, as Pete poured us all celebratory drinks. 'You're still behind target, of course. Seven weeks gone, over halfway through, with less than half the points you need. But I think Kirsty's sending you a message here. I think she's saying, "Last week was an aberration, but now you're back on course, and to show I want you to reach a thousand points, I'm symbolically giving you ten points more than your previous best score."'

George gave one of his ultra-thoughtful sniffs. 'Kirsty goes for the old symbolism, doesn't she? Last week it was a symbolic one, to keep Sam's hopes alive, this week it's a symbolic ten. Symbolism is the new rock 'n' roll.'

'And I like the sound it makes,' I said proudly. 'It's the sound of Kirsty saying she wants to be my wife.'

Amanda smiled and patted my arm, Pete emitted a gentle 'aaaahhh', and George drank his pint with a peaceful slurp that somehow chimed with the mood of love and optimism.

'It might not be,' came a rasping South African voice.

Oh God.

'It might be the sound,' continued Ray, who'd sneaked up without any of us noticing, 'of her stringing you along. I reckon this whole points thing is just her way of letting you down gently. She hasn't got the guts to say, "No, I don't want to marry you," so she's come up with this as a cop-out. You won't get enough points, she won't marry you, and you'll be left feeling you were the one to blame. Typical woman's trick. Shitty as anything, and you take the flak. I bet that's what it is.'

George leaned across to Ray. 'Don't take this the wrong way,' he said, 'but will you go and stick it up your arse?' It's not often he's roused to anger, but when it happens, he's magnificent.

'*Right* up your arse,' added Pete. 'Listen, Ray, I stand here day in, day out, watching your "investments" educate several bookies' kids, so it doesn't surprise me that that's your bet about all this. But some of us have got a bit more faith in Sam, and that's why we're in his Cabinet and you're not, so will you just *fuck off* and leave us to it?'

Ray hopped back to his end of the bar and sought solace in his Matt Monro tape. Cabinet discussions to the accompaniment of an out-of-tune 'From Russia With Love' could be seen as a bit of a challenge, but we'd been so offended by Ray's comment that we made an extra special effort to ignore him. I think the other three were even more offended than I was. Ray's theory was too stupid to take seriously. And after what I've worked out tonight, about the real reason Kirsty's put me on points, I know for absolute certain that he's wrong.

'A toast,' said Pete. 'To Sam's four hundred and eighty-two points.'

'To Sam's four hundred and eighty-two points,' echoed George and Amanda as the glasses chinked together.

Pete thought for a minute, and then added: 'That's four hundred and seventy-two louder, isn't it?'

George sniggered. I knew what was going to happen next. And I'm not judging them, because I've done it many times myself. Tonight, though, I was content to watch and laugh.

'You know,' said George, 'you're on ten, all the way on your guitar – where can you go? Where?'

Pete pretended to look dumb for a moment, although he was struggling not to crack up, and then said, 'I don't know.'

'Exactly,' replied George. 'But when we need that extra push, guess what we do?'

I could see that Amanda was dimly aware of what they were on about, but couldn't quite put her finger on it. I leaned over and whispered: '*Spinal Tap*.'

'I should have known,' she said despairingly. 'Every bloke under the age of forty can recite that film from beginning to end.'

'Haven't you seen it?' asked George.

'Of course I've seen it,' replied Amanda. 'I have had boyfriends who have had video recorders. Therefore I have seen *Spinal Tap*.'

Pete broke off from his mime of someone scraping a violin across the strings of a guitar. 'Didn't you think it was funny?'

'Yeah. Not to the extent that I lost control of my bladder, but then of course I'm not a man. That's also why I can't remember every single word of it. We women aren't as trivial as you lot.'

George looked offended. 'We're not trivial.'

'So how come you know that whole film off by heart? How come blokes always remember film scripts? Football scores? Trivia in general?'

'Ah,' he replied, 'Fundamental Female Misunderstanding number forty-seven. "Blokes remember trivia because they're trivial." No we don't, we remember it for precisely the opposite reason: because we're deep. Because we have a deep love of things.' When you spend as much of your time as George does pondering life, you come up with theories like this.

Amanda laughed, turned to face George properly and folded her arms. 'Come on, I want to hear this. This should be good.'

George pulled up his sleeves in a pre-rising-to-a-challenge way, then launched into his explanation. 'You think that Pete and I, and indeed Sam, know *Spinal Tap* off by heart because we've sat down and painstakingly learned it, ready for nights down the pub when we can act it all out and show off how good we are at remembering the lines. But it's not like that. The only reason I know the film so well is that I love it. I must have watched it . . . well, God knows, dozens, maybe even hundreds of times, and so it's not very surprising, is it, that I'm familiar with the dialogue?'

I'd never really thought of it like that, but now that I did I could see George had a point.

Amanda's arms remained folded. 'Carry on.'

'It's not a love of trivia for its own sake. It's just that when a bloke's interested in something he really loves it, gets to know it inside out, and all the information about it, all the, as you phrase it, "trivia", goes into his head and stays there. So you see, we're not superficial, we're deep.'

Amanda unfolded her arms. I sensed that she was beginning to engage with George's argument. I'd more than engaged with it, I'd signed up for it wholeheartedly. Blokes are exactly how he was describing them. At least this one is.

'Isn't it all just part of being a gang?' said Amanda. 'You all know *Spinal Tap* because it gives you something you can recite together.'

'No,' said George frustratedly. 'We all know *Spinal Tap* because we all love it. OK, maybe there's something about the male brain that means it stores information more easily. But we don't set out to memorise things for their own sake. It's just that when you've heard Nigel Tufnell complaining about the catering one hundred and fifty times, it sticks in your mind.'

I nearly starting quoting the scene in question, but stopped myself. It's rare to hear George get this animated about anything and I didn't want to interrupt him.

'It's a bit like dates,' he continued. 'I often remember dates. Like . . .' He paused to think of an example. 'Like the date Muhammad Ali won the world heavyweight title for the first time. Twenty-fifth of February, nineteen sixty-four. Now I know that not because I've purposely memorised it to impress people at parties—'

'Good job,' interrupted Amanda, 'because you wouldn't impress them, you'd scare them.'

'Hang on, let me finish. What I'm saying is the only reason that date's stuck in my mind is that I'm fascinated by Muhammad Ali, and I've read lots of books about him and watched lots of television programmes about him, and the fact that he won the world title on that date has been in most of them and so it's gone into my memory and stayed there.'

'Mmm,' said Amanda non-committally. I got the impression she hadn't been entirely convinced, but was perhaps beginning to consider the possibility that men aren't quite so trivial after all.

'There you go,' said Pete, jabbing a playful finger into her shoulder. 'Some traffic in the other direction for once. It's not just you who can reveal the secrets of your gender. Maybe this Cabinet might teach you a thing or two about men. If there's anything else you want clearing up, just let us know. No subject too delicate.'

'Delicate?' replied Amanda. 'Men don't do delicate. Their idea of delicate is turning the football off *before* they grab your breasts.'

'No,' said Pete, 'that's "romantic". "Delicate" is turning the sound down on the football.'

Amanda laughed, a little more readily than I felt comfortable with. Pete's quietened down on the flirting front recently and this was an unwelcome return to form. I'm sure Amanda's only playing along. She's got far too much taste to be seriously interested in an urchin like him. But even so, I don't want him jeopardising things. His flirting with her was a flagrant breach of Cabinet rules. Words will be had.

But that's for another day. Tonight I'm just happy to be on track for the points, and moreover to understand why I'm on points at all. I really think it's going to happen. The speeches, the cake, the drunken aunt making a fool of herself on the dancefloor – yes, that wedding will be mine.

Week Eight

If it's all the same to you, I'm going to stop the reports on how well I'm doing. I seem to have a habit of putting the commentator's curse on things.

The train of events started, now that I look back on it, on Monday morning, at work. Pete was due his reprimand, so I found an empty meeting room where no one would hear me and phoned him. The sound he made when he answered his mobile was a bit like the last one a really bad actor makes in a death scene.

'Why aren't you up yet?' I asked sternly.

'Raysopeninpub. Mgoneinfanoon.'

'Late night, was it?'

He yawned, and there was a scratching sound as the phone rubbed against his stubble.

'Listen, Pete,' I said, not giving him a chance to reply, 'I saw what you were up to with Amanda last night. How many times do I have to tell you that intra-Cabinet sex, or any attempt at arranging it, is banned? Not that you've got a snowball in hell's chance with her anyway.'

'So what are you worried about then?'

Damn, I'd walked straight into that one. 'I'm worried about her being alienated by your constant efforts at flirting with her.'

'Sam, it takes two to flirt. Amanda doesn't have to join in, you know.' There was a more distant scratching sound. I don't even want to speculate what that might have been. 'And I can understand you being annoyed by the suppressed sexual tension, but—'

'Pete, if you were suppressing it I wouldn't have a problem. Suppressing it is precisely what I'm asking you to do. No, not asking, I'm telling you. And if you don't do it yourself, I'm going to come round and suppress it for you, with a lump hammer.'

'All right, Mother Superior, I'll do as I'm told.' It sounded as though he was agreeing to avoid an argument rather than because he meant it. But I couldn't really press the issue any further.

Pete cleared his throat with quite revolting vigour. God, are all men like this when they wake up? I've never analysed my first-thing-in-the-morning behaviour, but maybe I should. It might be losing me points by the ton. 'Seeing as you're in such a bad mood with me, I don't suppose you'll be interested in helping me out?'

'What do you mean?'

'This Saturday. Another errand for Ter—'

I didn't even let him finish the name. I put the phone straight down.

Back at my desk, I remembered that Amanda had still been there when I left the Mitre last night. How late a night had it been? Irrational fears about whether Pete had been on his own during our phone call began to do their worst. Eventually I could contain myself no longer and sent Amanda a spurious e-mail about some minor work matter.

The three and a half minutes before she replied seemed a lot longer.

*

Pete's uncompleted sentence occupied not one iota of my brain power until Thursday night. I got back home, allegedly from a late finish at the office, in reality from an unproductive session with Danny. He knew that he'd let too much out of the bag last week and kept himself tight-lipped for the whole hour. The longest sentence he came out with was: 'Chemistry is a load of fucking rubbish.' Not necessarily something I'd disagree with, but hardly a cause for optimism that he'll do the course.

When I got in Kirsty was on the internet, looking up train times.

'Going somewhere nice?' I asked, standing behind her and giving her a relaxing shoulder-rub. (Twenty points at least, surely?)

'Home. For that reunion, remember?'

Of course. She'd mentioned it a while ago. Loads of her friends from school had piled on to Friends Reunited, and after a two-week period where Kirsty sat in front of the computer shrieking things like '*Aaaarrrgh!* No *way*! Michaela Brookes has got *three* children!', they all decided it would be fun to meet up. I advised against it, on the grounds that it's the very definition of playing with fire. They think they're all going to get pleasantly drunk and swap cosy reminiscences about ra-ra skirts. What's actually going to happen is that twenty years' simmering resentment about who snogged Gareth Hopkins first and who scratched whose Duran Duran album will boil venomously over, and grown women are going to fight in a car park in Newbury. But having pointed this out, I refrained from going on about it, as Kirsty's mind was clearly made up and any repetition of my doubts would have lost me points. So it had been arranged that on Saturday morning she was travelling down to her parents' house, where she'd be based for the weekend's revelry.

'The eleven forty-two, I think,' she said. 'Late lunch, hit the shops with Mum, then back to get changed for the party.'

Eleven forty-two, I thought. She'd be out of the flat by eleven. I'd have almost the whole of Saturday to myself. And that was when Pete's question came back to me. I swatted it from my mind instantly. But after a while it buzzed back in, and over the course of the evening, and then Friday morning, I started to ask myself what harm there was in finding out a bit more. Not that I was going to offer any help, of course. In fact, I told myself, I probably only wanted to hear about it to persuade myself that it was indeed too risky to get involved in, Kirsty being out of London or no Kirsty being out of London.

'Pete,' I said, having phoned him from the meeting room again, 'you know this thing tomorrow, for Terry?'

'Yeah.'

'Have you found anyone else to help?'

'Er, I think so.' Oh well, that was that then. 'Jack said he'd give me a hand. You know, the old guy who sits down Ray's end of the bar. Drinks whisky, shakes a lot.'

'Right, yeah. Just thought I'd ask.'

There was a pause. Then Pete said: 'Although I haven't run it past Terry yet. Don't know what he's going to think about Jack being involved. He has a laugh with him whenever he pops in. But this is business. And Terry did say how impressed Dino had been with us.'

'Dino? Impressed with us?' Maybe Dino hadn't updated Terry on the meeting's end. 'Not exactly something to be proud of, is it, Pete? It's a bit like getting a character reference from Robert Mugabe.'

'He said we both looked thoroughly professional.'

I wasn't letting myself get affected by this flattery, you know.

Thoroughly professional. Not just professional, but *thoroughly* professional.

'What is this job, anyway?'

'Oh, Sam, it's a doddle. It's collecting a rabbit.'

'A *rabbit*?'

'Yeah.'

'Terry's paying you to collect a rabbit?'

'Yeah.'

I paused. And then: 'A *rabbit*?'

'Sam, you want to get that phone of yours looked at. There's some sort of an echo on it.'

'But—'

'Look, for the last time, Terry is paying me to collect a rabbit. Called Vince.'

'Pete, stop taking the piss.'

'I'm serious. Vince is Terry's pride and joy. He loves that animal to bits. Never goes anywhere without him.'

'I thought people like him normally had white cats on their laps?'

'I'll pass that joke on to Terry if you want.'

'Don't bother. Where are you collecting this rabbit from?'

'Heathrow.'

'It's a flying rabbit?'

'It is on Saturday. Terry took it out to Spain with him. He's got a villa over there.' What a surprise. 'His wife made some sort of cock-up with the pet passport, though, so Vince couldn't come back with them. One of Terry's henchmen was staying out for a couple of weeks longer, said he'd look after the rabbit and bring it back when he returned. Which is going to be Saturday afternoon. All I have to do is pick him up, in the BMW Terry's lending me for the occasion, deliver him back home and collect the two hundred quid.'

'Two hundred? He only gave you a hundred and fifty last time.'

'Yeah, well, as I say, Vince is his pride and joy.'

'How much of that are you going to give to Jack?'

'Dunno. Seventy-five. Maybe not even that.' There was another pause, as though Pete was thinking of the best way of hinting at something. 'If it was someone I trusted a bit more, who I thought deserved a fair split of the cash, then of course I'd give them half.'

My turn to pause. Two figures kept flashing up in my mind: eleven and a hundred. The first was the time Kirsty would be leaving the house on Saturday. The second was the number of pounds that was on offer for collecting a rabbit from Heathrow, dropping it off in east London and . . . well, and nothing. That was it. That was the deal: a hundred quid for that. I really could do with the money. Not being able to afford treats for Kirsty isn't a very nice position to be in. You can buy a very nice dinner for two for a hundred quid. Points on a plate, quite literally.

But no. Winning points had been the aim before, and look what happened then.

A hundred quid, though.

But, I repeated to myself, no. That was 'no' as in the opposite of 'yes'. What I had to do here was confirm with Pete that the other collector of Vince really was going to be Jack and get off the line. It was perfectly simple.

'Who's driving the car? You or Jack?'

'Sam, he takes four attempts to get a cigarette into his mouth. And another four to light it. Do you seriously think I'm going to let him near the wheel of a BMW? I don't particularly want him coming along at all. But no one else I've asked is free on Saturday. Are you sure you're not interested in doing it? I'd split the money right down the middle with you.'

'What time does the flight get in?'

'Quarter-past one.'

'Pick me up at twelve.' I put the phone down.

Like I said, perfectly simple.

And so it came to pass that at half-past twelve yesterday afternoon I was in the fast lane of the M4, in the passenger seat of a dark blue BMW 7 series. Several times I'd thought about calling Pete to change my mind, but in the end I decided that this really was a no-risk arrangement. At the slightest sign of Kirsty altering her plans on Saturday morning I could ring Pete and get him to rouse Jack as a last-minute substitute. And thinking back to that hideous night in the Savoy, it had only been because of my greed that Kirsty ended up being there at all. If I'd been content just to take the eighty quid, it could safely have been credited to my points account at a later date and I'd have been wandering among the roses. As it was I'd ended up covered in the stuff that makes the roses grow quicker. So I'd learned my lesson: play it safe, get your wages, go home.

'Have a nice time,' I'd said to Kirsty at ten fifty-seven. We'd kissed, she'd walked down the path, overnight bag in hand, I'd closed the door and smiled at myself in the knowledge that next time I saw her, sometime on Sunday evening, I'd be a hundred poin . . . sorry, pounds richer.

A quick fiddle with the BMW's stereo produced 'Waterloo Sunset' by the Kinks. I turned up the volume, settled back in my seat and started to hum along.

'What are you doing?' snapped Pete, jabbing at the buttons. 'You can't play that stuff in a Beemer.'

'What do you suggest? Some Missy Elliot? Some Busta Rhymes? How about a couple of "hos" in the back seat, so we can "hang" with them?'

'You just want to watch what you're doing with Terry's pre-sets, that's all I'm saying.'

'Come on,' I replied. 'Put the Kinks back on.'

Pete responded by turning the radio off completely. 'We're nearly there now, I need some peace to find my way in. You know what a nightmare these terminals can be.'

I was reminded of Amanda's point about car radios and maps, but decided not to mention it as it would no doubt cause an argument, and I wanted to keep the atmosphere calm and professional. Thoroughly professional, indeed.

We made a couple of wrong turnings, but were still parked up and waiting in arrivals with time to spare.

'How will we know who we're looking for?' I asked.

Pete looked at me with an 'are you for real?' expression. 'He'll be the guy carrying a rabbit.'

'Oh, yeah. Of course.'

We stood without speaking, a muzak version of 'I Will Always Love You' by Whitney Houston playing in the background.

After a few minutes I said: 'Maybe one of us should be holding a piece of cardboard with "Vince" written on it?'

'If we did the rabbit would probably stand a better chance of reading it than Terry's henchman.'

Eventually the passengers from the Malaga flight began appearing through the arrivals gate. One of them was a well-built man in his fifties, tanned, wearing enough gold jewellery to open a small shop. In one hand he was carrying a briefcase, in the other a huge cage that looked as if it had been designed by Versace. It was made of shiny metal that had been painted red, gold and green, in a pattern so gaudy that even Michael Jackson would have thought twice. Through the wire mesh at the front I could see a large black shape. So large, in fact, that at first I thought I'd got the wrong guy, as this one was clearly carrying a dog. But as he got closer I saw that the cage's occupant was indeed an enormous black rabbit.

'Don?' asked Pete.

The guy nodded. 'Cop for that,' he said. 'Fuckin' thing's nearly taking me arm off.'

Pete took the cage and opened his mouth as if to introduce himself, but Don cut him short. 'Make sure you look after it proper, all right?' Then he turned and was gone.

We peered inside the cage. Vince interrupted his chewing of a carrot to peer nervously back, then decided we were friendly and carried on with his lunch. He really was huge, and his lush black coat shone beautifully. This was a prince among rabbits.

'Hello, Vince,' I said, in that gooey voice you always use to babies and pets. 'I'm Sam, and this is Pete, and we've come to take you back to your daddy.'

Vince moved to the back of the cage and turned away slightly, the better to concentrate on his carrot.

'Please yourself, you little bastard.'

'Don't talk to him like that,' hissed Pete.

'What's he going to do, report us to Terry for swearing at him?'

'I just don't want you putting him in a bad mood, that's all.'

I thought about questioning Pete on the likelihood of rabbits having moods at all, or even if they did how you could tell whether they were in a good one or a bad one, but I decided to hold my tongue. I had, after all, promised myself that this was to be as hassle-free a delivery as possible. Arguing with Pete now that we'd actually taken custody of Vince didn't seem a very good idea.

We got back to the car and used one of the rear seat belts to secure Vince's cage.

'Now stick to the slow lane on the way back,' I warned Pete. 'That belt looks strong enough, but it's better to be safe than sorry. And Vince catapulting through the windscreen just 'cos someone's cut you up would make us very sorry indeed.'

'Sam, I'm not going to take lessons in caution from someone who inadvertently pimped his girlfriend to a gangster.' He started the ignition. 'I was planning to stick to the slow lane anyway, as it happens.'

'Good.'

Pete remained true to his word. I occasionally leaned round to check that all was well with Vince. His contented chomping (all right, they do have moods) showed that it was. Then, just as we were reaching the outskirts of London, there came the sound of a mobile phone. After a couple of rings, I turned to Pete. 'Aren't you going to answer it?'

'It's not mine.'

'Well, it's not mine either.'

The sound seemed to be coming from somewhere near the gearstick. Looking down, we saw that there was a phone strapped into a holder. On the dashboard, the computerised display was flashing up the message, 'Hands-free?'

'I'd better answer it,' said Pete. 'Might be Terry.'

He pressed the point on the screen marked 'Yes' and the car was filled with a new voice. 'Hello? That you, Pete?'

'Yeah, Terry, it's me. Hi.' I looked around for the microphone, but couldn't see it. Must have been built into the steering wheel or something.

'All right, son? Everythin' sorted?'

'Yeah, Vince's safely on board. We're just getting back into town.'

'Nice one. Now listen, there's been a minor change of plan.' I felt my blood run about half a degree colder. 'I've gotta stay up north for an extra night, so you'll need to look after Vince till tomorrow. I'll be back about lunchtime.'

Pete looked at me. I purposefully directed my gaze out of the window. He tapped me on the knee. When I refused to acknowledge that, he hit me on the side of the head.

'Hello?' came Terry's voice. 'You still there, Pete?'

'Er, yeah, got you again now. Sorry, signal cut out for a minute.'

'I said I can't get back home tonight. You'll have to look after the rabbit until tomorrow. That all right, is it? There'll be more dosh in it for ya, 'course. Another ton, seein' as it's you.'

'Yeah, sure, no problem, Terry. Cheers.'

'Don't mention it. Now you keep a proper eye on Vince, won't you? He's very important to me.'

'Will do, Terry. You can rely on us.'

'Sweet. See ya then.' The phone went dead.

Still my fascination with the hard shoulder continued.

'Listen, Sam,' began Pete.

'I'm not interested.'

'No, hear me out. The thing is I've got this date, and—'

I put my fingers in my ears. 'Not interested,' I shouted. 'Not interested, not interested, not interested.' I took my fingers out. Pete was still speaking. I replaced my fingers. 'Not interested, not interested, not interested . . .' I watched him until I saw his lips stop moving. Then, very slowly and carefully, I took my fingers out of my ears again.

For five seconds there was silence.

'All I'm saying is—'

'Not interested, not interested, not interested . . .'

Out of the corner of my eye I saw his shoulders slump and I knew that he'd given up. I removed my fingers for a third time.

His next statement was so quick I didn't have time to block it. 'It'll mean more money.'

'No it won't. Because I'm not doing it.'

He didn't reply. He must have known that I was turning the money issue over and over in my mind. The whole reason I'm here, went my thinking, is to earn money to earn points. I've already earned a hundred quid. What's on offer isn't just another tenner, or even another twenty quid. It's another hundred quid. It's the same amount again. It's a hundred per cent increase on your original hundred. However many points the money you've already got is going to earn, this would earn you the same number of points again. We're not on about a marginal benefit here. This is the Double Your Points round.

And what, continued my thinking, are you being asked to do for those points? You're being asked to store, in your flat, the flat which you know for certain has been vacated by your girlfriend, you're being asked to store a rabbit. Not a boa constrictor, not a scorpion, not a tiger, but a rabbit. To look after that rabbit you will need a pound of carrots and some water. In terms of maintenance, this pet ranks some-where near a Furby. Even if Terry prolongs the storage any longer, you just get it back to Pete again and he takes the wages from then on.

However, even though that's what I was thinking, I refused to admit it to Pete. 'Who was this date going to be with?'

'Tamsin. She works in this barber's I've started going to.' He hit the steering wheel in frustration. 'I've been chatting her up for ages. She's really interested. You know when you can just tell? Honestly, tonight was going to be the night.'

'I've heard of hairdressers offering you something for the weekend, but never one who helps you use it.'

132

'Yeah, well, the only precaution I'll be taking now will be keeping that cage away from the radiator, won't it?'

I waited a while. I was in charge here and Pete knew it. Suddenly, though, a thought came to me that was so exciting it pushed me into action. 'You said it'll mean more money. How much more?'

He looked across, animated now that he knew I was thinking about it. 'A hundred quid. You heard Terry.'

'Yeah, I heard Terry, but I want to hear you.'

'Oh no, come on, Sam, you can't be serious.'

'Fine,' I said nonchalantly. 'It's just that I thought you wanted to take this Tamsin out.'

'I do,' he pleaded, 'but . . . Come on, you're getting two-thirds of the money as it is.'

'Yeah, because I'm doing two-thirds of the work.'

He ground his teeth, evidently trying to decide how important this date really was to him. 'All right, I'll give you twenty of my hundred.'

'Twenty?' I snorted. 'Grow up.' I was enjoying this.

Pete wasn't. 'All right, twenty-five.'

'Try seventy-five.'

His indignation nearly caused him to veer into the middle lane. 'You're telling *me* to grow up? That'd leave me with twenty-five quid out of the three hundred. I've got to have something left to spend on Tamsin.'

'I thought you said she was "really interested"?'

'She is, but you've got to show a bit of respect, haven't you? Where do you expect me to take her for dinner, a kebab van?'

'All right,' I said, 'I'll do it for fifty.'

'Forty.'

'Forty-five. You can share a starter.'

'OK,' he said, 'but you'll have to wait for it. Terry hasn't paid me for this one yet, has he?'

'Oh no you don't,' I replied. 'It's cash up front. Or you're sharing the night with Bugs Bunny.'

He was, I could sense, trying to give me a withering look, but I refused to take delivery of it. 'All right,' he said eventually. 'Two hundred and forty-five quid it is. Care for any of my teeth as well?'

I chuckled.

'It's a good job my cashpoint limit's just gone up.' Pete was clearly trying to prompt a late show of generosity on my part.

'Mmm,' I replied. 'It is.'

I heard him mutter a single word under his breath. I couldn't say for sure what it was, but it ended in a 't' sound.

Half an hour later, after Pete had stopped off at a bank whose hole-in-the-wall only gave him tenners so that I had to give him five pounds change, which I did in coins rather than with a note, which only added to his financial humiliation, we pulled up outside my flat and I carefully lifted Vince's cage out of the back.

'Hope you enjoy your evening with Tamsin.'

'Hope you enjoy your evening with Vince. Are you going to let him stay up late to watch the football?'

'I might show him *Fatal Attraction* for a laugh.'

Perhaps that was my comment too far, the one for which I was punished. Because punished I was. The cage was so heavy that I had to carry it with both hands, and so tall that I couldn't really see over the top of it. As a consequence I had to be extra-careful taking it into the flat. I shuffled along the corridor at zimmer-frame pace and edged into the sitting room, heading towards where I knew the table was.

'What is *that*?' came a shriek.

I nearly dropped the cage in shock, but thankfully just about managed to keep hold of it. I craned my neck to see who the unexpected occupant of my flat was. Even though the front door had shown no signs of being forced, and even though I'd recognised the high-pitched cry as coming from a very familiar voice, I was still harbouring the ridiculous hope that it might have been a burglar. Because that would have been preferable to who I thought it was.

But no. It was Kirsty. Or rather it was Kirsty and an unidentified female companion, sitting together on the sofa.

I froze in terror, unable to speak. All I could do, it seemed, was stare back at Kirsty and the other woman, whoever she was, holding the cage out in front of me, frantically trying to think of a response. Why in Christ's name had I agreed to do this? Two hundred and forty-five quid was the answer to that, of course, but just then I would happily have paid ten times that amount not to be where I was. Or should I say for Kirsty not to be where she was.

My silence, I felt sure, was compounding the guilt showing on my face. But as I stood there, I slowly began to register that all was not with Kirsty as I expected it to be, namely disbelief and points-jeopardising rage. In fact, her expression was one of merriness. A glassy-eyed, inanely grinning jolliness. Her companion's expression was much the same. I lowered my gaze to the table in front of them, where there was a bottle of Malibu and a litre bottle of Coke. Not much was left of the Coke, and although the Malibu bottle wasn't see-through I was prepared to place a hefty bet that not much remained in that either.

'Aaaaahhhhhhh,' said Kirsty. 'Isn't he *beautiful*?' She struggled as quickly to her feet as her drunken state would allow and walked, or rather weaved, towards me. She stopped in front of the cage and peered in through the mesh. 'You are *soooo* beautiful, aren't you? Aren't you, eh? Eh?' She turned to her friend. 'Come and say hello to him, Sonia.' Her friend also struggled and weaved, and soon they were standing together, cootchy-cooing at Vince, swaying slightly as they did so.

I couldn't believe I was seeing this. My confusion as to why Kirsty was back in the flat at all and who her companion was had been replaced by bewilderment at their reaction to the rabbit. Expecting an eruption, I'd got a love-in.

'What's his name?' asked Kirsty.

'Vince.'

In their fawning they didn't seem to notice what an unrabbit-like name this was. Kirsty looked up at me with an I-know-what-you're-playing-at smile. 'He's . . . You've . . . A surprise . . . Haven't you?'

Oh my God. She thought that . . . What could I say? The true sign of a panic-prone coward, a description which I'm proud to claim for myself, is that he will do whatever's necessary to get him out of the immediate pickle in which he finds himself, no matter what problems it'll lead to in the long term. So I gave a quick nod of my head. If Kirsty wanted to believe that I'd bought this rabbit as a present for her, and she was happy with that present, then I wasn't going to correct her. In my panic I don't think I even remembered that the thing belonged to Terry. If I did, I certainly couldn't think of an alternative explanation quickly enough. A present it was.

'Oh, I feel so terrible that I've ruined your surprise now,' she babbled. 'Sorry. But I promise you won't get any fewer p—.' She stopped herself, realising she'd been about to break her rule of not telling me how I'd earned and lost my points. I hadn't even had time to consider that this would earn me points at all. But now that she mentioned it, I saw that of course she'd see this as a deed worthy of reward. She'd obviously fallen instantly and deeply in love with Vince, and what's more he'd come completely out of the blue. It was a combination tailor-made to send my points-graph almost vertical.

My delight at this finally managed to snap me out of my trance. 'Well, the cat's out of the bag now,' I said, feigning disappointment. 'Or rather . . .' I thought better of finishing that joke off. It would have lost me some of the points I'd just earned.

'I don't care,' said Kirsty. 'He's lovely, and that's all that counts.' She grinned at me. Then she grinned at her friend. Her friend grinned back. Then they both grinned at me. In the absence of anything else to do, I grinned back.

'Oops, I'm sorry,' said Kirsty, 'I haven't introduced you, have I? Sam, this is Sonia. Sonia, Sam.'

'Hi,' I said, putting Vince's cage down on the table so I could shake Sonia's hand. She was quite short, with fairish hair and a friendly smile.

'Sonia's going to the reunion as well,' continued Kirsty as we all sat down. 'We bumped into each other at Paddington. The train was delayed, so we went for a drink, which made us miss the train, so then we went for lunch, and we had quite a few drinks with our lunch, and then Sonia had this idea that . . .'

They started giggling, so much that it prevented them from speaking. By way of explanation, Kirsty picked up a plastic bag that was lying on the floor. From inside she pulled out a small cardboard box and handed it to me. It was hair dye. Pink hair dye. Together with their eighties-throwback choice of alcohol, it gave a fair clue to what they had in mind.

Kirsty managed to pull herself together. 'Sonia said she wanted to get back into the spirit of it all, how we were at school, so we got some supplies . . .' She pointed at the Malibu bottle.

'And then we remembered how I got suspended for a week when I dyed my hair pink,' giggled Sonia, 'but now I can do it and no one can stop me. Kirsty said we should come back here to do it and then go straight to the party from the station. It's going to be very, very funny.'

Both girls collapsed into hysterics again. No it's not, I thought, it's going to be very, very stupid, and when you wake up tomorrow with a crippling hangover and pink hair you're going to realise just how stupid it was. But I didn't want to risk any of my freshly earned points by saying this. If Sonia wanted to take such drastic action to recreate her schooldays, that was her business.

'Do you want a drink?' asked Kirsty, pouring herself and Sonia another Malibu.

I thought about what that substance had done to their judgement. 'I'll stick to coffee, thanks.'

Kirsty downed her drink in one go. 'Right, well, we'd better get into that bathroom.' The girls paused by the rabbit's cage. 'Now you be a good Vincey while we're gone, won't you?' Vince twitched his nose at Kirsty, which made her smile and say 'aaaaahhhhh' again, and then they were off to commence hair-dyeing.

I went into the kitchen and made myself a coffee. After swinging from one extreme emotion to another – horror at discovering Kirsty in the flat, then joy at earning points from her misunderstanding – I now settled into a more realistic mood, somewhere between the two. The fact that Kirsty's new rabbit was in reality Terry's came back to me. At first sight it was a real quandary: only one of them could keep the thing. But such was my relief at having escaped the immediate problem, Kirsty catching me with Vince, that having time to work on this next problem made it seem a lot smaller. And sure enough, as I sipped my coffee, and the sound of running water and hysterical giggling came from the bathroom, a solution, of sorts, presented itself. I had to get another rabbit, one that looked exactly the same as Vince, which could take his place as Kirsty's new pet, allowing me to return the real Vince to Terry.

It might take a bit of finding, I thought, but rabbits are rabbits, aren't they? They're not like dogs or cats, which come in lots of different breeds. Most rabbits look pretty much the same to start with. Finding one that looked exactly the same shouldn't prove too difficult. Finding another cage like that would be almost impossible, but I could talk myself out of that easily enough. Say the pet shop had only loaned me the big one to carry Vince home in, something like that.

It was at this point that my plan hit its first snag. How was I going to know that the rabbit I was buying was a perfect double for Vince? I couldn't carry him around with me, he was too heavy. If I took him out of his cage to cut down on the weight I'd risk all sorts of escape/injury/death scenarios, and then I'd be looking for two doppelgänger Vinces with only a corpse, if that, to match them to.

This is where Polaroid cameras really come into their own. It was therefore a real pity that I didn't have a Polaroid camera. A quick estimate of how long it would take to go out, find a shop that sold them, come back to the flat, take a picture of Vince, go out again and start hawking his mugshot round the pet shops revealed that I'd be just as quick taking a picture with my normal camera, getting it developed on a one-hour service and then cutting straight to the pet shop stage. I found the camera, opened the door of Vince's cage and took a picture. Unfortunately the shock of the automatic flash sent him fleeing to the back of the cage, which meant I couldn't be sure I hadn't taken a picture of a black smudge showing its arse. So I had to entice him back to the door by reaching in, nicking the carrot he was currently munching on and placing it on the table. He responded by taking one from a whole pile at the back of the cage that I hadn't noticed before, which must have been put there to keep him happy on the flight home. So I had to nick the new carrot and the rest of the pile as well, and wait for Vince to come in search of them.

It took a couple of minutes for his mistrust of this malicious new owner to abate, but eventually he emerged into the cage's doorway and looked around suspiciously, like a wary cowboy at the end of a gunfight. When he was satisfied that his carrots weren't about to be stolen again, he craned his head forward to reach one of them.

Snap. 'Got you, you swine,' I muttered. The rabbit flinched, which I suppose was understandable, as normally when a rabbit sees a sudden bright light it means he's about to come second in an argument with a couple of Pirellis. But soon he realised that whatever this flashing was it wasn't going to hurt him, so I set about taking a whole load of pictures from various angles to make sure I'd got as complete a record of Vince's appearance as possible.

'What are you doing?'

I looked up to see that Kirsty had come out of the bathroom to fetch the Malibu. This hair-dyeing was obviously thirsty work. 'Er . . . he looked so cute that I wanted to get some pictures of him.'

Kirsty smiled, and went over to fuss him. 'You *are* cute, aren't you, my little darling? Cutey little Vincey.' The rabbit wiggled his ears to show how much he was enjoying the attention.

I took a couple more pictures with Kirsty in the shot to help give Vince some scale. Then I said, 'I think I'll go out and buy him some more carrots. He's really getting through the ones Terr— er, the pet shop gave me.'

'Well, he's a big lad, with a big appetite,' replied Kirsty. 'Aren't you, Vincey? Yes, you are.'

'I'll get these photos developed as well,' I said casually, as though it was an afterthought.

'We'll probably be gone by the time you get back.' Kirsty came over and gave me a boozy goodbye kiss.

'See you tomorrow,' I said.

'Mmm,' she replied vaguely, her attention already returning to the rabbit.

On my way out to the car I took shots of the ground to use up the rest of the film. My heart was certainly beating fast, but on the whole I still thought I had a fairly good chance of bringing this off. I'd have to be quick, though. It was ten to four, which meant I had very little retail time to play with.

Handing over my film in the chemist's, I asked how much the one-hour service was.

'Eight pounds forty-nine,' said the guy.

Normally I'd resent having to pay that much for someone swirling a bit of film around in a tray of chemicals, but with my newly acquired wad of cash it didn't seem too much. In fact, taking out the notes gave me an idea. 'How quickly could you get them done if I didn't want my change?' I asked, holding a twenty-pound note in front of him.

He looked around to see if his boss was in the vicinity. 'Come back in twenty minutes,' he murmured.

I spent some of that time nipping up to a pet shop on the same parade of shops. It had never struck me as the most upmarket establishment in the world, and the visit did nothing to change my mind. Apart from a few apathetic hamsters in the window and a parrot that looked as though its main priority should have been making a will, there weren't any actual living creatures on display. The shop mainly sold provisions like dog bowls and goldfish food, but the old lady who ran it gave me the names of three other pet shops within a fifteen-minute drive. Armed with this list, I went back to the chemist's.

Apart from the fact that in a couple of the later ones Vince had a nasty attack of red-eye (as indeed did Kirsty, although in her case it might have been the Malibu), the pictures had come out superbly. If they'd been on *Crimewatch*, the police would have got a conviction within hours. Whatever you needed to know about Vince, be it the length of his ears or the angle at which his back right leg stuck out, my photos had the answer.

Some nifty overtaking and an 'accidental' failure to notice a light turning red meant that I reached the first pet shop in just under ten minutes. It looked promising. There were at least half a dozen rabbits on a shelf right next to the door, and even though none of them was anywhere near as big as Vince, the shop stretched back for what seemed like miles. They must have some others, I thought.

'Can I help you, sir?' asked the owner, a tidy-looking man with a neat moustache.

'I'm looking for a rabbit.'

'Any particular sort?'

'Yeah, one that looks like this,' I replied, showing him a picture taken from Vince's left. I didn't know about Vince himself, but I thought it was his best side.

'My, that's a beauty,' said the man. 'A French Lop. You don't see many of those.'

Fuck. 'Don't you?'

'No. And when you do they cost a pretty penny.'

Double fuck. 'How pretty?'

'Oh, I've known them go for eighty, ninety pounds.'

'*Ninety quid?* For a rabbit?'

The man winced at my ignorance. 'These aren't just any old rabbits, you know. The French Lop is a very rare breed.'

Trust Terry to go for a top-of-the-range bunny. This bloody thing was going to eat into my wages more than I'd thought. Wowing someone with twenty quid had been enjoyable, but this was depleting my points-earning stash more severely. Still, I thought, you've been lucky to earn extra points for 'buying' Vince in the first place, so you shouldn't grumble about investing a bit of money to shore them up.

'I take it,' I said to the owner, 'that you haven't got any French Lops in at the moment?'

'Unfortunately I haven't. But I could order you one for next week.'

I shook my head. 'I need it today. Any ideas where else I could try?'

'If anywhere's going to have one it'll be Slater's.' This was one of the other two names on my list.

'Right, I'll try them,' I said, running out to my car.

The third shop on my list was on the way there, so I thought I might as well call in, but they only recommended Slater's as well. Christ, I thought, panic starting to set in again, if this shop doesn't have one I am well and truly shafted. By the time I screeched to a halt outside the shop it was nearly half-five. One of the shutters was already padlocked in place and a young lad, only about sixteen or so, was reaching to pull the other one down.

'Hold on,' I yelled, leaping out of my car and running across the road. So much adrenalin was pumping round me by this point that I scarcely even registered the two-ton truck managing to brake only yards away from me, or the robust language that flew in my direction from its driver. 'Hang on a minute,' I said, reaching the surprised-looking lad, 'I've got some business for you.'

'Oh.' He didn't look that happy about the news.

We both went into the shop.

'Have you got any French Lops?'

'What are they?'

This didn't quite fit in with the rabbit-expertise I'd been led to expect from Slater's. 'They're rabbits. Bloody big rabbits. Never heard of them?'

'Nah,' came the surly reply.

'This is Slater's the pet shop, not Slater's the hardware store?' I asked. The whole shop was filled with miaowing and scratching and tweeting noises, and we were standing right next to a stand packed with guinea pigs.

'Yeah,' said the lad, responding to my sarcasm with a truculent tone that reminded me uncomfortably of Danny, 'but I'm only looking after it while my parents are away.'

That explained his lack of enthusiasm. 'They're like this,' I said, trying to show him one of the photos of Vince.

But he wouldn't even look at it. 'Rabbits are over there,' he said, pointing to the back of the shop.

I made my way past a row of goldfish and found the rabbits. There was no doubt about it, Slater's seemed to be the best bunny people in town. Their selection was large and varied, and, importantly from my point of view, arranged by size. The bigger ones were at the far end of the row. *Please* let there be a Vince lookalike, I thought as I edged along towards them. I got a flutter of excitement as I saw a flash of black in one cage, but closer inspection revealed that, although big, the rabbit wasn't quite big enough. And its ears were far too short. Probably wasn't a French Lop at all. Damn. I carried on to the end of the row, but none of the

144

rabbits matched the photos in my hand. For the first time I really began to get scared. If this rabbit emporium didn't have what I needed, then nowhere would. So I refused to believe what I had just seen, or rather not seen, and did that stupid thing you always do when you can't find a book on a shelf: I went back and looked again. I examined every single cage, some of them as many as three or four times, but despite my furious prayers none of the rabbits turned miraculously into the one I wanted.

I tried to fend off my growing sense of alarm by coming up with an alternative plan. The major problem, I reasoned, was that tomorrow was Sunday. If it had been Monday, when the shops were open, I could have driven to every pet shop within the M25, and if necessary some of the ones outside it as well, until I found a rabbit that looked like Vince. Therefore if I could hang on to Vince until Monday, the switch could be made while Kirsty was at work. No one would be any the wiser and the points would still be in the bag. This meant that all I had to do was somehow fob Terry off . . . Ah. There are many things you do to people like Terry. Carry out their instructions to the letter. Smile nicely at them. Add 'sir' at the end of everything you say. But fobbing them off, about rabbits or anything else, is not one of those things. You avoid fobbing Terry off as though your life depends on it. For the very good reason that it does.

I'd just embarked on thinking through the next alternative plan – breaking the news of Vince's tragic and mysterious 'death' to Kirsty in as delicate a way as I could – when Surly Boy's face appeared round the corner. 'You buying any of these or what? I wanna lock up.'

I closed my eyes and concentrated on not throttling him. 'Don't you come your soft-soap sales patter with me, young man.'

I was expecting another burst of rudeness, but what I heard instead was: 'Why have you got pictures of Benson?'

I opened my eyes. 'What?'

'Those pictures. They're of Benson. Do you know my dad or something?'

Confused thoughts started to fly around my brain. I couldn't piece them together yet, but something in there was making me feel excited. 'No. Who's Benson?'

'What do you mean? You've got the photos.'

'These aren't photos of Benson. These are photos of Vince.'

Surly took the pictures from me and looked through them. 'Really? He looks just like Benson.'

'*Who* is Benson?'

'My dad's rabbit.'

'Right, I see.' I was trying to stay calm. 'And, er, where is Benson?'

'Upstairs, in the flat.'

I nodded, doing my best to appear normal. 'I couldn't, erm, take a look, could I?'

Surly gave me a suspicious look. Rightly so, I suppose. Here was a bloke twice his age asking if he could go upstairs with him. And while that sort of thing normally involves offering the youngster a look at your puppies rather than asking to see his bunny, Surly was no doubt thinking that you can never be too careful. 'I mean by you bringing Benson down here, rather than me going up there,' I added hurriedly.

He still didn't look too sure.

'It's just that if Benson really does look exactly the same as Vince, it'd be interesting to see him,' I said. 'For curiosity's sake, I mean.'

I think Surly concluded that offering this maniac what he

146

wanted was the quickest way of getting rid of him. 'Stay there,' he said.

I waited nervously. Would Benson really be an exact double for Vince? And if he was, would the boy agree to part with him? The first question was answered as soon as Surly reappeared. The rabbit's cage was a basic wire mesh job, which allowed you to see in from every angle. And whichever of those angles you chose, Benson was a perfect replica of the rabbit in my photos. It was quite spooky, in fact. Had I not left Vince at home myself only a couple of hours previously, I'd have sworn that the rabbit in the photos was the rabbit in the cage. I relayed this thought to Surly. He grunted.

I cleared my throat. 'How much would . . . Do you think your father would . . . If I was going to . . .' I took a deep breath. 'How much do you want for it?'

'He's not for sale.'

'How do you know?'

'If he was for sale he'd be in the shop, wouldn't he?'

You couldn't really argue with that. But I had to try. 'Maybe your father didn't have room. These rabbit shelves are packed solid, look.'

Surly looked sceptical. 'If he'd wanted to sell Benson he'd have made room.'

I clenched my teeth together in frustration. Trapped between Kirsty's wrath and Terry's baseball bat, I could see the answer to my problems right there in front of me – but I couldn't get my hands on it. What could I do or say that would change Surly's mind? There was only one thing for it.

I started to take the wad of notes from my pocket. Then, realising that if all my money came out into the open Surly would see it as up for grabs, I pushed my thumb into the middle of the notes and took out only half of them. I made a great play of counting the money. It came to a hundred and forty pounds, and did a very good job of catching Surly's attention. He couldn't take his eyes off it.

'This rabbit,' I said to him, 'is, as you now know, a French Lop. Clearly that's why your dad took a shine to it. It's also why I've taken a shine to it.'

Surly nodded.

'Now I've known Lops,' I continued, 'to sell for ni— for, erm, nigh on, er, nigh on fifty pounds. But never much more than fifty. So if you were to tell your dad that a customer had come in and offered you not fifty, not sixty, not even eighty, but a *hundred* pounds for Benson, I'm sure he'd put his attachment to the rabbit to one side and agree that you did the right thing in selling him. Don't you?'

'I'm not sure. He gets back on Tuesday. You could come in and talk to him then, if you want.'

'That'll be too late, I'm afraid.' Come on, lad, I thought, what I'm offering here isn't that hard to grasp. 'A hundred pounds for the rabbit,' I said, counting the notes into my left hand until I reached the stated amount. This left four ten-pound notes in my right hand. 'All you'll have to do is take this money,' I held both my hands towards Surly, 'and tell your dad that you've sold Benson for a hundred pounds, and give him that hundred pounds.'

But Surly wasn't looking at the hundred pounds. He was looking at the forty pounds. He reached out for it, but I snatched my hand back. 'Have we got a deal?'

He nodded.

'Well, can I take Benson then?'

He offered me the cage, which I took at precisely the same moment he took the money.

'Pleasure doing business with you,' I said as I left the shop. And despite the fact that my wad now contained only ninety pounds, I meant it. Benson was my saviour. Because of that, I made sure his cage was wedged tightly into the footwell of the front passenger seat before I set off. If I'd driven like I had on the way to the shop, I'd have made it home in about five minutes. As it was I didn't go above twenty miles an hour, and at one point pulled over to let a convoy of irritated drivers stream past me. I didn't care about the hand gestures several of them aimed at me. All I cared about was Benson. Benson was mine. Or rather he was Kirsty's. And he wasn't Benson, he was Vince. But the fact remained: he had saved the day.

Pulling up outside my flat I decided to leave Benson in the car while I nipped inside. I wanted to make sure that Kirsty really had left this time. To gain one unexpected rabbit had been unfortunate, to gain another would look suspicious, so suspicious that it couldn't be covered up by stories of surprise gift-buying. I went into the sitting room and shouted Kirsty's name. But there was no response. I shouted again. Still no response. Thank God for that. Vince's cage was open, and I could hear him scrabbling around behind the sofa, so as I went back to the car I made double-sure that the front door was shut. Escaping bunnies were the last thing I needed.

I carried Benson, still in his cage, into the flat. He looked excited about going on an adventure. I kicked the door shut behind me, and then for peace of mind's sake turned the deadlock as well. Setting Benson's cage down on the table next to Vince's, I bent down to address him. 'Now that sound behind the sofa,' I said, 'is Vince. It's important that you're prepared for when he comes out, because he looks exactly like you, and it might be a bit weird looking at your twin. I know I'd be freaked out by it.' I could hear behind me that Vince had emerged into the open. 'Let's say hello to him together, shall we?' Then I turned round to look at Vince.

I don't know if you've ever seen a pink rabbit, but trust me, it comes as a *very* big shock. The sight in itself is alarming enough. Vince, who had stopped in the middle of the floor to peer up at me and Benson, was now a violent shade of pink, apart, that is, from two black circles around his eyes. I found myself recoiling in fright. But equally, if not more, alarming than the sight itself was the set of consequences that went with it. Terry had entrusted his beloved rabbit to my safe-keeping, and I had managed to change its colour. Or at least allow its colour to be changed, by my drunken girlfriend and her schoolmate. And not just any colour. Pink. *Pink*.

A note on the table, which I hadn't spotted before, confirmed the chain of events that had led to this disaster:

Hi darling – hope you like Vince's new look – Sonia had some dye left, and we thought it'd be fun to give him a makeover! The little chap loved splashing about in the warm water and having the hairdryer on him. He and Sonia made quite a couple! Have a nice night. See you tomorrow, K. xx

Oh, what japes, I thought. Kirsty and Sonia neck too much Malibu, I get to have a conversation with Terry's knuckleduster. Wonderful.

I sat down on the floor, still not quite able to believe that I was seeing what I was seeing. I rubbed my eyes, opened them again . . . but Vince was still pink. Kirsty had really landed me in it here. How in the name of Christ was I going to explain this to Terry? I stared at Vince, and then at Benson, and then at Vince again. Finally, on the grounds that his colour was one of the standard ones associated with rabbits, I settled for staring at Benson.

And then I had an interesting thought.

Benson looked exactly like Vince used to. I'd been planning to substitute Benson for Vince without Kirsty noticing ... so why couldn't I do the same without Terry noticing? Return Benson to him tomorrow, instead of Vince? It made perfect sense. But it was one of those plans where even though you can't spot a flaw, you still feel slightly unsure about it. That, of course, was because of who I was planning to deceive. When Terry's involved, you think twice. And then twice more. Would he be tricked? Try as I might I couldn't think of any way he'd spot that Vince wasn't Vince. But still I wanted to check it with Pete. I rang him, apologised about interrupting the preenings for his hot date, and told him what had happened and what I intended to do about it.

The fact that he gulped, paused for a moment and then said: 'My hearing must be going, Sam, because I could swear you just said you were thinking of switching Vince for another rabbit,' told me that perhaps all was not going to be as straightforward as I'd hoped.

'It's all right, Pete, you've got to believe me, this other rabbit looks exactly the same as Vince. Absolutely identical. You cannot tell from looking at them which one's which. Well, apart from the fact that one of them's bright pink, but you get my drift.'

'Oh, I get your drift all right,' he replied. 'And I'm sure that you can't tell from looking at Benson that he's not Vince. But Terry won't just be looking at him.'

'What do you mean?'

'How can I put this ... You know that old saying about it not being how you look that counts, but what's inside you?'

A horrible comprehension of what Pete was hinting at began to seep over me, like rancid paint trickling slowly down a wall. 'You don't mean that . . .'

'Yes, Sam. I do.'

'Let me get this straight: the rabbit's a mule?'

He didn't reply. He didn't have to.

'Pete, you're saying that inside Vince is . . . well, what? Are we talking Bob Marley? Or Liam Gallagher?'

Pete answered the question with a hefty sniff.

'Oh no. Oh please no. Please, please, please, Pete, *please* tell me you're joking.'

'Sam, the one thing I've learned never to do where Terry's concerned is joke. It's very bad for your health.'

I tried to speak, but all that came from my mouth was a faint whining sound. My legs were no longer up to the job of supporting me. I collapsed into a chair. I desperately wanted a drink but the only alcohol I could see was the Malibu, and that had done quite enough damage for one day. Instead I began to pummel my fist into my forehead.

It managed to dislodge a thought. 'Hold on,' I said. 'You say the drugs are inside Vince?'

'Yeah.'

'Well, how come they haven't made an appearance yet? Just about everything else has. You should see the inside of his cage. It looks like someone's emptied a pepper mill into it.'

Pete sighed. 'Don't you think that Terry's a bit cleverer than that? He got the idea a few weeks ago. Vince was ill, had to have an operation. The vet was a good friend, and not that bothered about medical ethics, or any sort of ethics come to that, and when Terry said he'd had this idea and it seemed a shame to waste such an opportunity . . . well, to cut a long story short, Vince is having another operation next week. You can see it hasn't affected him. Enormous thing like him doesn't even notice a third of a kilo on his weight.'

'A third of a kilo?!'

'Yeah. By the time Terry's had it cut down that'll make a nice payday.'

'How much?'

'About fifty thousand quid.'

'*What?*'

'So you can see why Vince is so important to him.'

This was seriously scary now. I found myself getting angry. 'You mean to tell me, Pete, that you took me to Heathrow to collect that rabbit knowing what was inside it? What would have happened if we'd all been arrested?'

'That was precisely why I didn't tell you, you idiot. You could have honestly said that you didn't know anything. Besides which, no one was going to get arrested. Terry knows people. Terry talks to people. Terry pays people. Don't get yourself into such a state.'

'*Don't get myself into a state?*' I shouted. 'Pete, I've got a girlfriend who's put me on points, an engagement ring I might never get to use and a rabbit with a street value of fifty grand. What the *fuck* do I get myself into if not a state?'

'You get yourself into a really good frame of mind for thinking of plans,' replied Pete coldly. 'Good ones. Quick ones. Ones that stop Terry finding out you've dyed his rabbit pink.' Then the line went dead. The sod had hung up on me. I phoned him again but it went straight to voicemail. After a couple more tries, I gave up.

For a few minutes I couldn't move. I had that feeling you sometimes get in moments of utter hopelessness, the hope that if you stay still for long enough you might melt into your chair, and no one will be able to find you, and all your problems will go away. But then my forehead started to hurt from its earlier battering, and I had to make myself stand up and go to the bathroom, where I held a towel under the cold water and put it against my head. Sitting on the edge of the bath, I tried to analyse the situation. The 'give Benson to Terry' solution was now a non-starter. Vince had to go back to Terry, which meant that Benson had to go to Kirsty, but Terry was expecting his Vince to be black, whereas he was in fact pink, while Kirsty was expecting her Vince, who would in fact be Benson, to be pink, whereas he was in fact black.

Poking out from the top of the bin was Sonia's discarded bottle of hair dye. Lying by the side of the bin were a pair of swimming goggles that Kirsty must have found from somewhere. There were tinges of pink round the edges. Vince had obviously worn them when he was being 'done', to stop the dye getting in his eyes. I began to wonder: could he be dyed back to his original colour? And . . . now hold on, this was starting to make sense . . . could Benson be dyed pink? You'd need to do Benson first, to make sure you got the goggles in the right place so the black circles round his eyes looked right. But then, once that was done, you could do Vince . . .

What was I on about, 'you'? I'd never used hair dye in my life. I'd rather be in charge of cleaning a Van Gogh than have to interfere with Terry's rabbit. No, this was a job for an expert or it was a job for no one. But who did I know that was an expert in hair dye? Apart from Sonia, whose participation in this project, even if she agreed to give it, would ruin the whole point of it. I couldn't think of anyone. *Bloody* Pete. Why had I ever let him get me involved in another of these errands? Now I was left in the mire, and he was off on a date . . .

With a hairdresser.

I searched out his landline number and rang that. He wasn't expecting such persistence, because he answered it. 'Hello?'

'Pete it's Sam now don't hang up this is really important don't hang up I'm begging you listen it's not just me that's up the creek here you're in the boat as well think about it Terry asked you to sort the job out it was you that picked me so even though it was my girlfriend's friend who dyed his rabbit pink you're still responsible for me so if I can't get this sorted you're for the high jump as well and when I say high jump remember it's Terry we're talking about here and the high jump's going to be pretty fucking difficult with broken legs isn't it come on you've got to help me out.'

There was a pause. 'Terry won't take it out on me.'

He was bluffing, I knew he was. Terry would hold him responsible. All right, not as responsible as me, but at the very least his job in the Mitre would be under threat, if not several of his major organs. 'Come on, Pete, you know you've got a duty to help me with this.'

'"Duty" is putting it a bit strongly. I might be persuaded to help you with it.'

'Persuaded? By what?'

'By the same thing that persuaded you this afternoon.'

I couldn't really complain. I'd been in a position of strength then, and used it. Now he was in the same position, and doing likewise. 'How much?'

'The same amount that persuaded you.'

'Two hundred and forty-five? But that was because I was doing all the work. Now we'll be splitting the work.'

'No, Sam, we'll be splitting the work that you've created. And that's a "we" that includes Tamsin, of course, who's going to expect top money, I should think. If she agrees to do it at all.'

'But I've only got ninety quid left. Today's cost me an arm and a leg.'

'No, it's cost you a lot of money. If Terry finds out what you've done to Vince, then it'll cost you an arm and a leg.'

He had me over a barrel. 'OK then.'

'Right, I'm getting fifty-five tomorrow, so that means I need another hundred and ninety from you. Tonight. In cash.'

Here we go again, I thought. From being two hundred and forty-five quid ahead of the game, I was now going to be a hundred behind it. But at least I'd keep the points that Vince had earned me, and I wouldn't have to face any retribution from Terry. 'OK, one ninety it is.' Then I took Pete through what I had in mind.

'Tamsin's gonna love this,' he said.

'Yeah, well, at least she still gets to see you.'

'When she suggested we get together I don't think she meant "bring your mate and a couple of rabbits as well".' He sighed. 'Right, where are we going to do this?'

I hadn't thought of that. 'We can't do it round here. I don't think Kirsty's going to come back early, but even the slightest risk of it happening is too much. What about yours?'

'No chance. My flatmate's got someone coming round.'

Damn. 'I don't think I've got any friends who'd appreciate me bringing two strangers round to dye a pink rabbit black and a black rabbit pink.'

'Funny you should say that, Sam, neither have I.'

There was a silence as we both tried to think of a bunny-friendly venue. 'Listen,' said Pete eventually, 'Ray's doing the pub on his own tonight. Saturdays have been pretty quiet lately, so I can't imagine there'll be a lock-in. I'll go down there for about ten, and when it gets near to closing time I'll offer to lock up so he can get off home. You get there for half-eleven. I'll make sure everyone's gone by then.'

And so the Mitre it was. The rest of the evening was spent getting Pete's wages from the cashpoint, buying pink and black hair dye, as per instructions received from Tamsin via Pete, and waiting for eleven o'clock to come round. Having to drive to the pub stopped me having even a nerve-steadying drink, which in turn meant I stayed too on edge to eat anything. At eleven I packed the car boot with the hair dye, the goggles, the hairdryer, a plastic bowl and a few old towels, put Benson and Vince into the back seat and set off, sticking to the quiet streets at Sunday driver pace.

Pete was saying goodbye to the final regulars as I got there. I parked down the road, turned my lights off and waited for him to signal that the coast was clear. Then I drove right up to the pub and we took everything in from the car. While we waited for Tamsin I made sure that the blinds were right down so that no one passing by could accidentally witness what was going on. Even I wasn't totally convinced this was really happening, so God knows what nightmares someone would have who'd been drinking and then passed a pub containing two rabbits, one of them pink.

I put Vince, in his designer cage, on one table, and Benson, in his bog-standard one, on another. On the floor I put the bowl. Pete surveyed the scene, slowly shaking his head. 'Do you know what I was planning to be doing by now?'

'I'd rather not hear the details.'

He examined Vince. 'How did you manage to let her do this?'

'I know, Pete, I know, it's completely my fault. I should have seen it coming, shouldn't I? As I went out to the shops,

I should have thought, Woah, better not, because as soon as I'm gone my girlfriend and her mate are going to dye that rabbit pink. Because that's always happening, isn't it? Everywhere you go nowadays, people are dyeing rabbits pink. Turn your back for a minute and entire pet shops have been done. What do you mean, "manage to let her do this"?'

'You're given one simple job . . . Talking of jobs, where's my money?'

'I wondered when you'd want your pound of flesh,' I said, handing over the notes.

'Not like you did this afternoon, then.' He had a point there. 'And anyway, this isn't about my pound of flesh, it's about Terry's pound of cocaine.'

'No it's not. A third of a kilo is less than a pound.'

'Is it?'

'Yeah. I think.'

Our calculations on this evolved into a discussion on why cannabis is sold in ounces and cocaine in grams. Infantile, but at least it stopped us arguing. At about a quarter to twelve Tamsin arrived. I could see why Pete was annoyed at being denied his date with her. She was about twenty-two or so, blonde, and her good looks had an innocent quality about them, which had no doubt fuelled Pete's fantasies about corrupting her. The way she instantly starting directing us, though, showed that this girl was no shrinking violet. Pete was to lay the towels out on the floor, I was to fill the bowl with warm water.

'She's done a good job on her own hair,' I whispered to him as I put the full bowl down on the towels. 'I think it's dyed, isn't it?' I'd noticed the faintest signs of darkness among the roots.

'I was hoping to discover the answer to that tonight,' he muttered.

'Right, let's have a look at the patients,' said Tamsin.

'Yeah,' I replied, 'let the dog see the rabbits.' Oh bugger. 'Not that I'm saying—'

'We're dyeing the black one first?' asked Tamsin, not hearing, or pretending not to hear, my unintentional insult.

'That's right,' I said. 'The black bits around the eyes have got to exactly match Vince's. That shouldn't be a problem – these are the goggles my girlfriend used.'

Tamsin opened Benson's cage, took the goggles and, after a little fussing to gain the rabbit's trust, put them over his eyes. Benson gazed out from behind the plastic, looking a little apprehensive as Tamsin lifted him into the air. Vince scampered eagerly around his cage, as though he was offering encouragement. 'Go on, mate,' I imagined him saying, 'this water thing's great fun. I did it a few hours ago.' As soon as he went into the bowl, Benson found himself agreeing. He began to splash happily about.

'There's a good lad,' said Tamsin, scooping the water over him. 'There's a good boy.'

Benson kicked his back legs excitedly, and then rolled over so that the water could wash over his tummy. Pete and I took turns to give him a fuss. We looked at each other, exchanging simpering smiles at Benson's adorability, before realising how childish we must look. Hurriedly we composed ourselves and adopted serious expressions to show that we knew how grave the situation was.

Tamsin applied some shampoo to Benson and began to lather him up. By now the rabbit was clearly convinced that Christmas had come early. He closed his eyes, savouring every second of this all-over massage. Pete, in contrast, had started to look unhappy. He was obviously cursing the fact that by rights Tamsin's hands should have been all over his body, not the rabbit's.

'Anyone for a drink?' he asked, to give himself something to do other than punch me.

Tamsin replied that she'd have a bottle of Budweiser. Pete had the same. Seeing how safe the rabbits were going to be in Tamsin's hands, I decided to join them. It'd be a while before I was driving home. We drank our beers, Tamsin carrying on with the job in hand, all three of us chatting pleasantly away. At one point Vince began to look a touch glum, as though he was feeling left out, but he soon perked up when I assured him it'd be his turn again soon and gave him some dry-roasted peanuts to keep him going.

Soon Tamsin had applied the pink dye. On her instructions I'd bought exactly the same make that Sonia had used, together with some black from the same range. I'd gone for three bottles of each, which Tamsin told me was way more than enough, but as I hadn't been able to pluck up enough courage in the chemist's to ask how much hair dye one needed for a large rabbit, I'd played it safe.

'I wonder how long we should leave it in,' she said. 'I've never done a colour like this before.' I'm not surprised, I thought. It was the early 1980s that lacked enough taste for Sonia to pick that colour, and you were still in your pram then. 'Why don't we play it safe, and wash it out sooner rather than later? Then if it's not pink enough we can give him another blast.'

'Entirely up to you,' I said. 'You're the boss.'

So we waited twenty minutes, for most of which Pete and Tamsin chatted between themselves. In-jokes that had carried over from their previous meetings, comments about people who worked in her salon, material that allowed Pete to flirt with her while keeping me out of the conversation. But I didn't mind. As I sometimes do when Pete's up to his tricks, I fondly reminisced about how I used to be like him, the fun I had in my twenties, chasing girls, dodging commitment . . .

As soon as the time was up Tamsin rinsed Benson down and set to work with the hairdryer. He'd loved every part of the process, but the drying was without doubt his favourite. He closed his eyes in utter joy, thrusting his face up into the path of the dryer as though he never wanted it to stop. Even when he was dry Tamsin carried on for a little while, just to give him a treat. Then I took Vince from his cage and held him next to Benson.

'Not *quite* pink enough,' said Tamsin, in the manner of a perfectionist handyman deciding whether a shelf was level or not. 'I think we should do it again. For thirty minutes.'

Although I could see a minute difference in the shades, I didn't think Kirsty would be able to spot it after twenty-four hours, with a hangover and without the original rabbit there for comparison purposes. But if Tamsin was so keen to get the job bang-on, I wasn't going to stand in the way of her professional pride. She reapplied the goggles, checking once again that they were in exactly the right position, and gave Benson another dose of the dye. He, of course, was only too happy to cooperate.

By now we were all on our second bottles of beer – I think Pete might even have been on his third – and conversation was flowing quite freely. Almost all of it still between the other two, and most of it quite sexually charged. Pete had obviously sensed that far from ruining his chances with Tamsin, the rabbit project had put her in an especially good mood, and that accompanying her home after we'd finished was well and truly on the cards. I was happy to let them get on with their flirting. My concern, that Terry got his black Vince and Kirsty her pink 'Vince', had been taken care of, and was nearly in the bag.

After half an hour, Tamsin rinsed the dye out and dried Benson off. Ignoring his look of disappointment when she finished, I removed Vince from his cage and held him once more by Benson's side.

'That is surreal,' said Pete. 'Two pink rabbits, and you can't tell which one's which. They look *exactly* the same.'

Tamsin stood back, arms folded, to admire her handiwork. 'Even if I say so myself, he's right. That pink is a perfect match.'

'I can't really get the full effect from here,' I said to Pete. 'Come and hold Vince, will you?'

We swapped places. I had to admit it, Tamsin's work was faultless. The two rabbits were indistinguishable, right down to the little black circles around their eyes. There was absolutely no way on earth that Kirsty was going to be able to spot that Vince wasn't Vince.

'Tamsin,' I said, 'I want to thank you. For saving my life. And my marriage. Well, I mean my hopes of having a marriage. You're a miracle worker.'

She smiled. 'I have my talents.'

A look of intense longing came over Pete's face.

'OK,' I said, clapping my hands together, 'only the final bit of the job left. Namely the return of Vince to his proper colour. I'm just nipping to the loo, then I'll give you a hand emptying the bowl and everything.' In the Gents I breathed several sighs of relief that the end of the nightmare was in sight. Once Vince had been dyed black everything would be fine and I'd be able to bask in the glory of my points, free from the worry of upsetting Terry. I'd done it. I'd sorted out the rabbits. It was all going to be fine.

I returned to the bar, keen to get on with the second dyeing. As I burst through the door, Pete and Tamsin sprang apart, trying and failing to cover up the fact that they'd been snogging. I had to hand it to Pete: he's a speedy operator when he wants to be.

'Now now,' I said light-heartedly, 'there'll be plenty of time for that after we've finished.'

Unable to stop herself grinning, Tamsin began to unwrap a bottle of the black dye.

'Sorry, my lord,' said Pete, taking the bowl of water behind the bar to replace it.

'You're forgiven.' In my relaxed state I was secretly quite pleased for Pete. That only lasted, however, until I looked down at the floor. What I saw there wiped the smile from my face, emptied me of every last feeling of goodwill towards Pete, and filled me instead with a yearning to punch his lights out. There, gambolling around on the carpet in delighted abandon, were the two rabbits. Vince looked happy. Benson looked happy.

There was only one problem.

You couldn't tell which was which.

Pete looked at the rabbits. Pheromones must have addled his thinking, because for a second or two all he did was smile affectionately at the sight of them enjoying themselves. But then it dawned on him too. He looked up at me. 'Oh shit.'

'You could say that.'

'Sam,' he began to stammer, 'I'm *really* sorry. I am really, *really* sorry.'

'Apologies aren't enough!' I screamed. I was at his throat in something less than a tenth of a second. 'We were within sight of pulling it off there! We were one dye from safety!'

Pete looked genuinely frightened. 'Sam,' he squeaked, 'I'm sorry. I just didn't think.'

'*I know you didn't! If you'd thought, there wouldn't be two absolutely identical rabbits running around this fucking pub together, would there?*'

Tamsin, also looking alarmed by my outburst, edged herself gingerly between us. 'Now come on,' she said calmly. 'Let's try and sort this out, shall we?'

It took a moment for my grip on Pete's collar to slacken, but once it had he fell back against the wall. I got my breath back and then followed Tamsin out from behind the bar. Vince and Benson were having a high old time, chasing each other under bar stools and around table legs. But telling them apart was impossible. For a while I'd find myself imagining that one of the rabbits had an air of Vince about him, but then I'd look at the other and realise I could say exactly the same about him. They were exactly the same shade of pink. It was a bit like watching *Watership Down* on acid.

'There's got to be a way of solving this,' said Pete.

The only sound that answered him was the gentle scurrying of eight feet.

'There's just got to be,' he added after a while.

More scurrying.

'Hasn't there?' By now there was real desperation in his voice.

I sat down. As did Tamsin. The look on her face showed that she was trying just as hard as Pete and I were to think of a solution. I found this really impressive. She was nothing whatsoever to do with the mess we were in, in fact her only contribution had been to get us part of the way out of it, and still she seemed to be feeling our pain. I've got a nasty feeling that in her situation I'd have been out of there at the first opportunity.

'Hey!' cried Pete. 'What about this?'

He intercepted one of the rabbits mid-sprint and put it on the bar. It looked a bit unnerved for a second, but then accepted that there was no way it could leap to the floor from that height and got on with drinking the tonic water that Pete thoughtfully poured into an ashtray for it.

'Vince!' said Pete sharply.

The rabbit looked up in surprise. But Pete didn't say anything else. He waited until the rabbit got bored and returned to the water. Then he repeated his cry. 'Vince!'

Again the rabbit looked up. Pete turned to me in triumph. 'There you go. Job done.'

I stood up, walked across to him and put a hand on his shoulder. 'Pete, could I ask you to do something?'

''Course.'

'Could you just repeat that experiment, using the same name, but this time keep your eye not on the rabbit on the bar, but the one on the floor?'

Pete looked a bit confused, but nevertheless did as he was asked. 'Vince!' he shouted.

The rabbit on the floor looked up.

'Ah,' said Pete.

'And just in case you're in any doubt,' I continued, 'let's try this.' I cleared my throat. 'Benson!'

The rabbit on the floor looked up. As, of course, did the one on the bar.

'Norman!' I shouted. Both rabbits looked up. 'Fiona! Camshaft! Toothbrush!' At each word, the rabbits gave a little start. I turned to Pete. 'Are you getting the picture, Doctor Doolittle? You can say what you want with these things around, they're going to think you're talking to them.'

He nodded dumbly. I returned to my seat and carried on trying to think of a solution. The table next to me was the one with Benson's cage on it. It gave me an idea.

'How about . . .' I said, standing up and placing the cage on the floor at the far end of the pub. 'How about . . .' I put Vince's much grander cage next to it and opened the doors to both of them. Then I grabbed the rabbit that was still on the floor and held it about six feet away from the cages. 'Go on,' I said, 'run for home. Run for home.' I let go. The rabbit ran towards the cages, picked the ornate one and hopped inside.

'Hello,' I said, my hopes rising. 'That seemed a very definite choice.'

So I repeated the exercise, and once more the rabbit picked the larger cage. A third time: same result.

'This is looking promising,' I said, taking the other rabbit off the bar. I held it in the same position, gave it the same instructions – and it picked the same cage. The two rabbits sat side by side, gazing out at the world from the luxury of their very well-appointed home.

'Damn,' said Tamsin.

'You can't blame them,' I said miserably. 'They're rabbits, not homing pigeons. They're sensible, like us. Give them a mansion and a bedsit, they'll make the obvious choice.'

'You're not going to be in a mansion or a bedsit when Terry gets hold of you,' said Pete, matter-of-factly. 'You're going to be in intensive care.'

His lack of concern for my welfare infuriated me, but I was too drained to have a go at him. This problem had beaten me. And soon Terry would be doing the same. I might as well get used to it. I closed my eyes and started to work out the best way of rolling up into a ball, so that as few of the blows as possible would reach my head . . .

'Erm, lads,' said Tamsin quietly.

I didn't respond. I was too emotionally exhausted.

'This might interest you,' she added.

Still I kept my eyes shut. No doubt Tamsin thought she had a clever plan for telling these rabbits apart, but I really wasn't interested. I mean, I was touched she was trying to help, and I hated to appear ungrateful, but there was simply no way you could tell which of those rabbits was which. Not having any optimism left to invest in the matter, I ignored her.

Pete had obviously not ignored her, because soon he spoke too. 'You're right, Tamsin,' he said. 'That is quite interesting. Sam, you might want to take a look at this.'

I had to at least open my eyes, didn't I? It would be rude not to pay them that courtesy. Clearly there was going to be nothing worth looking at, not in the way of clues as to which rabbit was Benson and which Vince, but I had to look anyway, for good manners' sake. The first thing I saw was Pete, who directed my attention towards the cage. And what I saw in there were the two rabbits. Neither of them looked any different from before. But that wasn't important.

It was what they were doing that was important.

They were doing the thing that rabbits are famous for doing. They were doing it with great energy and not a little enjoyment, which I suppose is only to be expected, and they didn't seem at all bothered that there were three people watching them.

I looked across at Pete. He looked at Tamsin. Then she looked at me. There was a split second when none of us said or did anything. Then, at exactly the same moment, we all shot across to the cage like lightning.

'Grab the bastards!'

'I can't reach inside with that door there! Hold it RIGHT open!'

'I *am* doing!'

'Stand out of my way! I can't reach them!'

'How can I stand out of the way and hold the door open at the same time?!'

'Go round the back and hold it from there!'

'Come *here*, you shit!'

'They don't want to stop.'

'Would you?'

I've got to say that's the thing that impressed me most about the whole incident. I can't remember who finally managed to separate the rabbits and pull them into the open, but what I do remember is that in the midst of the chaos, with three giants crowded around their cage frantically trying to interrupt their love-making, the rabbits kept right at it. The one on top didn't miss a single stroke. It was a devotion to duty, or rather pleasure, of mind-boggling proportions. But in the end the poor bunny was fighting a lost cause. He ended up being held by Tamsin. I had the other one. Neither of them looked very happy.

'Before we go any further,' I said, speaking slowly and carefully, 'we've got to get these rabbits labelled. Tamsin, you are, I think, holding the one that was on top during . . . that?'

'I am.'

'Which means that unless that pet shop sold me the George Michael of the rabbit world, I am holding Benson. Correct?'

The other two nodded.

'Right,' I continued. 'While we continue to hold our rabbits, you, Pete, are going to write out the names of both rabbits on pieces of paper.'

Soon the rabbits had nametags attached to their back legs by elastic bands, which as an added precaution were of different colours, the codes for which were written out on a third piece of paper, kept in my pocket. We then put them in their correct cages, and sat down to recover ourselves over another drink.

Vince bore the look of a rabbit who was very unhappy at the way things had turned out. 'Look at him,' I laughed. 'He's annoyed at being denied his rights, isn't he?'

'I know how he feels,' mumbled Pete.

Although he didn't see it, Tamsin gave a smile which indicated that his frustration was only going to be temporary. 'Come on,' she said, 'let's get this dyeing finished. It's Vince from pink to black, right?'

As she filled the bowl with fresh water and set about returning Vince to his natural colour, a question occurred to me. 'Tamsin, I know I assumed that Benson was a male name, and so you weren't expecting her to be a her, but didn't you notice . . . you know . . . the absence of . . . While you were dyeing her?'

'The fur doesn't go all the way round there, you know. And even if I had been looking for it, I might have had a lot of difficulty in finding it. That can happen, you know.'

I directed a smirk at Pete. He replied with a scowl and a clenched fist, mouthing something threatening at me. But his bad mood didn't last for long. Once Vince was a black rabbit again, Tamsin came and sat next to Pete, her leg brushing his, a look in her eyes that showed she didn't expect to be sleeping alone that night. I thanked her again for her help, picked up Benson's cage and wished them both goodnight. I knew, even as I loaded the rabbit into my car outside, that Pete and Tamsin's coupling of earlier would already have been resumed. And again I got that reminiscey feeling, that desire to congratulate him, utter a gentle 'go on, my son'. He was going to have fun tonight, and that made me happy, partly for his sake, partly for my own, because it gave me an excuse to swim around in nostalgic memories of when I used to do that sort of thing. It was just what I needed to calm me down after the trauma of the previous few hours, and made the drive home a lot more pleasant.

Most of today was taken up with rehearsing my story about Benson, or, as she was of course now called, Vince. The cage was easy: the shop had only lent me the grand one to bring the rabbit home in and it had now been swapped for the plainer one. A minor fact. Kirsty wouldn't be at all surprised that it got lost in the general excitement of yesterday afternoon. The matter of a female rabbit being called Vince was a little more tricky, but then again it was very unlikely that Kirsty would ever find out. And even if she did I could blame it on the pet shop. Beyond that, it was simply a case of getting the name 'Benson' out of my head, forgetting about drugs and black hair-dye, and waiting for Kirsty's return.

How many points was I going to get for this? Some back-of-an-envelope scribblings told me that at this stage, week eight of twelve, I needed six hundred and sixty-seven points to be on track for marriage. I currently had four hundred and eighty-two. A hundred and eighty-five points in one week was what sports commentators would call a 'big ask'. My previous record was last week's one hundred and sixty. But that was before the days of fluffy, and more importantly unexpected, bunny rabbits. The delight in Kirsty's eyes when she saw Vince had been obvious. OK, those eyes were looking in slightly different directions at the time, but nevertheless, if the surprise present of a rabbit hadn't made this a one-eight-five week, nothing could.

Five o'clock found Vince and myself on the sofa together, watching a documentary about Bengal tigers. She seemed to be enjoying the roaring sounds and empathising with a fellow member of the animal kingdom, while I was trying to remember which sitcom the guy doing the voiceover was in. Then I heard the front door go.

I sat up straight. 'This is it,' I whispered to Vince. 'Look as cute as you can. I need maximum points here.' I waited for Kirsty to come into the room. But she didn't. Instead there was the sound of a bag being dropped in the hallway, and then slow, trudging footsteps making their way upstairs.

'Kirsty?'

Her reply was an elongated grunt which was obviously meant as 'hello, Sam, sorry for my rudeness but I'm very hungover and need to lie down straightaway'. Following Kirsty up to the bedroom a minute later, I found that she'd climbed under the duvet without taking her clothes off. Most of us have done that, granted, but Kirsty hadn't even taken her shoes off. Her eyes were no longer unfocused, they were simply bloodshot, which in one way was a good thing, because without them her face wouldn't have had any colour at all.

'Big night, was it?' I asked.

'Urrggh.'

'Did you stay on Malibu, or were there other Drinks Of Yesteryear? Snakebite, perhaps?'

'Urrgggh.'

This sound didn't answer the question, but I detected in it a note of warning that I was beginning to annoy her. To avoid losing points, I asked if she wanted a couple of Resolves.

'Urrgggh,' she said again, nodding her head to give me a clue.

A few minutes later I was back at the bedside. 'There we are,' I said, handing her the glass. 'I waited in the kitchen until the tablets had fully dissolved so that you wouldn't even have to listen to the hissing.' I didn't spell out that I expected at least ten points for this extreme attention to detail, but hoped that she'd register it anyway. The drink perked her up a bit, by which I mean she finally began to use words from the English language. 'God Almighty' were the first two, followed by, 'I am never going drinking with Stacy Astle again. Or seeing her at all, come to that.'

'Not a good reunion, then?'

'Oh, it was all right, I suppose. But we acted as though we were still fifteen. And we're not.'

Three little words. 'Told', 'you' and 'so'. They could have lost me hundreds of points. I kept them to myself. Besides which, I'd had a great idea. I rushed downstairs, gathered Vince in my arms and took 'him' up to the bedroom. 'Someone's been missing you,' I said.

Kirsty opened her eyes and nearly jumped out of her skin. The shock seemed to help her recover from her grogginess, but once she'd remembered about Vince, and dyeing him pink, her reaction was not the fond, cooing one of yesterday. That, I now learned, had been due not to the cuteness of Vince but the strength of the Malibu. In the cold light of a hangover, Kirsty was far less convinced by the rabbit's charms. 'I'd forgotten about that,' she said, recoiling to the other side of the bed.

That? Vince wasn't a 'that', he was a he. Or rather he was a she masquerading as a he. I suddenly felt very nervous. 'But yesterday you said you liked him.'

'Did I? God, I didn't realise I was that drunk that early. What the hell were we doing dyeing it pink?'

'You thought it was funny.'

Kirsty looked at the rabbit and winced. Gone was the love she'd shown for him (or rather his twin) yesterday. Then Vince had been a pet she could shower with love, a present that had earned me points aplenty. Now he was an abomination of nature. This was starting to look very, very bad.

Kirsty proceeded to confirm my fears. 'Why did you buy me a rabbit in the first place?' she asked suspiciously.

Oh Christ. Not only was she now questioning Vince's suitability as a present, she was doubting whether he'd really been a present at all. 'Because I thought you'd like it.' The inside of my mouth felt like the cloth on a pool table. Kirsty's eyes, bloodshot as they were, still managed to bore into me. I tried hard not to swallow guiltily, but couldn't help myself.

'You thought I'd like a rabbit?'

For a moment I seriously considered coming clean. I could quite truthfully say that at the time I brought the rabbit into our flat, I didn't know that it contained large quantities of a Class A drug. But it's always dodgy admitting to a lie and then claiming your new explanation is the truth. You've fibbed once, so why should they believe you this time? No, all I could do was hold out with the gift story. 'I just happened to be passing the pet shop and saw him in the window, and he looked . . . cuddly.'

'*Cuddly?* Sam, it's huge. And what do you mean, you were "just passing" the pet shop?'

This was going from bad to worse. I did the only thing I could think of. I ran away. 'Sorry that you don't like him,' I shouted over my shoulder, hurrying downstairs with Vince still in my arms. 'I'll take him back to the pet shop tomorrow.'

Kirsty didn't reply. I stewed downstairs for a while, angry that the points I'd expected from Vince weren't going to materialise, scared that Kirsty's suspicions would actually lose me points. She stayed in bed, nursing her hangover, although from the sound of the portable TV going on I could tell she wasn't actually asleep. The rabbit, scampering play-fully around the sitting-room floor, was the only happy one out of the three of us.

After a while I remembered that today was Sunday itself. The points were due to be dished out tonight. But was Kirsty feeling up to it? Would she rather leave it until tomorrow? If she tallied up my score tonight, her freshly brewed suspicion might make her penalise me too heavily. But then again, if she delayed until tomorrow, the suspicion would have all the more time to get stronger. Perhaps tonight was the better option? I tiptoed upstairs, ready to gauge the situation, under cover of offering her some more Resolve. But as I reached the bedroom, the answer was already waiting for me. On the carpet, outside the closed door, was a piece of paper that had been folded in two. Anxiously, I reached down and picked it up. Opening it out, I found this week's score.

Four hundred and eighty-five.

I couldn't believe this. Four hundred and eighty-five? That was a net score this week of three points. Kirsty's writing was a little bit shaky, but there was no mistaking any of the figures: four eight-five.

Hell. This was week eight. I was now two-thirds of the way through my allotted time but didn't have even half the number of points I needed. For a moment I began to feel angry. I wanted to barge into the bedroom and argue with Kirsty about this week's score. But that would be wrong, on at least two counts. Firstly it would show her I was rat-tled. I don't want her knowing how worried I am about this. Show that you're confident of victory and you're halfway to achieving it. That's why the All Blacks do that war dance thing before their rugby matches, isn't it? And secondly, as I said earlier, putting her straight about the rabbit might lose me even more points. 'I know you think there's something I'm not telling you about that rabbit, darling, but . . . well, actually, yes there is . . . but it's OK, it was all geared around earning money to treat you with, and although there was a criminal-prosecution quantity of cocaine involved, don't worry, it was only in our flat for a few hours . . .' Wouldn't exactly fill her with confidence. So I decided to head straight for the Mitre. Bring the Cabinet up to date, see what light they could shed on events.

Pete was in predictably chirpy form, exhibiting the jauntiness that young men always display the day after a fresh 'conquest'. Consequently he felt able to brush off my disastrous points total as a 'hiccup'.

'A hiccup?!' I shouted, my anger all the greater because it was him who'd got me involved with the rabbit in the first place. 'A *hiccup*?! I've got four weeks to get five hundred and fifteen points!'

'Calm down,' said George. 'Yes, you've got four weeks to get five hundred and fifteen points. But that's achievable if you score at last week's rate of one sixty. You can even do it if you score at your *second* highest rate, one fifty.'

'But this week I only got three!'

'Kirsty's obviously guessed that the rabbit wasn't really a present.'

Amanda nodded. 'Plus she had a hangover. I think they're right, Sam. You've got to let this week go. There's plenty of time left.' I was far from convinced, and it must have shown, because she put her arm round my shoulders and said: 'Come on, you know you're going to do this.'

'Am I?' I forced myself to think about the All Blacks again. Act strong, you'll be strong. 'OK, I'll stop worrying.' Amanda removed her arm, and I stood up. 'I *am* going to do this. I *am* going to get these points.' I sat down again. Just saying it had made me feel more optimistic. 'What song should we have our first dance to at the reception?'

'"Run Rabbit Run"?' suggested Pete.

I narrowed my eyes and fixed them on him. 'You're going to get such a slap in a minute.' He went off to serve a customer, chortling happily.

Later on the conversation split in two, Pete talking to George while Amanda and I chatted together.

'How's your Timepool thing going?' she asked.

'Danny? Pain in the backside.'

'Are you going to stop doing it?'

'I wish I could,' I said gloomily. 'But the annoying thing is, the kid's got to me. Even when he's really bad, like last week, pushing me so far that I just can't be bothered any more, and I vow that I'm going to tell Alan I've had enough and he can count me out, when it comes to it I can't say it. There's this course that we've got to get Danny to go on, and it's his last chance, and I know that I'm his only chance at the last chance. I can't abandon him now. Much as I want to. I mean, it's not as though I haven't got problems of my own at the moment.' I explained to Amanda the thing I noticed the first time I met Danny, how he seems like an adult rather than a child, how sad that makes me feel. It's been preying on my mind a bit.

'Missing out on childhood, you mean?' she said. 'That is sad.'

I nodded. 'But it's more than just the missing out on it. You need that experience of being a boy for when you grow up into a man. There's something childish about men.'

'Tell me something I don't know.'

'No, no, I'm serious. It's why blokes get on with other blokes, no matter what age they are.'

'Do they?' asked Amanda.

'Yeah. Much more than women do. I bet all your friends, your good friends, I mean, are the same sort of age as you.'

'Well . . . yeah, I suppose they are. I've never really thought about it.'

'All my adult life I've had mates who were older or younger than me. Pete, for instance. Six years younger than me, going through a completely different stage of his life, but I don't really notice the age difference. There's something about men, no matter how old they are, that remains childish. We can look at the world with a boy's eyes. Which means we can relate to other men in those terms. It gives a simplicity to our viewpoint. We're all boys, when we want to be.'

Amanda considered this for a moment. 'But women can remember what it's like to be a child too, you know.'

'Yeah, but you don't access it like we do. That's why you prefer friends your own age. Because you need other women who've lived as much as you, who see things the same way. Women who can understand the little complexities of life as much as you understand them. Whereas men can be friends with other blokes twenty years older than them, or twenty years younger, because they can all access that childish, simplistic part of themselves. A sort of emotional common ground, if you like.' I paused for a drink of my beer. 'We're not always like that, of course. Sometimes you do need a serious chat, advice, whatever, and that does have to be with a bloke your own age. Like when all this points thing started, George and I went for a chat one lunchtime, and he helped me get my head round it a bit. Couldn't have got that from Pete. Too young. But most of the time, when you're just talking with a few mates in the pub, age isn't an issue.'

'Well, well,' said Amanda. 'I've never looked at it like that.'

'There you go then,' I said. 'Another little insight into the male mind for you.'

'Bound to be a *little* insight,' she said with a teasing smile. 'They're little minds.'

Week Nine

A strange week. It started bizarrely, with me dropping Benson back off at the pet shop on my way to work. I was keen to avoid bumping into the owner's son. If the rabbit had been in its original condition I'd have tried to get at least some of my money back. But having to explain why Benson was now pink instead of black was more than I could face at that time on a Monday, so I parked down the road while Surly Boy opened the shutters, then drove quietly up, legged it across, put Benson's cage just inside the door-way, ran back to the car and Schumachered it away before Surly could make a note of my number. God knows what he's going to say when his father gets back. 'Honest, Dad, this bloke showed up, paid me a hundred quid for the rabbit, then brought it back two days later and it was pink.' But, without wishing to sound uncaring, I didn't care. It wasn't my problem. The lad had made forty quid, hadn't he? More if he fancied lying about the purchase price. So he could face the music. I'd got a marriage proposal to worry about.

And, of course, a thirteen-year-old boy. Having cleared it with Alan, I decided to give His Stubbornness a change of scenery on Wednesday by taking him into the West End. A risky strategy, you might think, after the way he behaved in

Clerkenwell. You'd be right. The risk was precisely what my plan depended on. It was a plan I felt uneasy about, and whether it was morally justifiable or not I'll leave for you to decide. But Danny's an unusually difficult case and I needed to think outside the box, or rather outside the park.

Alan dropped him off outside Selfridges just as the post-work shopping period was reaching its busiest point. The minute Danny and I walked through the door I could see his eyes light up. Kids are supposed to do this in toy stores, but Danny, as we know, is not a kid. His excitement was at the shelves and rails full of expensive clothing and jewellery, and at the handbags and pockets full of other people's money. This was the reaction my plan depended on. But not yet.

'Right, café on the first floor,' I said determinedly, standing behind him and gripping his arm to prevent any dashes for freedom. Thankfully Danny obeyed, and we walked up the stairs to the café. Over its balcony you get a wonderful panorama of the ground floor, with what seem like acres of retail activity spread out before you. Just what the plan called for. Whatever the morals, you can't say I hadn't thought it through.

'What do you want?'

'Do they do beer?'

'Yes, Danny, they do. But you're not having one. A Coke, perhaps?'

''Lrite then.'

We queued in silence, filing slowly past the baguettes and individual slices of tarte tatin until we reached the drinks section. Tapping my tray against the metal rail, I waited to get served.

Just as I was about to ask for our drinks, a huge weight forced itself in from my right, pushing me against Danny. There was a strong smell of aftershave.

'Two cappuccinos,' boomed the man, before turning to his female companion. He was in his forties, wearing an expensive suit that was straining at every seam, his tie covered with mementoes from several of the lunches (no doubt on expenses) that had contributed to his enormous waistline. The jacket pockets were bulging with sundry possessions. A mobile phone peeked out here, a wallet there, together with unopened letters, cigarette packets, ballpoint pens. Even if he hadn't just barged in front of me, the guy's appearance would have made me take an instant dislike to him. People who treat well-made suits like that shouldn't be allowed to own them.

But, in typically British fashion, I said nothing. Not only had the woman behind the counter already set to work on his coffees, the man himself was now canoodling, revoltingly, with his partner. She was also in her forties, a vision in peroxide, far too fond of sunbeds and showing an unwise amount of cleavage. It was obvious that they were married. It was equally obvious that they weren't married to each other. Only three sorts of people are that indecent in public: teenagers on escalators, couples in the first lust-filled month of a relationship, and people having affairs. Before I could complain about them pushing in I'd have needed to throw a bucket of cold water over them. So I marinated in my disgust, got served and sat Danny down at a table as far away from the adulterers as possible.

'Had a good week?'

'Shit.'

'Sorry to hear that, Danny. It's about to get even worse.' I took out the curriculum.

He groaned and looked away. 'I've fuckin' told you. You thick or what? I'm not doing that course. Don't fuckin' need to.'

I took a deep breath to stop myself giving any of the standard responses. These include 'I used to think that, but now I know better', 'this is your last chance, Danny', and 'once you've got your qualifications you can do whatever you want, you'll always have them to fall back on'. Not only have I tried all those and seen them fail, they're also what Danny gets from every other adult in his life, and he prides himself on being immune to them, on how much they harden his resistance. No, I had my plan. The first stage was to prepare the ground, soften Danny up, make him ready for the proposal when it came. 'Much rather be down there, wouldn't you?' I said, indicating the shop floor. 'All those opportunities to be taken. Or should I say purses? Better than having to sit up here with this boring old prat banging on about schoolwork.'

He replied without looking at me. 'You said it.' His eyes darted from one department to another, all of them packed with customers so entranced by the goodies on display that a small, speedy hand slipping into their bag would almost certainly go unnoticed. Danny was careful not to show anything as conventional as excitement at the prospect, but I knew his mind was racing. I gave him a while to take in the scene.

As he did so, I noticed the fat man asking a question of the girl clearing the tables. She pointed to the counter, and I could see from her smile that she was being perfectly polite, but the man stood up rudely, noisily scraping back his chair and brushing, if not actually pushing, the girl aside. 'At these prices?' he snarled. 'The least you could expect at these prices would be waitress service. Useless cow.'

I was filled with loathing. I didn't know whether the outburst had been intended to impress his girlfriend, or if he really was just that ignorant, but the poor girl looked shocked and turned away. A few people sitting nearby tutted, and an old woman said something to try and comfort her. The fat man, meanwhile, went and pushed his way to the front of the queue again.

I made myself forget about this odious lump and returned to the plan. 'What do you reckon to a deal, Danny?' I asked suddenly.

He looked round in surprise. This wasn't the way grown-ups normally spoke to him. It wasn't the way I'd just been speaking to him. What was I on about?

'Well,' I continued. 'Are you interested?'

'What do you mean, deal?'

'I offer you something, you offer me something else in return.'

'I know what "deal" means. What sort of deal?'

Inwardly I allowed myself a smile. His irritation showed that I was getting to him. He was biting. 'My side of the deal,' I said, 'is that you get five minutes to yourself. This evening, now. There'll be conditions, of course, and if you mess me around, even a tiny bit, on even one of them, then I'll go not just to Alan but to the police as well, and land you in a lot of very, very deep trouble. But as long as you play it straight, I'll tell no one. I'll leave you here for five minutes, meet you down the road, and whatever you get up to while we're apart is your business.'

He looked suspicious. 'Why would you do that? What's my side of the deal?'

I paused before answering and leafed through the curriculum. I wanted Danny to get it into his head that I was going to ask for a lot more than I really was. He had to think that I was going to insist on him signing up for the course. He'd never do that. No way was that worth five minutes' freedom in Selfridges on a busy shopping evening. He had to think that's what it was going to be so that when my real demand came, it would, by comparison, seem paltry.

Finally I spoke. 'You have to go through one section of this with me.'

My plan was working. I'd surprised him again. 'What do you mean?' Danny asked.

'We talk about one of the subjects in here, properly, with you taking it seriously. I decide when we've talked about it for long enough. I decide whether you've given it a good enough shot. If you haven't, we sit here in the usual point- less silence until it's time for Alan to collect you. If you have . . . like I say, five minutes.'

He weighed it up. Everything was happening on my terms, which no doubt annoyed him as much as it satisfied me. But he realised he had nothing to lose, apart from face. It wasn't that face wasn't important to him – the opposite, in fact – but equally he knew that the potential reward was worth it. 'Go on then.'

I opened up the curriculum. 'Module Four: Creative Writing.'

'Huh. That sounds really shit.'

'Is that you taking it seriously, Danny?' I asked threaten- ingly.

He couldn't actually bring himself to apologise, but my warning did at least keep him quiet as I read from the cur- riculum.

'"Pupils will be expected to use their imagination and creative powers in a variety of written exercises. These will be aimed at developing their descriptive writing, and making them better able to express themselves, their thoughts and their emotions." What do you think of that, then?'

Danny nearly repeated his last opinion, but then settled for a morose: 'What's it all mean?'

'You have to write things.'

'What sort of things?'

'Essays, I suppose. Stories.' I looked at the curriculum again. '"For their final exercise, pupils will be expected to write a five-hundred word essay on a subject of their choice." What would you pick, Danny? And you're not allowed shoplifting or lager.'

He considered the question. Clearly every fibre of his being was still rebelling against cooperating with an adult. For my part, I was still worried about proposing such a deal. But I told myself that Danny got up to his tricks for the rest of the week anyway, and so if I had to use those tricks as a bargaining chip in the one hour I had with him, so be it. There we were, this odd couple, neither of us really wanting to be there, both trying to cope with the situation as best we could.

Eventually Danny said: 'Architecture.'

'Sorry?'

'It means all to do with buildings and stuff.'

'Danny, you know what "deal" means, I know what "architecture" means. What I was asking was why you'd pick architecture as your subject.'

'I'd write about a building. A big building.'

This sounded promising, in the sense that it was better than 'really shit', so I uttered a gentle 'carry on' and hoped Danny would continue.

'Big palace sort of thing,' he said. 'Loads of different bits to it, you know, different sections, all with columns and arches, stuff like that. Made of marble and stone, like, really expensive stuff. All of it straight, you know, square angles and that. But only till you get to the roof. 'Cos on the roof are these onion-type things. Domes, like. Little ones, all over the different bits, and one big one, a big dome, a big onion, on top of the middle bit.'

'Sounds good.'

'And all round it are big gardens, full of flowers and grass and stuff. Hilly bits, flat bits, a path so you can walk round it all, path that leads up to the building itself, like. Yeah, enormous big palace, that's what I'd write about.'

'Where is this palace?'

Danny looked at me quickly, then looked away again. 'Don't matter, does it? I'm writing about the palace, not where it is.'

I'd stumbled on to something here. I had to be careful not to scare Danny back into his shell.

'Anyway,' he continued, 'it's not actually anywhere, it's a palace that I'd design, it's not real.'

'How would you design it?' I asked, trying to convince Danny that I believed him.

'I'd draw it all up first, draw it like I just told you, make all the plans and measurements and all that. Then you'd need to get blokes to build it.'

I proceeded to ask Danny more and more questions about the 'design' process to give him a chance to kick over the traces of his mistake. He had to think I believed him about this not being a real palace in a real location, or at least know that I wasn't going to press him about it. Softly, softly, catchee Danny.

After a few minutes of this, I closed the curriculum and put it back in my pocket to signify that Danny's side of the deal was finished. I braced myself for what I knew I had to say next. To maintain any respect from him, I had to honour the deal. Tricking him into cooperating with me would be wrong in itself and would also cut once and for all the ties, albeit fairly tenuous ones, that had built up between us. Even though I knew this deal was setting a dangerous precedent, that if I was to make any further progress with Danny it would depend on turning more blind eyes to more criminal behaviour, I had to keep my word.

'All right,' I said, 'you've done your bit. Now you've had a look at it I hope you realise you could do this course in your sleep.' He didn't respond. 'So, OK, it's your turn.' I lowered my voice. 'Five minutes. Not a second longer, right? I'll meet you down the street, by St Christopher's Place.'

'Got it,' he said, standing up.

'Hang on, not so quick. There are conditions, remember?'

Danny grudgingly sat down.

'Number one,' I said, 'if you get caught it's nothing to do with me. I'll say that you gave me the slip. Even if you tell them that I OKed it, they won't believe you. Number two . . .' I couldn't think of another condition. By saying that there were conditions I was merely trying to construct an edifice of respectability around something I knew to be wrong.

I looked over at Fat Man to see him still canoodling with his girlfriend. So that he could lean further across the table to her, he shoved the tray containing their cups out of the way, not caring that there was a woman sitting next to them, quietly eating a sandwich. The tray banged against hers, and if she hadn't grabbed her pot of tea it would have gone flying. Fat Man must have heard the clatter, but didn't bother to apologise. Instead he continued his slobbering, while the woman was left to mop up the spilt tea on her own.

'Number two,' I found myself saying, 'is that it's that bastard over there, all right?'

Danny turned to see who I meant. He spied Fat Man's jacket hanging over the back of his chair, the pockets gaping open with his possessions. 'Fuckin' hell, he's askin' for it.'

'Well, give it to him, then.' I stood up and walked out of the store, picking my way through the Oxford Street hordes until I reached the entrance to St Christopher's Place.

Danny obviously didn't mess around because two minutes and thirty seconds later he joined me.

'Stupid twat didn't even notice,' he grinned, brandishing a black leather wallet.

I imagined what Fat Man's face was going to be like when he discovered the loss. It couldn't have happened to a nicer bloke.

What made the rest of the week strange, and indeed stressful, was that my behaviour was completely at odds with how I was feeling. It had to be. I had to put on my strong act, show Kirsty how confident I was about getting these points. Whereas in reality the more I considered it, the less confident I became. I tried telling myself that George and Pete and Amanda were right, that I'd already had two weeks where I'd earned as many points as I needed to earn every week from now on, so there was nothing to worry about. My previous form, or at least some of it, was up to the job. But I couldn't help feeling scared that I wasn't going to make it, that I was going to lose the woman I love. Reveal that insecurity, though, and I'd scupper my chances completely. How could I expect Kirsty to have faith in me if I didn't show any in myself?

So it had to be a simple case of doing the best I could, hiding my fears behind an outward display of normality. Kirsty herself, funnily enough, made this relatively simple, in that her behaviour was normal as well. She wasn't in a mood with me, or at any rate it didn't seem she was. Whatever her suspicions about the rabbit incident, they appeared to have dissipated as quickly as her hangover. She still capped my jokes, still made me cups of coffee, still said yes when I offered to make her cups of coffee. Our cuddles – for still we cuddled – felt as genuine as they always had. But, and this is why the week was so strange, I was all the time trying to work out what I needed to do to earn these points. These five hundred and fifteen points. In four weeks. Which, if you need any help with the maths, equates to one hundred and twenty-eight point seven five points per week. Trust me on that one. It's a sum I've become very familiar with.

The small change was watched as never before. It's amazing what you can spot when you look really closely. On Friday night, as we were clearing up after dinner (tagliatelle with a fiendishly unusual sauce – finding the recipe for it must, I felt sure, have earned me at least thirty points), I found myself depositing an empty wine bottle in the bin. The swing-top lid failed to live up to its name when pressed, indicating that the bin was on the full side. So I did what I normally do in such situations: I took the whole lid off, to see how much scope there was for compacting the rubbish and making space for the bottle. It was as I gazed down on the two-day-old newspapers and dried-out teabags that a past conversation came back to me. Well, I say 'conversation'. I didn't contribute anything to it in the way of words. A more accurate description would be 'monologue'. It was delivered by Kirsty. Those of you who live within three miles of us will have heard it at the time. For the rest of you, here's a transcript:

'*Aaaarrrgh!* For the millionth time, Sam, *why* can you never empty this bin? Why do you *always* insist on packing stuff into it, whether or not there's room? This bin isn't a fucking Tardis, you know. There's just as much room on the inside as you'd expect from the outside. When it gets full, it needs *emptying*! *Understand?* You take the OLD bag OUT, and put a NEW one IN!'

Shocked by her sudden rage, I watched as Kirsty attempted to demonstrate the taking out of an old bag. But my final contribution to the bin's already overflowing load (an empty Pringles tube – I can see it now) had been rammed in with such force that when she lifted up the bag, the bin came with it.

'Arrrgh!' screamed Kirsty. 'Well, don't just stand there, come and help me!'

I hurried across and held on to the bin while Kirsty pulled the bag upwards. It took a real effort, and two or three times the bin slipped through my fingers, but eventually the bag started to behave and wormed its way free. The incredible thing was that there was so much rubbish in there, which had been compacted into every available bit of space, that for a good ten seconds the bag retained the exact shape of the bin's inside. Damien Hirst would have earned a fortune with it. Kirsty was unamused.

That memory earned me a few points on Friday. Instead of forcing the wine bottle down on to the heaving mass of rubbish, I took the bag out and replaced it with a fresh one. Letting the bottle drop noisily into the now-cavernous bin might, I grant you, have been gilding the lily a bit. But I wanted to be sure my achievement hadn't gone unnoticed.

After a week of such stress-inspired effort, my energy reserves were pretty well empty by this afternoon. And what was my new total? Five hundred and thirty-five. The week had seen my nerves ripped to shreds for a mere fifty points. I found it hard to understand. So hard that I began to feel angry. It only lasted a couple of minutes, and I'm sure it was only my puzzlement expanding temporarily into resentment, but that was how I felt. I don't know if it was anger at

Kirsty for not awarding me more points, or at myself for not being able to earn them. It was there, though, so I thought I should record it.

Once I'd taken my failure on board, I got down to the Mitre to see what help my Cabinet could provide.

George was the first to make a contribution. 'One hundred and fifty-five,' he said quietly.

'What?'

'One hundred and fifty-five points. It's your new required weekly rate. A thousand minus five-three-five is four-six-five, divided by three weeks is one-five-five.'

'You're very good on maths, George,' I said, 'but your English needs some work. Vocabulary. You could start by looking up the words "sympathy" and "tact".'

'At least one-five-five's a round number,' he replied.

Convinced he must be winding me up, I swivelled round, ready to lay into him. But I could tell from his uninspired expression that he'd been speaking out of desperation, not nastiness. Just as unable as I was to spot the explanation for my feeble score, he'd fallen back on the only comment that came to mind. And while it didn't exactly help my mood, at least it was a useful summary of the situation. I turned to Pete and asked if he could think of anything. But all he came up with was a suggestion that I change the bin bag twice a day, irrespective of how much rubbish was in it. Again, I couldn't be angry with him. It was a pathetic, indeed an illogical suggestion, but he wasn't making it to be facetious. You could tell that it was the best he could manage. In some ways I even felt guilty asking him. How can he be expected to understand these matters, when he's never been party to them? He's still young, he doesn't want to get married. If even I, the one who does want it, can't see where I'm going wrong, then what chance has he got?

The same, though, cannot be said of Amanda. Not only is she the right age to help me out, she's the right sex. There's obviously something I'm missing in all this, something bigger than the small change, more significant, more meaningful. And as I watched her tonight, sitting at the bar, a vodka and tonic fizzing quietly by her hand while she stared at my piece of paper, I sensed that she knew what it was. Something in her eyes compelled me to watch her. She didn't realise I was doing it – I was pretending to talk bins with Pete – but looking at her reading that score over and over again, I knew in my heart that she had something to say. Equally, though, I sensed that, a bit like Danny, she'd say it when she wanted to and not before. I was desperate to hear what was playing on her mind. But ask her straight out, I told myself, and she wouldn't answer.

'You still making a pig's knob of getting those points?'

The question irritated me not just because it was so vulgar, but also because it had torn my attention away from Amanda. There was no mystery, of course, about who'd been responsible for it. 'I've told you,' continued Ray, 'but you won't listen, will you? This isn't a challenge that you *can* win. She's stringing you along, mate. This is her way of giving you the push. You're not going to get enough points, she's going to be spared the guilt of telling you to piss off. Admit it, you're fucked.'

'Not only are you wrong, Ray,' I said, 'but you're offensive with it.' I was quite pleased that I'd avoided sinking to his level. No swearing, no personal abuse, just a simple statement of the facts.

Pete's approach was a little different. 'Shut your *fucking* mouth, you poxy little bastard,' he yelled, taking a threatening step down the bar and forcing Ray to hop backwards.

'That's my mate you're talking to, and just because you can't see how serious all this is, it doesn't give you the right to fuck everyone else off with your crap theories. Now keep out of our fucking way, all right? You're already one down in the leg stakes. You wouldn't want to lose any more, would you?'

Problem dealt with. I have to say, I couldn't help being touched by Pete calling me his mate. Having someone to stick up for me, even against Ray, who was an irritation rather than a threat, lifted my spirits. We may both have been lost without a map in the jungle of Kirsty's points-scheme, but at least Pete and I were lost together. It was a show of solidarity that had me springing to my feet. 'Come on,' I shouted, giving the bar a determined slap, 'I refuse to take this lying down. All hands to the pump. Every effort that can be made will be made. Right?'

'Right,' barked Pete.

'Yeah, come on,' said George, getting, by his standards, quite animated. 'We can do this.'

The bandwagon lurched a bit at that point, owing to the fact that I couldn't think of anything to do. But the problem didn't last too long. 'I tell you what,' said Pete, 'here's the answer. We all ask around, everyone we can think of, for every bit of intelligence we can lay our hands on about what annoys women in men's behaviour. We blitz the . . . the . . . what do you call it, Sam?'

'The small change.'

'That's it, the small change. George, you ask every female friend you've got, every ex-girlfriend, your mum, your sister, women you see on the bus, everyone. I'll do the same. Tamsin, for instance. I'm seeing her tomorrow night.'

Amanda gave a grin. 'So that romance has blossomed, has it?'

Pete replied with a grin of his own, before returning to the earnest look he'd adopted for his role as tactical leader. 'Amanda – you're vital here. You're our agent in the enemy camp. We need you, not just to list your own dislikes about men, but to get out there among your girlfriends. Every one of them. Quiz them, again and again. Quiz them until they've got nothing left to give. We need to know what annoys women about men.'

'You only do one thing that annoys us,' she said.

'What's that?'

'You breathe.'

Pete began to protest but Amanda cut him off. 'All right, I'll see what I can come up with.'

But I knew from the way she said it that her agreement was only to avoid offending Pete. Etched into her smile, which now I looked closer was slightly forced, there was an unmistakable conviction that Pete was barking up the wrong tree. Again I got that feeling: Amanda knew something she wasn't letting on. But what was it? I'd just have to wait. If she'd wanted to bring it up now, she would have done. She'd tell me in her own good time. All I could do was pray that that time would be soon. Because by Christ did I need her help.

Later, as I dried my hands on the towel rail in the Gents, Pete sidled in to join me. Keeping his back against the door so that no one could barge in, he started fishing in his pocket.

'What are you up to?'

'Present for you,' he said, taking out his wallet. 'It's a piece of paper, and it's folded. Don't worry though, there isn't a score written inside.'

'Ha-ha.'

He handed me what at first sight appeared to be a slip of shiny paper, cut from a glossy magazine, slightly smaller than a raffle ticket. But as I turned it over, and saw the complex folding arrangement that had made it into a miniature envelope, I realised that this was in fact a wrap of cocaine.

'It's from the boss,' he continued. 'Bonus for last weekend. Vince went to the vet's the other day, and Terry was so happy at how well his little scheme had worked that he thought he'd cut me in. If you'll forgive the expression. Gave me a couple of grams. Thought you might like one of them.'

I handed it straight back to him. 'Are you mad?'

Pete looked confused. 'What, don't you . . .?'

'Once in a while I have, yeah, but—'

'I was gonna say. There was that party at Jim's for a start. And—'

'Yes, all right, Pete, thank you. As I say, once in a while. But I haven't made a habit of it. Your turn to forgive an expression. I've only taken what's been offered me, I've never carried any of my own around. And I don't intend to start now. Three weeks to go, remember? That'd look really good, wouldn't it, Kirsty finding cocaine in my bloody wallet?'

'Does she ever look in your wallet?'

'Well, no, but . . . that's not the point. Anything could happen. I could lose my wallet, it'd get handed in to the police – what would I say then, eh? No, Pete, it's just not worth it.'

'Oh,' he mumbled. 'All right then. I was only trying to cheer you up a bit.'

'I know,' I replied gently. 'And I appreciate that, I really do, like I appreciate your help with the small change.' I didn't want to hurt his feelings, so I added: 'Tell you what, you look after it for me. Then if, somehow, I manage to pull these points out of the fire, we can have a "celebration" after that.'

'Yeah, good idea.' He went to open the door, but just before he did so he turned to me and said: 'Sorry, Sam. Didn't mean to mess things up for you. I was trying to help.'

Sometimes I can't help but love him. 'You do help, Pete. You do.'

Week Ten

I bet you didn't know flowers could talk, did you?

At least not to the person who's bought them. They're supposed to speak volumes to the recipient, I know that. But last Thursday I got a lesson in just how much of an ear-bending a bunch of lilies can give their purchaser. A mid-morning departmental meeting had been where the idea first arose. I hate meetings at the moment. Normally they're great, a chance to nod intelligently at everyone else's comments while secretly letting your mind wander, thinking about things other than bloody work for once. Which is precisely why I hate them now. At least when I'm slaving away at my desk, on the phone, my mind's occupied with that, rather than the imminent departure of my girlfriend. Or at least most of it is. I get a bit of a respite from the twenty-four-hour angst that my life has turned into. I think that's one of the reasons I've become so determined about Danny. He's something I *can* make progress on. Except weeks like this one, when he disappeared again. Annoying, because I'd managed to get somewhere in Selfridges. And I do worry about where he is, who he's with. But I'm sure he'll be back next week.

So, as I was saying, distractions are good. But in meetings, the points problem takes over my whole mind again. Kirsty fills my thoughts. My imagination becomes a cinema with only one seat. I'm strapped into it, and they only ever show one film: *Kirsty Leaves Sam*. It's a cross between a horror and a weepie. My response on Thursday, as someone from Human Resources prattled on about 'safety while using photo-copiers', was to think of positive moves I could make, big gestures that would earn me big points rather than small-change gestures (like bin-bag replacement) that only earn me small points. I remembered Steve's advice about the ini-tial proposal to Kirsty: keep it traditional, because some things are traditional for a reason, namely that women have always liked them and always will like them . . . such as flowers. That was it. Flowers.

But no sooner had the thought occurred to me than I began to worry. However much Steve might be right in normal circumstances, was now the time to buy Kirsty flow-ers? She might see it as the tactics of desperation. Of course she'd be right: I am desperate. It wasn't, of course, that I didn't feel the love those flowers would imply, rather that I was wary of showing Kirsty how petrified I was. I *had* to maintain my show of strength. But eventually I decided Steve was right. Flowers are flowers are flowers, and women love getting them.

There's a stall not far from our office. As I walked towards it, amid the bustle of a City lunchtime, I thought about some of the ways I've told Kirsty how much I love her. A message drawn in the steamed-up bathroom mirror; a self-penned poem inside a fortune cookie (she didn't know about my sneaky advance visit to the restaurant); a simple 'I love you' hidden underneath the Weetabix packet to make a Monday morning that bit easier to bear. Each time there'd been a real buzz in surprising her, bringing a smile to her face, and each time I'd felt glad about avoiding the cliché of flowers.

But now it was time to remind myself of Steve's reasoning. Clichés are only clichés because lots of people believe in them.

'All right, mate? What can I get you?' The guy in charge of the stall was quite short and also on the stocky side, but he had the market trader's breezy, come-on-girls-you-know-you-want-to confidence. I imagined him exchanging ripe one-liners with the female customers, and quite possibly getting phone numbers off some of them as well.

'I want to buy my girlfriend some flowers.'

'Flowers,' he replied, turning to look at the stall. 'Yeah, I think I've got some of those.'

You'll have gathered that flowers aren't my specialist subject. I know what a rose looks like, and a daffodil, and a daisy, but beyond that they're all the same to me. I knew the first of those three is a standard token of love, but it did seem a bit too standard. If I was going to be that predictable I might as well take Kirsty down the local Berni Inn and wait for the bloke to come round with plastic ones in a bucket.

I decided to make a clean breast of my ignorance. 'What would you recommend?'

'What you buying them for? Birthday? Anniversary?'

'You really wouldn't believe me if I told you.'

He laughed. 'You need to impress her, I take it?'

I nodded.

'These do the trick every time,' he said, lifting a bucket from the top shelf.

'What are they?'

'Lilies.'

Lilies. I knew Steve had mentioned a particular sort. 'Great. I'll have some of those.'

'How many do you want?'

'Tenner's worth?'

199

He surrounded the flowers with some of that green stuff they keep in a separate bucket and then wrapped it all in paper.

'Don't look massively impressive, do they?' I said.

'Well, er, I could put a bit more foliage round 'em . . .'

But it was clear from his hesitant tone that foliage wasn't the solution. 'Go on,' I said. 'Put another five in.'

'Another five it is. Fifteen quid, eh? What you done? Forgot the wedding anniversary?'

I didn't reply. The flowers were soon added, but it still wasn't a bouquet that was going to bowl anyone off their feet. 'Keep going. Round it up to twenty.'

'Twenty quid, get this. I dunno about the anniversary, you must have been playing away.' Was he like this with all his customers? What about the ones who really had forgotten their wedding anniversary or, even worse, been playing away? I wondered if anyone had ever hit him.

Twenty pounds' worth of lilies looked, I decided, sufficiently striking. Carrying them back to the office and storing them in an old vase in the little kitchen area where we make our coffee, I congratulated myself on some points well earned. Whether they'd be enough points, and whether they'd come soon enough, I had my doubts. But I was sure I'd done the right thing.

As the afternoon wore on, though, this certainty began to slip away. My earlier worries came back. Kirsty would see the flowers as the last, desperate attempt of a losing man trying to salvage the game. Wouldn't she? No, not if Steve was right. But what if Steve wasn't right? Oh *God*, why was this all so difficult? By half-four I'd decided, by the perfectly rational means of firing an elastic band into the air and seeing if it landed on a blue carpet tile or a grey one, that I wasn't going to give the flowers to Kirsty. So what should I do with them? Throw them away? No, I had a better idea.

'For me?' Amanda couldn't help beaming as she looked up from her desk.

'Yeah. To say thanks. For all your help in Cabinet.'

'Oh, Sam, that's really sweet of you. And you've put them in a vase as well. Here, let's put them on the windowsill.' She took a few seconds arranging the flowers, then turned and gave me a hug. 'Thanks, Sam. They're lovely.'

'Yeah, well . . . you know.' Oh, the eloquence of the man.

'And if this is what *my* flowers are like, imagine the bouquet you must be giving to Kirsty.'

Damn. I might have known. I looked at my watch. The stall might still be open. 'Mmm, yeah. Kirsty's bouquet. Of course. Lots of points there.'

Amanda didn't say anything for a second or two. Then she opened her mouth, but shut it again very quickly. She turned to look at the flowers. Finally she spoke. 'These really are . . . they're really pretty. Aren't they?'

I nodded and made some bland comment about the lilies. But inside I was worrying. What was it that Amanda had been about to say? My mention of points had triggered it, or rather nearly triggered it. It was about Kirsty, wasn't it? Kirsty, and me, and the points, and my chances of getting them. It was the same thing that had been on Amanda's mind in the Mitre. What could it be that she was so reluctant to say?

No! Not *that*. Not . . . But yes, that's what it had to be. Ray's theory. Amanda agreed with him. I was never going to earn these points, Kirsty was just using the whole thing as cover for wanting to leave me. That's why Amanda was so uncomfortable about saying it. Ray's an insensitive little creep who speaks his mind, or what passes for one, not caring how hurtful he's being to other people. Amanda, though, was frightened of saying she agreed with him. Quite rightly; her concern for people's feelings is one of the things I most admire about her. But the fact remained. *She agreed with him.*

Christ. I had to get away from her. Muttering something about watering the lilies properly, I dashed back downstairs and collapsed into my chair. Thankfully George was on the phone so didn't notice what a state I was in. I picked up some papers and tried to concentrate on them. But the words and figures swam before my eyes, making me dizzy. Then they started to blur – were those tears that were clouding my vision? I don't remember. All I know is that for a good fifteen minutes I felt worse, far worse, than I have felt during any of this.

No, more than that: I felt worse than I have ever felt in my whole life. Amanda's doubting me had shaken me more than I could have believed possible. My own doubts now had some chums they could get together with and, boy, were they having a party. Did Kirsty really not love me? Or was it that she didn't love me enough? Was she not the person I'd thought she was? Did I not know her well enough to pick up the signs that her feelings had cooled? Ray had said that Kirsty wanted me to take the blame, to feel that I'd been the one who'd failed and doomed our relationship, that I wasn't good enough for her. That, I still felt sure, was overly cynical. What do you expect from Ray? But maybe it was right to say that Kirsty couldn't face telling me she didn't love me *enough*, not enough to marry me. Maybe this was her way of letting me down gently, giving me twelve weeks to get used to the idea it was over.

On the shelf in our bathroom at home there's a picture of me and Kirsty, taken on the Wenceslas Bridge in Prague a couple of years ago. It was a hold-your-own-camera-at-arm's-length job, but somehow it came out wonderfully. We're both laughing, and it's one of those photos that manages to capture how you were feeling as well as how you looked. One night, as we were getting ready for bed, I glanced at it and said to Kirsty: 'That picture radiates love, doesn't it?' She smiled and gave me a toothpastey kiss, and said yes, she thought exactly the same. I felt so close to her when she said that. It was the most beautiful feeling I'd ever had. But now I was looking back on that night and wondering if she really had loved me as much as I thought, or as much as I loved her. And even if she did then, does she still feel it now? The document I'd been trying to read slipped from my fingers and my mind filled with an image of that photograph. It was being torn down the middle and the two halves were falling away in different directions, falling out of the bathroom, further and further away from each other, never to see each other again . . .

Stop it, I told myself. Just stop it, Sam, for God's sake stop it. Stand up, walk around, go and buy those flowers, do *something*. You can't be defeatist about this. So Amanda doubts you? Fine. You've doubted yourself, but the difference is this is your fight, not hers. You're the one whose happiness is at stake. You can't afford to let those doubts show. Not to Kirsty, and preferably not to yourself either. You're going to get back down to that flower stall, buy every lily he's got left, and this time you're bloody well going to go through with it.

There were twenty-eight of them. Kirsty's face when I gave them to her was, as you'd expect, a picture of delight. I tried hard not to overanalyse her expression, but I couldn't stop myself. How much happiness was there in her eyes? A lot, for sure, and I felt in my bones that it was genuine. Whatever Kirsty was playing at by putting me on points, it wasn't a total sham. There was at least some love there, that much I was certain of. How much? Couldn't say. The cumulative effect of nearly ten weeks' points-earning, and points-losing, had addled my brain, and with the afternoon I'd just suffered I was feeling particularly bewildered. But at least I knew there was a flame there to be fanned. I might not make it in time, in fact I might even blow it out altogether, but the flame was there.

Just how small it was got underlined tonight. As I unfolded the sheet of paper containing this week's score, it struck me that Kirsty, upstairs running a bath, was standing in the shadow of the Prague photo. Tearing images filled my mind again as I read the score: five hundred and eighty-five. Once again my weekly total had been fifty.

My reaction? The first thing I felt was anger. That had happened last week, but this time I knew what the target of my anger was: Kirsty herself. Why had my flowers not earned me a higher score than last week? Why were the details of her points scheme so arcane, so apparently inconsistent? Where was I going wrong? *Where?* Second-guessing, I'd come to learn, can be a very irritating hobby, and now my fury was being firmly directed at Kirsty herself. For a while I wrestled with the thought of running upstairs to confront her. But I decided against it. Not because it was forbidden to ask her what I'd earned points for. That didn't bother me. I've watched enough professional sport to know that you cheat if you think it'll help you. Rather it was because I knew it wouldn't help me. Showing Kirsty that I'm rattled, bothered, scared, is, as I keep saying, the one thing I can't do. Sharing those worries is what Cabinet's for.

'Only fifty again?' asked an astounded Pete.

I nodded. George's lips, I noticed, were silently moving. Obviously working out my new required points rate. This week, though, he had the sense to keep it to himself. His courtesy was appreciated. Besides which, I could have saved him the bother. It's two hundred and seven. And a half.

'That is out of order,' continued Pete. 'Completely out of order. But not to worry, Sam, because you know what's coming, don't you?'

The state I was in I couldn't have told you what day comes after Monday.

'What?'

He performed a trumpet-playing action as he sang out a fanfare. 'Dun, dun-dun-dun, dun, dun, DUNNN!' Then he clapped his hands. 'Yes, it's time for the results of our exhaustive, in-depth survey of the females of our acquaintance on the crucial matter of . . . What Annoys Women About Men!' He reached under the bar and pulled out a sheaf of papers. George, ferreting around in a plastic bag he'd brought with him, did likewise.

'Once we've gone through this lot,' said Pete eagerly, 'your small-change score is going to go through the roof.'

'Through the roof?' responded George. 'It's going to go into orbit. I've been collecting these during the week, Sam' – it's true, he's been up and down to that printer all the sodding time – 'and I have learned things that would never have occurred to me in a million years.'

I forced myself to smile. Sceptical as I was about the value of this exercise (surely my problem runs deeper than small change?), I couldn't appear ungrateful. The lads were doing their best to help, and it wasn't as though I had any better suggestions. Amanda was once again giving off her want-to-say-something-but-daren't vibes, and so to distract myself from that I threw myself wholeheartedly into the survey. George and Pete might not have had the answer to my prayers, but at least they weren't like Amanda, who didn't think there was any point in praying at all.

'The level of response to our appeal,' announced Pete, 'has been incredible. Phenomenal. Scary. In fact, having read all these girls' replies, I'm amazed that the human race continues to breed at all.'

George nodded. 'I can only echo Pete's sentiments there, Sam. From the moment you wake up in the morning to last thing at night, virtually everything you do has the potential to annoy a woman.'

'It's even worse than that,' said Pete. 'At least three replies I got mentioned snoring. So you can't even relax when you're asleep.'

'I stand corrected.'

Pete acknowledged this with a slight nod of the head and then turned back to me. 'Now, let's start with the basics, shall we? A lot of the feedback centred on predictable moans, which I'm sure you're well on top of, Sam. You know the sort of thing: missing the water and hitting the seat, or even the lino, damp towels on the bed, not washing up, leaving the sink covered in stubble after you've shaved . . . all the usual complaints.'

'If they're so usual why don't you stop doing them?' asked Amanda.

Pete gave an almost convincing impression of not having heard her. 'So I've moved beyond those and picked out the ones I thought had real potential. You know, the subtle ones you might not have spotted, that could still earn you points in the closing weeks.' He spread out his papers on the bar, revealing occasional stripes of green highlighter. 'Here, for instance: "So-called cunning variation on the not-changing-toilet-roll trick – deliberately leaving the last sheet of the old roll to avoid having to change it at all." Ring any bells?'

Even if I was the sort of guy who was that lazy, I like to think I'd have spotted it by this stage of my points-hunt. But I didn't want to discourage Pete. It was sweet of him to do all this, and apart from anything else it might give me a bit of a laugh. 'Don't think so. I'll bear it in mind, though. What else have you got?'

He searched for a moment. 'Here we are, this is a good one: "When you've made too much food, blokes refuse to freeze any of it. They insist on finishing it all by going back for seconds or even thirds, then they have stomach cramps for two days and lie around groaning."'

Pete gave me a questioning glance, but before I could respond George had jumped excitedly off his barstool. 'Hey, that reminds me of one I've got. Where is it? Erm, hang on . . . yeah, got it: "Buying totally inappropriate food when doing the weekly shop."'

The three of us exchanged puzzled expressions. What was 'inappropriate' food when it was at home? Then Amanda, staring in the other direction and speaking very quietly, as though she didn't realise her thoughts had reached her mouth, said: 'I sent a boyfriend of mine to do the shopping once. He came back with four kilos of parsnips and three venison sausages.'

Fearing that this was about to become terminally surreal, I hastened Pete on to his next item. 'This one came up a lot,' he said, 'so I'll just read you out a typical mention: "Pedantic shelving arrangements for CDs, books, et cetera. General analness about you disturbing their 'systems'."'

'Ha!' cried Amanda. 'You can say that again.' Her earlier indifference to this exercise was gone. The girls' responses had clearly tickled her irritation gland and she couldn't help but join in.

'"Analness"?' said George. 'What's she on about? There's no such bloody word. It should be . . . er, what? Anality?'

'That's a fairly anal point in itself, wouldn't you say?' asked Amanda. 'Stop avoiding the charge. Blokes are completely uptight about their bookshelves.'

'I'm not,' protested George. 'My books go on the shelf in any old order.'

'Same here,' I said. 'All my books are in the spare room and they're not in any particular order at all. Obviously the hardbacks are on a shelf of their own, because they'd look stupid intermingled with smaller paperbacks. But there's no system as such. Apart from I keep the biographies and the fiction separate.'

'Oh, well, yeah,' replied George, 'that's different, isn't it? I mean, I keep all my Bond novels together, but that's not being anal.'

'What is it then?' asked Amanda.

'It's . . . it's just . . . it makes *sense*,' said George, getting flustered.

'And have any of your girlfriends ever put a Bond novel back amongst the other books?' she asked.

'No.' He paused. 'Although Martina did put *Diamonds Are Forever* back before *Moonraker* once.'

'The problem being?'

'It was published after *Moonraker*.'

Amanda laughed. 'You've got them arranged in the order they were published?'

George nodded.

'Surely you admit that *that's* anal?'

'No, I don't, as it happens. That only came about because the first two I bought were *Casino Royale* and *Live and Let*

Die. Found them in a charity shop for fifty pence each. I really liked them, so I started buying the others, and it was only then that I found out, by accident, looking in the front of one of them, that – completely by coincidence – the first two I'd read were the first two to be published. So, after that, with them already on my bookshelf, in order as it were, it seemed a good idea to carry on shelving them in order. If you see what I mean.'

'Yes, we do see,' said Amanda. 'We see that you're completely anal.' And then, drowning out George's attempted protest: 'Come on, Pete, let's hear what else you've got.'

'This one's from the same girl. Follows on from the last point: "Why don't complaints of slovenliness with CDs, videos, books et cetera translate into bathroom hygiene?"'

Amanda shook her head sadly. 'A timeless question.'

'An unfair one in my case,' replied Pete, as he set about topping our drinks up. 'I regularly clean the bathroom.'

'Define "regularly",' said Amanda.

'Oh, at least once every three months. If not more.'

'And how long does it take you? On average?'

'About ten, maybe fifteen minutes.'

She grinned. 'In other words, you're the same as every other man on the planet. You think that wiping the sink and putting bleach down the loo counts as cleaning the bathroom.'

'No, that's where you're wrong. I wipe the bath itself as well.'

George saw that this one was slipping away from Pete so came to his rescue. 'Anyway,' he said, 'the only reason the average bathroom takes such a long time to clean properly is that every square inch of space in it is covered by the woman's moisturisers, hairgels, exfoliants . . .' – George's unfamiliarity with this type of product started to show through – '. . . and . . . and all that bloody stuff.'

'True,' echoed Pete. 'Very true. Before you can dust a woman's bathroom windowsill you've got to clear it of two hundred bottles of Carrot and Coriander Body Scrub.'

'Organic, of course,' added George.

Amanda took a sip of her wine, exhibiting the unflappability that I've come to see as her trademark. 'There are two things a man always says about your hairgel. One: "You spend far too much money on it." Two: "Do you mind if I use a bit?" Either that or they just use it without asking you.'

'Hairgel?' said Pete. 'You've been going out with the wrong blokes, Amanda.'

'I know that. But the problem was never that they used hairgel.'

'Come on,' interrupted George. 'Let's crack on. Here's one of mine: "Shouting advice at sportsmen on the telly. Do you think they can hear you? And even if they could, do you think they'd be interested in what you have to say? Your only regular sporting activity is PlayStation." Which leads nicely on to the next one. "PlayStation." That's all that one says, but I think we get the drift.'

'That won't affect Sam,' said Pete with a cruel smile. 'You're not really a PlayStation sort of guy, are you?'

'I still maintain you gave me a defective handset,' I replied. 'Carry on, George.'

'"Using the last bit of milk in the morning without a second thought." "Lighting a cigarette before realising they haven't offered you one." "Complete lack of interest in any household chore, unless it involves a power tool." "The unnecessary use of power tools." Then there's . . . erm . . .'

While George shuffled through his papers, Pete filled in. 'I noticed that illness got mentioned a lot. This one, for instance: "When I'm ill, he still expects me to fetch him cups of tea and cook his dinner. But when he gets a headache, it's a brain tumour." Women seem to think that we overreact when we're ill.'

'"Seem to think"?' snorted Amanda. 'Colds and flu just don't exist as far as men are concerned. You're either perfectly fit, or about to die. There's nothing in between. My brother made me take him to casualty one night. He swore blind that his appendix had burst.' She shook her head. 'It was trapped wind.'

'That reminds me,' said Pete. 'Something else that a lot of women complained about.'

'Having trapped wind?' I asked.

'No. Having wind and not keeping it trapped.'

Amanda cast her eye over Pete's papers. 'Any of those suggestions from Tamsin, were they?' she asked.

He suddenly looked uncomfortable. 'No.'

'Is that because she thinks you're the perfect man?'

'No, it's because she dum— because we're not seeing each other any more.' He started to pour us all fresh drinks. Our glasses weren't empty, it was just that he didn't want to catch anybody's eye.

Amanda laughed at his embarrassment. 'It's understandable, Pete. The first night you gave that girl was full of excitement and pink rabbits. It was bound to be downhill after that.'

He looked at her suspiciously. 'How did you know what she said?'

George and I joined in with Amanda's laughter. After we felt that we'd ribbed Pete enough, George went back to his list. '"Not changing gears at the proper time." They've got a nerve, haven't they? It's women who don't know about changing gears. They do it too much. Like when they're slowing down at traffic lights, they go down through all the gears until they get to neutral. What's the point of that? It's like they're trying to get marks for style. Don't bother. Just press the brake and the clutch down at the same time and stop before you hit the car in front. That's all that matters.' He realised that he was straying from the subject. 'Er, sorry, where was I? Right: "Faking dimness to get out of previously agreed social plans." "Real dimness regarding above." "Inability to watch television without holding own genitals." Oh, yeah, and there was this one as well: "Shouting out, at the moment of orgasm, 'Some people are on the pitch – they think it's all over – it is now!'"'

I stared at him in amazement. 'That can't be real, can it?'

Amanda gazed into her wine. 'You'd be surprised.'

'That's my lot,' said George, dropping his papers on to the bar. 'You got any more, Pete?'

'No really good ones, no.'

'How about you, Amanda?' asked George. 'Surely your girlfriends must have come up with a few complaints?'

She happened to catch my eye before replying and looked away again just as quickly. 'I'm sure they'd only have repeated what you got in all your research.' I thought as much. She hadn't bothered to ask anyone for information that could help my cause, because she didn't think I had a cause left to help. That was why she couldn't look me in the face. 'But I did find this in a shop the other day. Thought it might help.' She took a greetings card from her bag and read out what was written on the front of it. '"How To Impress A Woman: Wine her, dine her, call her, hug her, support her, hold her, surprise her, compliment her, smile at her, listen to her, laugh with her, cry with her, romance her, believe in her, cuddle her, shop with her, give her jewellery, buy her flowers, hold her hand, tell her that you love her. How To Impress A Man:'" She opened up the card, and read out what was inside. "'Arrive Naked.'"

George and Pete responded with more laughter than the joke deserved, although that was no doubt because the evening's drinking was catching up with them. I tried to join in, but not only had I stayed more sober than them, I also felt disappointed in Amanda. Not communicating her pessimism about my chances was understandable; her opinion wouldn't affect the outcome and she didn't want to offend me. But I thought she'd at least pretend to get some feedback from her girlfriends. OK, she knew as well as I did that small change wasn't going to help me now. Everything Pete and George had come up with I either never did in the first place (PlayStation, power tools, excessive parsnip-buying) or I've made sure I haven't done since going on points (using the last of the milk, not cleaning the bathroom properly, dimness re social arrangements). And even if they had come up with anything useful, the few points it'd earn me would be neither here nor there. Amanda knew that. But at least George and Pete had given me a bit of entertainment, and it was encouraging to know that they were still rooting for me. Amanda wouldn't even pretend to do that. Never had I felt so distant from her.

George took the card and read it, his drunken laughter gradually subsiding to nothing. Then he stared at the punchline, his mood becoming more and more serious, although no less tipsy. 'You know what?' he said after a while. 'That's not actually right.'

'What isn't?' asked Amanda.

'The bit about arriving naked. You know, as though that's the ultimate thing a bloke wants from a woman.'

'And it isn't?'

213

'Not *arriving* naked, no. That'd take half the fun out of it. When you're . . . you know . . . you want to discover all the delights gradually, don't you? Undress the girl. Or watch her undress herself. Or a bit of both, ideally.'

A smile appeared on Amanda's face. Seeing that drink had loosened George's tongue, she set about encouraging him to continue. But she was careful to keep it low-key so he wouldn't suddenly realise how frank he was being. 'I don't think you're right,' she said quietly.

'I *am*, I am,' replied George indignantly. 'Uncovering a woman's body gradually, bit by bit, it makes it all last longer, doesn't it? Makes the excitement mount, builds it up. That's much better than wham, bam, thank you ma'am.'

This was very funny. George was absolutely right, of course, but hearing another bloke being so honest about sex was unusual. He was only doing it because Amanda was there. Men would never be that frank with each other. With their girlfriend, yes. With someone they wanted to be their girlfriend, definitely – it's a great way of flirting. Talking to a woman makes things like this a lot easier to say.

As Pete proceeded to prove. 'It's true, Amanda,' he said. 'Like, the other year I went on holiday with this girl I was seeing. It was . . . oh, can't remember now, but one of those Mediterranean places where it's not a topless beach as such, but lots of the women do it anyway. So on the first day I'm petrified, thinking, How the hell am I going to keep my eyes on Louise all week, with all these other women lying around virtually starkers? 'Cos obviously I didn't want to offend her, you know, by being too much of a lech.'

'Obviously,' agreed Amanda, trying not to let her amusement show too clearly.

'So the first morning I was really careful, only looked at the other girls when Louise went for a swim. But do you know what? After a bit I realised they weren't doing any-thing for me. The breasts, I mean. There were dozens of them, hundreds even, but they weren't turning me on. Not one little bit. And I reckon it was 'cos they were . . . well, they were just there. You went to the beach, there they were, laid out in front of you. Not covered up at all. No bras, no bikini tops, no nothing. Normally when you get to see breasts, you've dreamed of them, longed for them. You know, seen them underneath a jumper, or maybe got a glimpse if she's wearing a low-cut top. But the crucial thing is, you haven't just been given access to them. That's where the attraction comes from. It's the dreaming that makes it all so pleasurable.'

Amanda was really enjoying this. 'You mean that antici-pation is half the pleasure?'

'Too right,' said Pete, unwittingly giving her what she wanted. 'I mean, why else do you think there's so much money in fancy underwear? I know women like wearing it and all that, but blokes like seeing them in it as well, don't they? If that card of yours was right, men would hate bras and knickers. They'd want their girlfriend to turn up in a shell-suit they could whip off straightaway. Or even better, a dressing-gown – no zips, you could get them naked as soon as look at them.'

'But we're not like that, are we?' said George. 'Bras and knickers are great. And stockings. And suspenders.'

Pete was nodding his head. Amanda was struggling to stop herself laughing, and I was similarly amused. It wasn't that I didn't agree with George and Pete. Every word they were saying was true. The card was unfair to men. We don't see sex as a race to achieve orgasm. If we did there'd be no shame in doing it prematurely, would there? We don't just want a woman to get naked as quickly as possible. The getting naked can be as pleasurable as what you do when you've got naked. In fact, sometimes you're not even totally naked when you do it, are you? And that can add to the fun.

No, George and Pete were speaking nothing but the truth. What was funny was that they didn't realise they were doing it. A combination of lager and Amanda's guile was drawing it all out of them. Although their conversation was largely with each other, they were looking at her as they spoke.

'Hold-ups are better than suspenders,' said Pete. 'Something simple about them. Classic. Easy on the eye. Suspenders are all very well from a distance, but when the woman's lying down and the dangly bits go all slack, things can get untidy.'

'Hmm,' responded George, turning the issue over in his mind. 'I dunno. Suspenders do have that certain something. They're out of the ordinary. Add to the sense of occasion. But then again, you see – tights. I think they get an unfair press.'

'Fiddly,' said Pete.

'Yeah, but on the right day, with the right girl, you don't mind that, do you?'

'Maybe. Going back to bras, though, I tell you what one of my favourite things is. When you're taking a girl's bra off, and she's lying on her front and you undo the strap and kiss her back right underneath where the clasp was.'

We all responded by staying absolutely silent. After a few seconds Pete looked up. He'd completely forgotten where he was and the shock on his face when he realised what he'd just said was magnificent to behold. George's expression was a mixture of relief that Pete had been the one to say it, and worry as he scanned back through all the things he'd just said himself.

Amanda's eyes shone roguishly as she grinned at Pete. 'Really? Is that one of your favourite things? Well, well, well.' Pete's face was getting redder and redder.

'Don't stop there,' she said, 'tell us more. I'm sure we're all dying to hear some of your other favourite things.'

Pete vigorously cleared his throat. 'Anyone for another drink? Another lager, George? Sam?'

Poor lad. Amanda teased him for a bit longer and then let the subject drop. The other subject that got dropped amid the general drunkenness was the small matter of my points-attempt. But I wasn't too bothered. George and Pete, bless them, couldn't do anything to help me, although their efforts were appreciated, and Amanda thought I was beyond help. My Cabinet was pretty well useless now. Whatever was going to happen in the last two weeks, it would be between me and Kirsty. Of course, I wasn't going to admit that to George, Pete, or least of all Amanda. I didn't want to hurt their feelings (however much Amanda might have hurt mine), and also I wanted to keep everything the same to help with my show of strength. Abandoning Cabinet, even for the one meaningful session it had left, would be an admission that something was fundamentally wrong with my gameplan. Kirsty wouldn't know about that, of course, but for my own sake I needed to carry on showing I was strong. And hope that somehow the fake strength would turn into real strength, and into points.

George was obviously settled in for a long night's drinking so at ten o'clock Amanda and I left together. As we walked to the Tube, I reflected how much had changed since she first joined the Cabinet. Back then she was the saviour, helping me, encouraging me, nudging me towards higher scores. Now she was a drag on my spirits. Admittedly they were so low they didn't need much dragging, but any fight that was left in this cause was now coming just from me. Amanda didn't think I could do it.

'Interesting discussion about underwear back there,' she said.

'Mmm. Pete's face was a picture.'

She laughed, and it occurred to me that her teasing of Pete might not have been solely for its own sake. You know I said earlier about sexual talk often being a way of flirting? Well, maybe that's what Amanda had been up to. Pete had, after all, told her that things were over between him and Tamsin. Had she seen her chance and gone for it? Briefly, as we descended the steps to the ticket hall, my old anxieties about intra-Cabinet affairs reared up. 'You don't fancy Pete, do you?'

We were by now standing at adjacent ticket machines. Amanda broke off from feeding her coins into the slot and looked across at me in . . . what? Surprise? Offence?

'I'm sorry,' I burbled. 'Sorry. I don't know what I was thinking of. I . . .'

We collected our tickets and moved across to the gates. 'Actually the reason I said that,' I continued, figuring that she deserved an explanation, 'was that when all this started I told Pete how important it was that you were in the Cabinet, and that he wasn't to . . . you know . . . jeopardise it.'

Amanda laughed. 'You mean you didn't want me to have a fling with anyone else in the Cabinet?'

I nodded.

'Well, that's a pity,' she replied.

I looked back at her. She held my gaze. A train rumbled on to the track beneath us, but neither of us turned to see which direction it was going in. Still Amanda smiled. And only then did it dawn on me what she could have meant by that last comment. Was it . . . Oh my God, no. Was it *me* she fancied? No, she couldn't. Could she? My mouth formed itself to pronounce a 'w', which I think was going to be the start of 'what do you mean by that?', but before I could say anything Amanda had looked down at the train.

'It's a westbound,' she said. 'That's me. See you.' And then she ran down to the platform and on to her train, leaving me with the ghost of her smile.

Oh no. I hadn't expected this. I *really* had not expected this.

Week Eleven

The beginning of the penultimate week of my points-attempt found me in pretty bad shape. Successful campaigns wind down as they reach their conclusion. With all the hard work done, you coast easily to a comfortable victory. But my campaign had had the arse torn out of it. Not only was I four hundred and fifteen points short of safety, a second front had opened up. Racked with doubts and worries about my relationship with Kirsty, I now had doubts and worries about my relationship with another woman. Could it really be that Amanda . . . well, what was I asking here? Did she fancy me? Did she have feelings for me that amounted to more than friendship? Had she – dare I even say it – fallen a little bit in love with me?

All I was going on was the look in her eyes at the Tube station. But having started from that, other things fell into place. Mainly her attitude to my chances with Kirsty. Perhaps that was the thing she hadn't had the courage to say. Not that she thought I was going to fail, but that she *wanted* me to fail. Maybe her opinion on whether I'd end up staying with Kirsty was coloured by a vested interest. The two things didn't exclude each other, of course. It was perfectly possible that she (Amanda) genuinely didn't think that she (Kirsty) was going to give me enough points, whether or not she (back to Amanda again) fancied/had feelings for/loved me. But if she did fancy/have feelings . . . et cetera, then that pessimism about my chances was a good thing, as it would give her hope about her own chances with me. And then – oh God, the memory made me wince – there'd been the lilies. Had I inadvertently boosted her hopes?

Assume, I told myself, for the sake of argument, that this was how Amanda felt about me. What did I think about that? Whatever feelings I had for her as a woman in her own right, the answer to the question hung on my feelings for Kirsty. And that's where I knew, for the first time, that I had real problems. If my love for Kirsty had been as uncomplicated, unconditional as it always used to be, attention from Amanda wouldn't have held any interest for me. I would have been Kirsty's, end of story. Amanda's feelings for me would have flattered, but not tempted. However, I found myself being intrigued by the possibility that Amanda wanted to be more to me than just a Cabinet minister. Because, and this now superseded that moment with the lilies on Thursday as the worst feeling of my life, I no longer felt sure, not absolutely sure, that Kirsty was the woman I wanted to spend the rest of my life with.

As the week drew on, I began to realise that this horrible, demoralising doubt was rooted in anger. The bursts of fury I'd felt on receiving the last two scores only lasted a short while, but now I had a vat of anger inside me that was bubbling away, a little more vigorously every day. It was condensed pain, I think. Kirsty is putting me through hell on a daily basis, but I have to keep my agony hidden from her. And so all that hurt and frustration hits the inside of my cool façade, turns into anger and runs back down into the vat. Each day sees the amount of anger get bigger, especially as I'm now so close to the end. I'm doing that thing you always do as a kid when Christmas is getting near: 'This is the last Thursday but one before Christmas, and next Thursday is Christmas Eve, which is nearly as exciting as Christmas itself, so today is the last non-exciting Thursday . . .' Except now it's all the other way round. 'Today,' I thought, 'is the last Monday but one before I split up with my girlfriend, and as by next Monday I might as well have started my packing, this is in effect the last Monday of living normally with the woman I thought I was going to marry . . .'

What *really* makes me angry is that Kirsty is still behaving just as she always has. Is it not a strain for her? Because Christ knows it's a strain for me. I'm still giving it the All Blacks routine, but now I'm not sure whether that's to keep myself in with a chance by appearing confident, or simply to spite Kirsty. I think that part of me might have given up on this attempt. Not voluntarily, you understand, but there's a dead area in my soul that's not responding to the calls for optimism. Perhaps the show of strength is just so I can say to Kirsty, 'I tried until the end, I kept it all the same as it had been, you were the one who walked away from it.' Do you know what I mean? If my anger burst to the surface and I went mad at Kirsty, she'd be able to say, 'See, it's not working, it's for the best that we separate.' Walking away from normality doesn't make sense. Walking away from a 'scene' does. And so perhaps my determination to stay cool is my way of denying Kirsty that scene.

God, is it hard work, though. On Tuesday, for instance, she got back from an evening out with some of the people who'd been at her school reunion.

'Hi, darling,' I said as she collapsed on to the sofa. 'Have a good time?'

She responded with that non-committal 'nnnn' sound you make through your nose, which signifies 'yes/no/but tending more towards no'. 'The whole point of tonight was that some of us really did get on in Newbury. We wanted to have a more grown-up evening together. But a few of the idiots latched on to it as well. Like Stacy Astle, for instance.'

'Did she get drunk?'

'Did she get drunk? You'll be asking me about the Pope's religious convictions next. That girl sees any unfinished bottle of wine as a challenge. She was embarrassing towards the end.'

'Oh dear. Did she ruin the night?'

'A bit.'

The reply that welled up inside me was: 'Ha, good! Serves you right to have your evening ruined, because my whole *life* is ruined at the moment by this points scheme of yours.' But of course that comment had to hit the façade and run down into the bubbling vat. What actually came out of my mouth was: 'Oh that's a shame. How about a Sam's Traditional Remedy to cheer you up?' Those of you hoping this is about to get risqué will be disappointed to hear that Sam's Traditional Remedy is an Irish coffee, for which, according to Kirsty, I have a particular knack.

The smile that appeared on her face was almost electrical in its brightness. 'You are *such* a star sometimes,' she said, reaching out to squeeze my hand as I passed her on the way to the kitchen.

How many points does this earn me, then? I wondered to myself as I poured the cream over the back of the spoon. Even if it's earned me a lot, I'm sure I'll miraculously lose them somewhere else, won't I? Heaven forfend that I should actually stand any chance of getting near those thousand points. But again, all that frustration had to turn itself into hidden anger, so that my outward expressions of interest in Kirsty's comments would sound genuine.

223

'A few of us got together at the end and said we must try again. Have a dinner round at someone's flat and not tell any of the Stacy crowd.'

'Good idea.'

'I said they could do it round here.'

'Fine.' Only after I'd said it did I realise that Kirsty hadn't necessarily been asking my permission. Unless they did it in the next week and a half I probably wouldn't even be around. That underlined even more how close we were to the relationship's end. Yet more anger boiled up inside me. But still I refused to let it show. 'There we are, my darling,' I said, handing Kirsty her coffee.

'Thanks,' she replied. 'You're so good to me.'

My smile was pure hypocrisy, and now I began to feel angry at myself for that, as well as at Kirsty for her calmness.

Perhaps all this anger influenced the way I dealt with Wednesday night, I don't know. But things didn't go as I was expecting, that's for sure. What I was expecting, indeed what Kirsty was expecting, was for us to accompany our friends Debbie and Stuart out to dinner. It had, after all, been in the diary for ages. But midway through the afternoon I got a call from Alan.

'You're stood down for another week, Sam.'

'He hasn't gone missing again?'

'Yeah. Well, I don't know if you could say "again". He's still missing from last week.'

'You mean he hasn't been home at all?'

'No.'

'Has he ever disappeared for this long before?'

'Er, no. His previous record was two days. Or maybe it was three . . .' There was a sound of another telephone ringing. 'Look, I've got to go. Danny'll be back soon, I'm sure. I'll keep you posted about next week. Bye.'

'Yeah, bye.'

Alan, I knew, was already on to his next problem, and didn't have time to worry about Danny. But I did. Over a week he'd been gone. And yes, maybe he would turn up soon. But what if he didn't? Why had he been gone so long? Who was he with? What was he doing with them? I couldn't stop myself going back over the clues I'd wheedled out of him. Someone called Spider, who lived by the beach. Which beach? Danny's trips were normally no more than twenty-four hours, so it had to be somewhere near London. The South Coast, then. Where would he have gone?

On the wall by our photocopier is a map of Britain, showing where all the company's offices are. I wandered over to it and scanned the South Coast. Any one of half a dozen places looked feasible. Bournemouth, Southampton, Portsmouth, Brighton, Eastbourne, Folkestone . . . I racked my brain. There was something I was forgetting. Something from Selfridges . . . That was it – the building. The one Danny had described in so much detail that it had to be a real place. A big palace, he'd called it. With domes on the roof that looked like onions . . . My eyes ran back and forth along the South Coast. A palace. Domes. Where could it be? Palace, domes, palace, domes, palace . . . My eyes stopped on Brighton.

The Pavilion.

Within a couple of minutes I'd found a webpage full of pictures of it. Onion-like domes, yes. It certainly looked like a palace. And the more I looked at it, the more of Danny's details came back to me. The columns, the arches, the gardens with a path running round them. Everything fitted. I had no way of being sure, of course. Danny might not be in Brighton at all. But wherever he was, something told me he was in danger. I could sit here and wonder whether my hunch about Brighton was correct. Or I could get down there and do something about it, at least have a go at helping this kid as I was supposed to be doing. This kid I'd found myself worrying about, caring about.

But what about Kirsty? The table was booked for eight, and the restaurant wasn't cheap. This wasn't a quick trip to Pizza Hut I'd be blanking. To ring up and cancel at this stage would lose me dozens of points. Or would it? I'd started to get a feeling about these points. In each of the last two weeks I'd scored fifty, with no real relation to what I'd done. My hunch was that even if I pulled out of the dinner, this week's score would be fifty as well. Forget the points, though, it'd still be rude. But mildly bothered as I was about Debbie and Stuart, I found that I couldn't care less about being rude to Kirsty. In fact, so great was my anger towards her that I quite enjoyed making the call.

'Darling, I don't know how to say this—'

'It's not about tonight, is it?'

'Erm, well, yeah. You see, our system's crashed, and you know we've got this presentation tomorrow?'

'No.'

Of course she didn't. I'd only invented it five seconds ago. 'Oh, I thought I'd mentioned it.'

'No, you didn't,' she said curtly. 'Anyway, what do you mean about tonight?'

'Erm, well . . . you see . . . we've got to redo all the work we've done for the presentation. Technical Support are working on the computers now, and they might be able to get all the data back at any moment, and if they do we can all go home, but—'

226

'Oh, Sam.'

'Look, darling, I'm really sorry. I'll try and get there as quickly as I can. But it might not be until quite late.'

'How late?'

'Well the worst case scenario is that I won't make it at all. But you can still have a nice time.'

'Yeah.'

'Kirsty, I'm really sorry. If there was any way of getting out of this I would . . .'

'Yeah.'

'I'll let you know if I'm going to make it. But it's not looking that hopeful.'

'OK.' She put the phone down.

Not looking that hopeful, I reflected. Story of my life at the moment. Thanks to your points.

Brighton had certainly changed since I went there last. Which was in the 1970s. I was wearing short trousers, and the town's idea of sophistication was not having curry sauce with your chips. But now it's all Coldplay and lattes and shades. I even saw a man, forty-five if he was a day, pushing himself along on one of those metallic skateboard-with-a-pole things. He was going slightly slower than an arthritic hedgehog and as usual with people like that I had to fight an urge to go up and tell him to act his age. Another difference from my childhood was the number of gay people around. Back then if you'd seen two men holding hands in the street the shock would have caused you to drop your candyfloss. Now Brighton looks like a Barbra Streisand concert in Sydney.

As I walked down the long, straight road from the station to the sea, the heat of the day gradually beginning to get less oppressive, I thought about the task facing me. How could I find Danny? How, even, could I be sure he was in Brighton at all? I couldn't. The one thing that was on my side, though, was that if it had been easy for Danny to come across 'Spider', it shouldn't be too difficult for me to do the same. This was a thirteen-year-old lad we were talking about, not a career criminal with an array of skills to offer. Danny wouldn't have found his way in with proper, hard-nut villains. His would have been very much a street-level entry. Literally.

I wandered along the seafront. The pier, seemingly Brighton's last haven of seaside tackiness, flashed its lights and blared out its crappy music. I made my way right along it, through the amusement arcade with its clanging and buzzing and whirring machines (all of them computerised, it seemed – what happened to those machines with thousands of two-pence pieces in?), and out to the funfair at the other end. Thirteen-year-olds abounded, but none of them was Danny. They were proper thirteen-year-olds, childish and loud. It was precisely because Danny wasn't like them that I was concerned about him. He'd found another way to pass his time, a more sinister, adult way.

I walked back along the pier. At its entrance sat a woman, begging. Next to her was a dog, an untidy mongrel. I squatted down and put fifty pence in her styrofoam cup.

'Do you know where I could find Spider?'

She looked at me in confusion. 'What?'

'Spider,' I said. 'Do you know who Spider is?'

She shook her head suspiciously and edged away from me.

I carried on along the seafront until I came to another beggar. This one was male, sitting with his back to the railings, a woollen hat on the ground in front of him, droning his chant at everyone who passed: 'Spare any change, spare any change, spare any change . . .' I looked at him closely, and realised that he couldn't have been much older than me. There but for the grace . . .

Not having another fifty-pence piece, and judging that anything less would be stingy, I threw him a quid.

'Thanks, mate.'

'You don't know anyone called Spider, do you?'

'Eh?'

'Spider. Do you know anyone called Spider?'

'No. Why?'

I turned away. 'It doesn't matter.'

The same answer came from the next three beggars. I began to doubt myself. Maybe Danny hadn't come to Brighton at all? Maybe Spider was by the beach in another town? But then I wandered into the grounds of the Pavilion and looked up at the building's roof. The domes were just like onions: it *had* to be this place Danny was talking about. I *had* to persevere.

I wandered the streets, asking every beggar I could find. Yet again I was shelling out cash. If my financial position got any worse, I'd have to start asking them for money. Time and again the answer came back that no, they'd never heard of anyone called Spider. My feet started to ache. I was getting hot, really, uncomfortably hot. I took off my jacket and carried it over my shoulder. Whenever it bounced it made my shirt cling sweatily to my back. And still no one had heard of Spider.

I came to a shopping centre. It was modern, air-conditioned. I went inside to cool down. Sitting on a bench outside Our Price was a middle-aged guy, drinking a can of cheap lager. He wasn't begging, but the mess his beard was in, and the fact that no one would sit next to him, told me he hadn't slept indoors last night. I went and sat next to him.

229

With no monetary donation to start our conversation off, I just had to come out with it. 'Excuse me. I don't suppose you know Spider, do you?'

He paused mid-swig. 'Who the fuck are you?'

This didn't answer my question as such, but the fact that there was suspicion as well as rudeness in his voice showed I was on to something. Desperately trying to sound street-wise, I replied: 'I'm someone who needs to find Spider.'

'Why?'

Now there was malice in his voice. I had to copy it to have any chance of being taken seriously. 'You don't need to know why. Either you know where he is or you don't. So do you?'

The guy was clearly confused. What does this suit want with Spider, he appeared to be thinking. Is he something to do with the law?

For my part, I was trying to look intimidating, hide the fact that I was scared at this contact with a world I wasn't used to. I scraped my foot across the floor to cover the throat-clear that my nerves suddenly made necessary.

'What's it worth?' asked the guy.

I hadn't got a clue what the rate of exchange was. 'You tell me.'

'Packet of fags?'

There was a kiosk near by. I went over to it. Then, before I could stop them, my middle-class sensibilities kicked in. 'What sort?' I called across to the guy, instantly cursing myself for being so un-street.

Sure enough he looked astonished at being given a choice, obviously having expected the cheapest brand I could fob him off with. 'Marlboro,' he said. 'The strong ones.' And then, as an afterthought: 'Kingsize.'

I bought the fags and took them over to him. 'Now, where can I find Spider?'

'Down by the West Pier,' he replied, greedily ripping at the cellophane with his gnarled fingernails. 'He's always there this time of night.'

Night? I looked at my watch: it was gone nine. Back outside, I saw how dark it had become. Wandering the streets before, I hadn't noticed the light going. I had to get a move on.

I made my way back down to the seafront. The half-collapsed West Pier lurked ominously in the distance, barely distinguishable from the dark blue sky and the black sea. No lights on this lumbering mass, unlike its modern cousin. As I walked towards it, I strained my eyes to see if I could make anyone out. But I couldn't. The wind whipping off the sea was quite cold now and I had to put my jacket back on. The expensive hotels went by on my right, giving way to the quieter part of town. Still I couldn't see any activity down by the pier.

By now I'd started to get nervous. I was in a strange place, in the dark and the cold, without really knowing how I'd got there. Sure, I could remember wanting to find Danny. But alien environments throw your certainties out of the window, and all I could think of was a restaurant in Mayfair where Kirsty was chatting and laughing with the others, her effortless charm concealing a grim fury at me letting her down. Had I done the right thing? Shouldn't I be with her, trying to earn every point I could instead of wasting my time like this on someone I owed absolutely nothing to, someone who probably wouldn't even listen to me? A gust of wind blew some spray in from the sea, wetting my face. What the hell was I doing here?

Something down on the beach caught my attention. It had looked like a spark, a small flame of some kind, about a hundred yards ahead, just on the other side of the pier. I stopped, and leaned over the railing to try and make it out. Through the dilapidated structure of the pier I saw the flame grow, dancing along some twigs. Someone had lit a fire. As it gained strength its light spread out, revealing more and more of the beach around it. At first I could just see pebbles, but then a figure came into view. It was a man, tall and wiry but strong-looking as well. Maybe it was the effect of the fire, maybe it wasn't, but there seemed something menacing about him.

The light spread to reveal seven or eight other people sitting round him on the beach. I carried on walking and as I got closer I could see that the main guy was in his late thirties. His clothes were filthy, his bleach-blond, dreadlocked hair even filthier. All over the backs of his hands and his forearms were faded tattoos. Two eyes, which managed to be bright blue and at the same time full of malevolence, looked out from his pale, haggard face. Which was covered, from chin to hairline, from ear to ear, with a tattoo of a spider's web.

The people around him were a lot younger, except for one woman who looked to be in her thirties as well. They were all equally filthy, with days, weeks, maybe even months of dirt caked into the lines on their faces. Around the eyes it gave the appearance of make-up, so that they reminded me of Alice Cooper. The thought would have made me laugh, had it not been such a frightening scene. Some of the youngsters were drinking from a plastic bottle of cider, others sharing a spliff. And there, on the edge of the group, with a can of lager in his hand, was Danny.

By now I was standing right above them, in the ultra-darkness around the edge of the fire's light, so that they couldn't see me. I watched Danny. His hair had reached the stage where it couldn't get any greasier. His fingernails were almost black. His jeans had got that plasticky look that comes from days and days of not being washed. Thin at the best of times, he was now emaciated. The flickering shadows made his whole appearance even more macabre. None of the others seemed to be talking to him. Instead he was watching them, monitoring one conversation then another, his eyes hungry for recognition that didn't come. In that instant all my doubts about being there disappeared. This kid needed help.

I walked a little further and found some steps down on to the beach. The pebbles scrunched under my feet as I marched towards the group, causing everyone to look up. I stepped into the circle of light and looked across at Danny. He could scarcely believe his eyes. This felt good. I had the initiative.

'Come on, Danny, we're going.'

Spider stood up. 'What d'you say?' He was about ten feet away, directly between me and Danny, who hadn't moved.

'I told Danny that we're going.'

'And what if I say he's not?' Spider took a step towards me.

'You can say what you like, mate. That kid's coming with me.'

Spider turned towards Danny, who was looking out to sea, refusing to acknowledge what was happening. Then he turned back to me. 'Doesn't look like it.'

'Listen, I know that kid's name. I know where he lives. I know where he is now. I've filled in all the blanks, which means the police won't have to do anything except listen to me.'

Spider exchanged a glance with the older woman. The mention of the 'p' word seemed to concentrate their minds.

Then he stared back at me, grinding his teeth, not saying anything.

'Now,' I continued, 'I don't care what you've got in mind for the rest of these poor bastards,' I looked round at the pathetic creatures sitting at our feet and tried not to think what Spider had in mind for them, or what people he knew would have in mind for them, 'but I want to talk to Danny. All right?'

I took a step towards Danny. Spider made as if to move but then thought better of it. The fire crackled as I walked round it, spitting tiny red-hot grains at me, as if it was a guard dog doing what Spider wanted to but couldn't. I'd got past the first obstacle. Now I just had to deal with Danny himself.

I stood over him. 'Come on.'

He didn't move, wouldn't even look at me.

'Danny, let's just have a talk about your course.'

As I hoped it would, this embarrassed him enough to provoke a response. 'Shut up,' he hissed at me. 'Don't talk about school and stupid shit like that. Not in front of Spider.'

I lowered my voice. 'If you don't go over there with me,' I indicated the pier where we'd be out of earshot, 'then I'll talk about school, and Alan, and lots of other "stupid shit", so loud and for so long that by the time I've finished Spider will be wetting himself laughing at you.'

Danny reluctantly accepted defeat. He got up and walked over to the pier with me.

'Come on,' I said to him. 'Why won't you come back to London with me?'

'I don't fuckin' need London any more,' he muttered. 'Don't need you, or my fuckin' family, or fuckin' Alan, or fuckin' school.'

'Don't you?'

'No. Got Spider. And my mates. Got it all here.'

Again, it would have been comical if it hadn't been so sickening. 'And what sort of future does Spider have in mind for you?'

'He says he knows people I can earn money from.'

The thought was hideous. I had to put it from my mind as soon as it had formed to stop myself attacking Spider in a blind rage. I was here to deal with Danny, not that piece of scum. 'Danny, I know you think it's big and clever, running away so that no one knows where you are—'

'Yeah, well I was wrong about that, wasn't I?'

'Yes you were, and you'd better thank your lucky stars you were. How long do you think you can last? You've done a week and a half. In the summer, that is. Even now it's starting to get cold. How are you going to cope in the winter?'

'Won't be out here then. Spider says he'll find me somewhere to stay.'

Another thought that made me shudder, that had to be forgotten as soon as I'd had it. This kid was teetering on the edge of his last chance. If I left him here now, if his desire to save 'face' won, then he'd be dragged into a dead-end world full of Spider's associates. And Danny would realise his mistake all right. But by then it'd be too late for him to do anything about it.

'Why are you doing this, Danny? Don't you realise how stupid you're being? Look at you. Look at the state you're in. This isn't kid's play any more. Don't try and prove you're an adult, not like this. You don't know what you're getting into. This won't be about nicking wallets in Selfridges, you know.'

'Whatever it is, it'll be better than some stupid fuckin' course.'

'Wrong.'

'Yeah, well, that's what you think.'

235

'No, Danny, it's what I know. What I used to think, when I was at school, is the same as you think now—'

'But you didn't have a domestic situation like me, did you? You don't know how much a domestic situation can affect you.'

That was it. That was the comment that made me lose control. The pat phrase 'domestic situation', hijacked from a social worker's report, sounded so alien coming from Danny's mouth that his self-pity leapt out at me, infuriating me. Before I knew what I was doing I'd grabbed him by the shoulders and slammed him against one of the pier's wooden uprights. 'DON'T YOU EVER TALK TO ME LIKE THAT!' I yelled at him, silencing the chatter that had started again among the group. 'What the FUCK makes you think you're so hard done by, eh?'

Danny looked seriously scared. In my rage I'd lifted him slightly into the air and he was struggling to reach the ground with the tips of his toes so that his T-shirt would loosen and allow him to breathe properly. But I didn't care. My face about two inches away from his, I spat my words at him. 'There was a girl at my secondary school, right? Her dad used to beat up her mum. And one night, when the girl was eleven, he beat up the mum so badly that he left her with brain damage. He got sent to prison. I remember it all happening, because that girl sat next to me, and she used to cry all day long, she didn't stop crying for *six fucking months*. But she didn't start playing truant. She didn't run off, or nick things, or go to the seaside to prove how hard she was. No, she kept working. She changed, totally, completely. Overnight she became the quietest girl you've ever known, and she wasn't the same girl, not for ages, in fact she was never going to be the same girl again, because something like that is a *real* fucking shock, Danny, it's way more than just your mum shacking up with someone you don't like. So will you *stop* coming out with that crap excuse for the fact that you're just too lazy to go to school, and will you get it into your *fucking* head that you've got one chance left to fix this mess you're in. Will you do that? *Eh?*'

With the final syllable I slammed him one last time against the pier. Then I remembered where I was, and became aware again of Spider, who was standing and watching in astonishment, and of the others, and I let Danny go. He tried to get his breath back. I did the same.

When I looked up, something seemed to have changed about him. Then it came to me: for the first time ever, Danny looked like a child. There was child-like fear in his eyes.

And I knew then that I'd got him. My outburst had shocked him, not just because of its intensity, but because it had made him realise where he was and what he was doing. I saw him looking round at Spider and the others, and in his eyes was a realisation that this was a different league. This wasn't shoplifting, or truancy, or telling Alan to piss off. This was serious. And it could get even more serious, past-the-point-of-no-return serious, if he didn't walk away from it now. Equally, though, I could see his pride was making him hate me for being the one to point all this out. Although he'd never convinced me by the 'domestic situation' routine, he'd convinced himself by it. And so now that the truth of his self-pity was hitting home, he felt ashamed, scared of admitting that he'd been wrong. I knew there was one more tactical endgame to be played.

'It's up to you now, Danny,' I said calmly. Then I turned round, walked past the fire, past Spider and up the steps. An unshakeable serenity had taken hold of me, the calm after the storm, and I walked slowly but steadily back up the hill to the station. Not once did I turn round. The London train was at the platform, with fifteen minutes to go before it departed. Right to the front end I walked, sitting in the furthest seat of the furthest carriage, facing back along the whole length of the train.

With two minutes to go, I saw Danny appear on the concourse. He slipped in behind someone at the gates to avoid buying a ticket, then got on the train. I'd be first off in London, well ahead of him, so he wouldn't have to see me then either.

I put my head back against the seat, and closed my eyes.

Alan called the next day, amazed at the fact that Danny had reappeared, saying he wanted to sign up for the course. I filled him in on what had happened, and his praise made me feel, I have to admit it, pretty good. It was needed as well, after the stony reception I'd got from Kirsty the previous night. Justified, of course, based on what she thought had happened. I toyed with the idea of coming clean about Danny, but then decided that it wasn't worth it. As I said, I'd already guessed what tonight's score was going to be.

And I wasn't wrong: six hundred and thirty-five. Yet another weekly score of fifty. But even though it was expected, the score still set my mind spinning with questions. Can it *really* be true that Kirsty is deliberately failing me? I now have seven days to get three hundred and sixty-five points. Over three times my current rate. Over twice my best ever score. In one week I need to earn over half as many points as I've done in the previous eleven put together. Whichever way you look at it, it's an impossible task. Not just because of the maths, but because there's something Kirsty isn't telling me. Whatever I've done in the last three weeks, it's made no difference to my score. But what the hell is that secret? Is it that Kirsty doesn't want me? Is the secret that there is no secret, that nothing I can do will earn these points, for the simple reason that Kirsty doesn't want me to earn them? The questions ricocheted around my brain as I made my way to the Mitre, and for the first time ever I understood just how much fear and anger are intertwined.

Cabinet itself was a pretty short affair. After last week, of course, I knew it would be. George murmured something about the 'Dunkirk spirit'. Pete made a desperate attempt to turn the 'not over until the fat lady sings' metaphor to my advantage, only to get sidetracked by an apology about not meaning that Kirsty was overweight. But what gave the lie to their bravado was that neither of them would look me in the eye. They knew as well as I did that this battle had gone beyond reasoning. If it's still a battle that can be won at all, that is. And so as soon as they decently could, they let the conversation glide away from my points-attempt, never to return. Needless to say, I was glad about this. And so, I noticed from the way she suddenly came to life, was Amanda.

All week long, at work, I'd hidden from her. Easy enough to do, as we're on different floors, and even when a meeting loomed at which I knew she'd be present, a strange headache suddenly took hold of me. It wasn't Amanda herself I was hiding from, of course, it was the possibility of her being interested in me. That was an emotional complication I could do without. But now that she was here, in the pub, sitting next to me, I couldn't help but wonder. Every word, every glance, every movement, I analysed the lot, searching for clues to her feelings. Maybe it wasn't me she was interested in? Maybe she really had been flirting with Pete?

The longer the evening drew on, the more her cloak of inscrutability was pulled away, ever so slightly, by white wine. Little signs were there – and they all pointed away from Pete being the object of her affection. He, of course, is a free agent again, after Tamsin's departure from the scene, and so was subjecting Amanda to a flirting offensive as vigorous as you'd expect from a lad in his twenties. Not that he'd abandoned the attempt even when he was seeing Tamsin. As I say, he's a lad in his twenties. But now his application levels had surged again, and every chance to divert himself and Amanda into another conversation about underwear was grabbed with both hands. She, though, resisted his advances and took every opportunity she could to talk to me. This, needless to say, irritated Pete no end. Normally that would have amused me but tonight I hated it. Every time Amanda made a private joke about something at work, or waited until Pete had to serve a customer to tell me about a film she wanted to see, or referred to a TV programme that we were old enough to remember but Pete wasn't, I wanted to run away.

Fancy a confession? I'm not sure, not by a long stretch, that my discomfort was because Amanda's attentions were unwelcome. It might well have been because they were welcome. The fact that I wanted her to stop talking to me and respond to Pete might not have been a sign that, still wanting Kirsty, I was embarrassed at her behaviour. It could have been a sign that, knowing deep down that I don't want Kirsty, I was tempted by Amanda. Perhaps I'm interested in her as well, and my awkwardness was just guilt making itself felt. One part of me wanted to shout, 'So what if I do feel something for Amanda? Why shouldn't I pursue that? After all, it's not her that's playing stupid games with a supposedly serious relationship, basing the future on some arbitrary system of points. That's Kirsty. Amanda's playing it the old-fashioned way, the normal way, the proper way. She's interested in me, she's talking to me, having a laugh with me, yeah, if you like, flirting with me. Why shouldn't I respond to that? Why should my happiness be held to ransom by these points? By someone who, for all I know, might be determined not to give me the points whatever happens?'

But I've been with Kirsty for a long time now, and eleven weeks ago she was the woman I proposed to, and just because a lot of what's gone on since then has passed my understanding, it doesn't mean I'm not interested in marrying her any more. Yes, I'm confused. Yes, I'm angry. But the 'sod Kirsty' part of me is only a part. Another is the 'somehow try and work this all out so that you and Kirsty can stay together' part. That hasn't been killed off by what's happened. I wanted to let Amanda know that my hopes were still alive, if not kicking. Why? To put a stop to the signs that were making me feel so uncomfortable? Maybe. Whatever the reason, my chance came as we again walked to the Tube together. There'd been a few seconds' silence. A memory shot out of nowhere and filled my mind. I had to tell Amanda about it.

'I had this plan to take Kirsty to the Millennium Wheel.'

She looked at me in confusion. 'Sorry?'

'When I'd proposed to her. I'd assumed she was going to say yes, you see. And for ages leading up to it, each time I imagined the "Will you marry me?", "Yes I will" scene, I had this supplementary plan, well, a dream I suppose you could call it, that I was going to whisk Kirsty straight into a cab and down to the Wheel and buy us tickets and get straight on it, and wait until our pod had got right to the top and we could see all over London and we were the highest thing for miles and miles around, and then I was going to hold her and say, "That's how you've made me feel."'

Amanda didn't say anything.

'On top of the world, I mean,' I added.

241

'Yeah, I did get it.'

I worried that she'd thought it sounded corny. As I described it to you just then I had the same fear. But way back then, when I had it as a dream to look forward to, I never worried that Kirsty would find it corny. I knew she wouldn't, because I knew her, I understood her. Way back then indeed.

My eyes filled with tears so that I couldn't look at Amanda, and as she still didn't speak I don't know what her reaction was to what I'd said. But to tell you the truth, I didn't really know what my reaction was either. What was I crying for? For myself? For my relationship with Kirsty? Was I crying because I was confused? Because I felt intrigued by the possibility of Amanda being interested in me and knew that I shouldn't?

How could one tiny question about a wedding have led to all this confusion and hurt and fear and anger?

Week Twelve

It was the beginning of my last week. And something incredible had happened.

I'd stopped worrying.

Surprised? I was bloody staggered. After the way I'd felt on Sunday night, and the weeks leading up to it, for all the worry suddenly to ebb away, as it did on Monday morning, seemed miraculous. As I puzzled on the strange sense of calm that had wrapped itself round me like a snug blanket, I realised that all the angst and stress had got me nowhere. The calmness was my subconscious telling me this wasn't a problem you could crack by working on it. It was immune to reasoning, however fevered that reasoning might be.

It reminded me of that time Kirsty was upset about her boss and I gave her a list of practical solutions to the problem when all she wanted, as Amanda pointed out, was a good mope. Both situations were about feeling instead of thinking. That was what I had to do here. All my anger, and hurt, and frustration, and fear, and worry, had welded together and produced calm. It was a calm that took hold of me and said, 'You're in dead trouble here, old son, no mistake about that, but there's no way you can think yourself out of it. Look at the last three weeks. Your brain's been working overtime and what difference has it made? None.

You've got the same score every week. This is a time for your heart, not your head.'

And what's more, the calm also revealed to me the way my heart could make itself heard, the setting in which my true feelings could emerge. That setting was to be Saturday night, and my sidekick would be George. But before I tell you all about it, let me explain why I knew it was a good idea. You know how extreme conditions are said to bring out the truth about someone? Soldiers, for example, men who six months ago had been working in a factory and now found themselves in a field in Belgium with bullets flying everywhere, said it was amazing how you discovered what you were really capable of. Mountaineers too – halfway up Everest, the mother of all storms kicks in, can you survive? And sportsmen always say that in the toughest matches, when it's gone right down to the wire, you discover what you're made of. That was how I felt about my own situation. Saturday night would amount to the most extreme conditions possible for a man trying to evaluate his feelings about the woman he'd proposed to. Because Saturday night was to be me, out on the pull, with George.

All of which, you say, sounds like an overly philosophical justification for going out on the pull. And yes, the origins of the plan were a bit more down to earth. They came on Monday afternoon, when George's mobile bleeped. He pulled it from his jacket pocket with an urgency that showed just how keenly the text message was awaited. His face as he read it told a story of disappointment. Putting the phone down on his desk, he muttered an involuntary, 'Shit'.

'Something wrong?' I asked.

'Argh, it's nothing important.' He was clearly trying to persuade himself as much as me.

Should I press the matter? Was it something he wanted to

talk about? Or should I keep my nose out? Risking a charge of prying, I said: 'Oh. You just seemed a bit annoyed, that's all.'

The way he leaned forward, so that no one else could hear, told me this was indeed a problem he wanted to share. 'That was from Beth. You remember, the girl I told you about the other week? Assistant manager at the gym?'

To be honest, which I will be with you but I wasn't with George, I didn't remember. But then I have been rather preoccupied lately. 'You got her mobile number? Well done.'

'That's all I'll be getting.' He handed me the phone, and I read the message: *Can't do Fri. V. bsy nr fut, will call.*

'I've seen candles blown out with more sensitivity than that,' he said morosely. 'But then why should she be any different from all the others?'

'Bit of a barren spell?'

'You could put it that way. You know, the other morning, I was eating my toast, watching breakfast television, and I realised I was trying to make out if the weather girl had a ring on the third finger of her left hand.' He took the phone back off me and deleted the text message. 'It's probably a good thing I'm not going to get intimate with Beth. I think I've forgotten what to do.' His eyes glazed over for a few unhappy seconds and then he came to his senses again. 'Sorry, Sam. That was really tactless. There you are trying to hang on to the woman you love, and I'm moaning about some stranger who doesn't want to go out for a drink with me.'

I laughed. Insulated from worry by my newfound peace of mind, I had no problem at all sympathising with George. 'Don't be stupid,' I told him. 'The two things are nothing to do with each other. And if a Cabinet member can't turn to his Prime Minister for help with a little local difficulty, then who can he turn to? Mmm?'

He smiled.

'Having said that,' I continued, 'I can't blame this Beth. I'm only surprised a specimen like you has ever had any success with women full stop.'

George's smile widened. He knew, as I did, that this wasn't a problem that required any solution. He'd had a bad run, and there was nothing more to it than that. Sooner or later the run would come to an end, but in the meantime a light bout of ribbing was what he needed to make him chuckle. Blokes are weird like that. If you want to cheer one up, all you have to do is have a go at him. You must do it with irony, of course, but even so, it seems strange, doesn't it? The habit often gets mistaken by women as men hiding from serious issues, retreating from a proper discussion of them, sheltering under the cover of immature banter. But I don't think that's true. We don't do it all the time, only when we know the problem's not that serious. It's a useful way of reminding ourselves that very little in this life is truly important, and the best approach to a lot of what goes on is to laugh at it.

George was cheerier for the rest of the afternoon, and that, as far I was concerned, was that. But something happened on Monday night to make me think again about George, and how his situation and mine could be linked. I was setting the video for a film that Kirsty and I wanted to watch but was on too late.

'Hang on,' she said, watching over my shoulder as I punched in the details. 'You've set that for next Monday, not tonight.'

She was right. The buttons on our video are so sensitive you can accidentally scroll through the entire menu just by looking at the sodding thing. I corrected the date, switched the timer on and the telly off, and went upstairs. Then it hit me that I'd nearly set that video to record on a day when I might not even live there any more. If I hadn't reached a thousand points by Sunday, then Monday was the first day of Kirsty and me having separate lives, and I didn't want to hang around to lead them under the same roof. It was yet another indication of just how close the end could be.

But the tranquillity I'd discovered allowed me to contemplate this without getting stressed about it. If that video mistake had happened in the first of my twelve weeks, I'd have been fretting about losing points for 'incompetence in a domestic task'. If it had happened in the last couple of weeks, I'd have got angry at Kirsty wanting to cuddle up and watch a film with me while our relationship could be just days from ending for good. But now, I looked at my girlfriend and simply wondered. It was no longer as though she was the woman I loved with all my heart, the woman I wanted more than anything else in the world to make my wife. Instead she was someone I'd known for a long time without really coming to know what I felt about her. All the uncertainty of the last few weeks, which at first had been about what Kirsty felt towards me – did she want to stay with me, or was the points scheme a way of ditching me? – now turned back on itself and made me wonder what I felt about her. Did I really love her? How would I feel if we split up? Would I be crushed? Or did I want to stroll off into pastures new? Maybe the pangs of nostalgia I'd felt watching Pete enjoy his promiscuous youth weren't nostalgia after all, but jealousy. Perhaps I wasn't as ready as I thought to commit myself to Kirsty.

That's where Saturday night came into it. Go out on the town with George, I reasoned, find some girls, get chatting to them, see what happens. Suggesting this to George, of course, would be like suggesting a banquet to a starving man. For me, a man who had twenty-four hours left to decide what he felt about the remnants of his once-sincere marriage proposal, a night on the pull would, I felt sure, make everything clear. Whatever my true feelings were, they would rise to the surface. If I wanted to stay with Kirsty, I'd reject the temptations of other women and return home to do three hundred and sixty-five points' worth of pleading. If I realised, as perhaps Kirsty had realised, that we didn't have spouse-potential, then those temptations would take me in their grasp. And if Kirsty was deceiving me and using the points as a way of dumping me without having to say so, then going off with another woman the night before it happened would be the perfect way of showing her how little I was bothered.

Of course, if my suspicions about Amanda were correct, she could play the 'another woman' role. But apart from the fact that I wasn't totally sure about that, getting up to anything with her, even if she did fancy me, would be too complicated. Amanda was a friend, a work colleague, someone I had feelings and respect for. That wasn't what this was all about. This was about the contrast of extremes: the woman you live with and proposed to, versus someone you've just met in a bar in the West End. Stamped all over it, in big red letters, were the words 'DANGEROUS' and 'WRONG'. But I knew, I *felt*, that it was the right thing to do. It was going to make sense of everything. It would show me what I wanted.

I let Tuesday morning pass uneventfully and chose my moment in the depths of the afternoon, when home-time seems so far away that you'll gladly talk about anything but work.

'What are you up to on Saturday night?' I asked.

George shrugged his shoulders. 'Dunno.'

'Do you fancy going out on—' Someone cut the power supply to my tongue. I'd forgotten, in the years since I did anything like this, that blokes never admit to each other that they're going out on the pull. That would be to admit the truth, namely that you're desperate. You don't want anyone to know that. Or rather, you don't want to spell it out. Everybody knows that everybody's desperate, but it's something you do your best to keep hidden, like verrucas. No, the phrase you use is the one I used to George after my near-mistake. 'Fancy going out for a few drinks?'

It's the plural that does it. 'Fancy going out for a drink?' means something different. It implies that it'll be just the two of you, drinking, talking to each other, maybe going for a curry as well, but, crucially, no girls. 'A few drinks', on the other hand, has a slightly hedonistic ring to it, and denotes a much more ambitious night, where the alcohol is incidental to a grander scheme, that of attracting women. 'A few drinks' has undertones of 'a few pubs', 'a few bars', 'a few girls', 'a few laughs'. And after that, who knows?

George paused before answering. He didn't look at me, but I could see the thoughts scrolling across his eyes like share prices on a ticker-tape screen. The first was:

Sam means do I want to go out on the pull with him?

And was closely followed by:

Obviously that's in response to my moan of yesterday.

Then came:

Of course I want to go out on the pull, talk about suggesting a banquet to a starving man.

Finally, and this is the reason his pause was quite as long as it was, he thought:

Hang on, why's Sam suggesting that we go out on the pull the night before his marriage proposal could be going up in flames?

That one hung around for a while, clogging up the ticker-tape, but soon enough it got shunted along by George's final consideration:

Don't worry about Sam, he must have his reasons. Whatever input I had on his points-attempt, it didn't do enough good. So shut up about that, worry about yourself, and say yes.

Which was exactly what he did say.

As I bathed and shaved and preened on Saturday evening, I could hear Kirsty on the phone, giving directions to the flat. Having been informed, earlier in the week, of my plans for the evening, she'd taken the opportunity to hold her Non-Stacy party.

I bounded down the stairs, holding a freshly laundered, waiting-to-be-ironed shirt.

Kirsty was between calls. 'Expecting a good turnout?' I asked her.

'Oh, there's only five of us,' she replied with a smile. It was, as ever, as bloody ever, that same friendly smile. This on the eve of the final day. However it turned out, that day was bound to be dramatic. Either the break-up of our relationship, or an amazing surge of points. But still Kirsty appeared to be her normal self. If she'd cracked, even at this late stage, if she'd said, 'Sam, let's stop pretending that tomorrow is just another day, let's talk about this,' then I'd have pulled the plug on my night out with George. I knew, though, that she wasn't going to say that. And my calmness still had hold of me. I had an absolute conviction that the night was going to teach me something, show me the way forward. Never in a thousand years could I have guessed just how that was going to happen. Looking back on it now, I still can't quite believe it. But right from the start, I knew *something* was in store for me.

Half an hour later I was shutting the front door behind me. Certain as I was that my Big Night Out was the right thing to do, I was still nervous about what its specific elements would turn out to be. My suit, not one that I normally use for work but one that I'd worn a dozen times before and always felt comfortable in, somehow managed to feel as though it still had the hanger in. My shoes, a much more recent purchase, looked up at me with a sneer. In the shop they'd cried, 'Buy us, you know we'll look good on you.' And indeed they had. Now, though, they felt awkward, about as stylish as a pair of oversized clogs, in orange, with lime-green spots.

My nerves, I realised on the Tube into town, were mostly due to the fact that I hadn't been out on the . . . out for a few drinks in a long time. So long that it had become very unfamiliar terrain. There's a simple answer to that sort of edginess. They sell it in pubs. Before I could have a few drinks, I needed to have a drink. And so a pint of Carlsberg in a cosy little place near Soho Square it was. Then, as my eight o'clock appointment with George was still twenty minutes away, I had another. By the time I wandered down to All Bar One on Charing Cross Road, the hanger was gone from my suit and I was full of optimism. This only increased when I caught sight of George. He too had gone for the suit-but-no-tie option. We were sartorially matched, and ready to strike.

'Evening.' Just as George spoke, a barman became free. 'What are you having?'

'Pint of Grolsch, I think.'

George turned to the barman. 'Make that two.'

This was good. It had all happened like it does in the movies, barman there whenever you want him, everything on cue. George and I chatted casually as the pints were poured, then retired to a table in the corner that had also read the script and thrown off its previous occupants just as we approached. George seemed as relaxed as I felt. Whether he'd prepared with a warm-up drink as well I wasn't sure, but it didn't matter: the game was afoot. Not that we admitted that, of course. We kept our conversation strictly non-pulling, contenting ourselves with idle chatter about work colleagues, films, sport and the like. All the time, though, our gazes were flitting over the bar and its other occupants. We both knew what we were playing at, so there was no need to spell it out. That would have been vulgar. Plus we'd both have been chronically embarrassed.

We finished our pints. Returning to the table with their replacements, I found that we'd been joined at the next table by three girls. They were a bit older than most of the other revellers; one of them might even have been as old as me and George. Sampling our new drinks, we eavesdropped on their conversation.

'Ah, it was dead good,' said one of the girls, whose Moschino handbag looked curiously substandard. 'He took me to this well posh rest'ron, said I could have anyfin I wan'ed, did'n have to stick to the set menu if I did'n wanna.'

The other girls cooed in wonderment. 'My Ron did that,' said the older one. 'But only once we'd been seein' each uvver for a bit. Not on our first date. This guy sounds real special.'

The first girl nodded.

George and I looked at each other. For the first time, the evening's real agenda broke its cover. 'I don't think this is quite the place for us, do you?'

'No,' he replied, smoothing the lapel of his jacket, as if to underline that we required somewhere altogether smarter.

'Where shall we go then?'

We both drank our pints while conducting mental searches of the West End map.

'Got it,' said George. 'The Mortimer Hotel. Upmarket, classy, cool.'

'No, George, we need somewhere that'll let us in.'

'This place will. It's not cheap, but it's not too exclusive either. Just what we need.'

And so off we went. It was only a short walk away. As we approached, I remembered that you enter the hotel through the biggest revolving doors in Christendom. They're about twenty feet tall. Ever since a nasty Christmas shopping incident when I was a child, I've never felt entirely comfortable with revolving doors. You have to be confident with them, otherwise you'll spend the rest of your life waiting for people to come through from the other side, but equally you can't be too rash, at least not if you like your nose the shape it is. Tonight, at a stylish venue where we were hoping to make a good impression, the potential for disaster was even higher. So I let George go first and resolved to follow in his tracks. But a couple of people nipped in before me, completely messing up my rhythm, and I got trapped in the same section as them. When the doors finally spewed me out into the huge open-plan lobby, I noticed that several of the staff (wearing black T-shirts – very postmodern) had registered my uncool behaviour. Fearing that we were about to be thrown out before we'd even got in, I hurried George across the lobby towards the bar.

It was the wrong bar, a sort of ante-bar where you waited while they got your table ready in the restaurant, I think. A member of staff directed us, with a 'one more mistake and you're out on your arses' frostiness, round to the other bar, which had been hidden from us when we first entered the lobby. It too had tables, but the centrepiece was the bar itself, a square set-up where you could get served on all four sides, a bit like the bar in *Cheers* except a lot hipper. The lighting was low enough to give even people like me a chance of looking presentable, while the mirrors lining the walls had that smoky tint which always makes things look good. All the people in there, most of them seated at the bar, a few standing up, were well-dressed and good-looking, and I can't imagine that any of them ever worried about paying the mortgage. Also the age bracket was one that would accommodate George and me more comfortably than All Bar One.

Having squeezed himself into a gap at the bar, George ordered us a couple of bottles of Budvar. He gave a momentary expression of alarm on receiving his change, but I'm sure no one noticed. They were all too busy engaging in urbane small talk. We stepped away from the bar. I took a few steps one way, George a few the other, to see if we could spot two free seats together. Neither of us could, so we stood there trying to look as urbane as everyone else. But either you can do urbane or you can't, and there is nothing less urbane than someone who can't do it trying to do it. Although George and I tried picking up a few threads from our earlier conversation, we both, I sensed, felt ill at ease on the edge of the group, and kept monitoring the other drinkers to see if they'd noticed how ill at ease we were, so that each of us would miss what the other had said and be forced to ask for a repeat.

After a few minutes, I noticed a couple on the far side of the bar standing up to leave. George noticed them too. He carried on with the point he was making, or rather went through the motions of doing so, because both of us were in fact giving all our attention to the people standing near the soon-to-be-vacated seats. Were any of them planning to jump in? It appeared not. Abandoning any pretence of still being in a conversation, we hastened round the bar, George in one direction, me in the other. This looked a little stupid, admittedly, but I didn't really mind, because as we took our respective final corners the seats were still free. It was only when we'd both got delayed by groups of drinkers standing near the seats that a smartly dressed couple came through from the lobby area and casually sat down on them.

George and I executed the braking motion you slide into when you've just missed a bus. Not merely a slowing of your actual speed, but an increasingly affected air of indifference, almost to the point of denying that you were ever hurrying in the first place. But it was no good. One or two of the beautiful people had noticed our synchronised dash and were muttering to each other about it, albeit with half-hidden smirks. Which meant that all the others had noticed and weren't muttering about it. George and I had just done a very good job of making complete fools of ourselves. This would have been bad enough at the best of times, but what was particularly annoying was the fact that a couple of groups of attractive women were nearby. In a single moment of crapness, so unchoreographed that it must have looked choreographed, we'd ruined any chance we might have had with them. Marvellous.

Anyway, there were always going to be new arrivals to the bar. By now it was nearing nine o'clock, and the turnover was quite high. Still no one had sat at any of the tables, and I wondered if they were for people who wanted to eat, or if anyone could sit there. But not wanting to commit any more gaffes, I stayed where I was. At about a quarter-past nine, the

255

issue was settled. By the most attractive woman we'd seen all night. She walked in behind me so that the first I knew of her was her perfume, which although noticeable wasn't overstrong. As the expensive aroma reached my nostrils, I turned round to see her buying a drink, then going to sit at a table a little distance from the bar. George and I shifted, very discreetly of course, so that we could see her more easily.

She raised sultriness to new levels: mid-, maybe even late-thirties, dark colouring, strong features and full lips, between which she placed a Marlboro Light. As she lit it, with Bacall-like assuredness, every unattached man in the bar was watching her. Quite a few of the attached ones were watching her too. Her dark brown hair fell in an exquisite tangle over her shoulders, which supported the straps of a dress that was obviously one of Knightsbridge's finest. Leaning back her head to blow out a thin stream of smoke, she reached in her bag for her mobile phone, on which she proceeded to make a call.

I don't know what gave me the courage to do it (the beer, I think, coupled with panic that someone else would approach her first), but I went and sat a couple of tables away from her. George followed. We weren't close enough to hear what she was saying, but it was definitely a base camp from which an expedition could be mounted. She didn't cast a single glance at either of us, or at anyone else in the bar.

'Do you think she's calling a friend to come and join her?' asked George.

'Could be.' I was trying to play it cool, although in reality the end of her cigarette was cooler than me. What I was doing felt unusual. It was a blast from my past and that made it exciting. But did it feel wrong? Did I feel that I should be back home with Kirsty? I couldn't tell. For now I was going to live on my instincts, my nerves, my gut feelings. And my gut feeling was that this woman attracted me. I wanted to act on it. I wanted to talk to her. The buzz this was giving me was incredible, all the more so because she was so stunning. This was a real challenge.

George was wittering on about something or other but I couldn't tell you what. I could see his lips moving, but my thoughts were swimming with how I was going to approach this woman, what I was going to say. Someone who looked like her was certain to have heard every chat-up line in the book, and quite a few from outside it as well, so I had to think of something good. But what? What would get me over that first fence and into a conversation with her? I imagined all the hundreds, the thousands of men who must have approached her in the past and tried to impress her with their wit, their charm, their sophistication. How could I hope to compete with them? Then the solution hit me. I'd compete with them by not competing with them. The very fact that she was so accustomed to smarmy advances meant she'd appreciate a straightforward one for a change. I would go up to her, say I was getting another drink for myself and my friend, would she like one? It wasn't my round, granted, but she wasn't to know that. I downed the rest of my Budvar in one, plucked up my courage and rose from the table.

'Back in a minute,' I said to George, while running through the line in my head: *I'm just getting a drink for myself and my friend – would you like one?* I hitched the waistband of my trousers. *I'm just getting a drink for myself and my friend – would you like one?* I tucked in my shirt. *I'm just getting a drink for myself and my friend – would you like one?*

I stepped away from the table. This was it. This was the first strike of the evening. I was going over to her.

Fifteen seconds later, I was in the Gents. It wasn't that my nerve had failed me, you understand. Any suggestion that it was will be dealt with by my lawyers. It was just that I had to run through the line one or two more times, and check to see that I looked OK, and . . . All right, my nerve had failed me. The reflection that gazed back at me from the mirror had a knowing look. You've remembered your time before Kirsty, it said to me, as one big happy holiday, when you could pull at will. It was a time, you've come to think, when you gambolled merrily through the meadow of single-dom, buxom young maidens prostrating themselves before you left, right and centre. Whenever you see a woman who attracts you now, you silently and briefly curse the fact that your commitment to Kirsty prevents you from pursuing the attraction, taking it for granted that were you not with Kirsty, fun and flirtation and frolics with that woman would happen automatically. But what you've forgotten is that life isn't like that. It never was. When you see Pete enjoying a dalliance with, say, Tamsin, you fondly remember yourself at his age, enjoying similar dalliances with similar girls. And so you did. But you also suffered rejections, far greater in number than your successes. That's what pulling is all about. It's a difficult, messy, desperate business, and most of the time it slaps you down and stamps on your face. Only once in a while do you get any success. The United States of Pulling has one main currency, and its name is Failure.

My reflection was right. I'd forgotten just how daunting it is when you're trying to pull. I hadn't even managed to speak to this woman, let alone get anywhere with her. The reminder of how mediocre I was at all this gave me a shock. I splashed cold water over my face, took a few deep breaths and asked myself how I was feeling. Shaken, came the answer. Shaken, but also determined. Tired of my confusion over the last few weeks, I wanted something definite. Tonight was supposed to be providing that, it was meant to be the extreme situation that would test me, teach me about myself, reveal my true emotions. And I couldn't even go up to a woman and ask her if she wanted a drink. Come on, Sam, you can do better than this.

I marched back out to the bar, determination powering my every step. But no sooner had I set my sights on the woman than I noticed the man bearing down on her. He'd just arrived and the huge smile on her face showed that she was expecting him. No doubt he was the one she'd been phoning. And this guy was cool. By which I don't just mean he was cool, I mean he was c-o-o-l. If you were to put a razor-sharp suit (*razor*-sharp, mind you) on the opening drum riff from 'Superstition' by Stevie Wonder, you would get this guy. Forty-something and tanned, his short, dark hair was tinged salt-and-pepper grey at the sides, and his face carried an hour-perfect amount of stubble. Women turned to look at him as he passed, in much the same way that men had turned to look at his companion. They kissed, a deep, bodies-pressed-together kiss that hovered for an instant on the edge of public indecency before reining itself in. But even as she stepped back, beaming, and listened to what appeared to be an explanation for his lateness, the woman still couldn't bring herself to let go of his hands. The tip of her tongue clinging suggestively to her top lip, seemingly without her realising it, she looked not into his eyes but at his mouth, yearning for the next time it would devour her, too eager for his loving to properly concentrate on his words.

I sat down. George too was watching the lovers. We saw him point briefly at her glass. She nodded her head, and I lip-read the word 'vodka'. But before he went to the bar, she pulled him back towards her, unable to stand another few seconds without kissing him, which she did with passion. Tearing himself away, the man went for their drinks.

George turned to me. 'I reckon he's in there.'

In one way I was annoyed, but in another relieved. Yes, my approach on Miss Sultry had been railroaded by the introduction of Diamond Bollocks over there, but equally it meant I wasn't going to waste time pursuing her in vain. That's assuming she'd even have looked at me when I offered her a drink, let alone replied, let alone replied with a 'yes'. The same could be said, I realised as I took another look around the place, of just about every woman in there. George and I could be as optimistic and determined as we liked, but when it came to pulling in the Mortimer, our faces simply weren't going to fit, and neither were our credit limits.

George finished his beer and placed the empty bottle next to mine. He must have come to the same conclusion as me, because he looked at his watch and said, 'Shall we move on?'

'Yeah, why not?'

On the way out we passed the member of staff who'd directed us to the bar. You could see him relax at the fact that his establishment was no longer to be contaminated by these oiks. I wanted to grab him by the T-shirt and shout, 'What's the matter, couldn't they afford proper uniforms?' But I decided not to. Confucius he say that man who lose composure not in right state of mind to be out on pull.

Returning to the All Bar One would have been too frank an admission of our failure in the hotel, so we found ourselves heading into the heart of Soho. Coupled with my determination now was a sense of urgency. It was half-past nine, and if we didn't get ourselves talking to some girls soon they'd all either be spoken for or too drunk to respond. Near the top of Frith Street we found a bar, not a pub where our suits would be over the top, but then not an unconquerable mountain like the hotel either. First signs were good. Although busy, the place wasn't sardined, which meant that you could spy, and approach, people easily. And many of the people that I did spy as George got the drinks in were female, attractive and about my own age. This was promising.

'There you go.'

Just as I turned to reach for my drink, a table on the far side of the room caught my attention. On it were two empty wine bottles, and one that was half empty, and standing next to it were four women. One of them in particular was the reason for my double-take. She was, I'd guess, just the other side of thirty from me, tall, with dark brown hair and a dazzling smile. The last of those qualities had been triggered by something said by one of her friends, but as she turned her head and found herself looking straight at me, the smile persisted. I managed to hold her gaze, and sure enough, even after we progressed, unmistakably, from 'happen to be in each other's line of sight' to 'making definite eye contact', she still didn't stop smiling. I smiled back . . .

'Do you want this beer or not?'

George's question jolted me to my senses. I took the bottle, and by the time I looked back at the woman she'd joined in with her friends' joking again. But three or four times over the next few minutes, as she talked to them and I talked to George, we found ourselves making eye contact. Was she interested in me? For the first time in years, since before I met Kirsty, I was reminded of the strange schizophrenia that characterises men when we're out on the pull.

Half of you feels you'll never attract another woman as long as you live, while the other half interprets the slightest glance from someone on the other side of a bar as a sure sign that she wants your body there and then. You know all the time that the truth is somewhere in between the two, but those tendencies are still there, fighting it out. Even allowing my pessimistic streak its maximum amount of slack, though, I still couldn't believe that all the glances this woman was giving me were accidental. After our initial look we weren't smiling at each other, but still, I told myself, you don't take that much notice of someone unless you want them to take notice of you.

I began to tingle with nerves. Eyeing someone up like this felt dangerous, perverse, exciting. Not wrong, though. It wasn't that Kirsty was completely absent from my thoughts; I did have her in mind, just not with any sense of guilt. Deep down inside I still had a conviction that I was going to learn from this night, that all my moves were geared towards finding out the truth. The right thing to do was to act on the looks this woman was giving me. What form should that action take? Going up to her, obviously, but what should I say? The quandary came back to me again: how should you pitch your first chat-up line? You've got to be confident, because no woman's going to respect a wimp, but you mustn't overdo it. Also to be avoided, and this is what the Miss Sultry planning had taught me, is the chat-up line that sounds like a chat-up line. 'Did it hurt? – Did what hurt? – When you fell from heaven.' – that sort of bullshit.

I realised that my beer hand was starting to shake. Come on, Sam, my optimistic side said to me, you can stand here all night analysing the situation, or you can get yourself across there and do something about it. Before my pessimistic side had a chance to reply, I was off, heading across to the women. 'Right,' I said to George as I went, 'we might as well start making some moves.' He looked a bit shocked at my sudden burst of energy, but soon followed when he saw where I was heading.

We parked ourselves next to the table and both took sips of our beer. I was standing nearest the woman who'd been looking at me, while George was in a prime position to talk to a couple of the others. To move right the way across the bar in such a pointed manner could only mean one thing, a fact that the women had obviously registered because after a whispered comment or two and some subtle grins they stood there saying nothing. This was my moment. An approach was being waited for, I had to provide it. I took another drink of beer, then moved half a step closer to my intended target. Even now, as my mouth was opening and she was looking across to hear what I had to say, I still didn't have the line formed in my head. It was improvisation time. Make it good, Sam. Make it count.

'I like your jeans.'

The second the words left my mouth I knew I'd got it horribly, horribly wrong. I like your jeans? What sort of line was that? There's 'non-corny' and then there's 'bland'. Worse, it was a bland line that still managed to sound desperate. I found myself gripping the keys in my pocket, as if my subconscious was telling me to cut my losses and get away from this bar *now*.

The woman stared at me in astonishment, and then decided that what she thought she'd heard was so incredible she must have got it wrong. 'I'm sorry?' The smile was no longer there. Her accent was pure Home Counties, her manner so assured that I suddenly felt about three feet tall. I gulped, desperately trying to think of a sentence I could substitute for what I'd said, which sounded like it but had more credibility. As if any line could have *less* credibility than 'I like your jeans'. But my mind, frozen by the horror of the moment, couldn't come up with anything. In the absence of my preferred option (the ground swallowing me up), I was forced to repeat the original comment. 'I said that I like your jeans.'

The woman fixed me with a look that somehow contrived to combine amazement, pity and distaste. 'You like my jeans.' Her tone walked the tightrope between polite and irritated. 'That's . . . that's nice.'

There was a pause, during which it became clear that if I didn't make myself scarce, she was going to jump off the tightrope and get very irritated, very quickly. So I made myself scarce. It was only as I traipsed back to the bar that I remembered George was with me. Such had been the embarrassment of the last few seconds that it seemed as if the woman and I were the only two people in existence, her representing all that was right and proper in the world, me symbolising all the annoying things that come along and mess it up.

'"I like your jeans"?' said George incredulously. '"*I like your jeans*"? Was that really the best you could manage?'

'Well, at least I made a fucking effort,' I exploded. 'How many women have you spoken to tonight, Casableedinnova?'

At first George was astonished by my rebuke, then he became fidgety. 'All right,' he said, rising to the provocation. 'All right, who do you want me to speak to? Come on, pick someone. Anyone. Any woman in this place. I'll go and speak to her now. And trust me, I'll think of something better to say than complimenting her on her fucking jeans.'

I scanned the bar. This mini-argument was the best thing that could have happened. It was going to make George eager to prove himself, and even if he didn't get us talking to some women at the first attempt, we were both now so determined that we wouldn't give in until we did succeed. Around the corner of the bar's L-shape were a couple of girls who looked to be nearer the beginning than the end of their twenties but who held themselves with a confidence that belied their youth. Dressed well, but not that expensively, they gave the impression of being out for a night that was rather more special than their usual Saturday routine.

'Them.'

'You mean the two brunettes?'

'Well, one of them's closer to auburn, I'd say, but yeah, them.'

'OK, you're on. Good choice. The fact they're over there means they won't have seen you getting blanked. We might still stand a chance of being taken seriously.'

'Well, you'd better get on with it then, hadn't you?'

George moved off, picking his way through the drinkers, me in tow, until he was next to the girls.

'Hi there,' he said with a smile. 'Having a good night?'

There was a gap of about point-three of a second as the girls evaluated us. They both looked at George, then at me, which necessitated a smile on my part that had to be friendly without being leery. I can't have looked too much of a creep because the girls quickly broke into smiles of their own. 'Great,' said the auburn-haired girl. 'How about you?'

Bloody hell. George had managed it. The simple approach had worked. I was staggered. After the dismal form we'd displayed all night, friendly smiles from two good-looking girls and a few civil words from one of them felt like an open invitation to an orgy.

'Yeah, not bad, er, you know,' said George, showing that he too was amazed at not having got a slap around the face.

'Where've you been?' asked the other girl.

Blimey, this was getting better. They were making the running. While George gave a heavily edited account of our evening to date, I watched the friendliness in their faces and remembered how easy it is, not just when you're out on the pull but in any social situation, to mistake other people's reticence for dislike. You see them not meeting your gaze, even moving so that they don't have to talk to you, and you assume that the problem is you. But it's them. They're shy. They're incapable of making the first approach. They're worried that you won't like them. They are, in short, just like you. They've got all the worries about you that you've got about them. Get over those worries, make that first approach and you'll find more often than not that they're glad to have someone to talk to. Common sense, really, but most of us have enough demons chipping away at us to forget it. You can go wrong, of course, as I'd just proved with my jeans comment, but by and large if you pick someone who's not too dissimilar to yourself and make a routine opening remark, common courtesy will see you through the initial stages.

These were the stages that George and I were now negotiating with, as it turned out, Alison and Carol. Alison, who had the auburn hair, was training to be a doctor, while Carol worked for the Inland Revenue. Both jobs were sufficiently out of the ordinary to provide scope for some lively conversation, and one or two hopefully-not-too-predictable jokes from me and George, and before I knew it I was asking the girls if they wanted another drink. They looked at each other and at their still half-full glasses (our beers were nearly finished), and for a moment I feared that I'd messed it up by being too forward.

But no, Carol nodded her head, and Alison smiled at me. 'That'd be nice,' she said. 'Thanks.'

Waiting to get served, I kept an eye on George and the girls. He was chatting more to Carol, who laughed at his jokes and maintained a significant amount of eye contact. Alison joined in from time to time, but already I sensed that George was less interested in her. Sure enough, when a table became free and they grabbed it, Carol and George positioned themselves at one end, leaving Alison and a free chair at the other. Returning with the drinks, I sat myself down and chinked my bottle against Alison's JD and Coke.

'Cheers.'

'Cheers.' Now that I was sitting quite close to her, I noticed how little make-up she was wearing. A touch of blusher on her slightly rounded cheeks, some mascara on the lashes of her blue eyes and a gentle coating of a pale pink lipstick, but apart from that she was content to let her looks speak for themselves. Which they did, in volumes. Alison had a vitality you couldn't help but get a charge from. At least I couldn't. The fact that she was sitting with her back half-turned to the other two, and that there were now two distinct conversations in progress, gave me a thrill. This girl was talking to me, and me alone.

'No wonder you're on whisky,' I said. 'Medical students are always the hardest drinkers.'

She gave a grin. 'Are we?'

'They always were when I was at university, anyway.'

'And when was that, exactly?' Her grin widened a little.

'Oh, before you were born, I'm sure.'

She laughed.

'But I'm right, aren't I?' I continued.

'Of course. Just because we're going to be doctors doesn't mean we can't have a good time.'

'Evidently.'

A pause.

'And what about you?' asked Alison.

'What about me?'

'How hard a drinker are you?'

'Oh, I'm a lightweight. Complete lightweight.'

'I thought so,' she said. 'That'll be your age.' Her expression remained deadpan for a split-second, before the grin returned and her eyes widened.

'Now, now, don't be rude. Not to your elders.'

'I'm sorry.' A pause. 'Grandad.'

My stomach gave a jolt. Not because the flirting was being stepped up a gear, although that in itself was exciting. No, my nerves were because of my reaction to the flirting – I was enjoying it. I began to contemplate something that up till now I hadn't, not really: going through with this. Going home with a girl, if she'd let me, or at any rate trying to. Or exchanging kisses, of whatever intensity, before we climbed into separate cabs. Or getting her number, with the intention of using it. The details didn't matter. What was important was that I'd started to be attracted by the thought, to weigh up, with a complete lack of guilt about Kirsty, the possibility of being unfaithful to her. Was this what the night was to teach me? Was this a lesson that I wanted to be taught?

Well, did I?

I wasn't walking away, was I?

Soon Alison was buying us, and the other two, another drink. As my next beer went down, I found that one word in ten was coming out slightly askew. A deep breath and lots of concentration provided enough sobriety to check on Alison. She seemed just as merry as me, and so with another slug of lager I dived back in and rejoined her in the drunkenness. Our laughs were coming thick and fast now. After the 'grandad' routine had run its course, we switched to teasing each other about work, with her making repeated use of the word 'suit' and me the phrase 'Florence Nightingale'. It was all childish stuff, which was exactly why it suited the moment. Carol beat George to the next round, and while she was gone Alison made a point of including him in our conversation. As soon as Carol got back, though, our separate conversations resumed. Some of Alison's jokes were now being accompanied by playful punches to my arm, and some of mine made her stick out her tongue. Glancing across at George and Carol from time to time, I saw they were getting on just as well. If these girls were winding us up, they were going miles out of their way to do it.

By the time we'd finished those drinks, we were all pissed enough to have difficulty remembering whose round it was. But tracing it back we worked out that it was George's, and he lurched off to the bar. Carol went to the loo.

Alison looked at her watch. 'It's twenty-past eleven. What time does this place close?'

'Twelve, I think.'

'Oh.' There was a note of disappointment in her voice, a longing for the fun to go on beyond midnight. Wasn't there? I listened. I could hear the single word she'd uttered dying away, and I analysed it for signals. Or was I analysing myself, my own feelings? Mingling into her 'oh' came other words: 'Kirsty', 'Alison', 'pulling', 'guilt', 'marriage', 'points', and, louder than any of these, 'desire'. That was what this was all about: desire. But what did I desire? Alison? No doubt about that. A guy can't flirt for that long with a girl who's that attractive and not feel even the tiniest bit of desire for her. But put that next to my desire to save my relationship with Kirsty and . . . well, and what? Still I had to drive myself on, still I wanted to know how I'd react in an extreme situation. 'What are you doing later on?' I asked.

Alison shrugged her shoulders. 'Who knows?'

269

The danger of what I was up to was utterly compelling. But Christ was it nerve-racking as well. Several times I opened my mouth to suggest that we go on somewhere together (her place? Could I really bring myself to say that?), but no words appeared. And then it was too late, because I saw that Carol was on her way back.

'Looks like she's enjoying herself with George,' I said.

Alison nodded. 'Yeah. I'm glad about that. She's had a rough time lately.'

'Why's that?'

'Her mum died a few months ago. Knocked her sideways for a while.'

'Oh, that's terrible,' I said.

'It was pretty bad. But I think she's back on her feet now. Tough old boot, really.'

We looked up. Without either of us realising it, Carol had sat down not in her own seat at the far end of the table but next to Alison, and so had heard most of what we'd said.

'I'm sorry,' Alison said to her. 'I didn't mean to—'

Carol laughed it off. 'Don't be silly. It's fine.'

It was a relief that we hadn't upset her, but still it wouldn't have been right to crank the jollity straight back up to its previous level. I felt that I should make a quick expression of sympathy, which would give Carol the chance to bring the subject to a close. Then the flirting could continue on George's return, which, I saw over her shoulder, was imminent. 'I was sorry to hear about your mum,' I said.

'Yeah, well,' said Carol, 'nothing you can do, is there?'

Crash! George's return had obviously been even more imminent than I thought. And, to judge by the force with which he'd walked into the table, more imminent than he thought. He didn't so much place the four drinks in front of us as throw them, and a small pool of lager and whisky formed around the glasses. I moved a couple of beermats over to soak up the worst of it and looked up at him.

'Shorry 'bout that.' He looked round at the three of us, and even in his condition could tell that the mood was a relatively serious one. 'You lot 'lright? Yuvall gone misuble.'

This was a delicate moment. It would have been unfeeling of me to gloss over the subject of Carol's mum completely, but neither could I make too big a thing of it for fear of bringing the mood down so low that we'd never raise it again. 'We're fine, George, fine. We were just talking about Carol . . . erm, Carol losing her mother.'

George swayed a little, then sat down. I was all ready to move on to another subject when suddenly he blurted out: 'I lost my mother when I was a kid.' He followed this dramatic statement with a hiccup.

The girls stared at him in surprise. So did I. George had never mentioned this before. OK, we weren't bosom buddies, but we'd had some deepish conversations and I thought I knew him pretty well. Surely I'd be aware of something like this? In fact, hadn't he mentioned going to see his mum a few months ago? Yeah, I was sure he'd said—

'Oh you poor thing.' It was Carol who'd translated her sympathy into words.

George's head jerked a little as he tried to focus on the table. 'I was six.'

The girls looked at each other, tears beginning to form in their eyes. 'That's . . . that's awful,' said Carol, her lip trembling.

George carried on staring at the table. Actually he was staring at the floor just beyond it, but he thought he was staring at the table. I, meanwhile, was beginning to sweat. Because I'd just realised what George had done. His misunderstanding was huge, it was disastrous, and in the emotional soup that was now brewing it had the potential to cause offence on a scale that was scaring me even before it had happened.

'We were in Debenhams . . .' said George. The first tear broke loose and trickled slowly down Carol's cheek. I was desperately trying to think of an acceptable way to interrupt George. But panic rendered me speechless and there was nothing I could do to stop the full horror unravelling. '. . . and she left me while she tried a dress on, and I wandered off to have a look for the toy department, but by the time I got back she'd come out and seen that I was gone, and the whole place was really crowded because it was Christmas week and we couldn't find each other . . .'

Carol's lip ceased its trembling and a look of revulsion appeared on her face. Alison shook her head in disgust. But George didn't see any of this, because he was still staring at the floor.

'I was really scared,' he continued. 'Eventually the store manager took me into his office and they put a call out, but it was a good fifteen minutes before it all got sorted. Petrified, I was.'

Carol stood up. 'And I suppose you think that's funny, do you?'

George looked up, his forehead creased in confusion.

'You sick bastard,' shouted Alison. 'You sick, sick bastard. Here's Carol getting over her terrible experience, and you're making jokes that you think are clever. Well they're not, they're just *sick*.' Her anger simmered, trying to find ways to express itself. For a second I thought she was going to clobber him, but with a 'Come on, Ali, don't waste your breath on him,' Carol dragged her away.

I watched them leave and then looked back at George. In less than a minute he'd turned my promising situation into a crash site. 'Thanks, mate,' I said. 'Thanks a million. That's really set the evening up nicely, that has.'

'What did I say?'

Did I have the patience to explain it all to him? Or would I explode, landing the punch on him that Alison had managed to restrain? I just about managed to control myself. 'Let's get out of here,' I said, dragging him to his feet. Everyone round us had heard the girls' rebuke and no doubt assumed that George was guilty as charged, whereas he'd been drunk and thick rather than cruel and twisted. And with everyone round the corner having seen my faux pas with Jeans Woman, George and I were dead ducks as far as this place was concerned.

We emerged on to Frith Street, George still not sure why the evening had taken such a nasty turn. Where could we go now? The pubs were closed, the few late bars that were open would be packed and/or charging a fortune to get in, and even then the people in them would no doubt have made their plans for the evening already. Streaming past us were plenty of couples who were obviously on their way home to carry out those plans. And here I was, the excitement of my flirting with Alison now a distant memory, standing in the cool night air with nothing to keep me warm but a burning sense of frustration.

I walked off. George, sensing that I was pissed off with him, followed a couple of paces behind. Going past Ronnie Scott's I got a glimpse of its lush red interior and heard smouldering, sex-charged notes from a saxophone. I thought of all the people in the audience, the men and women at cosy little tables for two . . . But no. I stopped myself. It was torture. Still I yearned to be in that extreme situation, although my chances of engineering it were now slimmer than a toothpick. Should I go home? Could I face

273

walking into the tail-end of Kirsty's party and having to be nice to everyone when inside I was seething with unreconciled desire? Because that was what I was feeling. I was bursting with the stuff. Desire for what, I didn't know. Desire for another woman? Desire to sort things out with Kirsty?

Across the street was Bar Italia. I'd forgotten about that. Not really a pulling place, but still it was somewhere to sit and have a drink, somewhere that gave me an excuse not to go home. We went in and sat at a table near the door. I ordered a beer, while George, who until the fresh air hit him had been too drunk to realise he was drunk, felt the need to sober up and asked for a coffee.

'Sorry I fucked it all up back there,' he said quietly.

'So am I.'

'Er – what happened, exactly?'

He was like a puppy who didn't know what it had done wrong. I couldn't help but feel sorry for him. I gave him a brief resumé of events.

He cringed. 'Oh fucking hell. What a wanker I am. *What* a wanker.'

I sighed. 'It's all right, George, I'm blaming the beer, not you. And I can hardly talk, can I? At least you got us started with some women. I couldn't even manage that.'

He sighed heavily. 'We're really shit at this, aren't we?'

I nodded and gave a sigh of my own. But inside I was feeling more on edge, more animated than George. He was resigned to our fate but I was still railing against it. The desire wouldn't let me go.

A group of thirty-somethings poured through the door. There were about eight of them, although over the next half an hour or so new people joined them and others left. All this time George and I sat moodily nursing our drinks, and the ones that followed (George switched back to beer), occasionally breaking the silence with a desultory burst of conversation. I watched the woman who seemed to be the centre of the group. She was, I'd guess, in her mid-thirties, but the fact that she was slight of build made her seem a lot younger. Her lack of feminine curves, together with her unisex clothes (T-shirt, jeans, trainers, all grungy but all bearing the most expensive logos) and her cropped hair, gave her a tomboyish quality. I'd say androgynous, but you might take from that that she wasn't attractive, and she certainly was. Something – Was it the sparkle in her eyes? Her thin, delicate wrists? The smallness of her feet? – formed a nugget of feminity which, although it didn't seize your attention in the first second, nevertheless kept drawing you back to look at her until you realised that, yes, you were sexually attracted to her.

The number of people with her had dwindled to three, two women and a camp-looking younger man. Then another guy turned up, at which point they saw that all their spare seats had been taken by adjoining tables. Tomboy noticed there was a chair free next to us.

'Mind if I take this?' she asked. Even her voice was somehow sexless, with a humming quality that on a civil servant would have been a drone but which on her was strangely attractive.

George answered without even looking up. 'No, feel free. Don't mind us. No fucker else has tonight.'

Unsurprisingly, the woman seemed shocked. 'I only asked,' she said, maintaining her composure but still administering the rebuke that George deserved. Then she lifted the chair away towards her own table.

'I'm sorry about my friend,' I said. 'He's only been released today. Still not used to being back in the community.'

She gave me a look as cold as the one she'd given George, but then registered my apology, and shabby attempt at humour, and softened a little. 'It's OK,' she replied. 'We all have our off moments.'

'True,' I said. 'Very true.'

I thought I detected the faintest signs of a smile, but I may have been mistaken. I watched, while pretending not to watch, as she sat down next to the new arrival in her group and listened to him briefly. Then they each dropped a hand below the level of the table and I assumed that any thoughts I'd been entertaining (had I?) of this woman being unattached were mistaken. But as soon as their hands had gone from view they reappeared, and Tomboy was on her feet again, heading for the loo. Did this indicate what I thought it indicated? The longer than average time she was gone, coupled with the way she was rubbing her nose when she returned, confirmed my suspicions.

The shuffling of chairs that had cleared her way meant that when she sat down again she was right next to me. Before she could join in with her friends' conversation, I took my desire and put it to use. 'When was your last off moment, then?'

She looked round at me, taking a couple of beats to get the reference. When she did, there was a further wait while she decided on a response. Had I overstepped the mark? Had her acceptance of my apology been all I could reasonably expect, and was I now in danger of annoying her? It appeared not. Call it generosity of spirit, or call it the cocaine she'd just taken, but she seemed ready to engage in conversation. 'Most of last week.' There was no smile to go with this, but I knew from observing her over the past half-hour that this woman didn't smile because she was expected to, she smiled as and when she wanted to.

'Why was that?'

'He was called Garth, he was from Dallas, he weighed eight stone more than he should and his breath smelt.'

'Doesn't strike me as your type.'

A smile, an almost grudging one, as though my joke, if it qualified as such, had forced it from her. 'He's the MD of a firm I'm representing.'

'Representing?'

'I'm a barrister. Specialise in employment law.'

Clearly a lawyer of the young, work-hard, play-hard variety. I guessed that the last thing she wanted to talk about at this time on a Saturday night was work. So I changed tack. 'What's your name?'

'Mel.' She took a drag on a cigarette that one of her girlfriends was holding out for her. 'You?'

'Sam.'

She nodded, as though deciding whether she wanted to carry on talking to me. Another drag on the cigarette. And then: 'Who's the guy feeling sorry for himself?'

'George. Needs a bit of work on his interpersonal skills, but not a bad lad at heart.'

George was staring out of the window at passers-by. He pretended not to hear us, but of course he was listening to every word.

'Where've you been tonight?'

'A few places,' I said. 'Couple of bars, the Mortimer Hotel . . .'

'I *hate* that place,' grimaced Mel.

'I wasn't that impressed with it, I have to say.'

'I used to go there when it first opened, but now it's full of rich tourists and wankers looking to pick up women.'

I coughed. 'Yeah, terrible, isn't it?' Was she having a go at us? Had she realised what our evening was all about? No, she wasn't that sort of person. If she was talking to me it was because she wanted to, either because of my magnetic personality, or her drugs kicking in. She wasn't the type to play games, to get my confidence up and then start taking the piss. 'What about you?'

'Not been anywhere yet. This is where we're all meeting.' Very cool. Don't start your evening until midnight, and even then start it somewhere low-key. 'We're going to Space.'

'Right.' Where the hell, and indeed what the hell, was Space? It was a question that didn't tax me too much. I was just pleased to be given the credit (albeit undeserved) for knowing the answer. This woman was taking me seriously.

'Or at least we will be going, when Alex gets off the phone.'

The guy who'd just turned up was talking on his mobile, although with his head turned away and his voice kept low. Gradually he got a little more agitated, and then suddenly ended the call.

'No good,' he said to Mel.

'Nothing at all?' She looked put out.

'Says he can't help us.'

At this Mel turned her back on me, literally, and started muttering to the others. Obviously their pharmaceutical supplier had let them down, and this snag took precedence over me. Oh well, nice to have been granted some respect, however shortlived. Back to reality . . .

Eh, hang on though.

Hang on just one cotton-pickin' minute.

Telling George to stay where he was, and keeping half an eye on the increasingly fraught discussions of Mel and her friends, I went outside and called Pete.

'Sam! How's things?'

'All right. Listen, where are you?'

'The Mitre. We're having a lock-in. D'you wanna come down?'

Weighing the prospect of Ray's 'Fly Me To The Moon' routine against what I was aiming at with Mel, I opted for the latter. 'No thanks, I'm up to something else.' Under my breath I added an 'I hope', and then continued: 'You remember my present?'

'What?'

'My present, the other week. From Terry.'

'Present? From Terr . . . oh, yeah, yeah. What about it?'

'Where is it?'

'It's in my wallet. Well, most of it is, anyway.'

'What do you mean?'

'Don't get your Y-fronts in a twist,' he said. 'I only had a bit. In fact, I didn't have any, a couple of girls did.'

'Which couple of girls?'

'Met them the other night, thought I was doing OK, my wrap was at home – well, at home and empty, actually – so I let them have a line each from yours. Long story.' He sighed. 'Disappointing ending.'

'I don't give a monkey's about your ending,' I growled, 'I just want to know how much of my coke is left.'

'*Will* you calm down? I've told you, haven't I? Almost all of it. They didn't have enormous lines.'

'Good. Because I need it.'

'What, now?'

'Yes, now. Probably. Hopefully.'

'Why?'

'Yours is not to reason why, Pete, yours is to deliver that coke, where I tell you, when I tell you. And I'll be telling you in a couple of minutes, so stand by that phone.' The answer to his question, of course, was that I wanted the drugs for precisely the same reason he had the other night. But I didn't want to admit that to him. Did I even want to admit it to myself?

'But, Sam, we're having a lock-in—'

'Yes, well, it won't take you long in a cab into the West End, will it? And I'm sure Ray'll let you back in.'

'But, Sam—'

'Pete, if you want to continue this discussion we can always sort out when you're going to top up that gram for me. But if you play along tonight, I'll turn a blind eye to the couple of lines and, more importantly, to the liberty you took in dishing them out without my permission.'

There was a silence. Then: 'All right. But don't be long.'

'I won't. In fact, you can call the cab now, come to think of it.' He could always cancel it if Mel declined my offer.

Back inside, Mel and her friends seemed to have finished their discussions, but from their disgruntled looks I could tell that no alternative supplier had been found.

'Are you OK?' I asked her. 'Everyone seems a bit subdued all of a sudden.'

She half looked at me, indicating a suspicion that I'd guessed what the problem was. 'Mmm,' she said. 'You could say that.'

This was an opening, of sorts. If she'd wanted to close the topic down completely she'd have denied there was a problem at all. 'Er, I don't want to be presumptuous,' I continued, feeling a little nervous, 'but if it's a question of . . . erm . . . Charles not being around . . .' – she turned to me, not saying anything, but showing that she'd understood, and was interested – '. . . then I think I might be able to help.'

'Really?'

'Yeah.' I leaned closer so that we could talk quietly. She did the same, and I could smell her scent. Whether it was perfume or deodorant or soap I couldn't tell, but I breathed in again to relish it. I covered this by looking as though I was thinking of what to say, although in reality I'd got it all mapped out. 'At this short notice I probably couldn't get my hands on more than a gram. But if it's any use to you . . .'

'Of course it is. That,' she pointed towards the loos, 'was the last we had.' She looked at me for a second. 'I didn't think you were . . . you know, a dealer.'

I laughed. 'I'm not. It's just that I know someone, and I wanted to . . . I wanted to help you. If that doesn't sound too crap.'

We were so close that I could hear the gentle smack of her lips parting before she spoke. 'No, it doesn't sound crap at all. I'm flattered to be someone you wanted to help.'

I didn't reply, I just let our words hang in the air.

Then Mel added: 'You are going to come to the club with us, aren't you?'

Gotcha. I nodded. We both sat up in our chairs, the moment of intimacy over, but noted.

'How quickly can you sort things out?'

'Shouldn't take very long at all.'

'We might as well wait here then,' she said. 'Stupid us turning up to the club separately.'

'Yeah,' I said, relieved I wouldn't have to admit that I didn't know where Space was. 'Let me just make the call.'

I went back outside and dialled Pete again. 'Right,' I said when he'd answered. 'Bar Italia. Quick as you like.'

'I'm in the car already.'

'Christ. Speedicabs living up to their name for once?'

'Surprising the effect it has when you tell them you work for Terry.'

'Good, I'll see you soon.'

And so I did, fifteen minutes later. They were minutes I filled talking to Mel, or rather listening to her, as her artificial advantage in the talking stakes began to tell. She introduced George and me to her friends, although as always when you meet more than three people at once, especially when you're drunk, the person doing the introductions might as well say, 'Someone whose name you'll instantly forget, someone else whose name you'll instantly forget, someone else . . .' She quietly asked me how much I wanted for the drugs, but I told her she could just buy me and George a few drinks. The kudos this earned me was, of course, entirely unjustified, as the drugs hadn't cost me a penny in the first place. At least not directly. But in view of the emotional strain I'd suffered in earning them, I told myself that any reward they brought me was more than deserved.

I deliberately kept an eye out for Pete and made sure I collared him before he came into the bar. The last thing I needed was Mel or either of her girlfriends taking a shine to him. The shine would be reciprocated, he'd lose his desire to get back to the Mitre, and my evening would be well and truly hijacked.

'Why d'you want this, then?' he asked as for reasons of subtlety I climbed into the back of the cab and sat next to him. 'You said you didn't want it anywhere near you while the points thing was still on. That doesn't end till tomorrow, does it?'

I stared at the tiny folded piece of paper. This was my ticket to Extreme, the magical place where you discover yourself. Taking drugs with a strange girl in a strange club, the night before a make-or-break day with your girlfriend: that was pretty extreme. My lesson was on its way. What was it going to be?

'I just need it, Pete.' And then, so that he wouldn't pursue the topic: 'How's it going down the pub?'

'Great, great,' he said. But his heart wasn't in it. I could tell that he could tell that something was up, and he was worried on my behalf. Maybe I should have been as worried as he was. But I wasn't. With desire as my friend, worries couldn't get near me.

The wrap safely in my pocket, I returned to the group. We were halfway through the drinks that were Mel's first down-payment on the coke, and George had, by the look of things, been thoroughly forgiven for his rudeness. He was getting on famously with her two girlfriends. Mel and I continued our conversation, which for some reason was about old leather suitcases and amounted to little more than statement after statement about how much each of us loved them, but we were blinded to the repetition by the substances flying round our bloodstreams. In her case, alcohol and cocaine, in mine, alcohol and desire.

When we'd finished our drinks, the non-camp guy, the one who'd been the last to arrive, announced that we could all go to Space in his car, which was parked just the other side of Oxford Street. It turned out to be a Cadillac. A genuine, 1950s, cherry-red, huge great Cadillac. I'd never been near a Cadillac before, let alone in one. Not that I'm particularly interested in Cadillacs, but the point was that the evening was rapidly becoming very, very different from any other evening I'd ever had. Truly I was heading for an extreme. It was great.

The car had one of those big front seats that go all the way across, so Non-Camp Guy and Camp Guy sat up there with one of the women. Squeezed into the back were the other woman, George, me and Mel. I was pressed up against the left-hand door, directly behind the driver. To create a bit more room I turned a little to my right, which meant that Mel was pressed up against my chest. Again I could smell her scent, and also now I felt her breath on my cheek whenever she turned to address me, which was often. The breath was beery, which should have been unpleasant, but as part of the intimacy that was developing between us it was thrilling. The nerves which had dogged me with the other women were gone. I was wrapped up in a great big ball of certainty, the combination of alcohol, the attention I was receiving from Mel and my conviction that a lesson was heading my way, that a signpost was soon to be reached.

There were so many people in the car and I was so happy to concentrate on Mel rather than the road that I completely lost track of where we were. The Cadillac eventually swung into an ad-hoc car park, which had been created by the demolition of a building. On either side towered huge Victorian warehouses. The buildings looked almost derelict, destined to go the same way as their one-time neighbour. Only two or three other cars were there. With the peeling fly-posters and torn wire fencing, it was a bit like being in a night-time scene in *Starsky and Hutch*. But as the roar of the Cadillac's engine died away and I filtered out the ongoing chatter of the others emerging on to the dusty, litter-strewn concrete, my ears picked up the faint throb of music.

Mel was leading the way across to one of the warehouses. Not out on to the street and in through the front, but via a small, steel-plated side-door, which had obviously been added to the building quite recently. She pressed a buzzer and waited. The door opened outwards a few inches, and then, when her identity had been ascertained, swung all the way open. A short middle-aged man, dressed entirely in black with long black hair tied in a ponytail, stood with his arms outstretched.

'Melissa!' he cried in a flamboyant East European accent. 'Melissa!'

'Nicolai,' she responded coolly. She hugged him, or at least stood there and allowed herself to be hugged.

'Eet's sor gude to shee you and your fraind!'

She smiled, and stood aside so that we could all file into the entrance area, which I guessed had once been a storage room within the warehouse. I don't know whether there was any question of a charge for getting in, but if there was Mel took care of it, either by paying or by being Mel and not having to pay. Then we were heading towards another metal door on the other side of the entrance area. The music had got a little louder than it had been outside, but was still not much more than a throb. When Nicolai opened the door for us, however, the effect was incredible. It was as though someone had simultaneously turned a stereo from one to ten and thrust your head inside the speaker. It hit more than your eardrums, it physically shook you. I could feel my chest vibrating in time to the beat. Walking through the door felt like entering a furnace of sound.

But the shock of how loud it was soon paled beside the shock of how big it was. The warehouse was four or five storeys high, and stretched away into the distance for what seemed like hundreds of yards. It was only by looking way, way up into the cavernous recesses of the roof that you could follow the building's entire length, because at ground level the place was packed with a heaving, perspiring, dancing mass of bodies. There were thousands and thousands and thousands of people in there. Peppering the walls were bars, seating areas, speaker stacks, and futuristic sculptures and paintings that looked utter messes but were no doubt by *the* artists of the moment. The lighting rigs must have cost millions, with hi-tech lasers that pierced the darkness, illuminating people for an instant before letting them return to their private self-indulgence.

So eclectic was the mix of people that George and I didn't look at all out of place in our suits. True, they were less outrageous than most of the suits on display, but no one seemed to notice us as being anything out of the ordinary, or should I say out of the extraordinary. Simply by virtue of being there, which we'd achieved by being with Mel, we were seen as cool enough to be acceptable. The moment she made her way into the throng, people were stopping her every few feet, most of them exhibiting the same sangfroid as her, but nonetheless communicating their pleasure at seeing her. I was vaguely aware that George and one of the other girls, pale with an angled blonde fringe, were somewhere close, but Mel was introducing only me to the people she met.

'Hi, this is Sam,' she'd say. 'He's a new friend of mine.'

And the man or woman would seem to register her phrase as some kind of codeword, and they'd look me up and down with greater-than-average interest, and greet me with greater-than-average respect, and Mel would stand noticeably close to me as though she was saying, 'You've got to evaluate him on how he looks with me – do we go well together?' I could feel my heart beating and now it wasn't just due to the music. It was beating with confidence, a huge, striding confidence that this was the right thing to be doing.

We moved over to the bar. It too was packed, but turning round I found myself right next to George and the girl who'd paired off with him. It was that sort of place, so busy, so loud, so dark that it disorientated you, made you forget who you were with, made you unsure as to how you'd got where you had. I began to feel dizzy, dizzier even than my drunkenness could account for, but also, at the same time, in

286

complete control of that dizziness. My lesson was on its way, quite close now, I sensed, although already I had the feeling that I knew what it was going to be. Mel was definitely attracting me, and attracted to me, sexually, and that attraction was becoming more urgent. I was quite happy now, as was she, for us to lock gazes for seconds at a time, not a word passing between us.

I remembered the cocaine in my pocket. But before I could mention it, Mel was ordering champagne. When they came, the bottles (she'd ordered two) were black, as were their labels, with gold lettering in a modern typeface, too tiny to read. No Moët here. We retired to a nearby table that was surrounded by a high-backed sofa, curved so that it formed almost a complete circle. I wondered why no one else had grabbed it until I saw a man standing near us flick the jacket of his black suit, accidentally revealing the curly wire running from his earpiece to his belt-mounted walkie-talkie. Bloody hell, I thought, even the bouncers here look like millionaires. Clearly he'd been guarding the table for the crème de la crème, of which Mel was certainly a member.

Cocooned inside the sofa, she expertly eased the cork from one of the champagne bottles. There was no fuss, no wide-eyed 'whoo!' at the popping sound, no reference to 'shampers' or 'poo'. Mel was obviously well used to champagne, drinking it not because tonight was anything special, but simply because it was her favourite drink. Then, sitting closer together than we had to, we drank the bottle's contents, aided by George and . . . his woman? Was that the implication now? The rest of the group had disappeared.

'How in the name of fuck,' said George in my ear, 'have we managed this?'

'Don't question it,' I replied. 'Just go with the flow.' At other times this would have been a nothing line, said for the sake of something to say. But now it was said in deadly earnest, a heartfelt piece of advice. Because that's how I was feeling myself. I was going with the flow, I wasn't questioning anything, I was letting my desire (desire for Mel? You bet) lead me on and on. Everything about the night felt vital, real, important.

The bottle emptied, Mel stood up and looked round. Spying a door, normal size, and mirrored, not metal, which was being guarded by another bouncer, she looked down at us. 'Shall we . . .?' This was it: time for the drugs. Grabbing the other bottle of champagne, she led us over to the door, and as we went through I noticed that the bouncer positioned himself in front of it to prevent anyone else following us in.

I could see why they'd have wanted to. Not to get any of our coke, but just to stand there and admire what was easily the most impressive toilet I had ever been in. It was a mind-boggling combination of the space-age and the traditional. A beautiful black marble unit containing a couple of sinks ran the entire length of one wall and supported a huge mirror that curled round at either end so that your reflections bounced off each other, throwing a million images of you into infinity. Opposite that were four cubicles made of a brushed bronze-coloured metal, inside which were toilets made of a deep maroon porcelain. Underfloor lights directed beams up towards the ceiling, where they hit tiny revolving mirrors and bounced off in constantly changing directions. It was a bit like going for a piss on the Starship Enterprise.

Not that that's what we were there for, of course. As the other girl opened the champagne, took a swig and offered the bottle to George, I handed Mel the cocaine. 'Be my guest,' I said with a smile.

'I'd love to.' She looked at the wrap thoughtfully for a moment or two. 'And you know what? I think tonight we should have a *really – big – night*.' She carefully unfolded the paper, checked that a portion of the sink unit was absolutely dry, then tipped out the entire gram (or, as I knew it to be, slightly less than a gram). Christ, we were going to do the lot in one go. Once I got over my shock at this, I became even more excited than I already had been. No, that's not quite the right word. I wasn't excited, not in the giggly, hyperactive, schooltrip-to-the-amusement-park sense. I was thrilled, gripped, hooked. Outwardly I was as calm and offhand as Mel and everyone else in the club, but inwardly my spirits were bursting at the sheer outrageousness of this evening, they were bursting so much that by rights I should have been yelling with joy. I wasn't though, and that was the point. I was soaking it up. I was, as I'd told George to do, going with the flow. Because I knew that my lesson was on its way, riding along on the back of this incredible night. My goal had been an extreme. And snorting huge lines of cocaine in a private loo in an ultra-cool club with two girls I'd only just met while swigging champagne from the bottle and receiving the strongest sexual vibes a woman can give off without removing her clothes . . . well, I think that counts as pretty extreme.

I jumped up on to the sink unit and sat with my back resting against the mirror, watching Mel start to work on the coke. The white powder stood out magnificently against the black marble, beams of light flashing across it from the ceiling, spotlights to emphasise that the drug was now the star of the show. Taking out her credit card – platinum – Mel scraped all the powder into a big heap, then into four or five smaller heaps, then back into one, and so on. With quick chopping movements she got rid of the lumps, bringing the edge of her card down again and again and again until all the powder was as fine as fine can be. George passed me the champagne and I took another swig, but when I offered it to Mel she didn't notice. She was too hypnotised by the cocaine. Her chopping had gone beyond what was necessary, she was just doing it because the act entranced her. Like a big child playing in a very expensive sand pit, she ran her card through the powder time after time, sweeping it into different patterns, the plastic riding behind lines of coke like a surfer on a wave, then ploughing through it and pushing it off in another direction. As I watched, I too became mesmerised, gazing at the designs Mel was creating in the drug, anticipating the rush it was going to give us. I was thrilled enough as it was – what was I going to feel like after taking the coke? Come on, I thought, I want to throw myself into the rest of this night and lose control, I want to carry on hearing that laughter from George and his girl, I want more champagne, I want Mel, I want all of this, come on, I want it now, that's it, there, Mel's shaping up the lines now, eight of them, two each, fucking huge lines of coke that are going to make us buzz like you wouldn't, couldn't, believe, that's it, Mel's finished toying with the coke now, there are those lines, side by side, degenerate soldiers waiting to carry us into battle, I can't stop looking at them, I can see out of the corner of my eye that Mel's rolling up a banknote, but I can't tear my gaze away from those lines, two of them are mine, I want them now, I want them both, and then I want more drink, and then I want Mel, this is it, this night is really going to come alive, I'm sitting up straight and stretching to flex myself for the rest of this night, and now Mel's bending over the coke, she's got the twenty to her nose, she's going to snort her first line and then it'll be my turn, I'm just going to lean against the mirror—

'What the *fuck* . . .?'

Mel's scream pierced the air like a firework. At first I didn't know what had happened, though I did know that it was very, very bad. And then the details started to get clearer. The first, and most crucial detail, was that the coke had gone. Disappeared. I don't mean just the line that Mel had been about to take, I mean all of it, all eight lines. They'd just vanished, in the blink of an eye. Literally the blink of an eye, because I hadn't seen where they'd gone. That was when the next detail hit me: there was a noise, a humming sound, coming from where my right arm had leaned against the mirror. Looking round I saw that my elbow had leaned not against the mirror itself but against some sort of button. It was the button of an electric hand-dryer, which was mounted on the wall, with the mirror built around it.

I had blown away our entire supply of cocaine.

I leapt to my feet, as if removing my weight from the hand-dryer would magically make time go backwards and rearrange the lines of coke on the sink unit. Not only did it not do that, it didn't even stop the blast of air, because it was one of those dryers that operate for a set number of seconds. Still the machine blew down on to the marble. Not that it made any difference, as the machine was so powerful that the gust of air had instantly shot every last grain of powder off the unit, scattering the coke so far and wide that it had completely ceased to exist. You couldn't see a single scrap of it anywhere. It hadn't even been as though Mel had arranged the lines from left to right, which might have allowed the ones at each end, or at least a fraction of them, to survive the hurricane. No, the lines had all been directly under the machine.

'What the *fucking* hell did you do that for?' hollered Mel, her eyes almost popping out of their sockets in rage, her

291

hand shaking as it continued to grip the now-redundant twenty-pound note.

I couldn't speak. I wanted to die. I would have paid every penny I had, and would ever have, just to reverse the events of the past few seconds. George and the other girl, who'd been sharing a joke, were slightly behind me in working out what had happened, but when they did their laughter came to a very abrupt end.

'You *cunt*!' yelled the other girl. 'You *absolute* cunt!' Then her shock caused her to start hyperventilating and she had to lean against the wall to recover. She had, I think, betrayed the fact that her longing for the cocaine had been more than just a wish and verged on a need. 'What are we going to do now?' she continued. 'What are we going to do *now*!'

George was looking at me more in shock than in anger, although I could tell he was pretty pissed off at his friend-ship with the girl being so suddenly and irretrievably ruined. But still I didn't speak.

Not because I couldn't, though. Because I didn't want to. I didn't need to. My lesson had come along. *This* was my lesson. As I stared at the empty cocaine wrap, at the girl whose interest in me had – *quelle surprise* – disappeared along with the drugs, at her friend whose enjoyment of the evening had been similarly dependent on the coke, at the room that I now saw was gaudy, not impressive, as I stared at all of this a lesson was ringing so loudly in my ears that the girls' rantings were powerless to attract my attention. The lesson, although deafening, was very simple. It was: *you have been such an arsehole. Just look at yourself, and the way you've spent this evening, and compare that to the love you feel – and you know you feel it, you cretin – for Kirsty. What in God's name do you think you've been playing at?*

It was funny – taking cocaine is supposed to sober you up, but now I felt sober because I hadn't taken it. The shock of what had happened was like a hundred cups of the strongest black coffee, and suddenly I was in complete control of my senses. Which was why I could pay such close attention to my lesson. *You are now less than twenty-four hours away from the moment that's going to decide whether or not you have a future with the woman you love like no other woman you have ever loved, and where are you? You're in a nightclub toilet, with two women you don't know, and don't want to know. This is what nights out on the pull are all about, you twat. They're shallow, they're pathetic, and even when they go right, which in your case is almost never, the pleasure they bring is temporary, and compared to what you've got with Kirsty it's the most synthetic, genetically modified, unpleasurable pleasure there is. At home is the woman you love. Something has been happening with this points system that you don't understand, but the solution to that is not to go out with your friend looking for casual sex, it's to go home and sort things out with Kirsty. Tell her that you'll do whatever it takes to get those points. Ask her to explain it to you. Phrase it whichever way you want, but just get home and sort it out, you snivelling little bastard. NOW.*

So that's what I did. I simply turned round and walked out of the room. Not a word did I address to anyone, not even to George. Maybe it was unfair to leave him facing the music on his own, but this was a time for priorities, and I only had one. Kirsty.

I walked out of the club, through the car park and on to the street, and tried to establish where I was. A street sign gave a name I'd never heard of. The postcode was SE1. Where was I? Bermondsey? Southwark? I headed for the end of the deserted, factory-lined street and tried to find something that looked like a main road. It took two more turnings before I saw any traffic, but gradually I worked my way out into civilisation, if pissed blokes falling out of kebab shops can be called civilisation. I was in Borough High Street. My watch told me it was nearly half-two, and the length of the nightbus queues told me I had absolutely no chance of getting a cab. I'd have to walk for ages before I could grab one. Not that I minded the walking – the shock of my lesson had given me lots of energy. It was the time that frustrated me, because I wanted to be at home with Kirsty this *instant*. I wanted to be sorting it all out *now*.

But I resigned myself to a trek, and headed into town, hoping to find a taxi somewhere en route. Each step made me feel better, because it was a step nearer to home, to Kirsty. I still hadn't got a clue how her points worked, or why I'd failed to get anywhere near enough of them, but at least now I was going to tackle it all head on, rather than fronting it out while I tried to second-guess her. I started to walk faster, my energy and optimism feeding off themselves. Don't get me wrong. I was still nervous, terrified, about what the outcome was going to be, but the fact that I was, at last, heading home to Kirsty to talk it through made me able to face those nerves. By the time I flagged down a cab the endorphins were rushing round my brain like manic commuters and I knew that I was going to sort this out once and for all. Kirsty and I were going to talk. I was going to find out whether or not I was to stay with the only woman I'd ever really loved. This was the most important moment of my life.

The cab pulled up outside the flat. Getting out, I glanced up at the windows and saw that none of the lights were on, not even our bedroom light. Kirsty's party had obviously finished a long time ago. I'd have to wake her up. But that was all right. This talk was going to be about our future, so momentous that it would soon have her wide awake. I waited for my change from the cabbie, feeling like an actor standing in the wings about to receive the cue for the biggest role of his career. The moment those coins were in my hand, that was it: that was my cue to go inside, up the stairs, into my flat and on to the stage that would determine my future.

I got the change. I turned and walked up the path, fiddling with my keys to find the right one. Which was why I didn't see the man coming out of the building. It was only as I got a step or two away from the door that he came hurtling out of it, leaving me just enough time to hop out of the way. Otherwise his momentum would have knocked me over and probably left me unconscious. By the time I looked up from my keys he was past me, and as he ran off into the distance I only got the briefest chance to form an impression: roughly my age, tall, well-built, well-dressed. That was it, apart from one tiny detail. One of his cufflinks was missing. Curious that I should register something like that, but it was hard not to notice because the double-cuff had fallen open and was flapping over his hand as he ran down the street.

Catching the door before it banged shut, I started to climb the stairs. I suppose that on a normal night I'd have been wondering about the guy running out of my building at three o'clock, asking myself which of our neighbours he was most likely to have been visiting, why he was in such a hurry to leave. But my thoughts, my emotions, my nerves were all taken up with Kirsty, and the points, and the future. *Our* future?

I reached our floor and made a deliberately noisy job of getting into the flat in the hope that I could wake Kirsty up by degrees. I shut the front door behind me, rattling my keys as I placed them on the hall table. I listened for signs of life upstairs. None.

'Kirsty?' I called.

No reply. I took off my watch and let it clatter on to the table. Then I dropped my phone next to it.

'Kirsty?'

From the bedroom came an almost-human sounding 'Mmm?'

'I've just got back.' I took my wallet out. 'You have a nice time with your friends?'

A yawn. 'Yeah. Quiet, though. Everyone left ages ago.'

'Right.' I collected myself, trying to formulate an opening line that I could use when I got upstairs. I'd decided not to get into bed but to stay dressed and sit on the chair, to signal how important this all was. But I still hadn't worked out the exact words I was going to use. Something simple was what I needed. 'Kirsty, I think we should talk about this.' Or maybe: 'Kirsty, I'm very worried, and I know I'm not allowed to ask you how I've earned or lost points, but I don't care, I want to sort this out.' Or maybe: 'Kirsty, could we talk about . . .'

I turned to place my wallet next to the other stuff. And only then did I notice it. It had been sitting on the table the whole time.

It was a cufflink.

I am never – and I mean never – going to forget how I felt catching sight of that thing. I felt dead. Physically and emotionally dead. Instead of blood I had stone inside me, and the only sensation anywhere was a slight tingling on the backs of my hands and the tops of my feet. Without knowing anything about it, I stepped back towards the stairs and sat heavily, my backside landing on the third or fourth step. Then my body slumped forward until my elbows hit my knees and supported me. Hunched over, staring at the floor, my emotions had shut down. It was as though my brain had told them that the news on its way through was bad, disastrous, the worst it could possibly be, and they'd better go on strike immediately so that they wouldn't have to deliver its poisonous message.

The tingling stayed in my hands and feet. It never quite died away, and gradually it started to spread again. I began to register where I was, what had just happened and what that cufflink meant. It belonged to the man that had run from the building. That man had been in my flat. He had been in my flat with my girlfriend, who was now pretending to have been asleep, claiming that everyone left 'ages ago'.

The horrible truth set to work on me. Kirsty had been . . . say it, Sam, it's not going not to be true just because you don't say it . . . Kirsty had been unfaithful to me. I'd come home, fired with a new certainty that Kirsty was the one for me, determined to do whatever it took to talk our relationship back from the brink, only to find that as far as Kirsty was concerned it was already over the brink. Kirsty didn't want me.

The feeling I had was beyond shock, or anger, or sadness. You're shocked by finding a mouse behind the fridge. You're angry when someone nicks your parking space. You're sad when ET goes home. This was way past any of that. But I didn't scream or shout or yell, or fight against it in any way at all, because I knew I couldn't. This was the worst thing that had ever happened to me, and it was smothering every other thing in my life. Without the love of Kirsty, nothing else mattered. This was hell, and I was in it, and I was staying in it. End of story.

So instead of bursting into tears, or running upstairs and confronting Kirsty, or smashing the place up in a rage, I simply stood up and started walking. Out of the door, down the stairs, out into the road and off into the night. For the second time that night I was walking, wordlessly, away from a girl. But whereas I'd done it in the nightclub because I'd realised something beautiful, now I was doing it because I'd realised something terrible.

I walked without knowing where I was going. Turnings came and I took them, or rather they took me. My direction was decided by which side of the road I happened to be on, or which way was downhill, or which way seemed, for whatever trivial reason, to be easier. There was no traffic about, save for the odd nightbus or taxi. I was alone in the streets, carrying my personal hell around with me. Passing suburban curtains drawn tightly against the loneliness of a dark night I thought back to the time – already it seemed like a different era – when Kirsty and I had been safe inside our own den. It was only minutes since I'd stumbled across the truth, but even so my relationship with her felt as though it was ancient history, a far-off period when there was sunshine and hope and love, instead of the darkness and torture and misery that had seized me now.

I walked without looking ahead, staring down at my feet eating up the miles, thinking about what had happened. What had this points thing been all about? Was Ray right? Had Kirsty started it as a smokescreen, knowing all along that she was going to leave me but trying to make me feel it was my fault? Or had she started it in good faith and realised halfway through that she didn't want me to succeed? Was that why I'd had good weeks and only fallen away in the second half?

When had she first been unfaithful to me? Was it ages ago, before I'd even proposed? Maybe not. Maybe she'd made up her mind that we were finished but hadn't had the nerve to sleep with anyone else. Maybe this points scheme, this convenient way of getting rid of me, if that's what it was, had given her the nerve. Certain that I'd be on my bike, she'd got on with the rest of her life before I'd even left.

Was Mr Cufflink really a schoolmate? Or was that a cover story? The other week, the reunion in Newbury, that had been genuine, surely? But had Saturday night really been a reunion of that reunion, at which her feelings for an old friend came to the fore, or was he someone she'd had her eye on more recently, who she'd invited around on his own, knowing that I'd be out? Had they fallen asleep, only to be woken just in time by the sound of my taxi pulling up? If he wasn't a schoolmate, how had she met him? Was he . . .

But there was no point in any of this. It didn't matter who this guy was, or whether tonight was the first time he'd slept with my girlf— . . . ex-girlfriend, or whether Kirsty had ever wanted me to succeed with the points. The only thing that mattered was that it was over. Kirsty didn't want me.

God knows how long I walked for, or which route I took, but when I looked up I found that I was standing on the south side of Trafalgar Square. Somehow I'd made my way right back into central London. I started to walk down Whitehall. Deserted as it was (even the policemen at the end of Downing Street were inside their little hut), my only companions were the statues of military leaders outside the Ministry of Defence. Tiredness was beginning to make my feet drag, and as I shuffled past the larger-than-lifesize heroes I felt the complete opposite of them. They'd defined themselves, affirmed their lives through their legendary acts of bravery. But I no longer felt I had a life to affirm. The defining thing about me had been my love for Kirsty, and that had been taken away from me. I was an empty shell. It also struck me how appropriate it was that I'd left the flat without my wallet. I was carrying nothing that could identify me. At school, you have your name sewn into your clothes. As an adult, you've always got your cards with you, a driving licence, something that tells the world who you are. But I had nothing. For the first time since I was a baby, I had no identity.

I reached Parliament Square. It was completely empty. Not a car, not a bus, not a taxi. No fellow wanderers. The traffic lights changed, from green to amber to red and back again, but there was nothing for them to direct. The futility of what they were doing sat perfectly with my mood. Pointlessly going through the motions. I knew that, without Kirsty, I had a lifetime of that ahead of me.

I walked out on to Westminster Bridge. My footsteps, although tired, no longer felt aimless. It was as though something was drawing me to this particular place. But what? Why was I heading this way? I looked up at Big Ben, and for the first time since I'd taken my watch off I knew what time it was: ten-past five. London was at its absolute deadest. Saturday night had finished, its revellers gone home. Sunday had yet to start, with even the keenest tourists still languishing in their beds. I looked down at the swishing waters of the Thames. Was that why I'd been drawn here? Was I yearning for the ultimate answer to it all: the rope, the breeze block and the final leap? I stopped in the middle of the bridge, on the side nearer Big Ben, and gazed into the river.

No. Whatever my subconscious was telling me, it wasn't telling me that. I turned around, sat down and leaned against the bridge, looking in the opposite direction, away from Big Ben. And then I knew what it was that had drawn me to this spot. There it was, on the other side of the river from Parliament, looking down on me like I'd look down on

300

an ant. The Millennium Wheel. My subconscious had brought me here to see the wreckage of my dream, to get it through to me that my life with Kirsty was over. I'd longed for the day when she'd say yes, when I could bring her to the Wheel and wait for our pod to get to the top and . . . well, you know the rest. And now I knew that it wasn't going to happen. That Wheel was always going to be a reminder of what I wanted but couldn't have. It was going to taunt me, peer down on me from its incredible height and say, 'Kirsty didn't want you. Kirsty wouldn't let you ride me to the top and say the line you dreamed of saying. Whatever else you do in your life, Sam, whatever else goes right for you, you're never going to have that. It'll never be yours. Kirsty will never be yours.'

I leaned my head back, looking up at the very top of the Wheel, motionless and forbidding. There wasn't a living soul anywhere in sight who could protect me. The Wheel's jibes rained down on me, and all the feelings that had been anaesthesised for the last two hours started to make themselves felt. I let my head fall forward and I cried like a baby. I sobbed and sobbed and sobbed, until I had no tears left.

'Time to get home, sir, don't you think?'

The policeman's comment, together with the gentle nudge from his boot, woke me up. A glance at Big Ben told me I'd only been asleep for ten minutes or so, but my slumped position meant that my neck had a painful crick. With the salty taste of tears still in my mouth, and my backside having soaked up the cold from the pavement, I felt almost as bad physically as I did emotionally.

'Yeah.' I hauled myself to my feet.

The copper examined my face. My eyes must have looked as red and puffy as they felt. 'Bad night, was it?'

301

I nodded. I thought about saying something along the lines of it having been so bad that now I didn't have a home to get to. But although my brain constructed the thought, my mouth wouldn't form the words. I walked off. What was I going to do? Where was I going to go? I couldn't go back to the flat. Not with Kirsty there. I just walked, down the Embankment, all the way to Blackfriars, up through Fleet Street, past the High Court, across into Covent Garden. Gradually London began to wake up. Street cleaners appeared, and café owners preparing for another day's business, and people walking their dogs, fetching newspapers, going out for a jog. Then, as the morning wore on and I meandered around town, there were tourists and coach parties and burger-stall attendants, and eventually the city was alive again.

Wherever I went, though, be it Bloomsbury or Waterloo or Lambeth, my feet would always find their way back to the Wheel. Every couple of hours I'd be standing there, watching the pods go round, inching their way to the top for a few brief minutes' superiority over London. The rest of the time, when I wasn't at the Wheel, I was thinking about practicalities. Immediate ones like when and how I was going to get back into the flat to collect my stuff (leave it until tomorrow, I thought, when Kirsty will be at work – I can collect my spare keys from the office), and more long-term ones, like where I was going to stay until I could find somewhere of my own. (With George? Would he still be talking to me after I'd ruined his chances at the club?) But when I was at the Wheel, my thoughts were about Kirsty herself. How did I feel about her? I knew that I should have been angry, because at the very least she'd been unfaithful to me, and quite possibly she'd constructed an elaborate twelve-week lie as well. But the strange thing was, I couldn't. Anger wouldn't come any more.

I thought about Danny, and wondered how he'd get on with his course. I tried to make myself feel better by focusing on my achievement with him. It hadn't been easy, after all, and Danny had got himself dangerously close to a life that was hardly worth the name. Hadn't I saved him from that? But I couldn't convince myself. My feelings for him were swamped by my own misery.

Morning turned into afternoon, and afternoon into evening. By nine o'clock, the effects of a night and a day out on the streets were beginning to make themselves felt. My feet were sore, my back ached and my appetite, which all day had been dulled by despair, was rearing up again, leaving me to wonder how I could get some money to buy food. Sitting on a bench on the South Bank, twenty yards away from the Wheel, which seemed to reach up almost to the stars in the sky, I even started to wonder if I had the courage to ask passers-by for change. That reminded me of Brighton, trying to find Danny, and I thought again about how I should be glad for him, and proud of myself, but still it didn't seem that important, still it was hidden by my misery.

'I thought I might find you here.'

There was no doubting whose voice it was. Even before I looked up, I knew it was her.

'Hello, Amanda.'

Without having to think about it, I knew exactly what had happened. When I didn't turn up for Cabinet, Amanda had realised that her pessimism had been well-founded and I'd been unable to face telling them all that I'd failed. Not getting any reply from my mobile, she'd remembered what I'd said last week about taking Kirsty on the Wheel, and how much the dream had meant to me, and she'd known that that's where I'd be. That part of it was easy to cope with. What was a lot harder was what I knew would be coming next. Amanda now saw me as fair game. My relationship with Kirsty was over, so she could tell me how she felt, admit she was interested in me . . . Oh God, this was the last thing I wanted. I was hurting. I couldn't even begin to think of looking for the first glimmerings of a hope that one day, in the distant future, I might be able to stop hurting about Kirsty and get on with my life.

'Sam, I'm glad I've found you—'

'Don't,' I interrupted, 'please don't. I know what you're going to say.' But as I spoke, Amanda was reaching into her bag, taking out an envelope and offering it to me. Confused, I took it. It was exactly the same as the envelopes that Kirsty had used to give me my score each Sunday night. How had Amanda got hold of one of those?

'I've got to go now,' she said. 'I'm off to the Mitre.'

'What? I thought you'd just come from there?'

She smiled. 'I have. But now I'm going back again, because . . . well, you'll see why. I told George he's not allowed to leave until I get there. Now that your Cabinet isn't happening any more, I can try and get it through to the stupid sod just how I feel about him.'

'How you feel about *George*?'

Again she smiled. 'Yes, about George. Look, I'm going. I'll see you soon.' She walked away.

So *that* was what she'd meant when she said it was a pity about not being allowed flings with anyone in the Cabinet. But what was this envelope all about? I opened it. Inside was a piece of paper. I unfolded it. On it were written just three words:

'One million points.'

I stared at the words, trying to make sense of them. And then a voice, one even more familiar than Amanda's, came to my ears. 'If you want them.'

I looked up. Kirsty was standing in front of me, her face pale, not a trace of make-up on it, but her eyes red in a way I knew only too well from early that morning.

'Kirsty, what's this all about?'

'It's a million points, Sam. You've got a million points, if you want them.'

'But last night . . .?'

'That's what earned you the million points.'

'How? I didn't do anything.'

'You did. You gave up.'

'What?'

'You gave up. Admittedly in a more dramatic way than I thought you would. I never thought you'd walk out. But then that was my fault for doing the cufflink thing.'

'Kirsty, will you please tell me what you're talking about?'

She sat next to me on the bench. 'Sam, what I've been waiting weeks for you to say is that you were giving up. That you didn't know, couldn't work out how to earn these points. You thought it was all about strength, showing me how strong you are, proving that you could fight your way through it. But that's not what love's about. It's not about being strong, it's about being weak. All I wanted to know was that you understood that.' She paused, trying to think of another angle to approach it from. 'Do you know what I feel every time you leave me, to go to work, to fetch a pint of milk from the shops, to go wherever you're going? I feel scared. I love you so much that I worry I'm never going to see you again. I long for the moment we'll be together again. I love you so much that it *hurts*. And that's what I wanted from you. I wanted to know that the loss of our love would hurt you as much as it'd hurt me. Being in love with you is the most wonderful thing that's ever happened to me, but it's the most frightening thing as well, because I'm always scared about what would happen if it's taken away from me. Being in love is about being weak, about accepting that things are out of your control, that you need the other person.'

'So that's why you put me on points? To see if I understood that?'

She sighed. 'I don't know if I'd quite realised what I was up to at the beginning. Getting the bathroom cleaned made a pleasant change. And as for the pillowcases – well, I never thought I'd see the day. But halfway through, yeah, it all worked itself out in my mind, and I knew that's what I was looking for. I wanted to know that you were scared, that you were weak like me. You kept putting on your show of strength, as though I was some girl you'd only just met who you had to impress. But when you're *really* in love with someone, that's not how it should be. The person you *really* love is the one you can be weak in front of. All I wanted was for you to give up, to admit that you didn't know how to earn the points. That would prove you weren't afraid to be weak in front of me.'

So much for my All Blacks routine.

'And then by last night I was so desperate for you to give up that I tried to provoke you. Gavin had taken his cufflinks out to help with the washing-up – yeah, that's how exciting the evening was – and I guess the Pinot Noir had gone to my head a bit, because I had the idea of making you think that we'd been . . . well, doing the other thing that would have meant him taking his cufflinks out . . . so while he wasn't looking I hid one of them. And then do you want to know how crap I am? I couldn't think of a way of delaying him, so I just had to say I'm playing a joke on my boyfriend, would you mind hanging around until he gets back and then legging it out of the flat? An hour and a half we were waiting. I'm sorry, Sam. That was a stupid thing to do.'

'Too fucking right it was.' I took a deep breath to control my temper. 'Your plan worked, though.'

'It worked too well. You gave up, but then you scarpered, so I couldn't tell you that you'd given up and earned the points. And I had no way of finding you. It was only when your mobile rang this evening, and I answered it and your friend Amanda asked where you were, that anything happened. She told me that she had a pretty good idea where you'd be, and that I should meet her here. Then she said there was something she had to explain first, something you'd probably got the wrong end of the stick about – George, was it? – and she asked if she could give you the envelope as well. As a surprise. I think she's quite fond of you.'

Yeah, but not as fond as I was worried she might be, I thought. And I'm glad that the bloke she's really fond of is George, because it'll stop him being annoyed at me for ruining his chances with Mel's mate. But I didn't say any of that. This was complicated enough as it was. In fact, I didn't say anything. I walked a few steps away from Kirsty and looked the other way to give myself a little privacy to work out what I felt about all this. Did I want Kirsty, after what she'd put me through? Did I want those million points?

Three thoughts came to me. The first was that, although Kirsty's behaviour the previous night hadn't exactly been above board, neither had mine. 'Pretending that you've been to bed with someone you haven't to elicit a reaction from your boyfriend' plays 'nearly snorting two enormous lines of cocaine with a strange girl in a nightclub toilet'. Call it a score draw.

The second thought, which was a slap-your-own-forehead-and-say-'dur' thought, was that this all explained the looks that Amanda had been giving me during Cabinet.

She'd obviously guessed what Kirsty was waiting for me to say. When I thought she was yearning to tell me 'you can't do this, there's no way you'll get these points', what was actually on her mind was 'the way to get these points is so simple you're staring straight past it'. But she couldn't tell me that. It was one of those lessons that was only of value if you learned it the hard way. Amanda saying 'go and tell Kirsty you've given up' wouldn't have worked. It wouldn't really have been me giving up. That was only going to happen if I did it for real.

But the final thought, the strongest one, crowding out the others and showing me the way forward, was that Kirsty was right. What she'd said to me didn't just make sense in my head, it made sense in my heart. Love is about being weak. At the core of my love for Kirsty was a very real weakness, a fear, a worry about losing her. I'd known that all along. You knew it, because I'd written it down. Amanda, George and Pete knew it, because I'd told them about it in Cabinet. The only person who didn't know it was Kirsty, because I was so determined to show her how bloody strong I was, how sure I was that I'd get those points. I understood her now. I'd never stopped loving her, even though I 'knew' after her 'infidelity' that I should have done. That was why I hadn't found it in myself to be angry, to hate her. I belonged with her.

I walked back to her. 'So if I take those million points, it's wedding bells?'

She nodded.

'For better for worse, till death us do part, all that?'

Another nod.

'Good,' I said, grabbing her handbag, 'because another part of the deal is that you endow me with all your worldly goods, and I haven't got any cash on me at the moment.' I marched off to the queue for the Wheel, which was as lengthy as it always is. Kirsty followed, clearly wondering what the hell I was doing.

'Now then,' I announced to the startled people near the front of the queue as I fiddled with the clasp of Kirsty's purse, 'do any of you want to sell your tickets for' – I fished out some notes – 'thirty quid? No? OK' – I took out another tenner – 'how about forty?' Still no one spoke, although I did notice the guy at the front of the queue whisper something to his wife. 'How about you, sir? Forty pounds for your tickets. That's over a hundred per cent profit.' I scrambled round in the bag and found another twenty-pound note at the bottom. 'No, make that sixty quid. Come on, sir, madam, sixty pounds for your tickets.'

I could tell from their respective expressions that he was well up for it, in fact, he'd been up for it at forty, but she was unsure. Following her eyeline, though, I saw the crucial factor that would make the difference. 'The bag, madam? I can see you're a fan of this bag. And why wouldn't you be? It's a lovely bag. Well, all right then, if that's what it takes, your tickets for sixty quid plus this bag. Can't say fairer than that, can I?'

The suspicion never entirely left their faces, but it didn't matter. The exchange was made, after I'd emptied the contents of Kirsty's bag into my jacket pockets, and dragging her by the hand I led her up the ramp into the next pod. As we climbed slowly up into the air I dealt with her very understandable confusion, explaining that it was part of a dream I'd had, and that it'd all become clear when we got to the top. Although we'd got there by a slightly tortuous route, I knew now that Kirsty was going to be my wife, and so I still wanted to live out that dream.

Higher and higher into the air we went, holding each other close. Then suddenly Kirsty remembered something.

'There was another call for you today,' she said.

'Oh yeah?'

'Some kid called Danny.'

I laughed. 'Really?'

'Yeah, he wanted to come and see you. I explained that I didn't know where you were, but he asked if he could drop something off for you anyway.' She searched in her pocket. 'When he came round he left a Thresher's bag and this note.'

I unfolded the piece of paper and read, in Danny's scrawled handwriting:

deer sam, this is to say sorry for wot I dun, messin you about and that, I realy meen it, and thanks for gettin me sorted with that corse, alan says it starts next week, and I realy am gonna do that bit about the place in brighton, thanks again, danny,

thought id get some good booze, not cheep stuff like lager, to say thanks proply,

will you help me with the corse, danny

The last line made me cry a little bit.

'Who is he?' asked Kirsty, wiping away my tears.

I explained about Timepool, and the park, and Brighton, and why I'd been afraid to tell her any of it, and she laughed at me. I could see why, now that I knew the real thinking behind the points. Kirsty asked if she could help with Danny's course as well. I said I'd love her to.

'What was the booze, by the way?'

Kirsty gave a chuckle. 'Bailey's.'

'Big bottle?'

'Yeah.'

'Fantastic.'

We were getting near the top now. But the dream demanded that I wait until we were at the very top before saying my line to her. I thought about it: 'That's how you've made me feel.' As the pod inched its way upwards, climbing and climbing and climbing, I looked down at Westminster Bridge and remembered how desolate I'd felt sixteen hours previously, sitting there with my world in tatters. And I realised that these two feelings were one and the same. My weakness down there had been because I loved Kirsty, as was my strength now, up here. Being on top of the world means being weak. That's what love is all about. Finally I'd come to understand that.

I looked out of each side of the pod. There was no part of the Wheel anywhere that was higher than us. We were right at the top. This was the moment. But it was time for a change of script.

'Kirsty,' I said, taking her hands in mine. 'Can we be weak together for the rest of our lives?'

She smiled, and pulled me close. 'Just let anyone try and stop us.'